Praise for Michael Moorcock

"A mythological cycle . . . highly relevant to the twentieth century . . . The figure of Elric often resembles many purely contemporary figureheads from Charles Manson to James Dean."
—*Time Out*

"Elric is back! Herald the event!"
—*Los Angeles Daily News,* on
The Fortress of the Pearl

"[The Elric] novels are totally enthralling."
—*Midwest Book Review*

"Among the most memorable characters in fantasy literature."
—*Science Fiction Chronicle*

"If you are at all interested in fantastic fiction, you must read Michael Moorcock. He changed the field single-handedly: He is a giant."
—TAD WILLIAMS

"A work of powerful and sustained imagination . . . The vast, tragic symbols by which Mr. Moorcock continually illuminates the metaphysical quest of his hero are a measure of the author's remarkable talents."
—J. G. BALLARD, author of *Crash*

"A giant of fantasy."
—*Kirkus Reviews*

"A superb writer."
—*Locus*

ELRIC
The Sleeping Sorceress

ELRIC
THE SLEEPING SORCERESS

CHRONICLES OF THE
LAST EMPEROR OF MELNIBONÉ

—— VOLUME 3 ——

MICHAEL MOORCOCK
ILLUSTRATED BY STEVE ELLIS

BALLANTINE BOOKS · NEW YORK

A Del Rey Trade Paperback Original

Copyright © 2008 by Michael Moorcock and Linda Moorcock
Foreword copyright © 2008 by Holly Black
Illustrations copyright © 2008 by Steven Ellis

Published in the United States by Del Rey,
an imprint of The Random House Publishing Group,
a division of Random House, Inc., New York.

DEL REY is a registered trademark and the Del Rey colophon is a
trademark of Random House, Inc.

The stories contained in this work originally appeared
in various science fiction magazines and books, as noted on
the following acknowledgments page.

Library of Congress Cataloging-in-Publication Data

Moorcock, Michael.
Elric : the sleeping sorceress / Michael Moorcock ;
illustrated throughout by Steve Ellis.
p. cm. — (Chronicles of the last emperor of Melniboné ; v. 3)
ISBN 978-0-345-49864-9 (trade pbk. : acid-free paper)   1. Elric of
Melniboné (Fictitious character)—Fiction.   2. Swordsmen—Fiction.
3. Albinos and albinism—Fiction.   4. Fantasy fiction, English.
I. Title.
PR6063.O59E467 2008
823'.914—dc22   2008028814

Printed in the United States of America

www.delreybooks.com

9 8 7 6 5 4 3 2

Book Design by Julie Schroeder

The Sleeping Sorceress was first published in the UK
by New English Library in 1971.

Elric of Melniboné was first published in the UK by Hutchinson in 1972.

"And So the Great Emperor Received His Education . . ." first appeared as a
spoken-word introduction to an audiobook edition of *Elric of Melniboné*
by AudioRealms in 2003 and appears here in print for the first time.

"Aspects of Fantasy (1)" first appeared in *Science Fantasy* magazine,
no. 61, October 1963, edited by John Carnell.

The introduction to *Elric of Melniboné*'s graphic adaptation,
First Comics, was published in 1986.

"El Cid and Elric" first appeared in Argentina, in *Comiqueando*
magazine, no. 100, August/September 2007.

Grateful acknowledgment is made to the following for
permission to reprint previously published material:

The Sleeping Sorceress cover artwork copyright © James Cawthorn, 1971.
Reprinted by permission of James Cawthorn.

Elric of Melniboné cover design copyright © Laurence Cutting, 1972.
Used by permission of The Random House Group Ltd.

"The Age of the Young Kingdoms" map, first published in *Elric of Melniboné*,
copyright © James Cawthorn. Reprinted by permission of James Cawthorn.

The Vanishing Tower cover painting by Michael Whelan © 1977.
All rights reserved. Reprinted by permission of DAW Books.

Previously unpublished page from graphic adaptation of *Stormbringer* copyright
© James Cawthorn, 1965. Reprinted by permission of James Cawthorn.

The Weird of the White Wolf cover artwork copyright © 1983 Berkley
Publishing Group. Reprinted by permission of Berkley Books.

"Мелнибонэ" ("Melniboné") map, by Н. Михайлов, 1992, appeared in
Хроники Элрика/Призрачный Горог (*The Dreaming City/The Sleeping
Sorceress*), Terra Fantastica, 2001. Original map drawn by James Cawthorn.
Reprinted by permission of James Cawthorn and Michael Moorcock.

Elric of Melniboné audiobook cover artwork copyright © Dalmazio
Frau, 2003. Reprinted by permission of AudioRealms.

Elric de Melniboné/La Fortaleza de la Perla (*Elric of Melniboné/The Fortress
of the Pearl*) cover artwork copyright © Chris Achilleos, 2007.
Reprinted by permission of Edhasa Books.

ALSO BY MICHAEL MOORCOCK

Behold the Man
Breakfast in the Ruins
Gloriana
The Metatemporal Detective

THE CORNELIUS QUARTET
The Final Program
A Cure for Cancer
The English Assassin
The Condition of Muzak

BETWEEN THE WARS: THE PYAT QUARTET
Byzantium Endures
The Laughter of Carthage
Jerusalem Commands
The Vengeance of Rome

And many more

If there's a Valhalla, where you'll find old editors who died in harness, I hope Ted Carnell, Larry Shaw, Don Wollheim, Michael Dempsey, and John Blackwell are having a very good time there. They are a few of the great editors who have helped me in my career.

CONTENTS

FOREWORD

by Holly Black

A boyfriend in high school recommended the Elric books to me. He was in a private school about an hour away, and we were doing that thing where you judge the entire future of the relationship by one single representative book choice.

I remember opening the books for the first time (they were the fat Science Fiction Book Club editions with the gorgeous Robert Gould covers) and poring over the pages as if hypnotized. Before Elric, my idea of a fantasy-novel hero was a strapping fellow who rose from simple circumstances to lofty heights. Elric was decadent, sickly, and doomed. I loved him instantly. I loved that Elric suffered, loved his milk-white hair and moody crimson eyes, loved that he was probably a bad boyfriend but a good king. He was tragic and I was hungry for tragedy.

The images that affected me the most deeply were Moorcock's descriptions of the Melnibonéan court in decline. There, in the dreaming city of Imrryr, are singers whose throats have been tortured so that each may produce one perfect haunting note. This told me something about Melniboné, something that I knew in my bones was true of Elfland and all worthy fantasy places, that their beauty entices you into terrible danger. And it told me everything about Melnibonéan culture—that a moment of perfection was worth any amount of cruelty. Just as the black blade Stormbringer told me something true about how the very thing that gives you strength and power may eat you away from the inside.

Those were good things for me to think about as a young writer.

When I met Michael and his charming wife, Linda, at a fantasy convention in Austin, Texas, we sat at a table in the bar, and Michael cheerfully recounted a horrific toe surgery. He is as skilled a raconteur as he is a writer, and soon more and more people crowded around, drawn in by the tale. When Michael and his wife left, we authors clutched each other's arms. *That was Michael Moorcock*, we said to one another, grinning like fools.

I envy you who are about to read these books for the first time. Not only did they change the genre, they influenced a generation of dreamers.

As for the high school boyfriend I was judging based on his book recommendation? What else could I do? Reader, I married him.

INTRODUCTION

By 1970 the Elric stories had become so popular that I was under considerable pressure from publishers to produce more. Given that I had killed Elric off in *Stormbringer*, all I could do was offer the public a prequel or two, drawing on events preceding the first magazine story ("The Dreaming City") or taking place between events published in *The Stealer of Souls*.

The first of these, "The Singing Citadel," was done for L. Sprague de Camp's *The Fantastic Swordsmen* anthology, and when my good friend Kenneth Bulmer, himself a fine writer of fantasy and science fiction, was asked to edit a new magazine called *Sword and Sorcery* the first thing he thought to do was phone me and ask if I could write a new Elric series. I sketched out an idea for three long linked novellas that would take place between early events in the series. He liked the idea, and I had completed the first and begun work on the second when the publisher, who had second thoughts about backing a fantasy magazine, canceled on him, leaving Ken with an inventory and no magazine.

To be honest, since I had publishers very keen to get new Elric stories from me, I was not especially put out by the news, but I felt very sorry for Ken, who had high hopes of producing a magazine in the literary tradition of the U.S. *Weird Tales* or U.K. *Science Fantasy,* where the Elric stories had first appeared. I think he would have done a first-class job; given the authors and illustrators he had lined up. His time had been wasted, and I completed the project as a novel, filling in some of the events between the stories.

Elric of Melniboné followed very shortly afterward. In writing *The Sleeping Sorceress* I had begun to think about Elric's early life and what old Melniboné might have been like, so I was ready to do this book. This was the first time I had written directly for book publication and had not been commissioned by a magazine editor. I wrote it for a publisher that had no previous policy of doing heroic fantasy, Hutchinson, but that had had some success with a series by Jane Gaskell and approached me for a novel.

Thus *Elric of Melniboné* came out only a year after *The Sleeping Sorceress*. I think this was the closest together any of the Elric books were published. I sent it to my old paperback publisher in the U.S., Lancer Books, since I felt I owed them a certain loyalty (they had published all the Elric and Hawkmoon books up to that time), but it was with some hesitation, since by then I was already being offered much larger advances elsewhere. I rather regretted it when they altered the early chapters and changed the title from *Elric of Melniboné* to, of all things, *The Dreaming City*. This seemed to show a singular stupidity, since, of course, the first published story in *The Stealer of Souls* had appeared under that title.

As soon as I could I got the rights back from Lancer (who in the meantime had gone bankrupt, taking most of my early titles with them), and when eventually Don Wollheim of DAW Books suggested reprinting the whole series with some brilliant new covers, I was at last able to publish the book as was originally intended. These are the books that most of my early readers from the 1970s remember best, with the matching Michael Whelan covers and matching type designs. I wrote a novella for my friend Bill Butler's Unicorn Books (*The Jade Man's Eyes*), which became part of a further addition to the series for DAW, *The Sailor on the Seas of Fate*. *The Sleeping Sorceress* was also at that time retitled as *The Vanishing Tower*.

These books went through many editions, establishing the chronology of the series, until Berkley Books made me an offer I couldn't refuse, together with the chance to use the work of Robert Gould on the covers, which is how those books and their later sequels appeared through the 1980s, again going into many editions. I wrote two new novels for Berkley. In the 1990s I again rearranged the sequence for the uniform omnibus editions of the Eternal Champion stories I published with Orion in the U.K. and White Wolf in the U.S., once more with some outstanding new covers. With the collapse of White Wolf's publishing program, I decided to "rest" my Eternal Champion books, including Elric, in the U.S. for a while and made no attempt to republish the books until Del Rey's publication of the Robert E. Howard titles inspired the present editions, published in the order the stories were originally done. As stated before, these, with their beautiful illustrations, are the definitive editions of the stories. One of the reasons I responded to Ken Bulmer's request for some new Elric adventures years ago was because he planned to ask Jim Cawthorn, with whom I had worked since the 1950s, to illustrate them. The chance of having these stories illustrated as I originally meant them to appear was too good to pass up! This will be the first time I have worked with Steve Ellis, a fine illustrator.

Some of the other pieces in this volume are collected in book form for the first time. The essay on Elric and El Cid, the great legendary champion of Spain, was done to celebrate the publication of the Elric series in Argentina. I have been especially fortunate over the years in having fine Spanish editions published. The original essay from my series Aspects of Fantasy is included because it appeared at the same time as the first Elric stories in *Science Fantasy* magazine and gives some idea of my attitudes toward fantasy at the time. A slightly more sophisticated version appeared as part of *Wizardry and Wild Romance,* my examination of heroic fantasy that was originally published in England by Victor Gollancz and in a revised edition by MonkeyBrain Press in 2004. These pieces were originally commissioned by John Carnell. The new introduction to the AudioRealms spoken-word edition of *Elric of Melniboné*, slightly changed from the original, is included here for obvious reasons, as is my introduction to the First Comics adaptation of the book. I am glad to say that the splendid Elric graphic versions drawn by P. Craig Russell and adapted by Roy Thomas will be appearing again soon from Dark Horse, who also, of course, does those great Conan graphic novels, reprinted the original Barry Windsor-Smith story in which Conan and Elric meet, and recently published the nonfiction *Conan: The Phenomenon,* for which I was privileged to write the introduction. Like it or not, the scowling barbarian and the mournful prince of a decadent nation are bound together by a destiny bigger than both of them! I hope you enjoy the stories here and that the additional material, carefully compiled by editor John Davey, will give you some idea of the excitement we felt when they were first exposed to the light of day!

Michael Moorcock
The Old Circle Squared, Lost Pines, Texas
September 2007

ELRIC
THE SLEEPING SORCERESS

THE SLEEPING SORCERESS

THE SLEEPING SORCERESS
(1971)

For Ken Bulmer, who, as editor of the magazine *Sword and Sorcery*, asked me to write this book as a serial for him. The magazine, which was to be a companion to *Vision of Tomorrow*, never appeared, due to the backer withdrawing his support from both magazines.

BOOK ONE

THE TORMENT OF THE LAST LORD

*... and then did Elric leave Jharkor in pursuit
of a certain sorcerer who had, so Elric claimed,
caused him some inconvenience ...*

—*The Chronicle of the Black Sword*

CHAPTER ONE

Pale Prince on a Moonlit Shore

IN THE SKY a cold moon, cloaked in clouds, sent down faint light that fell upon a sullen sea where a ship lay at anchor off an uninhabited coast.

From the ship a boat was being lowered. It swayed in its harness. Two figures, swathed in long capes, watched the seamen lowering the boat while they, themselves, tried to calm horses which stamped their hoofs on the unstable deck and snorted and rolled their eyes.

The shorter figure clung hard to his horse's bridle and grumbled.

"Why should this be necessary? Why could not we have disembarked at Trepesaz? Or at least some fishing harbour boasting an inn, however lowly ..."

"Because, friend Moonglum, I wish our arrival in Lormyr to be secret. If Theleb K'aarna knew of my coming—as he soon would if we went to Trepesaz—then he would fly again and the chase would begin afresh. Would you welcome that?"

Moonglum shrugged. "I still feel that your pursuit of this sorcerer is no more than a surrogate for real activity. You seek him because you do not wish to seek your proper destiny ..."

Elric turned his bone-white face in the moonlight and regarded Moonglum with crimson, moody eyes. "And what of it? You need not accompany me if you do not wish to . . ."

Again, Moonglum shrugged his shoulders. "Aye. I know. Perhaps I stay with you for the same reasons that you pursue the sorcerer of Pan Tang." He grinned. "So that's enough of debate, eh, Lord Elric?"

"Debate achieves nothing," Elric agreed. He patted his horse's nose as more seamen, clad in colourful Tarkeshite silks, came forward to take the horses and hoist them down to the waiting boat.

Struggling, whinnying through the bags muffling their heads, the horses were lowered, their hoofs thudding on the bottom of the boat as if they would stave it in. Then Elric and Moonglum, their bundles on their backs, swung down the ropes and jumped into the rocking craft. The sailors pushed off from the ship with their oars and then, bodies bending, began to row for the shore.

The late autumn air was cold. Moonglum shivered as he stared towards the bleak cliffs ahead. "Winter is near and I'd rather be domiciled at some friendly tavern than roaming abroad. When this business is done with the sorcerer, what say we head for Jadmar or one of the other big Vilmirian cities and see what mood the warmer clime puts us in?"

But Elric did not reply. His strange eyes stared into the darkness and they seemed to be peering into the depths of his own soul and not liking what they saw.

Moonglum sighed and pursed his lips. He huddled deeper in his cloak and rubbed his hands to warm them. He was used to his friend's sudden lapses of silence, but familiarity did not make him enjoy them any better. From somewhere on the shore a nightbird shrieked and a small animal squealed. The sailors grunted as they pulled on their oars.

The moon came out from behind the clouds and it shone on Elric's grim, white face, made his crimson eyes seem to glow like the coals of hell, revealed the barren cliffs of the shore.

The sailors shipped their oars as the boat's bottom ground on shingle. The horses, smelling land, snorted and moved their hoofs. Elric and Moonglum rose to steady them.

Two seamen leapt into the cold water and brought the boat up higher. Another patted the neck of Elric's horse and did not look directly at the albino as he spoke. "The captain said you would pay me when we reached the Lormyrian shore, my lord."

Elric grunted and reached under his cloak. He drew out a jewel that shone brightly through the darkness of the night. The sailor gasped and stretched out his hand to take it. "Xiombarg's blood, I have never seen so fine a gem!"

Elric began to lead the horse into the shallows and Moonglum hastily followed him, cursing under his breath and shaking his head from side to side.

Laughing among themselves, the sailors shoved the boat back into deeper water.

As Elric and Moonglum mounted their horses and the boat pulled through the darkness towards the ship, Moonglum said: "That jewel was worth a hundred times the cost of our passage!"

"What of it?" Elric fitted his feet in his stirrups and made his horse walk towards a part of the cliff which was less steep than the rest. He stood up in his stirrups for a moment to adjust his cloak and settle himself more firmly in his saddle. "There is a path here, by the look of it. Much overgrown."

"I would point out," Moonglum said bitterly, "that if it were left to you, Lord Elric, we should have no means of livelihood at all. If I had not taken the precaution of retaining some of the profits made from the sale of that trireme we captured and auctioned in Dhakos, we should be paupers now."

"Aye," returned Elric carelessly, and he spurred his horse up the path that led to the top of the cliff.

In frustration Moonglum shook his head, but he followed the albino.

By dawn they were riding over the undulating landscape of small hills and valleys that made up the terrain of Lormyr's most northerly peninsula.

"Since Theleb K'aarna must needs live off rich patrons," Elric explained as they rode, "he will almost certainly go to the capital, Iosaz, where King Montan rules. He will seek service with some noble, perhaps King Montan himself."

"And how soon shall we see the capital, Lord Elric?" Moonglum looked up at the clouds.

"It is several days' ride, Master Moonglum."

Moonglum sighed. The sky bore signs of snow and the tent he carried rolled behind his saddle was of thin silk, suitable for the hotter lands of the East and West.

He thanked his gods that he wore a thick quilted jerkin beneath his breastplate and that before he had left the ship he had pulled on a pair of woolen breeks to go beneath the gaudier breeks of red silk that were his outer wear. His conical cap of fur, iron and leather had earflaps which were now drawn tightly and secured by a thong beneath his chin and his heavy deerskin cape was drawn closely around his shoulders.

Elric, for his part, seemed not to notice the chill weather. His own cape flapped behind him. He wore breeks of deep blue silk, a high-collared shirt of black silk, a steel breastplate lacquered a gleaming black, like his helmet, and embossed with patterns of delicate silverwork. Behind his saddle were deep panniers and across this was a bow and a quiver of arrows. At his side swung the huge runesword Stormbringer, the source of his strength and his misery, and on his right hip was a long dirk, presented him by Queen Yishana of Jharkor.

Moonglum bore a similar bow and quiver. On each hip was a sword, one short and straight, the other long and curved, after the fashion of the men of Elwher, his homeland. Both blades were in scabbards of beautifully worked Ilmioran leather, embellished with stitching of scarlet and gold thread.

Together the pair looked, to those who had not heard of them, like free-traveling mercenaries who had been more successful than most in their chosen careers.

Their horses bore them tirelessly through the countryside. These were tall Shazaarian steeds, known all over the Young Kingdoms for their stamina and intelligence. After several weeks cooped up in the hold of the Tarkeshite ship they were glad to be moving again.

Now small villages—squat houses of stone and thatch—came in sight, but Elric and Moonglum were careful to avoid them.

Lormyr was one of the oldest of the Young Kingdoms and much of the world's history had been made there. Even the Melnibonéans had heard the tales of Lormyr's hero of ancient times, Aubec of Malador of the province of Klant, who was said to have carved new lands from the stuff of Chaos that had once existed at World's Edge. But Lormyr had long since declined from her peak of power (though still a major nation of the south-west) and had mellowed into a nation that was at once picturesque and cultured. Elric and Moonglum passed pleasant farmsteads, well-nurtured fields, vineyards and orchards in which the golden-leaved trees were surrounded by time-worn, moss-grown walls. A sweet land and a peaceful land in contrast to the rawer, bustling north-western nations of Jharkor, Tarkesh and Dharijor which they had left behind.

Moonglum gazed around him as they slowed their horses to a trot. "Theleb K'aarna could work much mischief here, Elric. I am reminded of the peaceful hills and plains of Elwher, my own land."

Elric nodded. "Lormyr's years of turbulence ended when she cast off Melniboné's shackles and was first to proclaim herself a free nation. I have a liking for this restful landscape. It soothes me. Now we have another reason for finding the sorcerer before he begins to stir his brew of corruption."

Moonglum smiled quietly. "Be careful, my lord, for you are once again succumbing to those soft emotions you so despise . . ."

Elric straightened his back. "Come. Let's make haste for Iosaz."

"The sooner we reach a city with a decent tavern and a warm fire, the better." Moonglum drew his cape tighter about his thin body.

"Then pray that the sorcerer's soul is soon sent to limbo, Master Moonglum, for then I'll be content to sit before the fire all winter long if it suits you."

And Elric made his horse break into a sudden gallop as grey evening closed over the tranquil hills.

CHAPTER TWO

White Face Staring Through Snow

Lormyr was famous for her great rivers. It was her rivers that had helped make her rich and had kept her strong.

After three days' traveling, when a light snow had begun to drift from the sky, Elric and Moonglum rode out of the hills and saw before them the foaming waters of the Schlan River, tributary of the Zaphra-Trepek which flowed from beyond Iosaz down to the sea at Trepesaz.

No ships sailed the Schlan at this point, for there were rapids and huge waterfalls every few miles, but at the old town of Stagasaz, built where the Schlan joined the Zaphra-Trepek, Elric planned to send Moonglum into town and buy a small boat in which they could sail up the Zaphra-Trepek to Iosaz where Theleb K'aarna was almost certain to be.

They followed the banks of the Schlan now, riding hard and hoping to reach the outskirts of the town before nightfall. They rode past fishing villages and the houses of minor nobles, they were occasionally hailed by friendly fishermen who trawled the quieter reaches of the river, but they did not stop. The fishermen were typical of the area, with ruddy features and huge curling moustaches, dressed in heavily embroidered linen smocks and leather boots that reached almost to their thighs; men who in past times had been ever ready to lay down their nets, pick up swords and halberds and mount horses to go to the defense of their homeland.

"Could we not borrow one of their boats?" Moonglum suggested. But Elric shook his head. "The fishermen of the Schlan are well known for their gossiping. The news of our presence might well precede us and warn Theleb K'aarna."

"You seem needlessly cautious . . ."

"I have lost him too often."

More rapids came in sight. Great black rocks glistened in the gloom and roaring water gushed over them, sending spray high into the air. There were no houses or villages here and the paths beside the banks were narrow and treacherous so that Elric and Moonglum were forced to slow their pace and make their way with caution.

Moonglum shouted over the noise of the water: "We'll not reach Stagasaz by nightfall now!"

Elric nodded. "We'll make camp below the rapids. There."

The snow was still falling and the wind drove it against their faces so that it became even more difficult to pick their way along the narrow track that now wound high above the river.

But at last the tumult began to die and the track widened out and the waters calmed and, with relief, they looked about them over the plain to find a likely camping place.

It was Moonglum who saw them first.

His finger was unsteady as he pointed into the sky towards the north.

"Elric. What make you of those?"

Elric peered up into the lowering sky, brushing snowflakes from his face.

His expression was at first puzzled. His brow furrowed and his eyes narrowed.

Black shapes against the sky.

Winged shapes.

It was impossible at this distance to judge their scale, but they did not fly the way birds fly. Elric was reminded of another flying creature—a creature he had last seen when he and the sea-lords fled burning Imrryr and the folk of Melniboné had released their vengeance upon the reavers.

That vengeance had taken two forms.

The first form had been the golden battle-barges which had waited for the attack as they left the Dreaming City.

The second form had been the great dragons of the Bright Empire.

And these creatures in the distance had something of the look of dragons.

Had the Melnibonéans discovered a means of waking the dragons before the end of their normal sleeping time? Had they unleashed their dragons to seek out Elric, who had slain his own kin, betrayed his own unhuman kind in order to have revenge on his cousin Yyrkoon who had usurped Elric's place on the Ruby Throne of Imrryr?

Now Elric's expression hardened into a grim mask. His crimson eyes shone like polished rubies. His left hand fell upon the hilt of his great black battle-blade, the runesword Stormbringer, and he controlled a rising sense of horror.

For now, in mid-air, the shapes had changed. No longer did they have the appearance of dragons, but this time they seemed to be like multicoloured swans, whose gleaming feathers caught and diffracted the few remaining rays of light.

Moonglum gasped as they came nearer.

"They are huge!"

"Draw your swords, friend Moonglum. Draw them now and pray to whatever gods rule over Elwher. For these are creatures of sorcery and they are doubtless sent by Theleb K'aarna to destroy us. My respect for that conjuror increases."

"What are they, Elric?"

"Creatures of Chaos. In Melniboné they are called the Oonai. They can change shape at will. A sorcerer of great mental discipline, of superlative powers, who knows the apposite spells can master them and determine their appearance. Some of my ancestors could do such things, but I thought no mere conjuror of Pan Tang could master the chimerae!"

"Do you know no spell to counter them?"

"None comes readily to mind. Only a Lord of Chaos such as my patron demon Arioch could dismiss them."

Moonglum shuddered. "Then call your Arioch, I beg you!"

Elric darted a half-amused glance at Moonglum. "These creatures must fill you with great fear indeed if you are prepared to entertain the presence of Arioch, Master Moonglum."

Moonglum drew his long, curved sword. "Perhaps they have no business with us," he suggested. "But it is as well to be prepared."

Elric smiled. "Aye."

Then Moonglum drew his straight sword, curling his horse's reins around his arm.

A shrill, cackling sound from the skies.

The horses pawed at the ground.

The cackling grew louder. The creatures opened their beaks and called to one another and it was very plain now that they were indeed something other than gigantic swans, for they had curling tongues. And there were slim, sharp fangs bristling in those beaks. They changed direction slightly, winging straight for the two men.

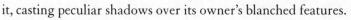

Elric flung back his head and drew out his great sword and raised it skyward. It pulsed and moaned and a strange, black radiance poured from it, casting peculiar shadows over its owner's blanched features.

The Shazaarian horse screamed and reared and words began to pour from Elric's tormented face.

"Arioch! Arioch! Arioch! Lord of the Seven Darks, Duke of Chaos, aid me! Aid me now, Arioch!"

Moonglum's own horse had backed away in panic and the little man was having great difficulty in controlling it. His own features were almost as pale as Elric's.

"Arioch!"

Overhead the chimerae began to circle.

"Arioch! Blood and souls if you will aid me now!"

Then, some yards away, a dark mist seemed to well up from nowhere. It was a boiling mist that had strange, disgusting shapes in it.

"Arioch!"

The mist grew still thicker.

"Arioch! I beg you—aid me now!"

The horse pawed at the air, snorting and screaming, its eyes rolling, its nostrils flaring. Yet Elric, his lips curled back over his teeth so that he looked like a rabid wolf, continued to keep his seat as the dark mist quivered and a strange, unearthly face appeared in the upper part of the shifting column. It was a face of wonderful beauty, of absolute evil. Moonglum turned his head away, unable to regard it.

A sweet, sibilant voice issued from the beautiful mouth. The mist swirled languidly, becoming a mottled scarlet laced with emerald green.

"Greetings, Elric," said the face. "Greetings, most beloved of my children."

"Aid me, Arioch!"

"Ah," said the face, its tone full of rich regret. "Ah, that cannot be . . ."

"You must aid me!"

The chimerae had hesitated in their descent, sighting the peculiar mist.

"It is impossible, sweetest of my slaves. There are other matters afoot in the Realm of Chaos. Matters of enormous moment to which I have already referred. I offer only my blessing."

"Arioch—I beg thee!"

"Remember your oath to Chaos and remain loyal to us in spite of all. Farewell, Elric."

And the dark mist vanished.

And the chimerae came closer.

And Elric drew a racking breath while the runesword whined in his hand and quivered and its radiance dimmed a little.

Moonglum spat on the ground. "A powerful patron, Elric, but a damned inconstant one." Then he flung himself from his saddle as a creature which changed its shape a dozen times as it arrowed towards him reached out huge claws which clashed in the air where he had been. The riderless horse reared again, striking out at the beast of Chaos.

A fanged snout snapped.

Blood vomited from the place where the horse's head had been and the carcass kicked once more before falling to the ground to pour more gore into the greedy earth.

Bearing the remains of the head in what was first a scaled snout, then a beak, then a sharklike mouth, the Oonai thrashed back into the air.

Moonglum picked himself up. His eyes contemplated nothing but his own imminent destruction.

Elric, too, leapt from his horse and slapped its flank so that convulsively it began to gallop away towards the river. Another chimera followed it.

This time the flying thing seized the horse's body in claws which suddenly sprouted from its feet. The horse struggled to get free, threatening to break its own backbone in its struggles, but it could not. The chimera flapped towards the clouds with its catch.

Snow fell thicker now, but Elric and Moonglum were oblivious of it as they stood together and awaited the next attack of the Oonai.

Moonglum said quietly: "Is there no other spell you know, friend Elric?"

The albino shook his head. "Nothing specific to deal with these. The Oonai always served the folk of Melniboné. They never threatened us. So we needed no spell against them. I am trying to think . . ."

The chimerae cackled and yelled in the air above the two men's heads.

Then another broke away from the pack and dived to the earth.

"They attack individually," Elric said in a somewhat detached tone, as if studying insects in a bottle. "They never attack in a pack. I know not why."

The Oonai had settled on the ground and it had now assumed the shape of an elephant with the huge head of a crocodile.

"Not an aesthetic combination," said Elric.

The ground shook as it charged towards them.

They stood shoulder to shoulder as it approached. It was almost upon them—

—and at the last moment they divided, Elric throwing himself to one side and Moonglum to the other.

The chimera passed between them and Elric struck at the thing's side with his runesword.

The sword sang out almost lasciviously as it bit deep into the flesh which instantly changed and became a dragon dripping flaming venom from its fangs.

But it was badly wounded.

Blood ran from the deep wound and the chimera screamed and changed shape again and again as if seeking some form in which the wound could not exist.

Black blood now burst from its side as if the strain of the many changes had ruptured its body all the more.

It fell to its knees and the lustre faded from its feathers, died from its scales, disappeared from its skin. It kicked out once and then was still—a heavy, black, piglike creature whose lumpen body was the ugliest Elric and Moonglum had ever seen.

Moonglum grunted.

"It is not hard to understand why such a creature should want to change its form . . ."

He looked up.

Another was descending.

This had the appearance of a whale with wings, but with curved fangs, like those of a stomach fish, and a tail like an enormous corkscrew.

Even as it landed it changed shape again.

Now it had assumed human form. It was a huge, beautiful figure, twice as tall as Elric. It was naked and perfectly proportioned, but its stare was vacant and it had the drooling lips of an idiot child. Lithely it ran at them, its huge hands reaching out to grasp them as a child might reach for a toy.

This time Elric and Moonglum struck together, one at each hand.

Moonglum's sharp sword cut the knuckles deeply and Elric's lopped off two fingers before the Oonai altered its shape again and began first to be an octopus, then a monstrous tiger, then a combination of both, until at last it was a rock in which a fissure grew to reveal white, snapping teeth.

Gasping, the two men waited for it to resume the attack. At the base of the rock some blood was oozing. This put a thought into Elric's mind.

With a sudden yell he leapt forward, raised his sword over his head and brought it down on top of the rock, splitting it in twain.

Something like a laugh issued from the Black Sword then as the sundered shape flickered and became another of the piglike creatures. This was completely cut in two, its blood and its entrails spreading themselves upon the ground.

Then, through the snowy dusk, another of the Oonai came down, its body glowing orange, its shape that of a winged snake with a thousand rippling coils.

Elric struck at the coils, but they moved too rapidly.

The other chimerae had been watching his tactics with their dead companions and they had now gauged the skill of their victims. Almost immediately Elric's arms were pinned to his sides by the coils and he found himself being borne upward as a second chimera with the same shape rushed down on Moonglum to seize him in an identical way.

Elric prepared to die as the horses had died. He prayed that he would die swiftly and not slowly, at the hands of Theleb K'aarna, who had always promised him a slow death.

The scaly wings flapped powerfully. No snout came down to snap his head off.

He felt despair as he realized that he and Moonglum were being carried swiftly northward over the great Lormyrian steppe.

Doubtless Theleb K'aarna awaited them at the end of their journey.

CHAPTER THREE

Feathers Filling a Great Sky

Night fell and the chimerae flew on tirelessly, their shapes black against the falling snow.

The coils showed no signs of relaxing, though Elric strove to force them apart, keeping tight hold of his runesword and racking his brains for some means of defeating the monsters.

If only there were a spell . . .

He tried to keep his thoughts from what Theleb K'aarna would do if, indeed, it was that wizard who had set the Oonai upon them.

Elric's skill in sorcery lay chiefly in his command over the various elementals of air, fire, earth, water and ether, and also over the entities who had affinities with the flora and fauna of the Earth.

He had decided that his only hope lay in summoning the aid of Fileet, Lady of the Birds, who dwelt in a realm lying beyond the planes of Earth, but the invocation eluded him.

Even if he could remember it, the mind had to be adjusted in a certain way, the correct rhythms of the incantation remembered, the exact words and inflections recalled, before he could begin to summon Fileet's aid. For she, more than any other elemental, was as difficult to invoke as the fickle Arioch.

Through the drifting snow he heard Moonglum call out something indistinct.

"What was that, Moonglum?" he called back.

"I only—sought to learn—if you still—lived, friend Elric."

"Aye—barely . . ."

His face was chill and ice had formed on his helmet and breast-plate. His whole body ached both from the crushing coils of the chimera and from the biting cold of the upper air.

On and on through the Southern night they flew while Elric forced himself to relax, to descend into a trance and to dredge from his mind the ancient knowledge of his forefathers.

At dawn the clouds had cleared and the sun's red rays spread over the snow like blood over damask. Everywhere stretched the steppe—a vast field of snow from horizon to horizon, while above it the sky was nothing but a blue sheet of ice in which sat the red pool of the sun.

And, tireless as ever, the chimerae flew on.

Elric brought himself slowly from his trance and prayed to his untrustworthy gods that he remembered the spell aright.

His lips were all but frozen together. He licked them and it was as if he licked snow. He opened them and bitter air coursed into his mouth. He coughed then, turning his head upwards, his crimson eyes glazing.

He forced his lips to frame strange syllables, to utter the old vowel-heavy words of the High Speech of Old Melniboné, a speech hardly suited to a human tongue at all.

"Fileet," he murmured. Then he began to chant the incantation. And as he chanted the sword grew warmer in his hand and supplied him with more energy so that the eldritch chant echoed through the icy sky.

> "Feathers fine our fates entwined
> Bird and man and thine and mine,
> Formed a pact that Gods divine
> Hallowed on an ancient shrine,
> When kind swore service unto kind.

> "Fileet, fair feathered queen of flight
> Remember now that fateful night
> And help your brother in his plight."

There was more to the Summoning than the words of the invocation. There were the abstract thoughts in the head, the visual images which had to be retained in the mind the whole time, the emotions felt, the memories made sharp and true. Without everything being exactly right, the invocation would prove useless.

Centuries before, the Sorcerer Kings of Melniboné had struck this bargain with Fileet, Lady of the Birds: that any bird that settled in Imrryr's walls should be protected, that no bird would be shot by any of the Melnibonéan blood. This bargain had been kept and dreaming Imrryr had become a haven for all species of bird and at one time they had cloaked her towers in plumage.

Now Elric chanted his verses, recalling that bargain and begging Fileet to remember her part of it.

> "Brothers and sisters of the sky
>   Hear my voice where'er ye fly
>   And bring me aid from kingdoms high . . ."

Not for the first time had he called upon the elementals and those akin to them. But lately he had summoned Haaashaastaak, Lord of the Lizards, in his fight against Theleb K'aarna and still earlier he had made use of the services of the wind elementals—the sylphs, the sharnahs and the h'Haarshanns—and the earth elementals.

Yet, Fileet was fickle.

And now that Imrryr was no more than quaking ruins, she could even choose to forget that ancient pact.

"Fileet . . ."

He was weak from the invoking. He would not have the strength to battle Theleb K'aarna even if he found the opportunity.

"Fileet . . ."

And then the air was stirring and a huge shadow fell across the chimerae bearing Elric and Moonglum northward.

Elric's voice faltered as he looked up. But he smiled and said:

"I thank you, Fileet."

For the sky was black with birds. There were eagles and robins and rooks and starlings and wrens and kites and crows and hawks and peacocks and flamingoes and pigeons and parrots and doves and magpies and ravens and owls. Their plumage flashed like steel and the air was full of their cries.

The Oonai raised its snake's head and hissed, its long tongue curling out between its front fangs, its coiled tail lashing. One of the chimerae not carrying Elric or Moonglum changed its shape into that of a gigantic condor and flapped up towards the vast array of birds.

But they were not deceived.

The chimera disappeared, submerged by birds. There was a frightful screaming and then something black and piglike spiraled to earth, blood and entrails streaming in its wake.

Another chimera—the last not bearing a burden—assumed its dragon shape, almost completely identical to those which Elric had once mastered as ruler of Melniboné, but larger and with not quite the same grace as Flamefang and the others.

There was a sickening smell of burning flesh and feathers as the flaming venom fell upon Elric's allies.

But now more and more birds were filling the air, shrieking and whistling and cawing and hooting, a million wings fluttering, and once again the Oonai was hidden from sight, once again a muffled scream sounded, once again a mangled, piglike corpse plummeted groundwards.

The birds divided into two masses, turning their attention to the chimerae bearing Elric and Moonglum. They sped down like two gigantic arrowheads, led, each group, by ten huge golden eagles which dived at the flashing eyes of the Oonai.

As the birds attacked, the chimerae were forced to change shape. Instantly Elric felt himself fall free. His body was numb and he fell like a stone, remembering only to keep his grip on Stormbringer, and as he fell he cursed at the irony. He had been saved from the beasts of Chaos only to hurtle to his death on the snow-covered ground below.

But then his cloak was caught from above and he hung swaying in the air. Looking up he saw that several eagles had grasped his clothing in their claws and beaks and were slowing his descent so that he struck the snow with little more than a painful bump.

The eagles flew back to the fray.

A few yards away Moonglum came down, deposited by another flight of eagles which immediately returned to where their comrades were fighting the remaining Oonai.

Moonglum picked up the sword which had fallen from his hand. He rubbed his right calf. "I'll do my best never to eat fowl again," he said feelingly. "So you remembered a spell, eh?"

"Aye."

Two more piglike corpses thudded down not far away.

For a few moments the birds performed a strange, wheeling dance in the sky, partly a salute to the two men, partly a dance of triumph, and then they divided into their groups of species and flew rapidly away. Soon there were no birds at all in the ice-blue sky.

Elric picked up his bruised body and stiffly he sheathed his sword Stormbringer. He drew a deep breath and peered upwards.

"Fileet, I thank thee again."

Moonglum still seemed dazed. "How did you summon them, Elric?"

Elric removed his helmet and wiped sweat from within the rim. In this clime that sweat would soon turn to ice. "An ancient bargain my ancestors made. I was hard pressed to remember the lines of the spell."

"I'm mightily pleased that you did remember!"

Absently, Elric nodded. He replaced his helmet on his head, staring about him as he did so.

Everywhere stretched the vast, snow-covered Lormyrian steppe.

Moonglum understood Elric's thoughts. He rubbed his chin.

"Aye. We are fairly lost, Lord Elric. Have you any idea where we may be?"

"I do not know, friend Moonglum. We have no means of guessing how far those beasts carried us, but I'm fairly sure it was well to the north of Iosaz. We are further away from the capital than we were . . ."

"But then so must Theleb K'aarna be! If we were, indeed, being borne to where he dwells . . ."

"It would be logical, I agree."

"So we continue north?"

"I think not."

"Why so?"

"For two reasons. It could be that Theleb K'aarna's idea was to take us to a place so far away from anywhere that we could not interfere with his plans. That might be considered a wiser action than confronting us and thus risking our turning the tables on him . . ."

"Aye, I'll grant you that. And what's the other reason?"

"We would do better to try to make for Iosaz where we can replenish both our gear and our provisions and enquire of Theleb K'aarna's whereabouts if he is not there. Also we would be foolish to strike further north without good horses and in Iosaz we shall find horses and perhaps a sleigh to carry us the faster across this snow."

"And I'll grant you the sense of that, too. But I do not think much of our chances in this snow, whichever way we go."

"We must begin walking and hope that we can find a river that has not yet frozen over—and that the river will have boats upon it which will bear us to Iosaz."

"A faint hope, Elric."

"Aye. A faint hope." Elric was already weakened from the energy spent in the invocation to Fileet. He knew that he must almost certainly die. He was not sure that he cared overmuch. It would be a cleaner death than some he had been offered of late—a less painful death than any he might expect at the hands of the sorcerer of Pan Tang.

They began to trudge through the snow. Slowly they headed south, two small figures in a frozen landscape, two tiny specks of warm flesh in a great waste of ice.

Chapter Four

Old Castle Standing Alone

A day passed, a night passed.

Then the evening of the second day passed and the two men staggered on, for all that they had long since lost their sense of direction.

Night fell and they crawled.

They could not speak. Their bones were stiff, their flesh and their muscles numb.

Cold and exhaustion drove the very sentience from them so that when they fell in the snow and lay motionless they were scarcely aware that they had ceased to move. They understood no difference now between life and death, between existence and the cessation of existence.

And when the sun rose and warmed their flesh a little they stirred and raised their heads, perhaps in an effort to catch one last glimpse of the world they were leaving.

And they saw the castle.

It stood there in the middle of the steppe and it was ancient. Snow covered the moss and the lichen which grew on its worn, old stones. It seemed to have been there for eternity, yet neither Elric nor Moonglum had ever heard of such a castle standing alone in the steppe. It was hard to imagine how a castle so old could exist in the land once known as World's Edge.

Moonglum was the first to rise. He stumbled through the deep snow to where Elric lay. With chapped hands he tried to lift his friend.

The tide of Elric's thin blood had almost ceased to move in his body. He moaned as Moonglum helped him to his feet. He tried to speak, but his lips were frozen shut.

Clutching each other, sometimes walking, sometimes crawling, they progressed towards the castle.

Its entrance stood open. They fell through it and the warmth issuing from the interior revived them sufficiently to allow them to rise and stagger down a narrow passage into a great hall.

It was an empty hall.

It was completely bare of furnishings, save for a huge log fire that blazed in a hearth of granite and quartz built at the far end of the hall. They crossed flagstones of lapis lazuli to reach it.

"So the castle is inhabited."

Moonglum's voice was harsh and thick in his mouth. He stared around him at the basalt walls. He raised his voice as best he could and called:

"Greetings to whoever is the master of this hall. We are Moonglum of Elwher and Elric of Melniboné and we crave your hospitality, for we are lost in your land."

And then Elric's knees buckled and he fell to the floor.

Moonglum stumbled towards him as the echoes of his voice died in the hall. All was silent save for the crackling of the logs in the hearth.

Moonglum dragged Elric to the fire and laid him down near it.

"Warm your bones here, friend Elric. I'll seek the folk who live here."

Then he crossed the hall and ascended the stone stair leading to the next floor of the castle.

This floor was as bereft of furniture or decoration as the other. There were many rooms, but all of them were empty. Moonglum began to feel uneasy, scenting something of the supernatural here. Could this be Theleb K'aarna's castle?

For someone dwelt here, in truth. Someone had laid the fire and had opened the gates so that they might enter. And they had not left the castle in the ordinary way or he should have noticed the tracks in the snow outside.

Moonglum paused, then turned and slowly began to descend the stairs. Reaching the hall, he saw that Elric had revived enough to prop himself up against the chimneypiece.

"And—what—found you . . ." said Elric thickly.

Moonglum shrugged. "Nought. No servants. No master. If they have gone a-hunting, then they hunt on flying beasts, for there are no signs of hoofprints in the snow outside. I am a little nervous, I must admit." He smiled slightly. "Aye—and a little hungry, too. I'll seek the pantry. If danger comes, we'd do as well to face it on full stomachs."

There was a door set back and to one side of the hearth. He tried the latch and it opened into a short passage at the end of which was another door. He went down the passage, hand on sword, and opened the door at the end. A parlour, as deserted as the rest of the castle. And beyond the parlour he saw the castle's kitchens. He went through the kitchens, noting that there were cooking things here, all polished and clean but none in use, and came finally to the pantry.

Here he found the best part of a large deer hanging and on the shelf above it were ranked many skins and jars of wine. Below this shelf were bread and some pasties and below that spices.

Moonglum's first action was to reach up on tiptoe and take down a jar of wine, removing the cork and sniffing the contents.

He had smelled nothing more delicate or delicious in his life.

He tasted the wine and he forgot his pain and his weariness. But he did not forget that Elric still waited in the hall.

With his short sword he cut off a haunch of venison and tucked it under his arm. He selected some spices and put them into his belt pouch. Under his other arm he put the bread and in both hands he carried a jar of wine.

He returned to the hall, put down his spoils and helped Elric drink from the jar.

The strange wine worked almost instantly and Elric offered Moonglum a smile that had gratitude in it.

"You are—a good friend—I wonder why . . ."

Moonglum turned away with an embarrassed grunt. He began to prepare the meat which he intended to roast over the fire.

He had never understood his friendship with the albino. It had always been a peculiar mixture of reserve and affection, a fine balance which both men were careful to maintain, even in situations of this kind.

Elric, since his passion for Cymoril had resulted in her death and the destruction of the city he loved, had at all times feared bestowing any tender emotion on those he fell in with.

He had run away from Shaarilla of the Dancing Mist, who had loved him dearly. He had fled from Queen Yishana of Jharkor, who had offered him her kingdom to rule, in spite of her subjects' hatred of him. He disdained most company save Moonglum's, and Moonglum, too, became quickly bored by anyone other than the crimson-eyed prince of Imrryr. Moonglum would die for Elric and he knew that Elric would risk any danger to save his friend. But was not this an unhealthy relationship? Would it not be better if they went their different ways? He could not bear the thought. It was as if they were part of the same entity—different aspects of the character of the same man.

He could not understand why he should feel this. And he guessed that, if Elric had ever considered the question, the Melnibonéan would be equally hard put to find an answer.

He contemplated all this as he roasted the meat before the fire, using his long sword as a spit.

Meanwhile Elric took another draft of wine and began, almost visibly, to thaw out. His skin was still badly blistered by chilblains, but both men had escaped serious frostbite.

They ate the venison in silence, glancing around the hall, puzzling over the non-appearance of the owner, yet too tired to care greatly where he was.

Then they slept, having put fresh logs on the fire, and in the morning they were almost completely recovered from their ordeal in the snow.

They breakfasted on cold venison and pasties and wine.

Moonglum found a pot and heated water in it so that they might shave and wash and Elric found some salve in his pouch which they could put on their blisters.

"I looked in the stables," Moonglum said as he shaved with the razor he had taken from his own pouch. "But I found no horses. There are signs, however, that some beasts have been kept there recently."

"There is only one other way to travel," Elric said. "There might be skis somewhere in the castle. It is the sort of thing you might expect to find, for there is snow in these parts for at least half the year. Skis would speed our progress back towards Iosaz. As would a map and a lodestone if we could find one."

Moonglum agreed. "I'll search the upper levels." He finished his shaving, wiped his razor and replaced it in his pouch.

Elric got up. "I'll go with you."

Through the empty rooms they wandered, but they found nothing.

"No gear of any kind." Elric frowned. "And yet there is a strong sense that the castle *is* inhabited—and evidence, too, of course."

They searched two more floors and there was not even dust in the rooms.

"Well, perhaps we walk after all," Moonglum said in resignation. "Unless there was wood with which we could manufacture skis of some kind. I might have seen some in the stables . . ."

They had reached a narrow stair which wound up to the highest tower of the castle.

"We'll try this and then count our quest unsuccessful," Elric said.

And so they climbed the stair and came to a door at the top which was half-open. Elric pushed it back and then he hesitated.

"What is it?" Moonglum, who was below him, asked.

"This room is furnished," Elric said quietly.

Moonglum ascended two more steps and peered round Elric's shoulder. He gasped.

"And occupied!"

It was a beautiful room. Through crystal windows came pale light which sparkled and fell on hangings of many-coloured silk, on embroidered carpets and tapestries of hues so fresh they might have been made only a moment before.

In the centre of this room was a bed, draped in ermine, with a canopy of white silk.

And on the bed lay a young woman.

Her hair was black and it shone. Her gown was of the deepest scarlet. Her limbs were like rose-tinted ivory and her face was very fair, the lips slightly parted as she breathed.

She was asleep.

Elric took two steps towards the woman on the bed and then he stopped suddenly. He was shuddering. He turned away.

Moonglum was alarmed. He saw bright tears in Elric's crimson eyes.

"What is it, friend Elric?"

Elric moved his white lips but was incapable of speech. Something like a groan came from his throat.

"Elric . . ."

Moonglum placed a hand on his friend's arm. Elric shook it off.

Slowly the albino turned again towards the bed, as if forcing himself to behold an impossibly horrifying sight. He breathed deeply,

straightening his back and resting his left hand on the pommel of his
sorcerous blade.

"Moonglum . . ."

He was forcing himself to speak. Moonglum glanced at the woman
on the bed, glanced at Elric. Did he recognize her?

"Moonglum—this is a sorcerous sleep . . ."

"How know you that?"

"It—it is a similar slumber to that in which my cousin Yyrkoon put
my Cymoril . . ."

"Gods! Think you that . . . ?"

"I think nothing!"

"But it is not—"

"—it is not Cy-
moril. I know. I—she
is like her—so like her.
But unlike her, too . . . It is
only that I could not have expected . . ."

Elric bowed his head.

He spoke in a low voice.
"Come, let's be gone from
here."

"But she must be
the owner of this
castle. If we
awakened
her we
could—"

"She cannot be awakened by such as we. I told you, Moonglum . . ."
Elric drew another deep breath. "It is an enchanted sleep she is in. I
could not wake Cymoril from it, with all my powers of sorcery. Unless
one has certain magical aids, some knowledge of the exact spell used,
there is nothing that can be done. Quickly, Moonglum, let us depart."

There was an edge to Elric's voice which made Moonglum shiver.

"But . . ."

"Then I will go!"

Elric almost ran from the room. Moonglum heard his footsteps
echoing rapidly down the long staircase.

He went up to the sleeping woman and stared down at her beauty.
He touched the skin. It was unnaturally cold. He shrugged and
made to leave the chamber, pausing for a moment only to notice that a
number of ancient battle-shields and weapons hung on one wall of the
room, behind the bed. Strange trophies with which a beautiful woman
should wish to decorate her bedroom, he thought. He saw the carved
wooden table below the trophies. Something lay upon it. He stepped
back into the room. A peculiar sensation filled him as he saw that it was
a map. The castle was marked and so was the Zaphra-Trepek river.

Holding the map down to the table was a lodestone, set in silver on
a long silver chain.

He grabbed the map in one hand and the lodestone in the other
and ran from the room.

"Elric! Elric!"

He raced down the stairs and reached the hall. Elric had gone. The
door of the hall was open.

He followed the albino out of the mysterious castle and into the
snow.

"Elric!"

Elric turned, his face set and his eyes tormented.

Moonglum showed him the map and the lodestone.

"We are saved, after all, Elric!"

Elric looked down at the snow. "Aye. So we are."

CHAPTER FIVE

Doomed Lord Dreaming

And two days later they reached the upper reaches of the Zaphra-Trepek and the trading town of Alorasaz with its towers of finely carved wood and its beautifully made timber houses.

To Alorasaz came the fur trappers and the miners, the merchants from Iosaz, down-river, or from afar as Trepesaz on the coast. A cheerful, bustling town with its streets lit and heated by great, red braziers at every corner. These were tended by citizens specially commissioned to keep them burning hot and bright. Wrapped in thick woolen clothing, they hailed Elric and Moonglum as they entered the city.

For all they had been sustained by the wine and meat Moonglum had thought to bring, they were weary from their walk across the steppe.

They made their way through the rumbustious crowd—laughing, red-cheeked women and burly, fur-swathed men whose breath steamed in the air, mingling with the smoke from the braziers, as they took huge swallows from gourds of beer or skins of wine, conducting their business with the slightly less bucolic merchants of the more sophisticated townships.

Elric was looking for news and he knew that if he found it anywhere it would be in the taverns. He waited while Moonglum followed his nose to the best of Alorasaz's inns and came back with the news of where it could be found.

They walked a short distance and entered a rowdy tavern crammed with big wooden tables and benches on which were jammed more traders and more merchants all arguing cheerfully, holding up furs to display their quality or to mock their worthlessness, depending on which point of view was taken.

Moonglum left Elric standing in the doorway and went to speak with the landlord, a hugely fat man with a glistening scarlet face.

Elric saw the landlord bend and listen to Moonglum. The man

nodded and raised an arm to bellow at Elric to follow him and Moonglum.

Elric inched his way through the press and was knocked half off his feet by a gesticulating trader who apologized cheerfully and profusely and offered to buy him a drink.

"It is nothing," Elric said faintly.

The man got up. "Come on, sir, it was my fault . . ." His voice tailed off as he saw the albino's face. He mumbled something and sat down again, making a wry remark to one of his companions.

Elric followed Moonglum and the landlord up a flight of swaying wooden stairs, along a landing and into a private room which, the landlord told them, was all that was available.

"Such rooms as these are expensive during the winter market," the landlord said apologetically.

And Moonglum winced as, silently, Elric handed the man another precious ruby worth a small fortune.

The landlord looked at it carefully and then laughed. "This inn will have fallen down before your credit's up, master. I thank thee. Trading must be good this season! I'll have drink and viands sent up at once!"

"The finest you have, landlord," said Moonglum, trying to make the best of things.

"Aye—I wish I had better."

Elric sat down on one of the beds and removed his cloak and his sword belt. The chill had not left his bones.

"I wish you would give me charge of our wealth," Moonglum said as he removed his boots by the fire. "We might have need of it before this quest is ended."

But Elric seemed not to hear him.

After they had eaten and discovered from the landlord that a ship was leaving the day after tomorrow for Iosaz, Elric and Moonglum went to their separate beds to sleep.

Elric's dreams were troubled that night. More than usual did phantoms come to walk the dark corridors of his mind.

He saw Cymoril screaming as the Black Sword drank her soul. He saw Imrryr burning, her fine towers crumbling. He saw his cackling cousin Yyrkoon sprawling on the Ruby Throne. He saw other things which could not possibly be part of his past . . .

Never quite suited to be ruler of the cruel folk of Melniboné, Elric had wandered the lands of men only to discover that he had no place there, either. And in the meantime Yyrkoon had usurped the kingship, had tried to force Cymoril to be his and, when she refused, put her into a deep and sorcerous slumber from which only he could wake her.

Now Elric dreamed that he had found a Nanorion, the mystic gem which could awaken even the dead. He dreamed that Cymoril was still alive, but sleeping, and that he placed the Nanorion on her forehead and that she woke up and kissed him and left Imrryr with him, sailing through the skies on Flamefang, the great Melnibonéan battle dragon, away to a peaceful castle in the snow.

He awoke with a start.

It was the dead of night.

Even the noise from the tavern below had subsided.

He opened his eyes and saw Moonglum fast asleep in the next bed.

He tried to return to sleep, but it was impossible. He was sure that he could sense another presence in the room. He reached out and gripped the hilt of Stormbringer, prepared to defend himself should any attackers strike at him. Perhaps it was thieves who had heard of his generosity towards the innkeeper?

He heard something move in the room and, again, he opened his eyes.

She was standing there, her black hair curling over her shoulders, her scarlet gown clinging to her body. Her lips curved in a smile of irony and her eyes regarded him steadily.

She was the woman he had seen in the castle. The sleeping woman. Was this part of the dream?

"Forgive me for thus intruding upon your slumber and your privacy, my lord, but my business is urgent and I have little time to spare."

Elric saw that Moonglum still slept as if in a drugged slumber.

He sat upright in his bed. Stormbringer moaned softly and then was silent.

"You seem to know me, my lady, but I do not—"

"I am called Myshella . . ."

"Empress of the Dawn?"

She smiled again. "Some have named me that. And others have called me the Dark Lady of Kaneloon."

"Whom Aubec loved? Then you must have preserved your youth carefully, Lady Myshella."

"No doing of mine. It is possible that I am immortal. I do not know. I know only one thing and that is that time is a deception . . ."

"Why do you come?"

"I cannot stay for long. I come to seek your aid."

"In what way?"

"We have an enemy in common, I believe."

"Theleb K'aarna?"

"The same."

"Did he place that enchantment upon you that made you sleep?"

"Aye."

"And he sent his Oonai against me. That is how—"

She raised her hand.

"I sent the chimerae to find you and bring you to me. They meant you no harm. But it was the only thing I could do, for Theleb K'aarna's spell was already beginning to work. I battle his sorcery, but it is strong and I am unable to revive myself for more than very short periods. This is one such period. Theleb K'aarna has joined forces with Prince Umbda, Lord of the Kelmain Host. Their plan is to conquer Lormyr and, ultimately, the entire Southern World!"

"Who is this Umbda? I have heard neither of him nor of the Kelmain Host. Some noble of Iosaz, perhaps, who . . ."

"Prince Umbda serves Chaos. He comes from the lands beyond World's Edge and his Kelmain are not men at all, though they have the appearance of men."

"So Theleb K'aarna was in the far south, after all."

"That is why I came to you tonight."

"You wish me to help you?"

"We both need Theleb K'aarna destroyed. His sorcery is what enabled Prince Umbda to cross World's Edge. Now that sorcery is strengthened by what Umbda brings—the friendship of Chaos. I protect Lormyr and I serve Law. I know that you serve Chaos, yet I hope your hatred of Theleb K'aarna overcomes that loyalty for the moment."

"Chaos has not served me, of late, lady, so I'll forget that loyalty. I would have my vengeance on Theleb K'aarna and if we can help each other in the matter, so much the better."

"Good."

She gasped then and her eyes glazed. When next she spoke it was with some difficulty.

"The enchantment is exerting its hold again. I have a steed for you near the town's north gate. It will bear you to an island in the Boiling Sea. On that island is a palace called Ashaneloon. It is there that I have dwelt of late, until I sensed Lormyr's danger . . ."

She pressed her hand to her brow and swayed.

". . . But Theleb K'aarna expected me to try to return there and he placed a guardian at the palace's gate. That guardian must be destroyed. When you have destroyed it you must go to the . . ."

Elric rose to help her, but she waved him away.

". . . to the eastern tower. In the tower's lower room is a chest. In the chest is a large pouch of cloth-of-gold. You must take that and—and bring it back to Kaneloon, for Umbda and his Kelmain now march against the castle. Theleb K'aarna will destroy the castle with their help—and destroy me, also. With the pouch, I may destroy them. But pray that I am able to wake, or the South is doomed and even you will not be able to go against the power that Theleb K'aarna will wield."

"What of Moonglum?" Elric glanced at his sleeping friend. "Can he accompany me?"

"Best not. Besides, he has a light enchantment upon him. There is no time to wake him . . ." She gasped again and flung her arms across her forehead. "No time . . ."

Elric leapt from the bed and began to pull on his breeks. He took his cloak from where it was draped across a stool and he buckled on his runesword. He went forward to help her, but she signaled him away.

"No . . . Go, please . . ."

And she vanished.

Still half asleep Elric flung open the door and dashed down the stairs, out into the night, racing for the north gate of Alorasaz, passing through it and running on through the snow, looking this way and that. The cold flooded over him like a sudden wave. He was soon knee-deep in snow. Peering about him he carried on until he stopped in his tracks.

He gasped in astonishment when he saw the steed which Myshella had provided for him.

"What's this? Another chimera?"

He approached it cautiously.

Chapter Six

Jeweled Bird Speaking

It was a bird, but it was not a bird of flesh and blood.

It was a bird of silver and of gold and of brass. Its wings clashed as he approached it and it moved its huge clawed feet impatiently, turning cold, emerald eyes to regard him.

On its back was a saddle of carved onyx chased in gold and copper and the saddle was empty, awaiting him.

"Well, I began all this unquestioningly," Elric said to himself. "I might as well complete it in the same manner."

And he went up to the bird and he climbed up its side and he lowered himself somewhat cautiously into the saddle.

The wings of gold and silver flapped with the sound of a hundred cymbals meeting and with three movements had taken the bird of metal and its rider high up into the night sky above Alorasaz. It turned its bright head on its neck of brass and it opened its curved beak of gem-studded steel.

"Well, master, I am commanded to take thee to Ashaneloon."

Elric waved a pale hand. "Wherever you will. I am at the mercy of you and your mistress."

And then he was jerked backward in the saddle as the bird's wings beat the stronger and it gathered speed and he was rushing through the freezing night, over snowy plains, over mountains, over rivers, until the coast came in sight and he saw the sea in the west which was called the Boiling Sea.

Down through the pitch blackness dropped the bird of gold and silver and now Elric felt damp heat strike his face and hands, heard a peculiar bubbling sound, and he knew they were flying over that strange sea said to be fed by volcanoes lying deep below its surface, a sea where few ships sailed.

Steam surrounded them now. Its heat was almost unbearable, but through it Elric began to make out the silhouette of a landmass, a small rocky island on which stood a single building with slender towers and turrets and domes.

"The palace of Ashaneloon," said the bird of silver and gold. "I will alight among the battlements, master, but I fear that thing you must meet before our errand is accomplished, so I will await you elsewhere. Then, if you live, I will return to take you back to Kaneloon. And, if you die, I will go back to tell my mistress of your failure."

Over the battlements the bird now hovered, its wings beating, and Elric reflected that there would be no advantage of surprise over whatever it was the bird feared so much.

He swung one leg from the saddle, paused, and then leapt down to the flat roof.

Hastily the bird retreated into the black sky.

Elric was alone.

All was silent, save for the drumming of warm waves on a distant shore.

He located the eastern tower and began to make his way towards the door. There was some chance, perhaps, that he could complete his quest without the necessity of facing the palace's guardian.

But then a monstrous bellow sounded behind him and he wheeled, knowing that this must be the guardian. A creature stood there, its red-rimmed eyes full of insensate malice.

"So you are Theleb K'aarna's slave," said Elric. He reached for Stormbringer and the sword seemed to spring into his hand at its own volition. "Must I kill you, or will you be gone now?"

The creature bellowed again, but it did not move.

The albino said: "I am Elric of Melniboné, last of a line of great Sorcerer Kings. This blade I wield will do more than kill you, friend demon. It will drink your soul and feed it to me. Perhaps you have heard of me by another name? By the name of the Soul Thief?"

The creature lashed its serrated tail and its bovine nostrils distended. The horned head swayed on the short neck and the long teeth gleamed in the darkness. It reached out scaly claws and began to lumber towards the prince of ruins.

Elric took the sword in both hands and spread his feet wide apart on the flagstones and prepared to meet the monster's charge. Foul breath struck his face. Another bellow and then it was upon him.

Stormbringer howled and spilled black radiance over both. The runes carved in the blade glowed with a greedy glow as the thing of hell slashed at Elric's body with its claws, ripping the shirt from him and baring his chest.

The sword came down.

The demon roared as the scales of its shoulder received the blow but did not part. It danced to one side and attacked again. Elric swayed back, but now a thin wound was opened in his arm from elbow to wrist.

Stormbringer struck for the second time and hit the demon's snout so that it shrieked and lashed out once more. Again its claws found Elric's body and blood smeared his chest from a shallow cut.

Elric fell back, losing his footing on the stones. He almost went down, but recovered his balance and defended himself as best he could. The claws slashed at him, but Stormbringer drove them to one side.

Elric began to pant and the sweat poured down his face and he felt desperation well in him and then that desperation took a different quality and his eyes glowed and his lips snarled.

"Know you that I am Elric!" he cried. "Elric!"

Still the creature attacked.

"I am Elric—more demon than man! Begone, you ill-shaped thing!"

The creature bellowed and pounced and this time Elric did not fall back, but, his face writhing in terrible rage, reversed his grip on the runesword and plunged it point first into the demon's open jaws.

He plunged the Black Sword down the stinking throat, down into the torso.

He wrenched the blade so that it split jaw, neck, chest and groin and the creature's life-force began to course along the length of the runesword. The claws lashed out at him, but the creature was weakening.

Then the life-force pulsed up the blade and reached Elric who gasped and screamed in dark ecstasy as the demon's energy poured into him. He withdrew the blade and hacked and hacked at the body and still the life-force flowed into him and gave greater power to his blows. The demon groaned and dropped to the flagstones.

And it was done.

And a white-faced demon stood over the dead thing of hell and its crimson eyes blazed and its pale mouth opened and it roared with wild laughter, flinging its arms upward, the runesword flaming with a black and horrid flame, and it howled a wordless, exultant song to the Lords of Chaos.

There was silence suddenly.

And then it bowed its head and it wept.

Now Elric opened the door to the eastern tower and stumbled through absolute blackness until he came to the lowest room. The door to the room was locked and barred, but Stormbringer smashed through it and the Last Lord of Melniboné entered a lighted room in which squatted a chest of iron.

His sword sundered the bands securing the chest and he flung open the lid and saw that there were many wonders in the chest, as well as the pouch made from cloth-of-gold, but he picked out only the pouch and tucked it into his belt as he raced from the room, back to the battlements where the bird of silver and gold stood pecking with its steel beak at the remnants of Theleb K'aarna's servant.

It looked up as Elric returned. In its eyes was an expression almost of humour.

"Well, master, we must make haste to Kaneloon."

"Aye."

Nausea had begun to fill Elric. His eyes were gloomy as he contemplated the corpse and that which he had stolen from it. Such life-force, whatever else it was, must surely be tainted. Did not he drink something of the demon's evil when his sword drank its soul?

He was about to climb back into the onyx saddle when he saw something gleaming amongst the black and yellow entrails he had spilled. It was the demon's heart—an irregularly shaped stone of deep blue and purple and green. It still pulsed, though its owner was dead.

Elric stooped and picked it up. It was wet and so hot that it almost burned his hand, but he tucked it into his pouch, then mounted the bird of silver and gold.

His bone-white face flickered with a dozen strange emotions as he let the bird bear him back over the Boiling Sea. His milk-white hair flew wildly behind him and he was oblivious of the wounds on his arm and chest.

He was thinking of other things. Some of his thoughts lay in the past and others were in the future. And he laughed bitterly twice and his eyes shed tears and he spoke once.

"Ah, what agony is this Life!"

Chapter Seven

Black Wizard Laughing

To Kaneloon they came in the early dawn and in the distance Elric saw a massive army darkening the snow and he knew it must be the Kelmain Host, led by Theleb K'aarna and Prince Umbda, marching against the lonely castle.

The bird of gold and silver flapped down in the snow outside the castle's entrance and Elric dismounted. Then the bird had risen into the air again and was gone.

The great gate of Castle Kaneloon was closed this time and he gathered his tattered cloak about his naked torso and he hammered on the gate with his fists and he forced a cry from his dry lips.

"Myshella! Myshella!"

There was no answer.

"Myshella! I have returned with that which you need!"

He feared she must have fallen into her enchanted slumber again. He looked towards the south and the dark tide had rolled a little closer to the castle.

"Myshella!"

Then he heard a bar being drawn and the gates groaned open and there stood Moonglum, his face strained and his eyes full of something of which he could not speak.

"Moonglum! How came you here?"

"I know not how, Elric." Moonglum stepped aside so that Elric could enter. He replaced the bar. "I lay in my bed last night when a woman came to me—the same woman we saw, sleeping, here. She said I must go with her. And somehow go I did. But I know not how, Elric. I know not how."

"And where is that woman?"

"Where we first saw her. She sleeps and I cannot wake her."

Elric drew a deep breath and told, briefly, what he knew of Myshella and the host that came against her Castle Kaneloon.

"Do you know the contents of that pouch?" Moonglum asked.

Elric shook his head and opened the pouch to peer inside. "It seems to be nothing but a pinkish dust. Yet it must be some powerful sorcery if Myshella believes it can defeat the entire Kelmain Host."

Moonglum frowned. "But surely Myshella must work the charm herself if only she knows what it is?"

"Aye."

"And Theleb K'aarna has enchanted her."

"Aye."

"And now it is too late, for Umbda—whoever he may be—nears the castle."

"Aye." Elric's hand trembled as he drew from his belt the thing he had taken from the demon just before he left the palace of Ashaneloon. "Unless this is the stone I think it is."

"What is that?"

"I know a legend. Some demons possess these stones as hearts." He held it to the light so that the blues and purples and greens writhed. "I have never seen one, but I believe it to be the thing I once sought for Cymoril when I tried to lift my cousin's charm from her. What I sought but never found was a Nanorion. A stone of magical powers said to be able to waken the dead—or those in deathlike sleep."

"And that is a Nanorion. It will awaken Myshella?"

"If anything can, then this will, for I took it from Theleb K'aarna's own demon and that must improve the efficaciousness of the magic. Come." Elric strode through the hall and up the stairs until he came to Myshella's room where she lay, as he had seen her before, on the bed hung with draperies, her wall hung with shields and weapons.

"Now I understand why these arms decorate her chamber," Moonglum said. "According to legend, these are the shields and weapons of all those who loved Myshella and championed her cause."

Elric nodded and said, as if to himself, "Aye, she was ever an enemy of Melniboné, was the Empress of the Dawn."

He held the pulsing stone delicately and reached out to place it on her forehead.

"It makes no difference," Moonglum said after a moment. "She does not stir."

"There is a rune, but I remember it not . . ." Elric pressed his fingers to his temples. "I remember it not . . ."

Moonglum went to the window. "We can ask Theleb K'aarna, perhaps," he said ironically. "He will be here soon enough."

Then Moonglum saw that there were tears again in Elric's eyes and that he had turned away, hoping Moonglum would not see. Moonglum cleared his throat. "I have some business below. Call me if you should require my help."

He left the room and closed the door and Elric was alone with the woman who seemed, increasingly, a dreadful phantom from his most frightful dreams.

He controlled his feverish mind and tried to discipline it, to remember the crucial runes in the High Speech of Old Melniboné.

"Gods!" he hissed. "Help me!"

But he knew that in this matter in particular the Lords of Chaos would not assist him—would hinder him if they could, for Myshella was one of the chief instruments of Law upon the Earth, had been responsible for driving Chaos from the world.

He fell to his knees beside her bed, his hands clenched, his face twisting with the effort.

And then it came back to him. His head still bent, he stretched out his right hand and touched the pulsing stone, stretched out his left hand and rested it upon Myshella's navel, and he began a chant in an ancient tongue that had been spoken before true men had ever walked the Earth . . .

"Elric!"

Moonglum burst into the room and Elric was wrenched from his trance.

"Elric! We are invaded! Their advance riders . . ."

"What?"

"They have broken into the castle—a dozen of them. I fought them off and barred the way up to this tower, but they are hacking at the door now. I think they have been sent to destroy Myshella if they could. They were surprised to discover me here."

Elric rose and looked carefully down at Myshella. The rune was finished and had been repeated almost through again when Moonglum had come in. She did not stir yet.

"Theleb K'aarna worked his sorcery from a distance," Moonglum said. "Ensuring that Myshella would not resist him. But he did not reckon with us."

He and Elric hurried from the room, down the steps to where a door was bulging and splintering beneath the weapons of those beyond.

"Stand back, Moonglum."

Elric drew the crooning runesword, lifted it high and brought it against the door.

The door split and two oddly shaped skulls were split with it.

The remainder of the attackers fell back with cries of astonishment and horror as the white-faced reaver fell upon them, his huge sword drinking their souls and singing its strange, undulating song.

Down the stairs Elric pursued them. Into the hall where they bunched together and prepared to defend themselves from this demon with his hell-forged blade.

And Elric laughed.

And they shuddered.

And their weapons trembled in their hands.

"So you are the mighty Kelmain," Elric sneered. "No wonder you needed sorcery to aid you if you are so cowardly. Have you not heard, beyond World's Edge, of Elric Kinslayer?"

But the Kelmain plainly did not understand his speech, which was strange enough in itself, for he had spoken in the common tongue, known to all men.

These people had golden skins and eye-sockets that were almost square. Their faces, in all, seemed crudely carved from rock, all sharp angles and planes, and their armour was not rounded, but angular.

Elric bared his teeth in a smile and the Kelmain drew closer together.

Then he screamed with dreadful laughter and Moonglum stepped back and did not look at what took place.

The runesword swung. Heads and limbs were chopped away. Blood gouted. Souls were taken. The Kelmain's dead faces bore expressions showing that before the life was drawn from them they had known the truth of their appalling fate.

And Stormbringer drank again, for Stormbringer was a thirsty hellsword.

And Elric felt his deficient veins swell with even more energy than that which he had taken earlier from Theleb K'aarna's demon.

The hall shook with Elric's insane mirth and he strode over the piled corpses and he went through the open gateway to where the great host waited.

And he shouted a name:

"Theleb K'aarna, Theleb K'aarna!"

Moonglum ran after him, calling for him to stop, but Elric did not heed him. Elric strode on through the snow, his sword dripping a red trail behind him.

Under a cold sun, the Kelmain were riding for the castle called Kaneloon and Elric went to meet them.

At their head, on slender horses, rode the dark-faced sorcerer of Pan Tang, dressed in flowing robes, and beside him was the prince of the Kelmain Host, Prince Umbda, in proud armour, bizarre plumes nodding on his helm, a triumphant smile on his strange, angular features.

Behind, the host dragged oddly fashioned war-gear which, for all its oddness, looked powerful—mightier than anything Lormyr could rally when the huge army fell upon her.

As the lone figure appeared and began to walk away from the walls of Castle Kaneloon, Theleb K'aarna raised his hand and stopped the host's advance, reining in his own horse and laughing.

"Why, it is the jackal of Melniboné, by all the Gods of Chaos! He acknowledges his master at last and comes to deliver himself up to me!"

Elric came closer and Theleb K'aarna laughed on. "Here, Elric—kneel before me!"

Elric did not pause, seemed not to hear the Pan Tangian's words.

Prince Umbda's eyes were troubled and he said something in a strange tongue. Theleb K'aarna sniffed and replied in the same language.

And still the albino marched through the snow towards the huge host.

"By Chardros, Elric, stop!" cried Theleb K'aarna, his horse shifting nervously beneath him. "If you have come to bargain you are a fool. Kaneloon and her mistress must fall before Lormyr is ours—and Lormyr shall be ours, there's no doubting that!"

Then Elric did stop and he brought up his eyes to burn into those of the sorcerer and there was a still, cold smile upon his pale lips.

Theleb K'aarna tried to meet Elric's gaze but could not. His voice trembled when he next spoke.

"You cannot defeat the whole Kelmain Host!"

"I have no wish to, conjuror. Your life is all I desire."

The sorcerer's face twitched. "Well, you shall not have it! Hai, men of the Kelmain, take him!"

He wheeled his horse and rode into the protective ranks of his warriors, calling out his orders in their own tongue.

From the castle another figure burst, rushing to join Elric.

It was Moonglum of Elwher, a sword in either hand.

Elric half-turned.

"Elric! We'll die together!"

"Stay back, Moonglum!"

Moonglum hesitated.

"Stay back, if you love me!"

Moonglum reluctantly retreated to the castle.

The Kelmain horsemen swept in, broad-bladed straight swords raised, instantly surrounding the albino.

They threatened him, hoping that he would lay down his sword and let himself be captured. But Elric smiled.

Stormbringer began to sing. Elric grasped the sword in both hands, bent his elbows then suddenly held the blade straight out before him.

He began to whirl like a Tarkeshite dancer, round and round, and it was as if the sword dragged him faster and faster while it gouged and gashed and decapitated the Kelmain horsemen.

For a moment they fell back, leaving their dead comrades heaped about the albino, but Prince Umbda, after a hurried conference with Theleb K'aarna, urged them upon Elric again.

And Elric swung his blade once more, but not so many of the Kelmain perished this time.

Armoured body fell against armoured body, blood mingled with brother's blood, horses dragged corpses away with them across the snow and Elric did not fall, yet something was happening to him.

Then it dawned upon his berserker brain that, for some reason, his blade was sated. The energy still pulsed in its metal, but it transferred nothing more to its master. And his own stolen energy was beginning to wane.

"Damn you, Stormbringer! Give me your power!"

Swords rained down upon him as he fought and slew and parried and thrust.

"More power!"

He was still stronger than normal and much stronger than any ordinary mortal, but some of the wild anger was leaving him and he felt almost puzzled as more Kelmain came at him.

He was beginning to waken from the blood-dream.

He shook his head and drew deep breaths. His back was aching.

"Give me their strength, Black Sword!"

He struck at legs and arms and chests and faces and he was covered from head to foot in the blood of his attackers.

But the dead now hampered him worse than the living, for their corpses were everywhere and he almost lost his footing more than once.

"What ails you, runesword? Do you refuse to help me? Will you not fight these things because, like you, they are of Chaos?"

No, it could not be that. All that had happened was that the sword desired no more vitality and therefore gave Elric none.

He fought on for another hour before his grip on the sword weakened and a rider, half-mad with terror, struck a blow at his head, failed to split it but stunned him so that he fell upon the bodies of the slain, tried to rise, then was struck again and lost consciousness.

Chapter Eight

A Great Host Screaming

"It was more than I hoped," murmured Theleb K'aarna in satisfaction, "but we have taken him alive!"

Elric opened his eyes and looked with hatred on the sorcerer who was stroking his black forked beard as if to comfort himself.

Elric could barely remember the events which had brought him here and placed him in the sorcerer's power. He remembered much blood, much laughter, much dying, but it was all fading, like the memory of a dream.

"Well, renegade, your foolishness was unbelievable. I thought you must have an army behind you. But doubtless it was your fear which unbalanced your poor brain. Still, I'll not speculate upon the cause of my own good fortune. There's many a bargain I can strike with the denizens of other planes, were I to offer them your soul. And your body I will keep for myself—to show Queen Yishana what I did to her lover before he died . . ."

Elric laughed shortly and looked about him, ignoring Theleb K'aarna.

The Kelmain were awaiting orders. They had still not marched on Kaneloon. The sun was low in the sky. He saw the pile of corpses behind him. He saw the hatred and fear on the faces of the golden-skinned host and he smiled again.

"I do not love Yishana," he said distantly, as if scarcely aware of Theleb K'aarna's presence. "It is your jealous heart that makes you think so. I left Yishana's side to find you. It is never love that moves Elric of Melniboné, sorcerer, but always hatred."

"I do not believe you," Theleb K'aarna tittered. "When the whole South falls to me and my comrades, then will I court Yishana and offer to make her Queen of all the West as well as all the South. Our forces united, we shall dominate the Earth!"

"You Pan Tangians were ever an insecure breed, forever planning conquest for its own sake, forever seeking to destroy the equilibrium of the Young Kingdoms."

"One day," sneered Theleb K'aarna, "Pan Tang will have an empire that will make the Bright Empire seem a mere flickering ember in the fire of history. But it is not for the glory of Pan Tang that I do this . . ."

"It is for Yishana? By the gods, sorcerer, then I am glad I'm motivated by hatred and not by love, for I do not half the damage, it seems, done by those in love . . ."

"I will lay the South at Yishana's feet and she may use it as she pleases!"

"I am bored by this. What do you intend to do with me?"

"First I will hurt your body. I will hurt it delicately to begin with, building up the pain, until I have you in the proper frame of mind. Then I will consort with the Lords of the Higher Planes to find which will give me most for your soul."

"And what of Kaneloon?"

"The Kelmain will deal with Kaneloon. One knife is all that's needed now to slit Myshella's throat as she sleeps."

"She is protected."

Theleb K'aarna's brow darkened. Then it cleared and he laughed again.

"Aye, but the gate will fall soon enough and your little red-haired friend will perish as Myshella perishes."

He ran his fingers through his oiled ringlets.

"I am allowing, at Prince Umbda's request, the Kelmain to rest a while before storming the castle. But Kaneloon will be burning by nightfall."

Elric looked towards the castle across the trampled snow. Plainly his runes had failed to counter Theleb K'aarna's spell.

"I would . . ." He began to speak when he paused.

He had seen a flash of gold and silver among the battlements and a thought without shape had entered his head and made him hesitate.

"What?" Theleb K'aarna asked him harshly.

"Nothing. I merely wondered where my sword was."

The sorcerer shrugged. "Nowhere you can reach it, reaver. We left it where you dropped it. The stinking hellblade is no use to us. And none to you, now . . ."

Elric wondered what would happen if he made a direct appeal to the sword. He could not get to it himself, for Theleb K'aarna had bound him tightly with ropes of silk, but he might *call* for it . . .

He lifted himself to his feet.

"Would you seek to run away, White Wolf?" Theleb K'aarna watched him nervously.

Elric smiled again. "I wished for a better view of the coming conquest of Kaneloon. Just that."

The sorcerer drew a curved knife.

Elric swayed, his eyes half-closed, and he began to murmur a name beneath his breath.

Theleb K'aarna leapt forward and his arm encircled Elric's head while the knife pricked into the albino's throat. "Be silent, jackal!"

But Elric knew that he had no other means of helping himself and, for all it was a desperate scheme, he murmured the words once more, praying that Theleb K'aarna's lust for a slow revenge would make the sorcerer hesitate before killing him.

Theleb K'aarna cursed, trying to prise Elric's mouth open.

"The first thing I'll do is cut out that damned tongue of yours!"

Elric bit the hand and tasted the sorcerer's blood. He spat it out.

Theleb K'aarna screamed. "By Chardros, if I did not wish to see you die over the months, I would . . ."

And then a sound came from the Kelmain.

It was a moan of surprise and it issued from every throat.

Theleb K'aarna turned and the breath hissed from between his clenched teeth.

Through the murky dusk a black shape moved. It was the sword, Stormbringer.

Elric had called it.

Now he cried aloud:

"Stormbringer! Stormbringer! To me!"

Theleb K'aarna flung Elric in the path of the sword and rushed into the security of the gathered ranks of Kelmain warriors.

"Stormbringer!"

The Black Sword hovered in the air near Elric.

Another shout went up from the Kelmain. A shape had left the battlements of Castle Kaneloon.

Theleb K'aarna shouted in hysteria. "Prince Umbda! Prepare your men for the attack! I sense danger to us!"

Umbda could not understand the sorcerer's words and Theleb K'aarna was forced to translate them.

"Do not let the sword reach him!" cried the sorcerer. Once more he shouted in the language of the Kelmain and several warriors ran forward to grasp the runesword before it could reach its albino master.

But the sword struck rapidly and the Kelmain died and none dared approach it after that.

Slowly Stormbringer moved towards Elric.

"Ah, Elric," cried Theleb K'aarna, "if you escape me this day, I swear that I shall find you."

"And if you escape me," Elric shouted back, "I will find you, Theleb K'aarna. Be sure of that."

The shape that had left Castle Kaneloon had feathers of silver and gold. It flew high above the host and hovered for a moment before moving to the outer edges of the gathering. Elric could not see it clearly, but he knew what it was. That was why he had summoned the sword, for he had an idea that Moonglum rode the giant bird of metal and that the Elwherite would try to rescue him.

"Do not let it land! It comes to save the albino!" screamed Theleb K'aarna.

But the Kelmain Host did not understand him. Under Prince Umbda's commands they were preparing themselves for the attack upon the castle.

Theleb K'aarna repeated his orders in their own tongue, but it was plain they were beginning not to trust him and could not see the need to bother themselves with one man and a strange bird of metal. It could not stop their engines of war. Neither could the man.

"Stormbringer," whispered Elric as the sword sliced through his bonds and gently settled in his hand. Elric was free, but the Kelmain, though not placing the same importance upon him as did Theleb K'aarna, showed that they were not prepared to let him escape now that the blade was in his grasp and not moving of its own volition.

Prince Umbda shouted something.

A huge mass of warriors rushed at Elric at once and he made no effort to take the attack to them this time for he was interested in fighting a defensive strategy until Moonglum could descend on the bird and help him.

But the bird was even further away. It appeared to be circling the outer perimeters of the host and showed no interest in his plight at all.

Had he been deceived?

He parried a dozen thrusts, letting the Kelmain warriors crowd in upon each other and thus hamper themselves. The bird of gold and silver was almost out of sight now.

And Theleb K'aarna—where was he?

Elric tried to find him, but the sorcerer was doubtless somewhere in the centre of the Kelmain ranks by now.

Elric killed a golden-skinned warrior, slitting his throat with the point of the runesword. More strength began to flow into him again. He killed another Kelmain with an overarm movement which split the man's shoulder. But nothing could be gained from this fight if Moonglum was not coming on the bird of silver and gold.

The bird seemed to change course and come back towards Kaneloon. Was it merely waiting for instructions from its sleeping mistress? Or was it refusing to obey Moonglum's commands?

Elric backed through the muddy, bloody snow so that the pile of corpses now lay behind him. He fought on, but with very little hope.

The bird went past, far to his right.

Elric thought ironically that he had completely mistaken the significance of the bird's leaving the castle battlements and by mistiming his decision had merely brought his death closer—perhaps Myshella's and Moonglum's deaths closer, too.

Kaneloon was doomed. Myshella was doomed. Lormyr and perhaps the whole of the Young Kingdoms were doomed.

And he was doomed.

It was then that a shadow passed across the battling men and the Kelmain screamed and fell back as a great din rent the air.

Elric looked up in relief, hearing the sound of the metal bird's clashing wings. He looked for Moonglum in the saddle and saw instead the tense face of Myshella herself, her hair blowing around her face as it was disturbed by the beating wings.

"Quickly, Lord Elric, before they close in again."

Elric sheathed the runesword and leapt towards the saddle, swinging himself behind the Dark Lady of Kaneloon. Then they rose into the air again, while arrows hurtled around their heads and bounced off the bird's metal feathers.

"One more circuit of the host and then we return to the castle," she said. "Your rune and the Nanorion worked to defeat Theleb K'aarna's enchantment, but they took longer than either of us would have liked. See, already Prince Umbda is ordering his men to mount and ride to Castle Kaneloon. And Kaneloon has only Moonglum to defend her now."

"Why this circuit of Umbda's army?"

"You will see. At least, I hope you will see, my lord."

She began to sing a song. It was a strange, disturbing chant in a language not dissimilar to the Melnibonéan High Speech, yet different enough for Elric to understand only a few words, for it was oddly accented.

Around the camp they flew. Elric saw the Kelmain form their ranks into battle order. Doubtless Umbda and Theleb K'aarna had by now decided on the best mode of attack.

Then back to the castle beat the great bird, settling on the battlements and allowing Elric and Myshella to dismount. Moonglum, his features taut, came running to meet them.

They went to look at the Kelmain.

And they saw that the Kelmain were on the move.

"What did you do to—" began Elric, but Myshella raised her hand.

"Perhaps I did nothing. Perhaps the sorcery will not work."

"What was it you . . .?"

"I scattered the contents of the purse you brought. I scattered it around their whole army. Watch . . ."

"And if the spell has not worked—" Moonglum murmured. He paused, straining his eyes through the gloom. "What is that?"

Myshella's satisfied tone was almost ghoulish as she said: "It is the Noose of Flesh."

Something was growing out of the snow. Something pink that quivered. Something huge. A great mass that arose on all sides of the Kelmain and made their horses rear up and snort.

And it made the Kelmain shriek.

The stuff was like flesh and it had grown so high that the whole Kelmain Host was obscured from sight. There were noises as they tried to train their battle-engines upon the stuff and blast their way through. There were shouts. But not a single horseman broke out of the Noose of Flesh.

Then the substance began to fold in over the Kelmain and Elric heard a sound such as none he had heard before.

It was a voice.

A voice of a hundred thousand men all facing an identical terror, all dying an identical death.

It was a moan of desperation, of hopelessness, of fear.

But it was a moan so loud that it shook the walls of Castle Kaneloon.

"It is no death for a warrior," murmured Moonglum, turning away.

"But it was the only weapon we had," said Myshella. "I have possessed it for a good many years but never before did I feel the need to use it."

"Of them all, only Theleb K'aarna deserved that death," said Elric.

Night fell and the Noose of Flesh tightened around the Kelmain

Host, crushing all but a few horses which had run free as the sorcery began to work.

It crushed Prince Umbda, who spoke no language known in the Young Kingdoms, who spoke no language known to the ancients, who had come to conquer from beyond World's Edge.

It crushed Theleb K'aarna, who had sought, for the sake of his love for a wanton queen, to conquer the world with the aid of Chaos.

It crushed all the warriors of that near-human race, the Kelmain. And it crushed all who could have told the watchers what the Kelmain had been or from where they had originated.

Then it absorbed them. Then it flickered and dissolved and was dust again.

No piece of flesh—man's nor beast's—remained. But over the snow was scattered clothing, arms, armour, siege engines, riding accoutrements, coins, belt-buckles, for as far as the eye could see.

Myshella nodded to herself. "That was the Noose of Flesh," she said. "I thank you for bringing it to me, Elric. I thank you, also, for finding the stone which revived me. I thank you for saving Lormyr."

"Aye," said Elric. "Thank me." There was a weariness on him now. He turned away, shivering.

Snow had begun to fall again.

"Thank me for nothing, Lady Myshella. What I did was to satisfy my own dark urges, to sate my thirst for vengeance. I have destroyed Theleb K'aarna. The rest was incidental. I care nought for Lormyr, the Young Kingdoms, or any of your causes ..."

Moonglum saw that Myshella had a skeptical look in her eyes and she smiled slightly.

Elric entered the castle and began to descend the steps to the hall.

"Wait," Myshella said. "This castle is magical. It reflects the desires of any who enter it—should I wish it."

Elric rubbed at his eyes. "Then plainly we have no desires. Mine are satisfied now that Theleb K'aarna is destroyed. I would leave this place now, my lady."

"You have none?" said she.

He looked at her directly. He frowned. "Regret breeds weakness which attacks the internal organs and at last destroys . . ."

"And you have no desires?"

He hesitated. "I understand you. Your own appearance, I'll admit . . ." He shrugged. "But are you—?"

She spread her hands. "Do not ask too many questions of me." She made another gesture. "Now. See. This castle becomes what you most desire. And in it, the things you most desire!"

And Elric looked about him, his eyes widening, and he began to scream.

He fell to his knees in terror. He turned pleadingly to her.

"No, Myshella! No. I do not desire this!"

Hastily she made yet another sign.

Moonglum helped his friend to his feet. "What was it? What did you see?"

Elric straightened his back and rested his hand on his sword and said grimly and quietly to Myshella:

"Lady, I would kill you for that if I did not understand you sought only to please me."

He studied the ground for a moment before continuing:

"Know this. Elric cannot have what he desires most. What he desires does not exist. What he desires is dead. All Elric has is sorrow, guilt, malice, hatred. This is all he deserves and all he will ever desire."

She put her hands to her own face and walked back to the room where he had first seen her. Elric followed.

Moonglum started after them but then he stopped and remained where he stood.

He watched them enter the room and saw the door close.

He walked back onto the battlements and stared into the darkness. He saw wings of silver and gold flashing in the moonlight and they became smaller and smaller until they had vanished.

He sighed. It was cold.

He went back into the castle and settled himself with his back against a pillar, preparing to sleep.

But a little while later he heard laughter come from the room in the highest tower.

And the laughter sent him running through the passages, through the great hall where the fire had died, out of the door, into the night to seek the stables where he could feel more secure.

But he could not sleep that night, for the distant laughter still pursued him.

And the laughter continued until morning.

BOOK TWO

TO SNARE THE PALE PRINCE

. . . but it was in Nadsokor, City of Beggars, that
Elric found an old friend and learned something
concerning an old enemy . . .

—*The Chronicle of the Black Sword*

CHAPTER ONE

The Beggar Court

NADSOKOR, CITY OF Beggars, was infamous throughout the
Young Kingdoms. Lying near the shores of that ferocious river,
the Varkalk, and not too far from the Kingdom of Org in which blos-
somed the frightful Forest of Troos, and exuding a stink which seemed
thick enough ten miles distant, Nadsokor was plagued by few visitors.

From this unlovely place sallied out her citizens to beg their way
about the world and steal what they could and bring it back to Nadsokor where half of their profits were handed over to their king in return for his protection.

Their king had ruled for many years. He was called Urish the
Seven-fingered, for he had but four fingers on his right hand and three
upon his left. Veins had burst all over his once handsome face and
filthy, infested hair framed that seedy countenance upon which age and
grime had traced a thousand lines. From out of all this ruin peered two
bright, pale eyes.

As the symbol of his power Urish had a great cleaver called Hackmeat which was forever at his side. His throne was of crudely carved
black oak, studded with bits of raw gold, bones and semi-precious

gems. Beneath this throne was Urish's Hoard—a chest of treasure which he let none but himself look upon.

For the best part of every day Urish would lounge on his throne, presiding over a gloomy, festering hall thronged with his Court: a rabble of rascals too foul in appearance and disposition to be tolerated anywhere but here.

For heat and light there burned permanently braziers of garbage which gave out oily smoke and a stink which dominated all the other stinks in the hall.

And now there was a visitor at Urish's Court.

He stood before the dais on which the throne was mounted and from time to time he raised a heavily scented kerchief to his red, full lips.

His face, which was normally dark in complexion, was somewhat grey and his eyes had something of a haunted, tortured look in them as they glanced from begrimed beggar to pile of rubbish to guttering brazier. Dressed in the loose brocade robes of the folk of Pan Tang, the visitor had black eyes, a great hooked nose, blue-black ringlets and a curling beard. Kerchief to mouth, he bowed low when he reached Urish's throne.

As always, greed, weakness and malice mingled to form King Urish's expression as he regarded the stranger whom one of his courtiers had but lately announced.

Urish had recognized the name and he believed he could guess the Pan Tangian's business here.

"I heard you were dead, Theleb K'aarna—killed beyond Lormyr, near World's Edge." Urish grinned to display the black crags which were the rotting remains of his teeth.

Theleb K'aarna removed the kerchief from his lips and his voice was strangled at first, gaining strength as he remembered the wrongs recently done him. "My magic is not so weak I cannot escape a spell such as was woven that day. I conjured myself below the ground while Myshella's Noose of Flesh engulfed the Kelmain Host."

Urish's disgusting grin widened.

"You crept into a hole, is that it?"

The sorcerer's eyes burned fiercely. "I'll not dispute the strength of my powers with—"

He broke off and drew a deep breath which he at once regretted. He stared warily around him at the Beggar Court, all mangled and maimed, which had deposited itself about the filthy hall, mocking him. The beggars of Nadsokor knew the power of poverty and disease— knew how it terrified those who were not used to it. And thus their very squalor was their safeguard against intruders.

A repulsive cough which might have been a laugh now seized King Urish. "And was it your magic that brought you here?" As his whole body shook his bloodshot eyes continued, beadily, to regard the sorcerer.

"I have traveled across the seas and all across Vilmir to be here," Theleb K'aarna said, "because I had heard there was one you hated above all others . . ."

"And we hate *all* others—all who are not beggars," Urish reminded him. The king chuckled and the chuckle became, once more, a throaty, convulsive cough.

"But you hate Elric of Melniboné most."

"Aye. It would be fair to say that. Before he won fame as the Kinslayer, the traitor of Imrryr, he came to Nadsokor to deceive us, disguised as a leper who had begged his way from the Eastlands beyond Karlaak. He tricked me disgracefully and stole something from my Hoard. And my Hoard is sacred—I will not let another even glimpse it!"

"I heard he stole a scroll from you," Theleb K'aarna said. "A spell which had once belonged to his cousin Yyrkoon. Yyrkoon wished to be rid of Elric and let him believe that the spell would release the Princess Cymoril from her sorcerous slumber . . ."

"Aye. Yyrkoon had given the scroll to one of our citizens when he went a-begging to the gates of Imrryr. He then told Elric what he had done. Elric disguised himself and came here. With the aid of sorcery he gained access to my Hoard—my Sacred Hoard—and plucked the scroll from it . . ."

Theleb K'aarna looked sideways at the Beggar King. "Some would say that it was not Elric's fault—that Yyrkoon was to blame. He deceived you both. The spell did not awaken Cymoril, did it?"

"No. But we have a Law in Nadsokor . . ." Urish raised the great cleaver Hackmeat and displayed its ragged, rusty blade. For all its battered appearance, it was a fearsome weapon. "That Law says that any man who looks upon the Sacred Hoard of King Urish must die and die most horribly—at the hands of the Burning God!"

"And none of your wandering citizens has yet managed to take this vengeance?"

"I must pass the sentence personally upon him before he dies. He must come again to Nadsokor, for it is only here that he may be acquainted with his doom."

Theleb K'aarna said: "I have no love for Elric."

Urish once more voiced the sound that was half laugh, half wheezing cough. "Aye—I have heard he has chased you all across the Young Kingdoms, that you have brought more and more powerful sorceries against him, yet every time he has defeated you."

Theleb K'aarna frowned. "Have a care, King Urish. I have had bad luck, yet I am still one of Pan Tang's greatest sorcerers."

"But you spend your powers freely and claim much from the Lords of Chaos. One day they will be tired of helping you and find another to do their work." King Urish closed soiled lips over black teeth. His pale eyes did not blink as he studied Theleb K'aarna.

There were stirrings in the hall, the Beggar Court moved in closer: the click of a crutch, the scrape of a staff, the shuffle of misshapen feet. Even the oily smoke from the braziers seemed to menace him as it drifted reluctantly into the darkness of the roof.

King Urish put one hand upon Hackmeat and the other upon his chin. Broken nails caressed stubble. From somewhere behind Theleb K'aarna a beggar woman let forth an obscene noise and then giggled.

Almost as if to comfort himself the sorcerer placed the scented kerchief firmly over his mouth and nostrils. He began to draw himself up, prepared to deal with an attack if it came.

"But you still have your powers now, I take it," said Urish suddenly, breaking the tension. "Or you would not be here."

"My powers increase . . ."

"For the moment, perhaps."

"My powers . . ."

"I take it you come with a scheme which you hope will result in Elric's destruction," continued Urish easily. The beggars relaxed. Only Theleb K'aarna now showed any signs of discomfort. Urish's bright, blood-shot eyes were sardonic. "And you desire our help because you know we hate the white-faced reaver of Melniboné."

Theleb K'aarna nodded. "Would you hear the details of my plan?"

Urish shrugged. "Why not? At least they may be entertaining."

Unhappily, Theleb K'aarna looked about him at the corrupt and tittering crew. He wished he knew a spell which would disperse the stink.

He took a deep breath through his kerchief and then began to speak . . .

Chapter Two

The Stolen Ring

On the other side of the tavern the young dandy pretended to order another skin of wine while actually taking a sly look towards the corner where Elric sat.

Then the dandy leaned towards his compatriots—merchants and young nobles of several nations—and continued his murmured discourse.

The subject of that discourse, Elric knew, was Elric. Normally he was disdainful of such behaviour, but he was weary and he was impatient for Moonglum to return. He was almost tempted to order the young dandy to desist, if only to pass the time.

Elric was beginning to regret his decision to visit Old Hrolmar.

This rich city was a great meeting place for all the imaginative people of the Young Kingdoms. To it came explorers, adventurers, mercenaries, craftsmen, merchants, painters and poets for, under the rule of
the famous Duke Avan Astran, this Vilmirian city-state was undergo-
ing a transformation in its character.

Duke Avan had been a man who had explored most of the world
and had brought back great wealth and knowledge to Old Hrolmar. Its
riches and its intellectual life attracted more riches, more intellectuals
and so Old Hrolmar flourished.

But where riches are and where intellectuals are, then gossip also
flourishes, for if there is any breed of man who gossips more than the
merchant or the sailor then it is the poet and the painter. And, naturally
enough, there was much gossip concerning the doom-driven albino,
Elric, already a hero of several ballads by poets not over-talented.

Elric had allowed himself to be brought to the city because
Moonglum had said it was the best place to find an income. Elric's care-
lessness with their wealth had made near-paupers of them, not for the
first time, and they were in need of provisions and fresh steeds.

Elric had been for skirting Old Hrolmar and riding on towards
Tanelorn, where they had decided to go, but Moonglum had argued
reasonably that they would need better horses and more food and
equipment for the long ride across the Vilmirian and Ilmioran plains to
the edge of the Sighing Desert, where mysterious Tanelorn was situ-
ated. So Elric had at last agreed, though, after his encounter with
Myshella and his witnessing of the destruction of the Noose of Flesh, he
had become weary and craved for the peace which Tanelorn offered.

What made things worse was that this tavern was rather too well-lit and
catering too much to the better end of the trade for Elric's taste. He
would have preferred a lowlier sort of inn which would have been
cheaper and where men were used to holding back their questions and
their gossip. But Moonglum had thought it wise to spend the last of their
wealth on a good inn, in case they should need to entertain someone . . .

THE SLEEPING SORCERESS 67

Elric left the business of raising treasure to Moonglum. Doubtless he intended to get it by thievery or trickery, but Elric did not care.

He sighed and suffered the sidelong looks of the other guests and tried not to overhear the young dandy. He sipped his cup of wine and picked at the flesh of the cold fowl Moonglum had ordered before he went off. He drew his head into the high collar of his black cloak, but succeeded only in emphasizing the bone-white pallor of his face and the milky whiteness of his long hair. He looked around him at the silks and furs and tapestries swirling about the tavern as their owners moved from table to table and he longed with all his heart to be on his way to Tanelorn, where men spoke little because they had experienced so much.

". . . killed mother and father, too—and the mother's lover, it is said . . ."

". . . and they say he lies with corpses for preference . . ."

". . . and because of that the Lords of the Higher Worlds cursed him with the face of a corpse . . ."

"Incest, was it not? I got it from one who sailed with him that . . ."

". . . and his mother had congress with Arioch himself, thus producing . . ."

". . . shortly before he betrayed his own people to Smiorgan and the rest!"

"He looks a gloomy fellow, right enough. Not one to enjoy a jest . . ."

Laughter.

Elric made himself relax in his chair and swallow more wine. But the gossip went on.

"They say also that he is an imposter. That the real Elric died at Imrryr . . ."

"A true prince of Melniboné would dress in more lavish style. And he would . . ."

More laughter.

Elric stood up, pushing back his cloak so that the great black broadsword at his hip was fully displayed. Most people in Old Hrolmar had heard of the runesword Stormbringer and its terrible power.

Elric crossed to the table where the young dandy sat.

"I pray you, gentlemen, to improve your sport! You can do much better now—for here is one who would offer you proof of certain things of which you speak. What of his penchant for vampirism of a particular sort? I did not hear you touch upon that in your conversation."

The young dandy cleared his throat and made a nervous little flirt of his shoulder.

"Well?" Elric feigned an innocent expression. "Cannot I be of assistance?"

The gossips had become dumb, pretending to be absorbed in their eating and drinking.

Elric smiled a smile which set their hands to shaking.

"I desire only to know what you wish to hear, gentlemen. Then I will demonstrate that I am truly the one you have called Elric Kinslayer."

The merchants and the nobles gathered their rich robes about them and, avoiding his eye, got up. The young dandy minced towards the exit—a parody of bravado.

But now Elric stood laughing in the doorway, his hand on the hilt of Stormbringer. "Will you not join me as my guests, gentlemen? Think how you could tell your friends of the meeting . . ."

"Gods, how boorish!" lisped the young dandy and then shivered.

"Sir, we meant no harm . . ." thickly said a fat Shazaarian herb trader.

"We spoke of another." A young noble with only the hint of a chin, but with an emphatic moustache, offered a feeble, placatory grin.

"We said how much we admired you . . ." stuttered a Vilmirian knight whose eyes appeared but recently to have crossed and whose face was now almost as pale as Elric's.

A merchant in the dark brocades of Tarkesh licked his red lips and attempted to conduct himself with more dignity than his friends. "Sir, Old Hrolmar is a civilized city. Gentlemen do not brawl amongst themselves here . . ."

"But like peasant women prefer to gossip," said Elric.

"Yes," said the youth with the abundance of moustache. "Ah—no . . ."

The dandy arranged his cloak about him and glowered at the floor.

Elric stepped aside. Uncertainly the Tarkeshite merchant moved forward and then ran for the darkness of the street, his companions tumbling behind him. Elric heard their footsteps running on the cobbles and he began to laugh. At the sound of his laugh the footfalls became a scamper and the party had soon reached the quayside where the water gleamed, turned a corner and disappeared.

Elric smiled and looked up beyond Old Hrolmar's baroque skyline at the stars. Now there were more footsteps coming from the other end of the street. He turned and saw the newcomers step into a pool of light thrown from the window of a nearby office.

It was Moonglum. The stocky Eastlander was returning in the company of two women who were scantily dressed and heavily painted and who were without doubt Vilmirian whores from the other side of the city. Moonglum had an arm about each waist and he was singing some obscure but evidently disgraceful ballad, pausing frequently to have one of the laughing girls pour wine down his throat. Both the whores had large stone flasks in their free hands and they were matching Moonglum drink for drink.

As Moonglum stepped unsteadily nearer he recognized Elric and hailed him, winking. "You see I have not forgotten you, Prince of Melniboné. One of these beauties is for you."

Elric made an exaggerated bow. "You are very good to me. But I thought you planned to find some gold for us. Was that not the reason for coming to Old Hrolmar?"

"Aye!" Moonglum kissed the cheeks of the girls. They snorted with laughter. "Indeed! Gold it is—or something as good as gold. I have rescued these young ladies from a cruel whoremaster on the other side of town. I have promised to sell them to a kinder master and they are grateful to me!"

"You stole these slaves?"

"If you wish to say so—I 'stole' them. Aye, then, 'steal' I did. I stole in with my steel and I released them from a life of degradation. A humanitarian deed. Their miserable life is no more! They may look forward to . . ."

"Their miserable lives will be no more—as, indeed, will be ours when the whoremaster discovers the crime and alerts the watch. How found you these ladies?"

"They found me! I had made my swords available to an old merchant, a stranger to the city. I was to escort him about the murkier regions of Old Hrolmar in return for a good purse of gold (better, I think, than he expected to give me). While he whored above, as he could, I had a drink or two below in the public rooms. These two beauties took a liking to me and told me of their unhappiness. It was enough. I rescued them."

"A cunning plan," Elric said sardonically.

"'Twas theirs! They have brains as well as—"

"I'll help you carry them back to their master before the city guards descend upon us."

"But Elric!"

"But first . . ." Elric seized his friend and threw him over his shoulder, staggering with him to the quay at the end of the street, taking a good hold on his collar and lowering him suddenly into the reeking water. Then he hauled him up and stood him down. Moonglum shivered and looked sadly at Elric.

"I am prone to colds, as you know."

"And prone to drunken plans, too! We are not liked here, Moonglum. The watch needs only one excuse to set upon us. At best we should have to flee the city before our business was done. At worst we shall be disarmed, imprisoned, perhaps slain."

They began to walk back to where the two girls still stood. One of the girls ran forward and knelt to take Elric's hand and press her lips against his thigh. "Master, I have a message . . ."

Elric bent to raise her to her feet.

She screamed. Her painted eyes widened. He stared at her in astonishment and then, following her gaze, turned and saw the pack of bravos who had stolen round the corner and were now rushing at himself and Moonglum. Behind the bravos Elric thought he saw the young dandy he had earlier chased from the tavern. The dandy wished for revenge. Poignards glittered in the darkness and their owners wore the black hoods of professional assassins. There were at least a dozen of them. The young dandy must therefore be extremely rich, for assassins were expensive in Old Hrolmar.

Moonglum had already drawn both his swords and was engaging the leader. Elric pushed the frightened girl behind him and put his hand to Stormbringer's pommel. Almost at its own volition the huge runesword sprang from its scabbard and black light poured from its blade as it began to hum its own strange battle-cry.

He heard one of the assassins gasp "Elric!" and guessed that the dandy had not made it plain whom they were to slay. He blocked the thrust of the slim longsword, turned it and chopped with a kind of delicacy at the owner's wrist. Wrist and sword flew into the shadows and the owner staggered back screaming.

More swords now and more cold eyes glittering from the black hoods. Stormbringer sang its peculiar song—half-lament, half-victory shout. Elric's own face was alive with battle-lust and his crimson eyes blazed from his bone-white face as he swung this way and that.

Shouts, curses, the screams of women and the groans of men, steel striking steel, boots on cobbles, the sounds of swords in flesh, of blades scraping bone. A confusion through which Elric fought, his broadsword clapped in both pale hands. He had lost sight of Moonglum and prayed that the Eastlander still stood. From time to time he glimpsed one of the girls and wondered why she had not run for safety.

Now the corpses of several hooded assassins lay upon the cobbles and the remainder were beginning to falter as Elric pressed them. They knew the power of his sword and what it did to those it struck. They had seen their comrades' faces as their souls were drawn from them by the hellblade. With every death Elric seemed to grow stronger and the black radiance from the blade seemed to burn fiercer. And now the albino was laughing.

His laughter rang over the rooftops of Old Hrolmar and those who

were abed covered their ears, believing themselves in the grip of nightmares.

"Come, friends, my blade still hungers!"

An assassin made to stand his ground and Elric swept the Black
Sword up. The man raised his blade to protect his head and Elric
brought the Black Sword down. It sheared through the steel and cut
down through the hood, through the neck, through the breastbone. It
clove the assassin completely in two and it stayed in the flesh, feasting,
drawing out the last traces of the man's dark soul. And then the rest
were running.

Elric drew a deep breath, avoided looking at the man his sword
had slain last, sheathed the blade and turned to look for Moonglum.

It was then that the blow came on the back of his neck. He felt nausea rise in him and tried to shake it off. He felt a prick in his wrist and
through the haze he saw a figure he thought at first was Moonglum.
But it was another—perhaps a woman. She was tugging at his left
hand. Where did she want him to go?

His knees became weak, and he fell to the cobbles. He tried to call
out, but failed. The woman was still tugging at his hand as if she sought
to take him to safety. But he could not follow her. He fell on his shoulder, then on his back, glimpsed a swimming sky . . .

. . . and then the dawn was rising over the crazy spires of Old Hrolmar
and he realized that several hours had passed since he had fought the
assassins.

Moonglum's face appeared. It was full of concern.

"Moonglum?"

"Thank Elwher's gentle gods! I thought you slain by that poisoned
blade."

Elric's head was clearing rapidly now. He rose to a sitting position.
"The attacker came from behind. How . . . ?"

Moonglum looked embarrassed. "I fear those girls were not all
they seemed."

Elric remembered the woman tugging at his left hand and he

stretched out his fingers. "Moonglum! The Ring of Kings is gone from my hand! The Actorios has been stolen!"

The Ring of Kings had been worn by Elric's forefathers for centuries. It had been the symbol of their power, the source of much of their supernatural strength.

Moonglum's face clouded. "I thought I stole the girls. But they were thieves. They planned to rob us. An old trick."

"There's more to it, Moonglum. They stole nothing else. Just the Ring of Kings. There's still a little gold left in my purse." He jingled his belt pouch, climbing to his feet.

Moonglum jerked his thumb at the street's far wall. There lay one of the girls, her finery all smeared with mud and blood.

"She got in the way of one of the assassins as we fought. She's been dying all night—mumbling your name. I had not told it to her. Therefore I fear you're right. They were sent to steal that ring from you. I was duped by them."

Elric walked rapidly to where the girl lay and he kneeled down beside her. Gently he touched her cheek. She opened her lids and stared at him from glazed eyes. Her lips formed his name.

"Why did you plan to rob me?" Elric asked. "Who is your master?"

"Urish . . ." she said in a voice that was a breeze passing through the grass. "Steal ring . . . take it to Nadsokor . . ."

Moonglum now stood on the other side of the dying girl. He had found one of the wine flasks and he bent to give her a drink. She tried to sip the wine but failed. It ran down her little chin, down her slim neck and onto her wounded breast.

"You are one of the beggars of Nadsokor?" Moonglum said.

Faintly, she nodded.

"Urish has always been my enemy," Elric told him. "I once recovered some property from him and he has never forgiven me. Perhaps he sought the Actorios ring in payment." He looked down at the girl. "Your companion—has she returned to Nadsokor?"

Again the girl seemed to nod. Then all intelligence left the eyes, the lids closed and she ceased to breathe.

Elric got up. He was frowning, rubbing at the hand on which the Ring of Kings had been.

"Let him keep the ring, then," said Moonglum hopefully. "He will be satisfied."

Elric shook his head.

Moonglum cleared his throat. "A caravan is leaving Jadmar in a week. It is commanded by Rackhir of Tanelorn and has been purchasing provisions for the city. If we took a ship round the coast we could soon be in Jadmar, join Rackhir's caravan and be on our way to Tanelorn in good company. As you know, it's rare for anyone of Tanelorn to make such a journey. We are lucky, for . . ."

"No," said Elric in a low voice. "We must forget Tanelorn for the moment, Moonglum. The Ring of Kings is my link with my fathers. More—it aids my conjurings and has saved our lives more than once. We ride for Nadsokor now. I must try to reach the girl before she gets to the City of Beggars. Failing that, I must enter the city and recover my ring."

Moonglum shuddered. "It would be more foolish than any plan of mine, Elric. Urish would destroy us."

"Nonetheless, to Nadsokor I must go."

Moonglum bent and began systematically to strip the girl's corpse of its jewelry. "We'll need every penny we can raise if we're to buy decent horses for our journey," he explained.

CHAPTER THREE

The Cold Ghouls

Framed against the scarlet sunset, Nadsokor looked from this distance more like a badly kept graveyard than a city. Towers tottered, houses were half-collapsed, the walls were broken.

Elric and Moonglum came up the peak of the hill on their fast Shazaarian horses (which had cost them all they had) and saw it.

Worse—they smelled it. A thousand stinks issued from the festering city and both men gagged, turning their horses back down the hill to the valley.

"We'll camp here for a short while—until nightfall," Elric said. "Then we'll enter Nadsokor."

"Elric, I am not sure I could bear the stench. Whatever our disguise, our disgust would reveal us for strangers."

Elric smiled and reached into his pouch. He took out two small tablets and handed one to Moonglum.

The Eastlander regarded the thing suspiciously. "What's this?"

"A potion. I used it once before when I came to Nadsokor. It will kill your sense of smell completely—unfortunately your sense of taste as well . . ."

Moonglum laughed. "I did not plan to eat a gourmet meal while in the City of Beggars!" He swallowed the pill and Elric did likewise.

Almost instantly Moonglum remarked that the stink of the city was subsiding. Later, as they chewed the stale bread which was all that was left of their provisions, he said:

"I can taste nothing. The potion works."

Elric nodded. He was frowning, looking up the hill in the direction of the city as the night fell.

Moonglum took out his swords and began to hone them with the small stone he carried for the purpose. As he honed, he watched Elric's face, trying to see if he could guess Elric's thoughts.

At last the albino spoke. "We'll need to leave the horses here, of course, for most beggars disdain their use."

"They are proud in their perversity," Moonglum murmured.

"Aye. We'll need those rags we brought."

"Our swords will be noticed . . ."

"Not if we wear the loose robes over all. It will mean we'll walk stiff-legged, but that's not so strange in a beggar."

Reluctantly Moonglum got the bundles of rags from the saddle-panniers.

So it was that a filthy pair, one stooped and limping, one short but with a twisted arm, crept through the debris which was ankle deep around the whole city of Nadsokor. They made for one of the many gaps in the wall.

Nadsokor had been abandoned some centuries before by a people fleeing from the ravages of a particularly virulent pox which had struck down most of their number. Not long afterwards the first of the beggars had occupied it. Nothing had been done to preserve the city's defenses and now the muck around the perimeters was as effective a protection as any wall.

No-one saw the two figures as they climbed over the messy rubble and entered the dark, festering streets of the City of Beggars. Huge rats raised themselves on their hind legs and watched them as they made their way to what had once been Nadsokor's senate building and which was now Urish's palace. Scrawny dogs with garbage dangling in their jaws warily slunk back into the shadows. Once a little column of blind men, each man with his right hand on the shoulder of the man in front, tapped their way through the night, passing directly across the street Elric and Moonglum were in. From some of the tumble-down buildings came cacklings and titterings as the maimed caroused with the crippled and the degenerate and corrupted coupled with their crones. As the disguised pair neared what had been Nadsokor's forum there came a scream from one shattered doorway and a young girl, barely over puberty, dashed out pursued by a monstrously fat beggar who propelled himself with astounding speed on his crutches, the livid stumps of his legs, which terminated at the knee, making the motions of running. Moonglum tensed, but Elric held him back as the fat cripple bore down on his prey, abandoned his crutches which rattled on the broken pavement, and flung himself on the child.

Moonglum tried to free himself from Elric's grasp but the albino whispered: "Let it happen. Those who are whole either in mind, body or spirit cannot be tolerated in Nadsokor."

There were tears in Moonglum's eyes as he looked at his friend.

"Your cynicism is as disgusting as anything they do!"

"I do not doubt it. But we are here for one purpose—to recover the stolen Ring of Kings. That, and nought else, is what we shall do."

"What matters that when ...?"

But Elric was continuing on his way to the forum and after hesitating for a moment Moonglum followed him.

Now they stood on the far side of the square looking at Urish's palace. Some of its columns had fallen, but on this building alone had there been some attempt at restoration and decoration. The archway of the main entrance was painted with crude representations of the Arts of Begging and Extortion. An example of the coinage of all the nations of the Young Kingdoms had been imbedded in the wooden door and above it had been nailed, perhaps ironically, a pair of wooden crutches, crossed as swords might be crossed, indicating that the weapons of the beggar were his power to horrify and disgust those luckier or better endowed than himself.

Elric stared through the murk at the building and he had a calculating frown on his face.

"There are no guards," he said to Moonglum.

"Why should there be? What have they to guard?"

"There were guards last time I came to Nadsokor. Urish protects his Hoard most assiduously. It is not outsiders he fears but his own despicable rabble."

"Perhaps he no longer fears them."

Elric smiled. "A creature like King Urish fears everything. We had best be wary when we enter the hall. Have your swords ready to draw at any hint that we have been lured into a trap."

"Surely Urish would not suspect we'd know where the girl came from?"

"Aye, it seemed good chance that one of them told us, but nonetheless we must make allowances for Urish's cunning."

"He would not willingly bring you here—not with the Black Sword at your side."

"Perhaps . . ."

They began to walk across the forum. It was very still, very dark. From far away came the occasional shout, a laugh or an obscene, indefinable sound.

Now they were at the door, standing beneath the crossed crutches. Elric felt beneath his ragged robes for the hilt of his sword and with his left hand pushed at the door. It squeaked open a fraction. They looked about them to see if anyone had heard the sound, but the square was as still as it had been.

More pressure. Another squeak. And now they could squeeze their bodies through the aperture.

They stood in Urish's hall. Braziers of garbage gave off faint light. Oily smoke curled towards the rafters. They saw the dim outlines of the dais at the far end and on the dais stood Urish's huge, crude throne. The hall seemed deserted, but Elric's hand did not leave the hilt of the Black Sword.

He stopped as he heard a sound, but it was a great, black rat scuttling across the floor.

Silence again.

Elric moved forward, step by cautious step, along the length of the slimy hall, Moonglum behind him.

Elric's spirits began to rise, as they neared the throne. Perhaps Urish had, after all, grown complacent of his strength. He would open the trunk beneath the throne, remove his ring and then they would leave the city and be away before dawn, riding across country to join the caravan of Rackhir the Red Archer on its way to Tanelorn.

He began to relax but his step was just as cautious. Moonglum had paused, cocking his head to one side as if hearing something.

Elric turned. "What is it you hear?"

"Possibly nothing. Or maybe one of those great rats we saw earlier. It is just that—"

A silver-blue radiance burst out from behind the grotesque throne and Elric flung up his left hand to protect his eyes, trying to disentangle his sword from his rags.

Moonglum yelled and began to run for the door, but even when Elric put his back to the light he could not see. Stormbringer moaned in its scabbard as if in rage. Elric tugged at it, but felt his limbs grow weaker and weaker. From behind him came a laugh which he recognized. A second laugh—almost a throaty cough—joined it.

His sight came back but now he was held by clammy hands and when he saw his captors he shuddered. Shadowy creatures of limbo held him—ghouls summoned by sorcery. Their dead faces smiled but their dead eyes remained dead. Elric felt the heat and the strength leaving his body and it was as if the ghouls sucked it from him. He could almost feel his vitality traveling from his own body to theirs.

Again the laugh. He looked up at the throne and saw emerging from behind it the tall, saturnine figure of Theleb K'aarna, whom he had left for dead near the castle of Kaneloon a few months since.

Theleb K'aarna smiled in his curling beard as Elric struggled in the grasp of the ghouls. Now from the other side of the throne came the

filthy carcass of Urish the Seven-fingered, the cleaver Hackmeat cradled in his left arm.

Elric could barely hold his head up as the ghouls' cold flesh absorbed his strength, but he smiled at his own foolishness. He had been right in suspecting a trap, but wrong in entering it so poorly prepared.

And where was Moonglum? Had he deserted him? The little Eastlander was nowhere to be seen.

Urish swaggered round the throne and sprawled his begrimed person in it, placing Hackmeat so that it lay across the arms. His pale, beady eyes stared hard at Elric.

Theleb K'aarna remained standing by the side of the throne, but triumph flamed in his eyes like Imrryr's own funeral fires.

"Welcome back to Nadsokor," wheezed Urish, scratching himself between the legs. "You have returned to make amends, I take it."

Elric shivered as the cold in his bones increased. Stormbringer stirred at his side but it could only help him if he drew it with his own hands. He knew he was dying.

"I have come to regain my property," he said through chattering teeth. "My ring."

"Ah! The Ring of Kings. It was yours, was it? My girl mentioned something of that."

"You sent her to steal it!"

Urish sniggered. "I'll not deny it. But I did not expect the White Wolf of Imrryr to step so easily into my trap."

"He would have stepped out again if you had not that amateur magic-maker's spells to help you!"

Theleb K'aarna glowered but then his face relaxed. "Are you not discomforted, then, by my ghouls?"

Elric was gasping as the last of the heat fled his bones. He now could not stand, but hung in the hands of the dead creatures. Theleb K'aarna must have planned this for weeks, for it took many spells and pacts with the guardians of limbo to bring such ghouls to Earth.

"And so I die," Elric murmured. "Well, I suppose I do not care . . ."

Urish raised his ruined features in what was a parody of pride.

"You do not die yet, Elric of Melniboné. The sentence has yet to be passed! The formalities must be suffered! By my cleaver Hackmeat I must sentence you for your crimes against Nadsokor and against the Sacred Hoard of King Urish!"

Elric hardly heard him as his legs collapsed altogether and the ghouls tightened their grip on him.

Dimly he was aware of the beggar rabble shuffling into the hall.

Doubtless they had all been waiting for this. Had Moonglum died at their hands when he fled the hall?

"Put his head up!" Theleb K'aarna instructed his dead servants. "Let him see Urish, King of All Beggars, make his just decree!"

Elric felt a cold hand beneath his chin and his head was raised so he could watch, through misting eyes, as Urish stood up and grasped the cleaver Hackmeat in his four-fingered hand, stretching it towards the smoky ceiling.

"Elric of Melniboné, thou art convicted of many crimes against the Ignoblest of the Ignoble—myself, King Urish of Nadsokor. Thou has offended King Urish's friend, that most pleasingly degenerate villain Theleb K'aarna—"

At this Theleb K'aarna pursed his lips, but did not interrupt.

"—and, moreover, did come a second time to the City of Beggars to repeat thy crimes. By my great cleaver Hackmeat, the symbol of my dignity and power, I condemnest thee to the Punishment of the Burning God!"

From all sides of the hall came the foul applause of the Beggar Court. Elric remembered a legend of Nadsokor—that when the original population were first struck by the disease they summoned aid from Chaos—begging Chaos to cleanse the disease from the city—with fire if necessary. Chaos had played a joke upon these folk—sent their Burning God who had burned what was left of their possessions. A further summons to Law to help them had resulted in the Burning God's being imprisoned by Lord Donblas in the city. Having had enough of the Lords of the Higher Worlds the remnants of the citizens had abandoned their city. But was the Burning God still here in Nadsokor?

Faintly he still heard Urish's voice. "Take him to the labyrinth and give him to the Burning God!"

Theleb K'aarna spoke but Elric did not hear what he said, though he heard Urish's reply.

"His sword? How will that avail him against a Lord of Chaos? Besides, if the sword is released from the scabbard, who knows what will happen?"

Theleb K'aarna was evidently reluctant, by his tone, but at last agreed with Urish.

Now Theleb K'aarna's voice boomed commandingly.

"Things of limbo—release him! His vitality has been your reward! Now—begone!"

Elric fell to the muck on the flagstones but was now too weak to move as beggars came forward and lifted him up.

His eyes closed and his senses deserted him as he felt himself borne from the hall and heard the united voices of the wizard of Pan Tang and the King of the Beggars giving vent to their mocking triumph.

CHAPTER FOUR

Punishment of the Burning God

"By Narjhan's droppings he's cold!"

Elric heard the rasping voice of one of the beggars who carried him. He was still weak but some of the beggars' body heat had transferred itself to him and the chill of his bones was now by no means as intense.

"Here's the portal."

Elric forced his eyes open.

He was upside down but could see ahead of him through the gloom.

Something shimmered there.

It looked like the iridescent skin of some unearthly animal stretched across the arch of the tunnel.

He was jerked backwards as the beggars swung his body and hurled it towards the shimmering skin.

He struck it.

It was viscous.

It clung to him and he felt it was absorbing him. He tried to struggle but was still far too weak. He was sure that he was being killed.

But after long minutes he was through it and had struck stone and lay gasping in the blackness of the tunnel.

This must be the labyrinth of which Urish had spoken.

Trembling, he tried to rise, using his scabbarded sword as a support. It took him some time to get up but at last he could lean against the curving wall.

He was surprised. The stones seemed to be hot. Perhaps it was because he was so cold and in reality the stones were of normal heat.

Even this speculation seemed to weary him. Whatever the nature of the heat it was welcome. He pressed his back harder against the stones.

As their heat passed into his body he felt a sensation almost of ecstasy and he drew a deep breath. Strength was returning slowly.

"Gods," he murmured, "even the snows of the Lormyrian steppe could not compare with such a great cold."

He drew another deep breath and coughed.

Then he realized that the drug he had swallowed was beginning to wear off.

He wiped his mouth with the back of his hand and spat out saliva. Something of the stink of Nadsokor had entered his nostrils.

He stumbled back towards the portal. The peculiar stuff still shimmered there. He pressed his hand against it and it gave reluctantly but then held firm. He leaned his whole weight on it but it would still not give any further. It was like a particularly tough membrane but it was not flesh. Was this the stuff with which the Lords of Law had sealed off the tunnel, entrapping their enemy, the Lord of Chaos? The only light in the tunnel came from the membrane itself.

"By Arioch, I'll turn the tables on the Beggar King," Elric murmured. He threw back his rags and put his hand on Stormbringer's pommel. The blade purred as a cat might purr. He drew the sword from its scabbard and it began to sing a low, satisfied song. Now Elric hissed as its power flowed up his arm and into his body. Stormbringer was giving him the strength he needed—but he knew that Stormbringer must be paid soon, must taste blood and souls and thus replenish its energy. He aimed a great blow at the shimmering wall. "I'll hack down this portal and release the Burning God upon Nadsokor! Strike true, Stormbringer! Let flame come to devour the filth that is this city!"

But Stormbringer howled as it bit into the membrane and it was held fast. No rent appeared in the stuff. Instead Elric had to tug with all his might to get the sword free. He withdrew, panting.

"The portal was made to withstand the efforts of Chaos," Elric murmured. "My sword's useless against it. And so, unable to go back I must, perforce, go forward." Stormbringer in hand, he turned and began to make his way along the passage. He took one turn and then another and then a third and the light had disappeared completely. He reached for his pouch where his flint and tinder were kept, but the beggars had cut that from his belt as they carried him. He decided to retrace his steps. But by now he was deeply within the labyrinth and he could not find the portal.

"No portal—but no god, it seems. Mayhap there's another exit from this place. If it's blocked by a door of wood, then Stormbringer will soon carve me a path to freedom."

And so he pressed further into the labyrinth, taking a hundred twists and turns in the darkness before he paused again.

He had noticed that he was growing warmer. Now, instead of feeling horribly cold, he felt uncomfortably hot. He was sweating. He removed some of the upper layers of his rags and stood in his own shirt and breeks. He had begun to thirst.

Another turning and he saw light ahead.

"Well, Stormbringer, perhaps we are free after all!"

He began to run towards the source of the light. But it was not daylight, neither was it the light from the portal. This was firelight—of brands, perhaps.

He could see the sides of the tunnel quite clearly in the firelight. Unlike the masonry in the rest of Nadsokor, this was free of filth—a plain, grey stone stained by the red light.

The source of the light was around the next bend. But the heat had grown greater and his flesh stung as the sweat sprang from his pores.

"AAH!"

A great voice suddenly filled the tunnel as Elric rounded the bend and saw the fire leaping not thirty yards distant.

"AAH! AT LAST!"

The voice came from the fire.

And Elric knew he had found the Burning God.

"I have no quarrel with you, my lord of Chaos!" he called. "I, too, serve Chaos!"

"But I must eat," came the voice. "CHECKALAKH MUST EAT!"

"I am poor food for one such as you," Elric said reasonably, putting both his hands around Stormbringer's hilt and taking a step backward.

"Aye, beggar, that thou art—but thou art the only food they send!"

"I'm no beggar!"

"Beggar or not, Checkalakh will devour thee!"

The flames shook and a shape began to be made of them. It was a human shape but composed entirely of flame. Flickering hands of fire stretched out towards Elric.

And Elric turned.

And Elric ran.

And Checkalakh, the Burning God, came fast as a flash fire behind him.

Elric felt pain in his shoulder and he smelled burning cloth. He increased his speed, having no notion of where he ran.

And still the Burning God pursued him.

"Stop, mortal! It is futile! Thou canst not escape Checkalakh of Chaos!"

Elric shouted back in desperate humour. "I'll be no-one's roast pork!" His step began to falter. "Not—not even a god's!"

Like the roar of flames up a chimney, Checkalakh replied, "Do not defy me, mortal! It is an honour to feed a god!"

Both the heat and the effort of running were exhausting Elric. A plan of sorts had formed in his brain when he had first encountered the Burning God. That was why he had started to run.

But now, as Checkalakh came on, he was forced to turn.

"Thou art somewhat feeble for so mighty a Lord of Chaos," he panted, readying his sword.

"My long sojourn here has weakened me," Checkalakh replied, "else I would have caught thee ere now! But catch thee I will! And devour thee I must!"

Stormbringer whined its defiance at the enfeebled Chaos god and blade struck out at flaming head and gashed the god's right cheek so that paler fire flickered there and something ran up the black blade and into Elric's heart so that he trembled in a mixture of terror and joy as some of the Burning God's life-force entered him.

Eyes of flame stared at the Black Sword and then at Elric. Brows of flame furrowed and Checkalakh halted.

"Thou art no ordinary beggar, 'tis true!"

"I am Elric of Melniboné and I bear the Black Sword. Lord Arioch is my master—a more powerful entity than you, Lord Checkalakh."

Something akin to misery passed across the god's fiery countenance. "Aye—there are many more powerful than me, Elric of Melniboné."

Elric wiped sweat from his face. He drew in great gulps of burning air. "Then why—why not combine your strength with mine? Together we can tear down the portal and take vengeance on those who have conspired to bring us together."

Checkalakh shook his head and little tongues of fire fell from it. "The portal will only open when I am dead. So it was decreed when Lord Donblas of Law imprisoned me here. Even if we were successful in destroying the portal—it would result in my death. Therefore, most powerful of mortals, I must fight thee and eat thee."

And again Elric began to run, desperately seeking the portal, knowing that the only light he could hope to find in the labyrinth came from the Burning God himself. Even if he were to defeat the god, he would still be trapped in the complex maze.

And then he saw it. He was back at the place where he had been thrown through the membrane.

"It is only possible to enter my prison through the portal, not leave it!" called Checkalakh.

"I'm aware of that!" Elric took a firmer grip on Stormbringer and turned to face the thing of flame.

Even as his sword swung back and forth, parrying every attempt of the Burning God's to seize him, Elric felt sympathy for the creature. He had come in answer to the summonings of mortals and he had been imprisoned for his pains.

But Elric's clothes had begun to smoulder now and even though Stormbringer supplied him with energy every time it struck Checkalakh, the heat itself was beginning to overwhelm him. He sweated no more. Instead his skin felt dry and about to split. Blisters were forming on his white hands. Soon he would be able to hold the blade no longer.

"Arioch!" he breathed. "Though this creature be a fellow Lord of Chaos, aid me to defeat him!"

But Arioch lent him no extra strength. He had already learned from his patron demon that greater things were being planned on and above the Earth and that Arioch had little time for even the most favourite of his mortal charges.

Yet, from habit, still Elric murmured Arioch's name as he swept the sword so that it struck first Checkalakh's burning hands and then his burning shoulder and more of the god's energy entered him.

It seemed to Elric that even Stormbringer was beginning to burn and the pain in his blistered hands grew so great that it was at last the only sensation of which he was aware. He staggered back against the iridescent membrane and felt its fleshlike texture on his back. The ends of his long hair were beginning to smoke and large areas of his clothes had completely charred.

Was Checkalakh failing, though? The flames burned less brightly and there was an expression of resignation beginning to form on the face of fire.

Elric drew on his pain as his only source of strength and he made the pain take the sword and bring it back over his head and he made the pain bring Stormbringer down in a massive blow aimed at the god's head.

And even as the blow descended the fire began to die. Then Stormbringer had struck and Elric yelled as an enormous wave of energy poured into his body and knocked him backwards so that the sword fell from his hand and he felt that his flesh could not contain what it now held. He rolled, moaning, on the floor and he kicked at the air, raising his twisted, blistered hands to the roof as if in supplication to some being who had the power to stop what was happening to him. There were no tears in his eyes, for it seemed that even his blood had begun to boil out of him.

"Arioch! Save me!" He was shuddering, screaming. "Arioch! Stop this thing happening to me!"

He was full of the energy of a god and the mortal frame was not meant to contain so much force.

"Aaaah! Take it from me!"

He became aware of a calm, beautiful face looking down upon him as he writhed. He saw a tall man—much taller than himself—and he knew that this was no mortal at all, but a god.

"It is over!" said a pure, sweet voice.

And, though the creature did not move, soft hands seemed to caress him and the pain began to diminish and the voice continued to speak.

"Long centuries ago, I, Lord Donblas the Justice Maker, came to Nadsokor to free it from the grip of Chaos. But I came too late. Evil brought more evil, as evil will, and I could not interfere too much with the affairs of mortals, for we of Law have sworn to let mankind make its own destiny if that is possible. Yet the Cosmic Balance swings now like the pendulum of a clock with a broken spring and terrible forces are at work on the Earth. Thou, Elric, art a servant of Chaos—yet thou hast served Law more than once. It has been said that the destiny of

mankind rests within thee and that may be true. Thus, I aid thee—though I do so against mine own oath . . ."

And Elric closed his eyes and felt at peace for the first time that he remembered.

The pain had gone, but great energy still filled him. When he opened his eyes again there was no beautiful face looking down on him and the scintillating membrane which had covered the archway had disappeared. Nearby Stormbringer lay and he sprang up and seized the sword, returning it to his scabbard. He noticed that the blisters had left his hands and that even his clothes were no longer charred.

Had he dreamed it all—or most of it?

He shook his head. He was free. He was strong. He had his sword with him. Now he would return to the hall of King Urish and take his vengeance both on Nadsokor's ruler and Theleb K'aarna.

He heard a footfall and withdrew into the shadows. Light filtered into the tunnel from gaps in the roof and it was plain that at this point it was close to the surface. A figure appeared and he recognized it at once.

"Moonglum!"

The little Eastlander grinned in relief and sheathed his swords. "I came here to aid you if I could, but I see you need no aid from me!"

"Not here. The Burning God is no more. I'll tell you of that later. What became of you?"

"When I realized we were in a trap I ran for the door, deciding it would be best if one of us were free and I knew it was you they wanted. But then I saw the door opening and realized they had been waiting there all along." Moonglum wrinkled his nose and dusted at the rags he still wore. "Thus I came to find myself lying at the bottom of one of those heaps of garbage littered about Urish's hall. I dived into it and stayed there, listening to what passed. As soon as I could, I found this tunnel, planning to help you however I could."

"And where are Urish and Theleb K'aarna now?"

"It appears that they go to make good Theleb K'aarna's bargain with Urish. Urish was not altogether happy with the plan to lure you here for he fears your power—"

"He has reason to! Now!"

"Aye. Well, it seems that Urish had heard what we had heard, that the caravan for Tanelorn was on its way back to that city. Urish has knowledge of Tanelorn—though not much, I gather—and fosters an unreasoning hatred for the place, perhaps because it is the opposite of what Nadsokor is."

"They plan to attack Rackhir's caravan?"

"Aye—and Theleb K'aarna is to summon creatures from hell to ensure that their attack is successful. Rackhir has no sorcery to speak of, I believe."

"He served Chaos once, but no more—those who dwell in Tanelorn can have no supernatural masters."

"I gathered as much from the conversation."

"When do they make this attack?"

"They have gone already—almost as soon as they had dealt with you. Urish is impatient."

"It is unlike the beggars to make a direct attack on a caravan."

"They do not always have a powerful wizard for an ally."

"True." Elric frowned. "My own powers of sorcery are limited without the Ring of Kings upon my hand. Its supernatural qualities identify me as a true member of the royal line of Melniboné—the line which made so many bargains with the elementals. First I must recover my ring and then we go at once to aid Rackhir."

Moonglum glanced at the floor. "They said something of protecting Urish's Hoard in his absence. There may be a few armed men in the hall."

Elric smiled. "Now that we are prepared and now I have the strength of the Burning God in me, I think we shall be able to deal with a whole army, Moonglum."

Moonglum brightened. "Then I'll lead the way back to the hall. Come. This passage will take us to a door which is let into the side of the hall, near the throne."

They began to run along the passage until they came at length to the door Moonglum had mentioned. Elric did not pause but drew his sword and flung the door open. It was only when he was in the hall that he stopped. Daylight now lit the gloomy place, but it was again deserted. No sword-bearing beggars awaited them.

Instead, there sat in Urish's throne a fat, scaly thing of yellow and green and black. Brown bile dripped from its grinning snout and it raised one of its many paws in a mockery of a salute.

"Greetings," it hissed, "and beware—for I am the guardian of Urish's treasure."

"A thing of hell," Elric said. "A demon raised by Theleb K'aarna. He has been brewing his spells for a long time, methinks, if he can command so many foul servants." He frowned and weighed Stormbringer in his hand but, oddly, the blade did not seem to hunger for battle.

"I warn thee," hissed the demon, "I cannot be slain by a sword— not even that sword. It is my wardpact . . ."

"What is that?" whispered Moonglum, eyeing the demon warily.

"He is of a race of demons used by all with sorcerous power. He is a guardian. He will not attack unless himself attacked. He is virtually invulnerable to mortal weapons and, in his case, he has a ward against swords—be they supernatural or no. If we attempted to slay him with our swords, we should be struck down by all the powers of hell. We could not possibly survive."

"But you have just destroyed a god! A demon is nothing compared with that!"

"A weak god," Elric reminded him. "And this is a strong demon—for he is a representative of all demons who would mass with him to preserve his wardpact."

"Is there no chance of defeating him?"

"If we are to help Rackhir, there is no reason for trying. We must get to our horses and try to warn the caravan. Later, perhaps, we can return and think of some sorcery which will aid us against the demon." Elric bowed sardonically to the demon and returned his salute. "Farewell unlovely one. May your master not return to release you and thus ensure you squat in this filth for ever!"

The demon slobbered in rage. "My master is Theleb K'aarna—one of the most powerful sorcerers amongst your kind."

Elric shook his head. "Not my kind. I shall be slaying him soon and you will be left there until I discover the means of destroying you."

Somewhat pettishly, the demon folded its multitude of arms and closed its eyes.

Elric and Moonglum strode through the muck-strewn hall towards the door.

They were close to vomiting by the time they reached the steps leading into the forum. The rest of Elric's potions had been taken when his purse was taken and they had no protection now against the stink. Moonglum spat on the steps as they descended into the square and then he looked up and drew his two swords in a cross-arm motion.

"Elric!"

Some dozen beggars were rushing at them, bearing an array of clubs, axes and knives.

Elric laughed. "Here's a titbit for you, Stormbringer!" He drew his sword and began to swing the howling blade around his head, moving implacably towards the beggars. Almost immediately two of their number broke and ran, but the rest came in a rush at the pair.

Elric brought the sword lower and took a head from its shoulders and had bitten deep into the next man's shoulder before the first's blood had begun to spout.

Moonglum darted in with his two slim swords and engaged two of the beggars at the same time. Elric stabbed at another and the man screamed and danced, clutching at the blade which remorselessly drew out his soul and his life.

Stormbringer was singing a sardonic song now and three of the surviving beggars dropped their weapons and were off across the square as Moonglum neatly took both his opponents simultaneously in their hearts and Elric hacked down the rest of the rabble as they shouted and groaned for mercy.

Elric sheathed Stormbringer, looked down at the crimson ruin he had caused, wiped his lips as a man might who had just enjoyed a fine meal, caused Moonglum to shudder, and clapped his friend on the shoulder.

"Come—let's to Rackhir's aid!"

As Moonglum followed the albino, he reflected that Elric had absorbed more than just the Burning God's life-force in the encounter in the labyrinth. Much of the callousness of the Lords of Chaos was in him today.

Today Elric seemed a true warrior of ancient Melniboné.

CHAPTER FIVE

Things Which Are Not Women

The beggars had been too absorbed in their triumph over the albino and their plans for their attack on the caravan of Tanelorn to think to seek the mounts on which Elric and Moonglum had come to Nadsokor.

They found the horses where they had left them the previous night. The superb Shazaarian steeds were cropping the grass as if they had been waiting only a few minutes.

They climbed into their saddles and soon were riding as fast as the fleet horses could carry them—north-north-east to the point the caravan was logically due to reach.

Shortly after noon they had found it—a long sprawl of wagons and horses, awnings of gay, rich silks, brightly decorated harness, it stretched across the floor of a shallow valley. And surrounding it on all sides was the squalid and motley beggar army of King Urish of Nadsokor.

Elric and Moonglum reined in their horses when they reached the brow of the hill and they watched.

Theleb K'aarna and King Urish were not immediately visible and at last Elric saw them on the opposite hill. By the way in which the sorcerer was stretching out his arms to the deep blue sky Elric guessed he was already summoning the aid he had promised Urish.

Below Elric saw a flash of red and knew that it must be the scarlet garb of the Red Archer. Peering closer he saw one or two other shapes he recognized—Brut of Lashmar with his blond hair and his huge, burly body almost dwarfing his warhorse; Carkan, once of Pan Tang himself, but now dressed in the chequered cloak and fur cap of the barbarians of Southern Ilmiora. Rackhir himself had been a Warrior Priest from Moonglum's country beyond the Weeping Waste, but all these men had forsworn their gods to go to live in peaceful Tanelorn where, it was said, even the greatest Lords of the Higher Worlds could not enter—Eternal Tanelorn, which had stood for uncountable cycles and would outlive the Earth herself.

Knowing nothing of Theleb K'aarna's plan Rackhir was plainly not too worried by the appearance of the beggar rabble which was as poorly armed as those Elric and Moonglum had fought in Nadsokor.

"We must ride through their army to reach Rackhir now," Moonglum said.

Elric nodded but he made no move. He was watching the distant hill where Theleb K'aarna continued his incantation, hoping that he might guess what kind of aid the sorcerer was summoning.

A moment later Elric yelled and spurred his horse down the hill at a gallop. Moonglum was almost as startled as the beggars as he followed his friend into the thick of the ragged horde, slashing this way and that with the longest of his swords.

Elric's Stormbringer emitted black radiance as it carved a bloody path through the beggar army, leaving in its wake a mess of dismembered bodies, entrails and dead, horrified eyes.

Moonglum's horse was splashed with blood to the shoulder and it snorted and balked at following the white-skinned demon with the howling black blade, but Moonglum, afraid that the beggar ranks would close, forced it on until at last they were both riding towards the caravan and someone was yelling Elric's name.

It was Rackhir the Red Archer, clothed in scarlet from head to foot, with a red bone bow in his hand and a red quiver of crimson-fletched arrows on his back. On his head was a scarlet skull-cap decorated with a single scarlet feather. His face was weather-beaten and all but flesh-less. He had fought with Elric before the Fall of Imrryr and together they had discovered the black swords. Rackhir had gone on to seek Tanelorn and find it at last.

Elric had not seen Rackhir since then. Now he noted an enviable look of peace in the archer's eyes. Rackhir had once been a Warrior Priest in the Eastlands, serving Chaos, but now he served nothing but his tranquil Tanelorn.

"Elric! Have you come to help us send Urish and his beggars back to where they came from?" Rackhir was laughing, evidently pleased to see his old friend. "And Moonglum! When did you two meet? I have not seen thee since I left the Eastlands!"

Moonglum grinned. "Much has come to pass since those days, Rackhir."

Rackhir rubbed at his aquiline nose. "Aye—so I've heard."

Elric dismounted swiftly. "No time for reminiscence now, Rackhir. You're in greater danger than you know."

"What? When did the beggar rabble of Nadsokor offer anything to fear? Look how poorly armed they are!"

"They have a sorcerer with them—Theleb K'aarna of Pan Tang. See—that's him on yonder hill."

Rackhir frowned. "Sorcery. These days I've little guard against that. How good is the sorcerer, do you know?"

"He is one of the most powerful in Pan Tang."

"And the wizards of Pan Tang almost equal your folk, Elric, in their skills."

"I fear he more than equals me at present, for my Actorios Ring has been stolen from me by Urish."

Rackhir looked strangely at Elric, noting something in the albino's face which he had evidently not seen there when they last parted. "Well," he said, "we shall have to defend ourselves as best we can . . ."

"If you cut loose your horses so that all your folk could be mounted we might be able to escape before Theleb K'aarna invokes whatever supernatural aid it is he seeks." Elric nodded as the giant, Brut of Lashmar, rode up grinning at him. Brut had been a hero in Lashmar before he had disgraced himself.

Rackhir shook his head. "Tanelorn needs the provisions we carry."

"Look," said Moonglum quietly.

On the hill where Theleb K'aarna had been standing there had now appeared a billowing cloud of redness, like blood in clear water.

"He is successful," Rackhir murmured. "Brut! Let all be mounted. We've no time to prepare further defenses, but we'll have the advantage of being on horseback when they attack."

Brut thundered off, yelling at the men of Tanelorn. They began to unharness the wagon horses and ready their weapons.

The cloud of redness above was beginning to disperse and out of it shapes were emerging. Elric tried to distinguish the shapes but could not at that distance. He climbed back into his saddle as the horsemen of Tanelorn now formed themselves into groups which would, when the attack came, race through the unmounted beggars striking swiftly and passing on. Rackhir waved to Elric and went to join one of these divisions. Elric and Moonglum found themselves at the head of a dozen warriors armed with axes, pikes and lances.

Then Urish's voice cawed out over the waiting silence.

"Attack, my beggars! They are doomed!"

The beggar rabble began to move down the sides of the valley. Rackhir raised his sword as the signal to his men. Then the first groups of cavalry rode out from the caravan, straight at the advancing beggars.

Rackhir replaced his blade and took up his bow. From where he sat on his horse he began to send arrow after arrow into the beggar ranks.

There was shouting everywhere now as the warriors of Tanelorn met their foes, driving wedges everywhere in their mass.

Elric saw Carkan's chequered cape in the midst of a sea of rags, filthy limbs, clubs and knives. He saw Brut's great blond head towering over a cluster of human filth.

And Moonglum said: "Such creatures as these are unfit opponents for the warriors of Tanelorn."

Elric pointed firmly up the hill. "Perhaps they'll prefer their new foes."

Moonglum gasped. "They are women!"

Elric drew Stormbringer from its scabbard. "They are not women. They are Elenoin. They come from the Eighth Plane—and neither are they human. You will see."

"You recognize them?"

"My ancestors fought them once."

A strange, shrill ululation reached their ears now. It came from the hillside where Theleb K'aarna's figure could again be seen. It came from the shapes which

Moonglum was sure were women. Red-haired women whose tresses fell almost to their knees and covered their otherwise completely naked bodies. They danced down the hill towards the besieged caravan and they whirled about their heads swords which must have been over five feet long.

"Theleb K'aarna is clever," Elric muttered. "The warriors of Tanelorn will hesitate before striking at women. And while they hesitate the Elenoin will rip and slash and slay them."

Rackhir had already seen the Elenoin and he, too, recognized them for what they were. "Do not be deceived, men!" he called. "These creatures are demons!" He glanced across at Elric and there was a look of resignation on his face. He knew the power of the Elenoin. He spurred his horse towards the albino. "What can we do, Elric?"

Elric sighed. "What can mortals do against the Elenoin?"

"Have you no sorcery?"

"With the Ring of Kings I could summon the Grahluk, perhaps. They are the ancient enemies of the Elenoin. Theleb K'aarna has already made a gateway from the Eighth Plane."

"Could you not try to call the Grahluk?" Rackhir begged.

"While I tried my sword would not be aiding you. I think Stormbringer is more use today than spells."

Rackhir shuddered and turned his horse away to order his men to re-form their ranks. He knew now that they were all to die.

And now the beggars fell back, as horrified by the Elenoin as were the men of Tanelorn.

Still singing their shrill, chill song, the Elenoin lowered their swords and spread out along the hill, each one smiling at them.

"How can they . . .?" Then Moonglum saw their eyes. They were huge, orange, animal eyes. "Oh, by the gods!" And then he saw their teeth—long, pointed teeth which glinted like metal.

The horsemen of Tanelorn fell back to the wagons in a long, ragged line. Horror, despair, uncertainty was on every face save Elric's—and on his face was a look of grim anger. His crimson eyes smouldered as he held Stormbringer across his saddle pommel and regarded the demon women, the Elenoin.

The singing grew louder until it made their ears fill with sharp pain and made their stomachs turn. The Elenoin raised their slender arms and began to whirl their long swords about their heads again, staring at them all the while through beastlike, insensate eyes—malicious, unblinking eyes.

Then Carkan of Pan Tang, his fur cap askew, his chequered cloak billowing, gave a strangled yell and urged his heavy horse at them, his own sword waving.

"Back, demons! Back, spawn of hell!"

"Aaaaaaaah!" gasped the Elenoin in anticipation. "Eeeeeeeh!" they sang.

And Carkan was suddenly in the midst of a dozen slender, slashing swords and he and his horse were cut all to tiny morsels of flesh which lay in a heap at the feet of the Elenoin. And their laughter filled the valley as some of them bent to pop the flesh into their fanged mouths.

A groan of horror and hatred went up from the ranks of Tanelorn then and screaming men, hysterical with fear and disgust, began to fling themselves at the Elenoin who laughed the more and whirled their sharp swords.

Stormbringer murmured as it seemed to hear the sounds of battle, but Elric did not move as he stared at the scene. He knew that the Elenoin would kill all as they had killed Carkan.

Moonglum moaned. "Elric—there must be some sorcery against them!"

"There is! But I cannot summon the Grahluk!" Elric's chest was heaving and his brain was in turmoil. "I cannot, Moonglum!"

"For the sake of Tanelorn, you must try!"

Then Elric was riding forward, Stormbringer howling, riding at the Elenoin and screaming Arioch's name as his ancestors had screamed it since the founding of Imrryr!

"Arioch! Arioch! Blood and souls for my Lord Arioch!"

He parried the whirling blade of an Elenoin and glared into the bestial eyes as Stormbringer sent a shudder down his arm. He struck and his own blow was parried by the demon that was not a woman.

Red hair swung and curled around his throat. He hacked at it and it loosened its grip. He thrust at the naked body and the Elenoin danced aside. Another whistling blow from the slim sword and he flung himself backwards to avoid it, toppling from his saddle and springing instantly to his feet to parry a second attack, gripped Stormbringer in both hands and stepped forward under the blade to plunge the Black Sword into the smooth belly. The Elenoin shouted with anger and green foulness billowed from the wound. The Elenoin fell, still glaring and snarling, still living. Elric chopped at the neck and the head sprang off, its hair thrashing at him. He dashed forward, picked up the head and began to run up the hill to where the beggars were gathered, watching the destruction of Tanelorn's warriors. As he approached the beggars broke and began to run, but he caught one in the back with his blade. The man fell, tried to crawl on, but his twisted knees would not support him and he collapsed into the stained grass. Elric picked the wretch up and flung him over his shoulder. Then he turned and began to run down the hill back to the camp. The warriors of Tanelorn were fighting well, but half their number had already been slain by the Elenoin. Almost unbelievably there were also several Elenoin corpses on the field.

Elric saw Moonglum defending himself with both swords. He saw Rackhir, still mounted, shouting orders to his men. He saw Brut of Lashmar in the thick of the fight. But he ran on until he stood behind one of the wagons and had dropped both his bloody bundles to the ground. With his sword he split open the twitching body of the beggar and he gathered up the hair of the Elenoin and soaked it in the man's blood.

Again he stood upright, looking towards the west, with the bloody hair in one hand and Stormbringer in the other. He raised both sword and head and began to speak in the ancient High Speech of Melniboné.

Held to the West and soaked in the blood of an enemy, the hair of an Elenoin must be used to summon the enemies of the Elenoin—the Grahluk. He remembered the words he had read in his father's ancient grimoire.

And now the invocation:

> Grahluk come and Grahluk slay!
> Come kill thine ancient enemy!
> Make this thy victory day.

All the strength of the Burning God was leaving him as he used the energy to perform the invocation. And perhaps without the Ring of Kings he was wasting that strength for nothing.

> Grahluk speed without delay!
> Come kill thine ancient enemy!
> Make this thy vengeance day.

The spell was far less complex than many he had used in the past. Yet it took as much from him as any spell ever had.

"Grahluk, I summon thee! Grahluk, here you may take vengeance on your foes!"

Many cycles since, the Elenoin were said to have driven the Grahluk from their lands in the Eighth Plane and the Grahluk sought revenge now at every opportunity.

All around Elric the air shivered and turned brown, then green, then black.

"Grahluk! Come destroy the Elenoin!" Elric's voice was weakening. "Grahluk—the gateway is made!"

And now the ground trembled and strange winds blew at the blood-soaked hair of the Elenoin and the air became thick and purple and Elric fell to his knees, still croaking the invocation.

"Grahluk . . ."

A shuffling sound. A grunting noise. The stink of something unnamable.

The Grahluk had come. They were apelike creatures as bestial as the Elenoin. They carried nets and ropes and shields. Once, it was said, both Grahluk and Elenoin had had intelligence—had been part of the same species which had devolved and divided.

They moved out of the purple mist in their scores and they stood looking at Elric who was still on his knees. Elric pointed at where the remaining warriors of Tanelorn were still fighting the Elenoin.

"There . . ."

The Grahluk snorted with battle-greed and shambled towards the Elenoin.

The Elenoin saw them and their shrill wailing voices changed in quality as they retreated a short distance up the hill.

Elric forced himself to his feet and gasped: "Rackhir! Withdraw your warriors. The Grahluk will do their work now . . ."

"You helped us after all!" Rackhir yelled, turning his horse. His clothes were all in tatters and there were a dozen wounds on his body.

They watched as the Grahluk's nets and nooses flashed towards the screaming Elenoin whose sword blows were stopped by the Grahluk shields. They watched as the Elenoin were crushed and throttled and parts of their entrails devoured by the grunting, apelike demons.

And when the last of the Elenoin was dead, the Grahluk picked up the fallen swords and reversed them and fell upon them.

Rackhir said: "They are killing themselves. Why?"

"They live only to destroy the Elenoin. Once that is done, they have nothing left for which to exist." Elric swayed and Rackhir and Moonglum caught him.

"See!" Moonglum laughed. "The beggars are running!"

"Theleb K'aarna," Elric muttered. "We must get Theleb K'aarna . . ."

"Doubtless he has gone back with Urish to Nadsokor," Moonglum said.

"I must—I must retrieve the Ring of Kings."

"Plainly you can work your sorcery without it," Rackhir said.

"Can I?" Elric looked up and showed his face to Rackhir who lowered his eyes and nodded.

"We will help you get back your ring," Rackhir said quietly. "There'll be no more trouble from the beggars. We'll ride with you to Nadsokor."

"I had hoped you would." Elric climbed with difficulty into the saddle of a surviving horse and jerked at its reins, turning it towards the City of Beggars. "Perhaps your arrows will slay what my sword cannot . . ."

"I do not understand you," Rackhir said.

Moonglum was mounting now. "We'll tell you on the way."

Chapter Six

The Jesting Demon

Through the filth of Nadsokor now rode the warriors of Tanelorn.

Elric, Moonglum and Rackhir were at the head of the company but there was no ostentatious triumph in their demeanour. The riders looked neither to left nor to right and the beggars offered no threat now, not daring to attack but instead cowering into the shadows.

A potion of Rackhir's had helped Elric recover some of his strength and he no longer leaned over his horse's neck but sat upright as they crossed the forum, came to the palace of the Beggar King.

Elric did not pause. He rode his horse up the steps and into the gloomy hall.

"Theleb K'aarna!" Elric shouted.

His voice boomed through the hall, but Theleb K'aarna did not reply.

The braziers of garbage guttered in the wind from the opened door and threw a little more light on the dais at the end.

"Theleb K'aarna!"

But it was not Theleb K'aarna who knelt there. It was a wretched, ragged figure and it sprawled before the throne and it was sobbing, imploring, whining at something on the throne.

Elric walked his horse a little further into the hall and now he could see what occupied the throne.

Squatting in the great chair of black oak was the demon which had
been there earlier. Its arms were folded and its eyes were shut and it
seemed, somewhat theatrically, to be ignoring the pleadings of the creature kneeling at its feet.

The others, also mounted, entered the hall now and together they
rode up to the dais and stopped.

The kneeling figure turned its head and it was Urish. It gasped
when it saw Elric and stretched out a maimed hand for its cleaver,
abandoned some distance away.

Elric sighed.

"Do not fear me, Urish. I'm weary of bloodletting. I do not want
your life."

The demon opened its eyes.

"Prince Elric, you have returned," it said. There seemed to be an
indefinable difference in its tone.

"Aye. Where is your master?"

"I fear he has fled Nadsokor for ever."

"And left you to sit here for eternity."

The demon inclined its head.

Urish put a grimy hand on Elric's leg. "Elric—help me! I must
have my Hoard. It is everything! Destroy the demon and I will give
you back the Ring of Kings."

Elric smiled. "You are generous, King Urish."

Tears streamed down the filth on Urish's ruined face. "Please,
Elric, I beg thee . . ."

"It is my intention to destroy the demon."

Urish looked nervously about him. "And aught else?"

"That decision lies with the men of Tanelorn whom you sought to
rob and whose friends you caused to be slain in a most foul manner."

"It was Theleb K'aarna, not I!"

"And where is Theleb K'aarna now?"

"When you unleashed those ape things on our Elenoin he fled the
field. He went towards the Varkalk River—towards Troos."

Without looking behind him Elric said, "Rackhir? Will you try the
arrows now?"

There was the hum of a bowstring and an arrow struck the demon in the breast. It quivered there and the demon looked at it with mild interest, then breathed in deeply. As he breathed the arrow was drawn further into him and was eventually absorbed altogether.

"Aaah!" Urish scuttled for his cleaver. "It will not work!"

A second arrow sped from Rackhir's scarlet bow and it, too, was absorbed, as was the third.

Urish was gibbering now, waving his cleaver.

Elric warned him: "He has a wardpact against swords, King Urish!"

The demon rattled its scales. "Is that thing a sword, I wonder?"

Urish hesitated. Spittle ran down his chin and his red eyes rolled. "Demon—begone! I must have my Hoard—it is mine!"

The demon watched him sardonically.

With a yell of terror and anguish Urish flung himself at the demon, the cleaver Hackmeat swinging wildly. Its blade came down on the hell-thing's head, there was a sound like lightning striking metal and the cleaver shivered to pieces. Urish stood staring at the demon in quaking anticipation. Casually the demon reached out four of its hands and seized him. Its jaws opened wider than should have been possible, the bulk of the demon expanded until it was suddenly twice its original size. It brought the kicking Beggar King to its maw and suddenly there were only two legs waving from the mouth and then the demon gave a mighty swallow and there was nothing at all left of Urish of Nadsokor.

Elric shrugged. "Your wardpact is effective."

The demon smiled. "Aye, sweet Elric."

Now the tone of voice was very familiar. Elric looked narrowly at the demon. "You're no ordinary . . ."

"I hope not, most beloved of mortals."

Elric's horse reared and snorted as the demon's shape began to alter. There was a humming sound and black smoke coiled over the throne and then another figure was sitting there, its legs crossed. It had the shape of a man but it was more beautiful than any mortal. It was a being of intense and majestic beauty—unearthly beauty.

"Arioch!" Elric bowed his head before the Lord of Chaos.

"Aye, Elric. I took the demon's place while you were gone."

"But you have refused to aid me . . ."

"There are larger affairs afoot, as I've told you. Soon Chaos must engage with Law and such as Donblas will be dismissed to limbo for eternity."

"You knew Donblas spoke to me in the labyrinth of the Burning God?"

"Indeed I did. That was why I afforded myself the time to visit your plane. I cannot have you patronized by Donblas the Justice Maker and his humourless kind. I was offended. Now I have shown you that my power is greater than Law's." Arioch stared beyond Elric at Rackhir, Brut, Moonglum and the rest who were protecting their eyes from his beauty. "Perhaps you fools of Tanelorn now realize that it is better to serve Chaos!"

Rackhir said grimly: "I serve neither Chaos nor Law!"

"One day you will be taught that neutrality is more dangerous than side-taking, renegade!" The harmonious voice was now almost vicious.

"You cannot harm me," Rackhir said. "And if Elric returns with us to Tanelorn, then he, too, may rid himself of your evil yoke!"

"Elric is of Melniboné. The folk of Melniboné all serve Chaos— and are greatly rewarded. How else would you have rid this throne of Theleb K'aarna's demon?"

"Perhaps in Tanelorn Elric would have no need of his Ring of Kings," Rackhir replied levelly.

There was a sound like rushing water, the boom of thunder and Arioch's form began to grow larger. But as it grew it also began to fade until there was nothing left in the hall but the stench of its garbage.

Elric dismounted and ran to the throne. Reaching under it he drew out dead Urish's chest and hacked it open with Stormbringer. The sword murmured as if resenting the menial work. Gems, gold, artifacts scattered through the muck as Elric sought his ring.

And then at last he held it up in triumph, replacing it on his finger. His step was lighter as he returned to his horse.

Moonglum had in the meantime dismounted and was scooping the best of the jewels into his pouch. He winked at Rackhir, who smiled.

"And now," Elric said, "I go to Troos to seek Theleb K'aarna there. I have still to take my vengeance upon him."

"Let him rot in Troos's sickly forest," Moonglum said.

Rackhir placed a hand on Elric's shoulder. "If Theleb K'aarna hates you so, he will find you again. Why waste your own time in the pursuit?"

Elric smiled slightly at his old friend. "You were ever clear in your arguments, Rackhir. And it is true that I am weary—both gods and demons have fallen to my blade in the little while since I came to Nadsokor."

"Come, rest in Tanelorn—peaceful Tanelorn, where even the greatest Lords of the Higher Worlds cannot come without permission."

Elric looked down at the ring on his finger. "Yet I have sworn Theleb K'aarna shall perish . . ."

"There will be time yet to fulfill your oath."

Elric ran his hand through his milk-white hair and it seemed to his friends that there were tears in his crimson eyes.

"Aye," he said. "Aye. Time yet . . ."

And they rode away from Nadsokor, leaving the beggars to brood in the stink and the foulness and regret that they had aught to do with sorcery or with Elric of Melniboné.

They rode for Eternal Tanelorn. Tanelorn, which had welcomed and held all troubled wanderers who came upon it. All save one.

Doom-haunted, full of guilt, of sorrow, of despair, Elric of Melniboné prayed that this time Tanelorn might hold even him . . .

THREE HEROES WITH A SINGLE AIM

*. . . Elric, of all the manifestations of the Champion Eternal,
was to find Tanelorn without effort. And of all those
manifestations he was the only one to choose to
leave that city of myriad incarnations . .*

—*The Chronicle of the Black Sword*

CHAPTER ONE

Tanelorn Eternal

TANELORN HAD TAKEN many forms in her endless existence, but all those forms, save one, had been beautiful.

She was beautiful now, with the soft sunlight on her pastel towers
and her curved turrets and domes. And banners flew from her spires,
but they were not battle-banners, for the warriors who had found
Tanelorn and had stayed there were weary of war.

She had been here always. None knew when Tanelorn had been
built, but some knew that she had existed before time and would exist
after the end of time and that was why she was known as Eternal
Tanelorn.

She had played a significant role in the struggles of many heroes
and many gods and because she existed beyond time she was hated by
the Lords of Chaos who had more than once sought to destroy her. To
the south of her lay the rolling plains of Ilmiora, a land where justice
was known to prevail, and to the north of her lay the desolation which
was the Sighing Desert, endless wasteland over which hissed a constant
wind. If Ilmiora represented Law, then the Sighing Desert certainly

mirrored something of the barrenness of Ultimate Chaos. Those who dwelled in Tanelorn had loyalty neither to Law nor to Chaos and they had chosen to have no part in the Cosmic Struggle which was waged continuously by the Lords of the Higher Worlds. There were no leaders and there were no followers in Tanelorn and her citizens lived in harmony with each other, even though many had been warriors of great reputation before they chose to stay there. But one of the most admired citizens of Tanelorn, one who was often consulted by the others, was Rackhir of the ascetic features who had once been a fierce Warrior Priest in the Eastlands where he had gained the name of the Red Archer because his skill with a bow was great and he dressed all in scarlet. His skill and his dress remained the same, but his urge to fight had left him since he had come to live in Tanelorn.

Close to the low west wall of the city lay a house of two storeys surrounded by a lawn in which grew all manner of wild flowers. The house was of pink and yellow marble and, unlike most of the other dwellings in Tanelorn, it had a tall, pointed roof. This was Rackhir's house and Rackhir sat outside it now, sprawled on a bench of plain wood while he watched his guest pace the lawn. The guest was his old friend the tormented albino prince of Melniboné.

Elric wore a simple white shirt and britches of heavy black silk. He had a band of the same black silk tied around his head to keep back the mane of milk-white hair which grew to his shoulders. His crimson eyes were downcast as he paced and he did not look at Rackhir at all.

Rackhir was unwilling to intrude upon his friend's reverie and yet he hated to see Elric as he was now. He had hoped that Tanelorn would comfort the albino, drive away the ghosts and the doubts inhabiting his skull, but it seemed that even Tanelorn could not bring Elric tranquility.

At last Rackhir broke his silence. "It has been a month since you came to Tanelorn, my friend, yet still you pace, still you brood."

Elric looked up with a slight smile. "Aye—still I brood. Forgive me, Rackhir. I am a poor guest."

"What occupies your thoughts?"

"No particular subject. It seems that I cannot lose myself in all this peace. Only violent action helps me drive away my melancholy. I was not meant for Tanelorn, Rackhir."

"But violent action—or the results of it—produces further melancholy, does it not?"

"It is true. It is the dilemma with which I live constantly. It is a dilemma I have been in since the burning of Imrryr—perhaps before."

"It is a dilemma known to all men, perhaps," Rackhir said. "At least to some degree."

"Aye—to wonder what purpose there is to one's existence and what point there is to purpose, even if it should be discovered."

"Tanelorn makes such problems seem meaningless to me," Rackhir told him. "I had hoped that you, too, would be able to dismiss them from your thoughts. Will you stay on in Tanelorn?"

"I have no other plans. I still thirst for vengeance upon Theleb K'aarna, but I now have no idea of his whereabouts. And, as you or Moonglum told me, Theleb K'aarna is sure to seek me out sooner or later. I remember once, when you first found Tanelorn, you suggested that I bring Cymoril here and forget Melniboné. I wish I had listened to you then, Rackhir, for now, I think, I would know peace and Cymoril's dead face would not be infesting my nights."

"You mentioned this sorceress who, you said, resembled Cymoril . . . ?"

"Myshella? She who is called Empress of the Dawn? I first saw her in a dream and when I left her side it was I who was in a dream. We served each other to achieve a common purpose. I shall not see her again."

"But if she—"

"I shall not see her again, Rackhir."

"As you say."

Once more the two friends fell silent and there was only birdsong and the splash of fountains in the air as Elric continued his pacing of the garden.

Some while later Elric suddenly turned on his heel and went into the house followed by Rackhir's troubled gaze.

When Elric came out again he was wearing the great wide belt around his waist—the belt which supported the black scabbard containing his runesword Stormbringer. Over his shoulders was flung a cloak of white silk and he wore high boots.

"I go riding," he said. "I will go by myself into the Sighing Desert and I will ride until I am exhausted. Perhaps exercise is all I need."

"Be careful of the desert, my friend," Rackhir cautioned him. "It is a sinister and treacherous wilderness."

"I will be careful."

"Take the big golden mare. She is used to the desert and her stamina is legendary."

"Thank you. I will see you in the morning if I do not return earlier."

"Take care, Elric. I trust your remedy is successful and your melancholy disappears."

Rackhir's expression had little of relief in it as he watched his friend stride towards the nearby stables, his white cloak billowing behind him like a sea fog suddenly risen.

Then he heard the sound of Elric's horse as its hoofs struck the cobbles of the street and Rackhir got to his feet to watch as the albino urged the golden mare into a canter and headed for the northern wall beyond which the great yellow waste of the Sighing Desert could be seen.

Moonglum came out of the house, a large apple in his hand, a scroll under his arm.

"Where goes Elric, Rackhir?"

"He looks for peace in the desert."

Moonglum frowned and bit thoughtfully into his apple. "He has sought peace in all other places and I fear he'll not find it there, either."

Rackhir nodded his agreement. "But it is my premonition he'll discover something else, for Elric is not always motivated by his own wishes. There are times when other forces work within him to make him take some fateful action."

"You think this is such a time?"

"It could be."

CHAPTER TWO

Return of a Sorceress

The sand rippled as the wind blew it so that the dunes seemed like waves in an almost petrified sea. Stark fangs of rock jutted here and there—the remains of mountain ranges which had been eroded by the wind. And a mournful sighing could just be heard, as if the sand remembered when it had been rock and the stones of cities and the bones of men and beasts and longed for its resurrection, sighed at the memory of its death.

Elric drew the cloak's cowl over his head to protect it from the fierce sun which hung in the steel-blue sky.

One day, he thought, I too shall know this peace of death and perhaps then I shall also regret it. He let the golden mare slow to a trot and took a sip of water from one of his canteens.

Now the desert surrounded him and it seemed infinite. Nothing grew. No animals lived there. There were no birds in the sky.

For some reason he shuddered and he had a presentiment of a moment in the future when he would be alone, as he was now, in a world even more barren than this desert, without even a horse for company. He shook off the thought, but it had left him so stunned that for a little while he achieved his ambition and did not brood upon his fate and his situation. The wind dropped slightly and the sighing became little more than a whisper.

Dazed, Elric fingered the pommel of his blade—Stormbringer, the Black Sword—for he associated his presentiment with the weapon but could not tell why. And it seemed to him that he heard an ironic note in the murmuring of the wind. Or did the sound emanate from his sword itself? He cocked his head, listening, but the sound became even less audible, as if aware that he listened.

The golden mare began to climb the gentle slope of a dune, stumbling once as her foot sank into deeper sand. Elric concentrated on guiding her to firmer ground.

Reaching the top of the dune he reined his horse in. The desert dunes rolled on, broken only by the occasional rock. He had it in mind then to ride on and on until it would be impossible to return to Tanelorn, until both he and his mount collapsed from exhaustion and were eventually swallowed by the sands. He pushed back his cowl and wiped sweat from his brow.

Why not? he thought. Life was not bearable. He would try death.

And yet would death deny him? Was he doomed to live? It sometimes seemed so.

Then he considered the horse. It would not be fair to sacrifice it to his desire. Slowly he dismounted.

The wind grew stronger and the sound of its sighing increased. Sand blew around Elric's booted feet. It was a hot wind and it tugged at his voluminous white cloak. The horse snorted nervously.

Elric looked towards the north-east, towards the edge of the world.

And he began to walk.

The horse whinnied enquiringly at him when he did not call it, but he ignored the sound and had soon left his mount behind him. He had not even bothered to bring water with him. He flung back his cowl so that the sun beat directly upon his head. His pace was even, purposeful, and he marched as if at the head of an army.

Perhaps he did sense an army behind him—the army of the dead, of all those friends and enemies whom he had slain in the course of his pointless search for a meaning to his existence.

And still one enemy remained alive. An enemy even stronger, even more malevolent than Theleb K'aarna—the enemy of his darker self, of that side of his nature which was symbolized by the sentient blade still resting at his hip. And when he died, then that enemy would also die. A force for evil would be removed from the world.

For several hours Elric of Melniboné tramped on through the Sighing Desert and gradually, as he had hoped, his sense of identity began to leave him so that it was almost as if he became one with the wind and the sand and, in so doing, was united at last with the world which had rejected him and which he had rejected.

Evening came, but he hardly noticed the sun's setting. Night fell, but he continued to march, unaware of the cold. Already he was weakening. He rejoiced in the weakness where previously he had fought to retain the strength he enjoyed only through the power of the Black Sword.

And sometime around midnight, beneath a pale moon, his legs buckled and he fell sprawling in the sand and lay there while the remains of his sensibilities left him.

"Prince Elric. My Lord?"

The voice was rich, vibrant, almost amused. It was a woman's voice and Elric recognized it. He did not move.

"Elric of Melniboné."

He felt a hand on his arm. She was trying to pull him upright. Rather than be dragged he raised himself with some difficulty to a sitting position. He tried to speak, but at first no words would come from his mouth which was dry and full of sand. She stood there as the dawn rose behind her and brightened her long black hair framing her beautiful features. She was dressed in a flowing gown of blue, green and gold and she was smiling.

As he cleared the sand from his mouth he shook his head, saying at last: "If I am dead, then I am still plagued by phantoms and illusions."

"I am no more illusion than anything else in this world. You are not dead, my lord."

"You are, in that case, many leagues from Castle Kaneloon, my lady. You have come from the other side of the world—from edge to edge."

"I have been seeking you, Elric."

"Then you have broken your word, Myshella, for when we parted you said that you would not see me again, that our fates had ceased to be twined."

"I thought then that Theleb K'aarna was dead—that our mutual enemy had perished in the Noose of Flesh." The sorceress spread her arms wide and it was almost as if the gesture summoned the sun, for it appeared over the horizon, suddenly. "Why did you walk thus in the desert, my lord?"

"I sought death."

"Yet you know it is not your destiny to die in such a way."

"I have been told as much but I do not *know* it, Lady Myshella. However," he stumbled upright and stood swaying before her, "I am beginning to suspect that it is so."

She came forward, bringing a goblet from beneath her robes. It was full to the brim with a cool, silvery liquid. "Drink," she said.

He did not lift his hands towards the cup. "I am not pleased to see you, Lady Myshella."

"Why? Because you are afraid to love me?"

"If it flatters you to think that—aye."

"It does not flatter me. I know you are reminded of Cymoril and that I made the mistake of letting Kaneloon become that which you most desire—before I understood that it is also what you most fear."

He lowered his head. "Be silent!"

"I am sorry. I apologized then. We drove away the desire and ter-ror together for a little while, did we not?"

He looked up and she was staring intently into his eyes. "Did we not?"

"We did." He took a deep breath and stretched out his hands for the goblet. "Is this some potion to sap my will and make me work for your interests?"

"No potion could do that. It will revive you, that is all."

He sipped the liquid and immediately his mouth was clean and his head clear. He drained the goblet and he felt a glow of strength in all his limbs and vitals.

"Do you still wish to die?" she asked as she received back the cup, replacing it beneath her robes.

"If death will bring me peace."

"It will not—not if you die now. That I know."

"How did you find me here?"

"Oh, by a variety of means, some of them sorcerous. But my bird brought me to you." She extended her right arm to point behind him.

He turned and there was the bird of gold and silver and brass which he himself had once ridden while in Myshella's service. Its great metallic wings were folded but there was intelligence in its emerald eyes as it waited for its mistress.

"Have you come, then, to return me to Tanelorn?"

She shook her head. "Not yet. I have come to tell you where you may discover our enemy Theleb K'aarna."

He smiled. "He threatens you again?"

"Not directly."

Elric shook sand from his cloak. "I know you well, Myshella. You would not interfere in my destiny unless it had again become in some way linked with your own. You have said that I am afraid to love you. That may be true, for I think I am afraid to love any woman. But you make use of love—the men to whom you give your love are men who will serve your purpose."

"I do not deny that. I love only heroes—and only heroes who work to ensure the presence of the power of Law upon this plane of our Earth . . ."

"I care not whether Law or Chaos gains predominance. Even my hatred of Theleb K'aarna has waned—and that was a personal hatred, nothing to do with any cause."

"What if you knew Theleb K'aarna once again threatens the folk of Tanelorn?"

"Impossible. Tanelorn is eternal."

"Tanelorn is eternal—but its citizens are not. I know. More than once has some catastrophe fallen upon those who dwell in Tanelorn. And the Lords of Chaos hate Tanelorn, though they cannot attack it directly. They would aid any mortal who thought he could destroy those whom the Chaos Lords regard as traitors."

Elric frowned. He knew of the enmity of the Lords of Chaos to Tanelorn. He had heard that on more than one occasion they had made use of mortals to attack the city.

"And you say Theleb K'aarna plans to destroy Tanelorn's citizens? With Chaos's aid?"

"Aye. Your thwarting of his schemes concerning Nadsokor and

Rackhir's caravan made him extend his hatred to all dwelling in Tanelorn. In Troos he discovered some ancient grimoires—things which survived from the Age of the Doomed Folk."

"How can that be? They existed a whole time cycle before Melni-boné!"

"True—but Troos itself has lasted since the Age of the Doomed Folk and these were people who had many great inventions, a means of preserving their wisdom . . ."

"Very well. I will accept that Theleb K'aarna found their gri-moires. What did those grimoires tell him?"

"They showed him the means of causing a rupture in the division which separates one plane of Earth from another. This knowledge of the other planes is largely mysterious to us—even your ancestors only guessed at the variety of existences obtaining in what the ancients termed the 'multiverse'—and I know only a little more than do you. The Lords of the Higher Worlds can, at times, move freely between these temporal and spacial layers, but mortals cannot—at least not in this period of our being."

"And what has Theleb K'aarna done? Surely great power would be needed to cause this 'rupture' you describe? He does not have that power."

"True. But he has powerful allies in the Chaos Lords. The Lords of Entropy have leagued themselves with him as they would league them-selves with anyone who was willing to be the means of destruction of those who dwell in Tanelorn. He found more than manuscripts in the forest of Troos. He discovered those buried devices which were the in-ventions of the Doomed Folk and which ultimately brought about their destruction. These devices, of course, were meaningless to him until the Lords of Chaos showed him how they could be activated using the very forces of creation for their energy."

"And he has activated them? Where?"

"He brought the device he wanted to these parts, for he needed space to work where he thought he could not be observed by such as myself."

"He is in the Sighing Desert?"

"Aye. If you had continued on your horse you would have found him by now—or he you. I believe that is what drove you into the desert—a compulsion to seek him out."

"I had no compulsion save a need to die!" Elric tried to control his anger.

She smiled again. "Have it thus if you will . . ."

"You mean I am so manipulated by Fate that I cannot choose to die if I wish?"

"Ask yourself for that answer."

Elric's face was clouded with puzzlement and despair. "What is it, then, which guides me? And to what end?"

"You must discover that for yourself."

"You want me to go against Chaos? Yet Chaos aids me and I am sworn to Arioch."

"But you are mortal—and Arioch is slow to aid you these days, perhaps because he guesses what lies in the future."

"What do you know of the future?"

"Little—and what I know I cannot speak of to you. A mortal may choose whom he serves, Elric."

"I have chosen. I chose Chaos."

"Yet much of your melancholy is because you are divided in your loyalties."

"That, too, is true."

"Besides, you would not fight for Law if you fought against Theleb K'aarna—you would merely be fighting against one aided by Chaos—and those of Chaos often fight among themselves do they not?"

"They do. It is also well known that I hate Theleb K'aarna and would destroy him whether he served Law or Chaos."

"Therefore you will not unduly anger those to whom you are loyal—though they may be reluctant to help you."

"Tell me more of Theleb K'aarna's plans."

"You must see for yourself. There is your horse." She pointed again and this time he saw the golden mare emerge from the other side of a dune. "Head north-east as you were heading, but move cautiously lest Theleb K'aarna becomes aware of your presence and traps you."

"Suppose I merely return to Tanelorn—or choose to try to die again?"

"But you will not, will you, Elric? You have loyalties to your friends, you wish in your heart to serve what I represent—and you hate Theleb K'aarna. I do not think you would wish to die for the moment."

He scowled. "Once more I am burdened with unwanted responsibilities, hedged by considerations other than my own desires, trapped by emotions which we of Melniboné have been taught to despise. Aye—I will go, Myshella. I will do what you wish."

"Be careful, Elric. Theleb K'aarna now has powers which are unfamiliar to you, which you will find difficult to combat." She gave him a lingering look and suddenly he had stepped forward and had seized her, kissed her while tears flowed down his white face and mingled with hers.

Later he watched as she climbed into the onyx saddle of the bird of silver and gold and called out a command. The metal wings beat with a great clashing, the emerald eyes turned and the gem-studded beak opened. "Farewell, Elric," said the bird.

But Myshella said nothing, did not look back.

Soon the metal bird was a speck of light in the blue sky and Elric had turned his horse towards the north-east.

CHAPTER THREE

The Barrier Broken

Elric reined in behind the cover of a crag. He had found the camp of Theleb K'aarna. A large tent of yellow silk had been erected beneath the protection of an overhang of rock which was part of a formation making a natural amphitheatre amongst the dunes of the desert. A wagon and two horses were close to the tent, but all this was dominated by the thing of metal which reared in the centre of the clearing. It was contained in an enormous bowl of clear crystal. The bowl was almost globular with a narrow opening at the top. The device itself was asymmetrical and strange, composed of many curved and angular surfaces which seemed to contain myriad half-formed faces, shapes of beasts and buildings, illusive designs coming and going even as Elric looked upon it. An imagination even more grotesque than that of Elric's ancestors had fashioned the thing, amalgamating metals and other substances which logic denied could ever be fused into one thing. A creation of Chaos which offered a clue as to how the Doomed Folk had come to destroy themselves. And it was alive. Deep within it something pulsed, as delicate and tentative as the heartbeat of a dying wren. Elric had witnessed many obscenities in his life and was moved by few of them, but this device, though superficially more innocuous than much he had seen, brought bile into his mouth. Yet for all his disgust he remained where he was, fascinated by the machine in the bowl, until the flap of the yellow tent was drawn back and Theleb K'aarna emerged.

The sorcerer of Pan Tang was paler and thinner than when Elric had last seen him, shortly before the battle between the beggars of Nadsokor and the warriors of Tanelorn. Yet unhealthy energy flushed the cheeks and burned in the dark eyes, gave a nervous swiftness to the movements. Theleb K'aarna approached the bowl.

As he came closer Elric could hear him muttering to himself.

"Now, now, now," murmured the sorcerer. "Soon, soon will die Elric and all who league with him. Ah, the albino will rue the day when he earned my vengeance and turned me from a scholar into what I am today. And when he is dead, then Queen Yishana will realize her mistake and give herself to me. How could she love that pale-faced anachronism more than a man of my great talents? How?"

Elric had almost forgotten Theleb K'aarna's obsession with Queen Yishana of Jharkor, the woman who had wielded a greater power over the sorcerer than could any magic. It had been Theleb K'aarna's jealousy of Elric which had turned him from a relatively peaceful student of the dark arts into a vengeful practitioner of the most frightful sorceries.

He watched as Theleb K'aarna began with his finger to trace complicated patterns upon the glass of the bowl. And with every completed rune the pulse within the machine grew stronger. Oddly coloured light began to flow through certain sections, bringing them to life. A steady thump issued from the neck of the bowl. A peculiar stink began to reach Elric's nostrils. The core of light became brighter and larger and the machine seemed to alter its shape, sometimes becoming apparently liquid and streaming around the inside of the bowl.

The golden mare snorted and began to shift uneasily. Elric automatically patted her neck and steadied her. Theleb K'aarna was now merely a silhouette against the swiftly changing light within the bowl. He continued to murmur to himself but his words were drowned by the heartbeats which now echoed among the surrounding rocks. His right hand drew still more invisible diagrams upon the glass.

The sky seemed to be darkening, though it was some hours to sunset. Elric looked up. Above his head the sky was still blue, the golden sun still strong, but the air around him had grown dark, as if a solitary cloud had come to cover the scene he witnessed.

Now Theleb K'aarna was stumbling back, his face stained by the strange light from the bowl, his eyes huge and mad.

"Come!" he screamed. "Come! The barrier is down!"

Elric saw a shadow then, behind the bowl. It was a shadow which dwarfed even the great machine. Something bellowed. It was scaly. It lumbered. It raised a huge and sinuous head. It reminded Elric of a dragon from one of his own caves, but it was bulkier and upon its enormous back were two rows of flapping ridges of bone. It opened its mouth to reveal row upon row of teeth and the ground shook as it walked from the other side of the bowl and stood staring down at the tiny figure of the sorcerer, its eyes stupid and angry. Another came pounding from behind the bowl, and another—great reptilian monsters from another Age of Earth. And following them came those who controlled them. The horse was snorting and prancing and desperately trying to escape, but Elric managed to calm her down again as he looked at the figures which now rested their hands on the obedient heads of the monsters. The figures were even more terrifying than the reptiles—for although they walked upon two legs and had hands of sorts they, too, were reptilian. They bore a peculiar resemblance to the dragon creatures and their size, also, was many times greater than a man's. In their hands they had ornate instruments which could only be weapons—instruments attached to their arms by spirals of golden metal. A hood of skin covered their black and green heads and red eyes glared from the shadows of their faces.

Theleb K'aarna laughed. "I have achieved it. I have destroyed the barrier between the planes and, thanks to the Lords of Chaos, have found allies which Elric's sorcery cannot destroy because they do not obey the sorcerous rules of this plane! They are invincible, invulnerable—and they obey only Theleb K'aarna!"

A huge snorting and screaming came from beasts and warriors alike.

"Now we shall go against Tanelorn!" Theleb K'aarna shouted. "And with this power I shall return to Jharkor, to make fickle Yishana my own!"

Elric felt a certain sympathy for Theleb K'aarna at that moment. Without the aid of the Lords of Chaos, his sorcery could not have achieved this. He had given himself up to them, had become one of their tools all because of his weak-minded love for Jharkor's aging queen. Elric knew he could not go against the monsters and their monstrous riders. He must return to Tanelorn to warn his friends to leave the city, to hope that he might find a means of returning these frightful interlopers back to their own plane. But then the mare screamed suddenly and reared, maddened by the sights, the sounds and the smells she had been forced to witness. And the scream sounded in a sudden silence. The rearing horse revealed itself to Theleb K'aarna as he turned his mad eyes in Elric's direction.

Elric knew he could not outride the monsters. He knew those weapons could easily destroy him from a distance. He drew the black hellsword Stormbringer from its scabbard and it shouted as it came free. He drove his spurs into the horse and he rode directly down the rocks towards the bowl while Theleb K'aarna was still too startled to give orders to his new allies. His one hope was that he could destroy the device—or at least break some important part of it—and in so doing return the monsters to their own plane.

His white face ghastly in the sorcerous darkness, his sword raised high, he galloped past Theleb K'aarna and struck a mighty blow at the glass protecting the machine.

The Black Sword collided with the glass and sank into it. Carried on by the momentum, Elric was flung from his saddle and he, too, passed through the glass without apparently breaking it. He glimpsed the dreadful planes and curves of the Doomed Folk's device. His body struck them. He felt as if the fabric of his being was disintegrating . . .

. . . and then he lay sprawled upon sweet grass and there was nothing of the desert, of Theleb K'aarna, of the pulsing machine, of the horrible beasts and their dreadful masters, only waving foliage and warm sunshine. He heard birdsong and he heard a voice.

"The storm. It has gone. And you? Are you called Lord Elric of Melniboné?"

He picked himself up and turned. A tall man stood before him. The man was clad in a conical silver helm and was encased to the knee in a byrnie also of silver. A scarlet, long-sleeved coat partly covered the byrnie. The man bore a scabbarded longsword at his side. His legs were encased in breeks of soft leather and there were boots of green-tinted doeskin on his feet. But Elric's attention was caught primarily by the man's features (which resembled those of a Melnibonéan much more than those of a true man) and the fact that he wore upon his left hand a six-fingered gauntlet encrusted with dark jewels, while over his right eye was a large patch which was also jeweled and matched the hand. The eye not covered by the patch was large and slanting and had a yellow centre and purple surrounds.

"I am Elric of Melniboné," the albino agreed. "Are you to thank for rescuing me from those creatures Theleb K'aarna summoned?"

The tall man shook his head. "'Twas I that summoned you, but I know of no Theleb K'aarna. I was told that I had only one opportunity to receive your aid and that I must take it in this particular place at this particular time. I am called Corum Jhaelen Irsei—the Prince in the Scarlet Robe—and I ride upon a quest of grave import."

Elric frowned. The name had a half-familiar ring, but he could not place it. He half-recalled an old dream . . .

"Where is this forest?" he asked, sheathing his sword.

"It is nowhere on your plane or in your time, Prince Elric. I summoned you to aid me in my battle against the Lords of Chaos. Already I have been instrumental in destroying two of the Sword

Rulers—Arioch and Xiombarg—but the third, the most powerful, remains . . ."

"Arioch of Chaos—and Xiombarg? You have destroyed two of the most powerful members of the company of Chaos? Yet but a month since I spoke with Arioch. He is my patron. He . . ."

"There are many planes of existence," Prince Corum told him gently. "In some the Lords of Chaos are strong. In some they are weak. In some, I have heard, they do not exist at all. You must accept that here Arioch and Xiombarg have been banished so that effectively they no longer exist in my world. It is the third of the Sword Rulers who threatens us now—the strongest, King Mabelode."

Elric frowned. "In my—plane—Mabelode is no stronger than Arioch and Xiombarg. This makes a travesty of all my understanding . . ."

"I will explain as much as I can," said Prince Corum. "For some reason Fate has selected me to be the hero who must banish the domination of Chaos from the Fifteen Planes of Earth. I am at present traveling on my way to seek a city which we call Tanelorn, where I hope to find aid. But my guide is a prisoner in a castle close to here and before I can continue I must rescue him. I was told how I might summon aid to help me effect this rescue and I used the spell to bring you to me. I was to tell you that if you aided me, then you would aid yourself—that if I was successful then you would receive something which would make your task easier."

"Who told you this?"

"A wise man."

Elric sat down on a fallen tree trunk, his head in his hands. "I have been drawn away at an importunate time," he said. "I pray that you speak the truth to me, Prince Corum." He looked up suddenly. "It is a marvel that you speak at all—or at least that I understand you. How can this be?"

"I was informed that we should be able to communicate easily because 'we are part of the same thing.' Do not ask me to explain more, Prince Elric, for I know no more."

Elric shrugged. "Well this may be an illusion. I may have killed myself or become digested by that machine of Theleb K'aarna's, but plainly I have no choice but to agree to aid you in the hope that I am, in turn, aided."

Prince Corum left the clearing and returned with two horses, one white and one black. He offered the reins of the black horse to Elric.

Elric settled himself in the unfamiliar saddle. "You spoke of Tanelorn. It is for the sake of Tanelorn that I find myself in this dream-world of yours."

Prince Corum's face was eager. "You know where Tanelorn lies?"

"In my own world, aye—but why should it lie in this one?"

"Tanelorn lies in all planes, though in different guises. There is one Tanelorn and it is eternal with many forms."

They were riding through the gentle forest along a narrow track.

Elric accepted what Corum said. There was a dreamlike quality about his presence here and he decided that he must regard all events here as he would regard the events in a dream. "Where go we now?" he asked casually. "To the castle?"

Corum shook his head. "First we must have the Third Hero—the Many-Named Hero."

"And will you summon him with sorcery, too?"

"I was told not. I was told that he would meet us—drawn from whichever age he exists in by the necessity to complete the Three Who Are One."

"And what mean these phrases? What is the Three Who Are One?"

"I know little more than you, friend Elric, save that it will need all three of us to defeat him who holds my guide prisoner."

"Aye," murmured Elric feelingly, "and it will need more than that to save my Tanelorn from Theleb K'aarna's reptiles. Even now they must march against the city."

CHAPTER FOUR

The Vanishing Tower

The road widened and left the forest to wander among the heather of high and hilly moorland country. Far away to the west they could see cliffs, and beyond the cliffs was the deeper blue of the ocean. A few birds circled in the wide sky. It seemed a particularly peaceful world and Elric could hardly believe that it was under attack from the forces of Chaos. As they rode Corum explained that his gauntlet was not a gauntlet at all, but the hand of an alien being, grafted onto his arm, just as his eye was an alien eye which could see into a terrifying nether-world from which Corum could bring aid if he chose to do so.

"All you tell me makes the complicated sorceries and cosmologies of my world seem simple in comparison," Elric smiled as they crossed the peaceful landscape.

"It only seems complicated because it is strange," Corum said. "Your world would doubtless seem incomprehensible to me if I were suddenly flung into it. Besides," he laughed, "this particular plane is not my world, either, though it resembles it more than do many. We have one thing in common, Elric, and that is that we are both doomed to play a role in the constant struggle between the Lords of the Higher Worlds—and we shall never understand why that struggle takes place, why it is eternal. We fight, we suffer agonies of mind and soul, but we are never sure that our suffering is worthwhile."

"You are right," Elric said feelingly. "We have much in common, you and I, Corum."

Corum was about to reply when he saw something on the road ahead. It was a mounted warrior. He sat perfectly still as if he awaited them. "Perhaps this is the Third of whom Bolorhiag spoke."

Cautiously, they rode forward.

The man they approached stared at them from a brooding face. He was as tall as them, but bulkier. His skin was jet black and he wore upon his head and shoulders the stuffed head and pelt of a snarling bear. His plate armour was also black, without insignia, and at his side was a great black-hilted sword in a black scabbard. He rode a massive roan stallion and there was a heavy round shield attached to the back of his saddle. As Elric and Corum came closer the man's handsome negroid features assumed an astonished expression and he gasped.

"I know you! I know you both!"

Elric, too, felt he recognized the man, just as he had noticed something familiar in Corum's features.

"How came you here to Balwyn Moor, friend?" Corum asked him.

The man looked about him as if in a daze. "Balwyn Moor? This is Balwyn Moor? I have been here but a few moments. Before that I was—I was . . . Ah! The memory starts to fade again." He pressed a large hand to his forehead. "A name—another name! No more! Elric! Corum! But I—I am now . . ."

"How do you know our names?" Elric asked him. A mood of dread had seized the albino. He felt that he should not ask these questions, that he should not know the answers.

"Because—don't you see?—I am Elric—I am Corum—oh, this is the worst agony . . . Or, at least, I have been or am to be Elric or Corum . . ."

"Your name, sir?" Corum said again.

"A thousand names are mine. A thousand heroes I have been. Ah! I am—I am—John Daker—Erekosë—Urlik—many, many, many more . . . The memories, the dreams, the existences." He stared at them suddenly through his pain-filled eyes. "Do you not understand? Am I the only one to be doomed to understand? I am he who has been called the Champion Eternal—I am the hero who has existed for ever—and, yes, I am Elric of Melniboné—Prince Corum Jhaelen Irsei—I am you, also. We three are the same creature and a myriad other creatures besides. We three are one thing—doomed to struggle for ever and never understand why. Oh! My head pounds. Who tortures me so? Who?"

Elric's throat was dry. "You say you are another incarnation of myself?"

"If you would phrase it so! You are both other incarnations of *myself*!"

"So," said Corum, "that is what Bolorhiag meant by the Three Who Are One. We are all aspects of the same man, yet we have tripled our strength because we have been drawn from three different ages. It is the only power which might successfully go against Voilodion Ghagnasdiak of the Vanishing Tower."

"Is that the castle wherein your guide is imprisoned?" Elric asked, casting a glance of sympathy at the groaning black man.

"Aye. The Vanishing Tower flickers from one plane to another, from one age to another, and exists in a single location only for a few moments at a time. But because we are three separate incarnations of a single hero it is possible that we form a sorcery of some kind which will enable us to follow the tower and attack it. Then, if we free my guide, we can continue on to Tanelorn . . ."

"Tanelorn?" The black man looked at Corum with hope suddenly flooding into his eyes. "I, too, seek Tanelorn. Only there may I discover some remedy to my dreadful fate—which is to know all previous incarnations and be hurled at random from one existence to another! Tanelorn—I must find her!"

"I, too, must discover Tanelorn," Elric told him, "for on my own plane her inhabitants are in great danger."

"So we have a common purpose as well as a common identity," Corum said. "Therefore we shall fight in concert, I pray. First we must free my guide, then go on to Tanelorn."

"I'll aid you willingly," said the black giant.

"And what shall we call you—you who are ourselves?" Corum asked him.

"Call me Erekosë—though another name suggests itself to me— for it was as Erekosë that I came closest to knowing forgetfulness and the fulfillment of love."

"Then you are to be envied, Erekosë," Elric said meaningly, "for at least you have come close to forgetfulness . . ."

"You have no inkling of what it is I must forget," the black giant told him. He shook his reins. "Now Corum—which way to the Vanishing Tower?"

"This road leads to it. We ride down now to Darkvale, I believe."

*   *   *

Elric's mind could hardly contain the significance of what he had heard. It suggested that the universe—or the multiverse, as Myshella had named it—was divided into infinite layers of existence, that time was virtually a meaningless concept save where it related to one man's life or one short period of history. And there were planes of existence where the Cosmic Balance was not known at all—or so Corum had suggested—and other planes where the Lords of the Higher Worlds had far greater powers than they had on his own world. He was tempted to consider the idea of forgetting Theleb K'aarna, Myshella, Tanelorn and the rest and devoting himself to the exploration of all these infinite worlds. But then he knew that this could not be for, if Erekosë spoke the truth, then he—or something which was essentially himself—existed in all these planes already. Whatever force it was which he named 'Fate' had admitted him to this plane to fulfill one purpose. An important purpose affecting the destinies of a thousand planes it must surely be if it brought him together in three separate incarnations. He glanced curiously at the black giant on his left, at the maimed man with the jeweled hand and eye on his right. Were they really himself?

Now he fancied he felt some of the desperation Erekosë must feel—to remember all those other incarnations, all those other mistakes, all that other pointless conflict—and never to know the purpose for it all, if purpose indeed there were.

"Darkvale," said Corum pointing down the hill.

The road ran steeply until it passed between two looming cliffs, disappearing in shadow. There was something particularly gloomy about the place.

"I am told there was a village here once," Corum said to them. "An uninviting spot, eh, brothers?"

"I have seen worse," murmured Erekosë. "Come, let's get all this done with . . ." He spurred his roan ahead of the others and galloped at great speed down the steep path. They followed his example and soon they had passed between the lowering cliffs and could barely see ahead of them as they continued to follow the road through the shadows.

And now Elric saw ruins huddled close to the foot of the cliffs on either side. Oddly twisted ruins which had not been the result of age or warfare—these ruins were warped, fused, as if Chaos had touched them while passing through the vale.

Corum had been studying the ruins carefully and at length he reined in. "There," he said. "That pit. Here is where we must wait."

Elric looked at the pit. It was ragged and deep and the earth in it seemed freshly turned as if it had been but lately dug. "What must we wait for, friend Corum?"

"For the tower," said Prince Corum. "I would guess that this is where it appears when it is in this plane."

"And when will it appear?"

"At no particular time. We must wait. And then, as soon as we see it, we must rush it and attempt to enter before it vanishes again, moving on to the next plane."

Erekosë's face was impassive. He dismounted and sat on the hard ground with his back against a slab of rock which had once belonged to a house.

"You seem more patient than I, Erekosë," said Elric.

"I have learned patience, for I have lived since time began and will live on at the end of time."

Elric got down from his own black horse and loosened its girth strap while Corum prowled about the edge of the pit. "Who told you that the tower would appear here?" Elric asked him.

"A sorcerer who doubtless serves Law as I do, for I am a mortal doomed to battle Chaos."

"As am I," said Erekosë the Champion Eternal.

"As am I," said Elric of Melniboné, "though I am sworn to serve it."

Elric looked at his two companions and it was possible to believe that these were two incarnations of himself. Certainly their lives, their struggles, their personalities, to some extent, were very similar.

"And why do you seek Tanelorn, Erekosë?" he asked.

"I have been told that I may find peace there—and wisdom—a means of returning to the world of the Eldren where dwells the woman I love, for it has been said that since Tanelorn exists in all planes at all times it is easier for a man who dwells there to pass between the planes, discover the particular one he seeks. What interest have you in Tanelorn, Lord Elric?"

"I know Tanelorn and I know that you are right to seek it. My mission seems to be the defense of that city upon my own plane—but even now my friends may be destroyed by that which has been brought against them. I pray Corum is right and that in the Vanishing Tower I shall find a means to defeat Theleb K'aarna's beasts and their masters."

Corum raised his jeweled hand to his jeweled eye. "I seek Tanelorn for I have heard the city can aid me in my struggle against Chaos."

"But Tanelorn will fight neither Law nor Chaos—that is why she exists for eternity," Elric said.

"Aye. Like Erekosë I do not seek swords but wisdom."

Night fell and Darkvale grew gloomier. While the others watched the pit Elric tried to sleep, but his fears for Tanelorn were too great. Would Myshella try to defend the city? Would Moonglum and Rackhir die? And what could he possibly find in the Vanishing Tower which would aid him? He heard the murmuring of conversation as his other selves discussed how Darkvale had come to exist.

"I heard that Chaos once attacked the town which at that time lay in a quiet valley," Corum told Erekosë. "The tower was then the property of a knight who gave shelter to one whom Chaos hated. They brought a huge force of creatures against Darkvale, raising and compressing the walls of the valley, but the knight sought the aid of Law which enabled him to shift his tower into another dimension. Then Chaos decreed that the tower should shift for ever, never being on one plane longer than a few moments. The knight and the fugitive went mad at last and killed each other. Then Voilodion Ghagnasdiak found the tower and became resident therein. Too late he realized his mistake as he was shifted from his own plane to an alien one. Since then he has been too fearful to leave the tower but desperate for company. He has taken to the habit of capturing whomever he can and forcing them to be his companions in the Vanishing Tower until they bore him. When they bore him, he slays them."

"And your guide may soon be slain? What manner of creature is this Voilodion Ghagnasdiak?"

"He is a monstrous evil creature commanding great powers of destruction, that is all I know."

"Which is why the gods have seen fit to call up three aspects of myself to attack the Vanishing Tower," said Erekosë. "It must be important to them."

"It is to me," said Corum, "for the guide is also my friend and the very existence of the Fifteen Planes is threatened if I cannot find Tanelorn soon."

Elric heard Erekosë laugh bitterly. "Why cannot I—we—ever be faced with a small problem, a domestic problem? Why are we forever involved with the destiny of the universe?"

Corum replied just as Elric began to nod into a half-doze. "Perhaps domestic problems are worse. Who knows?"

CHAPTER FIVE

Jhary-a-Conel

"It is here! Hasten, Elric!"

Elric sprang up.

It was dawn. He had already stood watch once during the night.

He drew his black sword from its scabbard noticing with some astonishment that Erekosë had already drawn his own blade and that it was almost identical to his own.

There was the Vanishing Tower.

Corum was running towards it even now.

The tower was in fact a small castle of grey and solid stone, but about its battlements played lights and its outline was not altogether clear at certain sections of its walls.

Elric ran beside Erekosë.

"He keeps the door open to lure his 'guests' in," panted the black giant. "It is our only advantage, I think."

The tower flickered.

"Hasten!" Corum cried again and the Prince in the Scarlet Robe dashed into the darkness of the doorway.

"Hasten!"

They ran into a small antechamber which was lit by a great oil lamp hanging from the ceiling by chains.

The door closed suddenly behind them.

Elric glanced at Erekosë's tense black features, at Corum's blemished face. All had swords ready, but now a profound silence filled the hall. Without speaking Corum pointed through a window-slit. The view beyond it had changed. They seemed now to be looking out over blue sea.

"Jhary!" Corum called. "Jhary-a-Conel!"

A faint sound came back. It might have been a reply or it might have been the squeak of a rat in the castle walls. "Jhary!" Corum cried again. "Voilodion Ghagnasdiak? Am I to be thwarted? Have you left this place?"

"I have not left it. What do you want with me?" The voice came from the next room. Warily the three heroes who were one hero went forward.

Something like lightning flickered in the room and in its ghastly glare Elric saw Voilodion Ghagnasdiak.

He was a dwarf clad all in puffed multicoloured silks, furs and satins, a tiny sword in his hand. His head was too large for his body, but it was a handsome head with thick black eyebrows which met in the middle. He smiled at them. "At last someone new to relieve my ennui. But lay down your swords, gentlemen, I beg you, for you are to be my guests."

"I know what fate your guests may expect," Corum said. "Know this, Voilodion Ghagnasdiak, we have come to release Jhary-a-Conel whom you hold prisoner. Give him up to us and we will not harm you."

The dwarf's handsome features grinned cheerfully at these words. "But I am very powerful. You cannot defeat me. Watch."

He waved his sword and more lightning lashed about the room. Elric half-raised his sword to ward it off, but it never quite touched him. He stepped angrily towards the dwarf. "Know this, Voilodion Ghagnasdiak, I am Elric of Melniboné and I have much power. I bear the Black Sword and it thirsts to drink your soul unless you release Prince Corum's friend!"

Again the dwarf laughed. "Swords? What power have they?"

"Our swords are not ordinary blades," Erekosë said. "And we have been brought here by forces you could not comprehend—wrenched from our own ages by the power of the gods themselves—specifically to demand that this Jhary-a-Conel be given up to us."

"You are deceived," said Voilodion Ghagnasdiak, "or you seek to deceive me. This Jhary is a witty fellow, I'd agree, but what interest could gods have in him?"

Elric raised Stormbringer. The Black Sword moaned in anticipation of a quenching.

Then the dwarf produced a tiny yellow ball from nowhere and flung it at Elric. It bounced on his forehead and he was flung backward across the room, Stormbringer clattering from his hand. Dizzily Elric tried to rise, reached out to take his sword, but he was too weak. On impulse he began to cry for the aid of Arioch, but then he remembered that Arioch had been banished from this world. There were no supernatural allies to call upon here—none but the sword and he could not reach the sword.

Erekosë leapt backward and kicked the Black Sword in Elric's direction. As the albino's hand encircled the hilt he felt strength come back to him, but it was no more than ordinary mortal strength. He climbed to his feet.

Corum remained where he was. The dwarf was still laughing. Another ball appeared in his hand. Again he flung it at Elric, but this time he brought up the Black Sword in time and deflected it. It bounced across the room and exploded against the far wall. Something black writhed from the fire.

"It is dangerous to destroy the globes," said Voilodion Ghagnas-diak equably, "for now what is in them will destroy you."

The black thing grew. The flames died.

"I am free," said a voice.

"Aye." Voilodion Ghagnasdiak was gleeful. "Free to kill these fools who reject my hospitality!"

"Free to be slain," Elric replied as he watched the thing take shape.

At first it seemed all made of flowing hair which gradually com-pressed until it formed the outline of a creature with the heavily mus-cled body of a gorilla, though the hide was thick and warted like that of a rhinoceros. From behind the shoulders curved great black wings and on the neck was the snarling head of a tiger. It clutched a long, scythe-like weapon in its hairy hands. The tiger head roared and the scythe swept out suddenly, barely missing Elric.

Erekosë and Corum began to move forward to Elric's aid. Elric heard Corum cry: "My eye—it will not see into the netherworld. I can-not summon help!" It seemed that Corum's sorcerous powers were also limited on this plane. Then Voilodion Ghagnasdiak threw a yel-low ball at the black giant and the pale man with the jeweled hand. Both barely managed to deflect the missiles and, in so doing, caused them to burst. Immediately shapes emerged and became two more of the winged tiger-men, and Elric's allies were forced to defend them-selves.

As he dodged another swing of the scythe Elric tried to think of some rune which would summon supernatural aid to him, but he could think of none which would work here. He thrust at the tiger-man but his blow was blocked by the scythe. His opponent was enormously strong and swift. The black wings began to beat and the snarling thing flapped upwards to the ceiling, hovered for a moment and then rushed down on Elric with its scythe whirling, a chilling scream coming from its fanged mouth, its yellow eyes glaring.

Elric felt something close to panic. Stormbringer was not supply-ing him with the strength he expected. Its powers were diminished on this plane. He barely managed to dodge the scythe again and lash at the creature's exposed thigh. The blade bit but no blood came. The tiger-man did not seem to notice the wound. Again it began to flap towards the ceiling.

Elric saw that his companions were experiencing a similar plight. Corum's face was full of consternation as if he had expected an easy victory and now foresaw defeat.

Meanwhile Voilodion Ghagnasdiak continued to scream his glee and flung more of the yellow balls about the room. As each one burst there emerged another snarling winged tiger-creature. The room was full of them. Elric, Erekosë and Corum backed to the far wall as the monsters bore down on them, their ears full of the fearful beating of the giant wings, the harsh screams of hatred.

"I fear I have summoned you two to your destruction," Corum panted. "I had no warning that our powers would be so limited here. The tower must shift so fast that even the ordinary laws of sorcery do not apply within its walls."

"They seem to work well enough for the dwarf," Elric said as he brought up his blade to block first one scythe and then another. "If I could slay but a single . . ."

His back was hard against the wall, a scythe nicked his cheek and drew blood, another tore his cloak, another slashed his arm. The tiger faces were grinning now as they closed in.

Elric aimed a blow at the head of the nearest creature, struck off its ear so that it howled. Stormbringer howled back and stabbed at the thing's throat.

But the sword hardly penetrated and served only to put the tiger-man slightly off balance.

As the thing staggered Elric wrenched the scythe from its hands and reversed the weapon, drawing the blade across the chest. The tiger-man screamed as blood spurted from the wound.

"I was right!" Elric shouted at the others. "Only their own weapons can harm them!" He moved forward with the scythe in one hand and Stormbringer in the other. The tiger-men backed off and then began to flap upwards to hover near the ceiling.

Elric ran towards Voilodion Ghagnasdiak. The dwarf gave a yell of terror and disappeared through a doorway too small easily to admit Elric.

Then, with thundering wings, the tiger-creatures descended again.

This time the other two strove to capture scythes from their enemies. Driving back those who attacked him, the albino prince took Corum's main assailant from behind and the thing fell with its head sliced off. Corum sheathed his longsword and plucked up the scythe, killing a third tiger-man almost immediately and kicking the fallen scythe towards Erekosë. Black feathers drifted in the stinking air. The flagstones of the floor were slippery with blood. The three heroes drove a path through their enemies into the smaller room they had lately left. Still the tiger-creatures came on, but now they had to pass through the door and this was more easily defended.

Glancing back Elric saw the window slit of the tower. Outside the scenery altered constantly as the Vanishing Tower continued its erratic progress through the planes of existence. But the three were wearying and all had lost some blood from minor wounds. Scythes clashed on scythes as the fight continued, wings beat loudly and the snarling faces spat at them and spoke words which could barely be understood. Without the strength supplied him by his hell-forged sword Elric was weakening rapidly. Twice he staggered and was borne up by the others. Was he to die in some alien world with his friends never knowing how he had perished? But then he remembered that his friends were even now under attack from the reptilian beasts Theleb K'aarna had sent against Tanelorn, that they, too, would soon be dead. This knowledge gave him a little more strength and enabled him to sweep his scythe deep into the belly of another tiger-creature.

This gap in the ranks of the sorcerous things enabled him to see the small doorway on the far side of the other room. Voilodion Ghagnasdiak was crouched there, hurling still more of the yellow globes. New winged tiger-men grew up to replace those who had fallen.

But then Elric heard Voilodion Ghagnasdiak give a yell and saw that something was covering his face. It was a black-and-white animal with small black wings which beat in the air. Some offspring of the beasts who attacked him? Elric could not tell. But Voilodion Ghagnasdiak was plainly terrified of it, trying to drag it from his face.

Another figure appeared behind the dwarf. Bright eyes peered from an intelligent face framed by long black hair. He was dressed as ostentatiously as the dwarf, but he was unarmed. He was calling to Elric and the albino strained to catch the words even as another tiger-creature came at him.

Corum saw the newcomer now. "Jhary!" he shouted.

"The one you came to save?" Elric asked.

"Aye."

Elric made to press forward into the room, but Jhary-a-Conel waved him back. "No! No! Stay there!"

Elric frowned, was about to ask why when he was attacked from two sides by the tiger-creatures and had to retreat, slashing his scythe this way and that.

"Link arms!" Jhary-a-Conel cried. "Corum in the centre—and you two draw your swords!"

Elric was panting. He slew another tiger-man and felt a new pain shoot through his leg. Blood gushed from his calf.

Voilodion Ghagnasdiak was still struggling with the thing which clung to his face.

"Hurry!" cried Jhary-a-Conel. "It is your only chance—and mine!"

Elric looked at Corum.

"He is wise, my friend," Corum said. "He knows many things which we do not. Here, I will stand in the centre."

Erekosë linked his brawny arm with Corum's and Elric did the same on the other side. Erekosë drew his sword in his left hand and Elric brought forth Stormbringer in his right.

And something began to happen. A sense of energy came back, then a sense of great physical well-being. Elric looked at his companions and laughed. It was almost as if by combining their powers they had made them four times stronger—as if they had become one entity.

A peculiar feeling of euphoria filled Elric and he knew that Erekosë had spoken the truth—that they were three aspects of the same being.

"Let us finish them!" he shouted—and he saw that they shouted
the same. Laughing the linked three strode into the chamber and now
the two swords wounded whenever they struck, slaying swiftly and
bringing them more energy still.

The winged tiger-men became frantic, flapping about the room as
the Three Who Were One pursued them. All three were drenched in
their own blood and that of their enemies, all three were laughing, invulnerable, acting completely in unison.

And as they moved the room itself began to shake. They heard
Voilodion Ghagnasdiak screaming.

"The tower! The tower! This will destroy the tower!"

Elric looked up from the last corpse. It was true that the tower was
swaying wildly from side to side like a ship in a storm.

Jhary-a-Conel pushed past the dwarf and entered the room of
death. The sight seemed obnoxious to him but he controlled his feelings. "It is true. The sorcery we have worked today must have its effect.
Whiskers—to me!"

The thing on Voilodion Ghagnasdiak's face flew into the air and
settled on Jhary's shoulder. Elric saw that it was a small black-and-
white cat, ordinary in every detail save for its neat pair of wings which
it was now folding.

Voilodion Ghagnasdiak sat crumpled in the doorway and he was
weeping through sightless eyes. Tears of blood flowed down his handsome face.

Elric ran back into the other room, breaking his link with Corum.
He peered through the window slit. But now there was nothing but a
wild eruption of mauve and purple cloud.

He gasped. "We are in limbo!"

Silence fell. Still the tower swayed. The lights were extinguished
by a strange wind blowing through the rooms and the only illumina-
tion came from outside where the mist still swirled.

Jhary-a-Conel was frowning to himself as he joined Elric at the
window.

"How did you know what to do?" Elric asked him.

"I knew because I know you, Elric of Melniboné—just as I know

Erekosë there—for I travel in many ages and on many planes. That is why I am sometimes called Companion to Champions. I must find my sword and my sack—also my hat. Doubtless all are in Voilodion's vault with his other loot."

"But the tower? If it is destroyed shall we, too, be destroyed?"

"A possibility. Come, friend Elric, help me seek my hat."

"At such a time, you look for a—hat?"

"Aye." Jhary-a-Conel returned to the larger room, stroking the black-and-white cat. Voilodion Ghagnasdiak was still there and he was still weeping. "Prince Corum—Lord Erekosë—will you come with me, too."

Corum and the black giant joined Elric and they squeezed into the narrow passage, inching their way along until it widened to reveal a flight of stairs leading downward. The tower shuddered again. Jhary lit a brand and removed it from its place in the wall. He began to descend the steps, the three heroes behind him.

A slab of masonry fell from the roof and crashed just in front of Elric. "I would prefer to seek a means of escape from the tower," he said to Jhary-a-Conel. "If it falls now, we shall be buried."

"Trust me, Prince Elric," was all that Jhary would say.

And because Jhary had already shown himself to possess great knowledge Elric allowed the dandy to lead him further into the bowels of the tower.

At last they reached a circular chamber and in it was set a huge metal door.

"Voilodion's vault," Jhary told them. "Here you will find all the things you seek. And I, I hope, will find my hat. The hat was specially made and is the only one which properly matches my other clothes . . ."

"How do we open a door like that?" Erekosë asked. "It is made of steel, surely!" He hefted the black blade he still bore in his left hand.

"If you link arms again, my friends," Jhary suggested with a kind of mocking deference, "I will show you how the door may be opened."

Once again Elric, Corum and Erekosë linked their arms together. Once again the supernatural strength seemed to flow through them and they laughed at each other, knowing that they were all part of the same creature.

Jhary's voice seemed to come faintly to Elric's ears. "And now, Prince Corum, if you would strike with your foot once upon the door . . ."

They moved until they were close to the door. That part of them which was Corum struck out with his foot at the slab of steel—and the door fell inward as if made of the lightest wood.

This time Elric was much more reluctant to break the link which held them. But he did so at last as Jhary stepped into the vault chuckling to himself.

The tower lurched. All three were flung after Jhary into Voilodion's vault. Elric fell heavily against a great golden chair of a kind he had once seen used as an elephant saddle. He looked around the vault. It was full of valuables, of clothes, shoes, weapons. He felt nauseated as he realized that these had been the possessions of all those Voilodion had chosen to call his guests.

Jhary pulled a bundle from under a pile of furs. "Look, Prince Elric. These are what you will need where Tanelorn is concerned." It seemed to be a bunch of long sticks rolled in thin sheets of metal.

Elric accepted the heavy bundle. "What is it?"

"They are the banners of bronze and the arrows of quartz. Useful weapons against the reptilian men of Pio and their mounts."

"You know of those reptiles? You know of Theleb K'aarna, too?"

"The sorcerer of Pan Tang? Aye."

Elric stared almost suspiciously at Jhary-a-Conel. "How can you know all this?"

"I have told you. I have lived many lives as a Friend of Heroes. Unwrap this bundle when you return to Tanelorn. Use the arrows of quartz like spears. To use the banners of bronze, merely unfurl them. Aha!" Jhary reached behind a sack of jewels and came up with a somewhat dusty hat. He smacked off the dust and placed it on his head. "Ah!" He bent again and displayed a goblet. He offered this to Prince Corum. "Take it. It will prove useful, I think."

From another corner Jhary took a small sack and put it on his shoulder. Almost as an afterthought he hunted about in a chest of jewels and found a gleaming ring of unnamable stones and peculiar metal. "This is your reward, Erekosë, in helping to free me from my captor."

Erekosë smiled. "I have the feeling you needed no help, young man."

"You are mistaken, friend Erekosë. I doubt if I have ever been in greater peril." He looked vaguely about the vault, staggering as the floor tilted alarmingly.

Elric said: "We should take steps to leave."

"Exactly." Jhary-a-Conel crossed swiftly to the far side of the vault. "The last thing. In his pride Voilodion showed me his possessions, but he did not know the value of all of them."

"What do you mean?" asked the Prince in the Scarlet Robe.

"He killed the traveler who brought this with him. The traveler was right in assuming he had the means to stop the tower from vanishing, but he did not have time to use it before Voilodion had slain him." Jhary picked up a small staff coloured a dull ochre. "Here it is. The Runestaff. Hawkmoon had this with him when I traveled with him to the Dark Empire . . ."

Noticing their puzzlement, Jhary-a-Conel, Companion to Champions, apologized. "I am sorry. I sometimes forget that not all of us have memories of other careers . . ."

"What is the Runestaff?" Corum asked.

"I remember one description—but I am poor at naming and explaining things . . ."

"That has not escaped my notice," Elric said, almost smiling.

"It is an object which can only exist under a certain set of spacial and temporal laws. In order to continue to exist, it must exert a field in which it can contain itself. That field must accord with those laws—the same laws under which we best survive."

More masonry fell.

"The tower is breaking up!" Erekosë growled.

Jhary stroked the dull ochre staff. "Please gather near me, my friends."

The three heroes stood around him. And then the roof of the tower fell in. But it did not fall on them for they stood suddenly on firm ground breathing fresh air. But there was blackness all around them. "Do not step outside this small area," Jhary warned, "or you will be doomed. Let the Runestaff seek what we seek."

They saw the ground change colour, breathed warmer, then colder, air. It was as if they moved from plane to plane of the multiverse, never seeing more than the few feet of ground upon which they stood.

And then there was harsh desert sand beneath their feet and Jhary shouted. "Now!" The four of them rushed out of the area and into the blackness to find themselves suddenly in sunlight beneath a sky like beaten metal.

"A desert," Erekosë murmured. "A vast desert . . ."

Jhary smiled. "Do you not recognize it, friend Elric?"

"Is it the Sighing Desert?"

"Listen."

And sure enough Elric heard the familiar sound of the wind as it made its mournful passage across the sands. A little way away he saw the Runestaff where they had left it. Then it was gone.

"Are you all to come with me to the defense of Tanelorn?" he asked Jhary.

Jhary shook his head. "No. We go the other way. We go to seek the device Theleb K'aarna activated with the help of the Lords of Chaos. Where lies it?"

Elric tried to get his bearings. He lifted a hesitant finger. "That way, I think."

"Then let us go to it now."

"But I must try to help Tanelorn."

"You must destroy the device after we have used it, friend Elric, lest Theleb K'aarna or his like try to activate it again."

"But Tanelorn . . ."

"I do not believe that Theleb K'aarna and his beasts have yet reached the city."

"Not reached it! So much time has passed!"

"Less than a day."

Elric rubbed at his face. He said reluctantly: "Very well. I will take you to the machine."

"But if Tanelorn lies so near," Corum said to Jhary, "why seek it elsewhere?"

"Because this is not the Tanelorn we wish to find," Jhary told him.

"It will suit me," Erekosë said. "I will remain with Elric. Then, perhaps . . ."

A look almost of terror spread over Jhary's features then. He said sadly: "My friend—already much of time and space is threatened with destruction. Eternal barriers could soon fall—the fabric of the multiverse could decay. You do not understand. Such a thing as has happened in the Vanishing Tower can only happen once or twice in an eternity and even then it is dangerous to all concerned. You must do as I say. I promise that you will have just as good a chance of finding Tanelorn where I take you. Your opportunity lies in Elric's future."

Erekosë bowed his head. "Very well."

"Come," Elric said impatiently, beginning to strike off to the north-east. "For all your talk of time, there is precious little left for me."

CHAPTER SIX

Pale Lord Shouting in Sunlight

The machine in the bowl was where Elric had last seen it, just before he had attacked it and found himself plunged into Corum's world.

Jhary seemed completely familiar with it and soon had its heart beating strongly. He shepherded the other two up to it and made them stand with their backs against the crystal. Then he handed something to Elric. It was a small vial.

"When we have departed," he said, "hurl this through the top of the bowl, then take your horse which I see is yonder and ride as fast as you can for Tanelorn. Follow these instructions perfectly and you will serve us all."

Elric accepted the vial. "Very well."

"And," Jhary said finally as he took his place with the others, "please give my compliments to my brother Moonglum."

"You know him? What—?"

"Farewell, Elric! We shall doubtless meet many times in the future, though we may not recognize each other."

Then the beating of the thing in the bowl grew louder and the ground shook and the strange darkness surrounded it—then the three figures had gone. Swiftly Elric hurled the vial upwards so that it fell through the opening of the bowl, then he ran to where his golden mare was tethered, leapt into the saddle with the bundle Jhary had given him under his arm, and galloped as fast as he could go towards Tanelorn.

Behind him the beating suddenly ceased. The darkness disappeared. A tense silence fell. Then Elric heard something like a giant's gasp and blinding blue light filled the desert. He looked back. Not only the bowl and the device had gone—so also had the rocks which had once surrounded it.

He came up behind them at last, just before they reached the walls of Tanelorn. Elric saw warriors on those walls.

The massive reptilian monsters bore their equally repulsive masters upon their backs, their feet leaving deep marks in the sand as they moved. And Theleb K'aarna rode at their head on a chestnut stallion— and there was something draped across his saddle.

Then a shadow passed over Elric's head and he looked up. It was the metal bird which had borne Myshella away. But it was riderless. It wheeled over the heads of the lumbering reptiles whose masters raised their strange weapons and sent hissing streams of fire in its direction, driving it higher into the sky. Why was the bird here and not Myshella? A peculiar cry came again and again from its metal throat and Elric realized what that cry resembled—the pathetic sound of a mother bird whose young is in danger.

He stared hard at the bundle over Theleb K'aarna's saddle and suddenly he knew what it must be. Myshella herself! Doubtless she had given Elric up for dead and had tried to go against Theleb K'aarna only to be beaten.

Anger boiled in the albino. All his intense hatred for the sorcerer revived and his hand went to his sword. But then he looked again at the vulnerable walls of Tanelorn, at his brave companions on the battlements, and he knew that his first duty was to help them.

But how was he to reach the walls without Theleb K'aarna seeing him and destroying him before he could bring the banners of bronze to his friends? He prepared to spur his horse forward and hope that he would be lucky. Then a shadow passed over his head again and he saw that it was the metal bird flying low, something like agony in its emerald eyes. He heard its voice. "Prince Elric! We must save her."

He shook his head as the bird settled in the sand. "First I must save Tanelorn."

"I will help you," said the bird of gold and silver and brass. "Climb up into my saddle."

Elric cast a glance towards the distant monsters. Their attention was now wholly upon the city they intended to destroy. He jumped from his horse and crossed the sand to clamber into the onyx saddle of the bird. The wings began to clash and with a rush they swept into the sky, turning towards Tanelorn.

More streaks of fire hissed around them as they neared the city, but the bird flew rapidly from side to side and avoided them. Down they drifted now to the gentle city, to land on the wall itself.

"Elric!" Moonglum came running along the defenses. "We were told you were dead!"

"By whom?"

"By Myshella and by Theleb K'aarna when he demanded our surrender."

"I suppose they could only believe that," Elric said, separating the staffs around which were furled the thin sheets of bronze. "Here, you must take these. I am told that they will be useful against the reptiles of Pio. Unfurl them along the walls. Greetings, Rackhir." He handed the astounded Red Archer one of the banners.

"You do not stay to fight with us?" Rackhir asked.

Elric looked down at the twelve slender arrows in his hand. Each one was perfectly carved from multicoloured quartz so that even the fletchings seemed like real feathers. "No," he said. "I hope to rescue Myshella from Theleb K'aarna—and I can use these arrows better from the air, also."

"Myshella, thinking you dead, seemed to go mad," Rackhir told him. "She conjured up various sorceries against Theleb K'aarna—but he retaliated. At last she flung herself from the saddle of that bird you ride—flung herself upon him armed only with a knife. But he overpowered her and has threatened to slay her if we do not allow ourselves to be killed without retaliating. I know that he will kill Myshella anyway. I have been in something of a quandary of conscience . . ."

"I will resolve that quandary, I hope." Elric stroked the metallic neck of the bird. "Come, my friend, into the air again. Remember, Rackhir—unfurl the banners along the walls as soon as I have gained a good height."

The Red Archer nodded, his face puzzled, and once again Elric was rising into the air, the arrows of quartz clutched in his left hand.

He heard Theleb K'aarna's laughter from below. He saw the monstrous beasts moving inexorably towards the walls. The gates opened suddenly and a group of horsemen rode out. Plainly they had hoped to sacrifice themselves in order to save Tanelorn and Rackhir had not had time to warn them of Elric's message.

The riders galloped wildly towards the reptilian monsters of Pio, their swords and lances waving, their yells rising to where Elric drifted high above. The monsters roared and opened their huge jaws, their masters pointed their ornate weapons at the horsemen of Tanelorn. Flames burst from the muzzles, the riders shrieked as they were devoured by the dazzling heat.

In horror Elric directed the metal bird downwards. And at last Theleb K'aarna saw him and reined in his horse, his eyes wide with fear and rage. "You are dead! You are dead!"

The great wings beat at the air as the bird hovered over Theleb K'aarna's head. "I am alive, Theleb K'aarna—and I come to destroy you at long last! Give Myshella up to me."

A cunning expression came over the sorcerer's face. "No. Destroy me and she is also destroyed. Beings of Pio—turn your full strength against Tanelorn. Raze it utterly and show this fool what we can do!"

Each of the reptilian riders directed their oddly shaped weapons at Tanelorn where Rackhir, Moonglum and the rest waited on the battlements.

"No!" shouted Elric. "You cannot—"

There was something flashing on the battlements. They were unfurling at last the banners of bronze. And as each banner was unfurled a pure golden light blazed out from it until there was a vast wall of light stretching the whole length of the defenses, making it impossible to see the banners themselves or the men who held them. The beings of Pio aimed their weapons and released streams of fire at the barrier of light which immediately repelled them.

Theleb K'aarna's face was suffused with anger. "What is this? Our earthly sorcery cannot stand against the power of Pio!"

Elric smiled savagely. "This is not our sorcery—it is another sorcery which *can* resist that of Pio! Now, Theleb K'aarna, give up Myshella!"

"No! You are not protected as Tanelorn is protected. Beings of Pio—destroy him!"

And, as the weapons began to be directed at him, Elric flung the first of the arrows of quartz. It flew true—directly into the face of the leading reptilian rider. A high whining escaped the rider's throat as it raised its webbed hands towards the arrow embedded in its eye. The beast the rider sat upon reared, for it was plain that it was only barely controlled. It turned away from the blinding light, from Tanelorn, and it galloped at earth-shaking speed away into the desert, the dead rider falling from its back. A streak of fire barely missed Elric and he was forced to take the bird up higher, flinging down another arrow and seeing it strike a rider's heart. Again the mount went out of control and followed its companion into the desert. But there were ten more of the riders and each now turned his weapon against Elric, though finding it hard to aim as all the mounts grew restive and sought to accompany the two who had fled. Elric left it to the metal bird to duck and to dive through the criss-cross of beams and he hurled down another arrow and another. His clothes and his hair were singed and he remembered another time when he had ridden the bird across the Boiling Sea. Part of the bird's right wing-tip had been melted and its flight was a little more erratic. But still it climbed and dived and still Elric threw the arrows of quartz into the ranks of the beings of Pio. Then, suddenly, there were only two left and they were turning to flee, for nearby a cloud of unpleasant blue smoke had begun to erupt where Theleb K'aarna had been. Elric flung the last arrows after the reptiles of Pio and took each rider in the back. Now there were only corpses upon the sand.

The blue smoke cleared and Theleb K'aarna's horse stood there. And there was another corpse revealed. It was that of Myshella, Empress of the Dawn, and her throat had been cut. Theleb K'aarna had vanished, doubtless with the aid of sorcery.

Sickened, Elric descended on the bird of metal. On the walls of Tanelorn the light faded. He dismounted and he saw that the bird was weeping dark tears from its emerald eyes. He knelt beside Myshella.

An ordinary mortal could not have done it, but now she opened her lips and she spoke, though blood bubbled from her mouth and her words were hard to make out.

"Elric . . ."

"Can you live?" Elric asked her. "Have you some power to . . ."

"I cannot live. I am slain. Even now I am dead. But it will be some comfort to you to know that Theleb K'aarna has earned the disdain of the great Chaos Lords. They will never aid him again as they aided him this time, for in their eyes he has proved himself incompetent."

"Where has he gone? I will pursue him. I will slay him the next time, that I swear."

"I think that you will. But I do not know where he went. Elric—I am dead and my work is threatened. I have fought against Chaos for centuries and now, I think, Chaos will increase its power. Soon the great battle between the Lords of Law and the Lords of Entropy will take place. The threads of destiny become much tangled—the very

structure of the multiverse seems about to transform itself. You have some part in this . . . some part . . . Farewell, Elric!"

"Oh, Myshella!"

"Is she dead now?" It was the sombre voice of the bird of metal.

"Aye." The word was forced from Elric's tight throat.

"Then I must take her back to Kaneloon."

Gently Elric picked up Myshella's bloody corpse, supporting the half-severed head on his arm. He placed the body in the onyx saddle.

The bird said: "We shall not see each other again, Prince Elric, for my death shall follow closely upon Lady Myshella's."

Elric bowed his head.

The shining wings spread and, with the sound of cymbals clashing, beat at the air.

Elric watched the beautiful creature circle in the sky and then turn and fly steadily towards the south and World's Edge.

He buried his face in his hands, but he was beyond weeping now. Was it the fate of all the women he loved to die? Would Myshella have lived if she had let him die when he had wanted to? There was no rage left in him, only a sense of impotent despair.

He felt a hand on his shoulder and he turned. Moonglum stood there, with Rackhir beside him. They had ridden out from Tanelorn to find him.

"The banners have vanished," Rackhir told him. "And the arrows, too. Only the corpses of those creatures remain and we shall bury them. Will you come back with us, now, to Tanelorn?"

"Tanelorn cannot give me peace, Rackhir."

"I believe that to be true. But I have a potion in my house which will deaden some of your memories, help you forget some of what has happened lately."

"I would be grateful for such a potion. Though I doubt . . ."

"It will work. I promise. Another would achieve complete forgetfulness from drinking this potion. But you may hope to forget a little."

Elric thought of Corum and Erekosë and Jhary-a-Conel and the implications of his experiences—that even if he were to die he would be reincarnated in some other form to fight again and to suffer again. An eternity of warfare and of pain. If he could forget that knowledge it would be enough. He had the impulse to ride far away from Tanelorn and concern himself as much as he could in the pettier affairs of men.

"I am so weary of gods and their struggles," he murmured as he mounted his golden mare.

Moonglum stared out into the desert.

"But when will the gods themselves weary of it, I wonder?" he said. "If they did, it would be a happy day for Man. Perhaps all our struggling, our suffering, our conflicts are merely to relieve the boredom of the Lords of the Higher Worlds. Perhaps that is why when they created us they made us imperfect."

They began to ride towards Tanelorn while the wind blew sadly across the desert. The sand was already beginning to cover up the corpses of those who had sought to wage war against eternity and had, inevitably, found that other eternity which was death.

For a while Elric walked his horse beside the others. His lips formed a name but did not speak it.

And then, suddenly, he was galloping towards Tanelorn dragging the screaming runesword from its scabbard and brandishing it at the impassive sky, making the horse rear up and lash its hoofs in the air, shouting over and over again in a voice full of roaring misery and bitter rage:

"Ah, damn you! Damn you! Damn you!"

But those who heard him—and some might have been the gods he addressed—knew that it was Elric of Melniboné himself who was truly damned.

AND SO THE GREAT EMPEROR
RECEIVED HIS EDUCATION . . .

AND SO THE GREAT EMPEROR
RECEIVED HIS EDUCATION ...
(2003)

L EARNING HIS WIZARD'S craft on the dream couches, where one might live a thousand years in a single night, Elric was trained in the ancient traditions of Melniboné's Sorcerer Kings.

No mortal could learn all there was to learn in a single lifetime, and thus it was that the lords of the Bright Empire conceived a means by which their sons might gain all their inherited wisdom. A wisdom of millennia.

These sons (and sometimes daughters) dreamed the long dreams of Imrryr the Beautiful, the Dreaming City. They made pacts with the great elementals of fire, water, air and earth.

In these dreams, while they lay upon the dream couches of the Dreaming City, they consorted with demons, with angels and with violent, desperate men, with cruel warlocks, powerful witches and all manner of supernatural beings.

In these dreams they walked with the denizens of hell and made bargains with the Lords of Chaos, even indulged in compacts with the Dukes and Duchesses of Law.

In sublime terror they made love to the undying. With horrible joy they made war against the never-to-be-born. They explored the corridors of measureless palaces and wandered through unmappable landscapes without horizon or end.

They journeyed beneath the earth, into the lands of sunless, crystalline beauty, where vast, glowing rivers roared and strange, unhuman beings ruled.

They walked the moonbeam roads, the astral roads between the worlds. They fell into burning suns and froze on silver moons. They learned the histories of all their pasts and all their futures.

In these dreams no pain was unfamiliar to them. No pleasure went untasted. Dream followed dream. Knowledge was heaped on knowledge. Terror on terror and joy on joy. And by this means they learned their magic, their power over all men and all the forces of nature. They learned to summon great winds, to throw fire, to raise the waters, to break open the very surface of the earth. They learned to destroy the living and to resurrect the dead. They learned to survive dangers no ordinary mortal might ever hope to experience and live . . .

Not all survived. Many died on the dream couches, trapped in some nameless spell, victims of some voracious immortal, torn apart by unimaginable creatures, destroyed by some appalling force.

Of course, no mortal brain could absorb so many experiences or hold so many memories and remain sane and it was frequently argued that there were few sane emperors of Melniboné.

Was Elric sane?

Elric of Melniboné, son of Sadric, would never be certain of his own sanity, nor indeed of his own moral choices. These were questions forever in his conscious mind, filling his waking hours, just as the terrors and wisdom of his dream-quests remained in his *un*conscious mind, to disturb his sleeping hours.

Elric of Melniboné had received the most rigorous education of all. For almost every hour of his lifetime he had lived ten years upon the dream couches. Those who saw a young man, just reaching maturity, could not possibly know, unless they had experienced it themselves, what an ancient near-immortal dwelled within.

Yet in some ways, the ordinary ways of the world, its certainties and its deceits, Elric *was* a young man. He had a young man's ambitions, a young man's ideals, a young man's need for spontaneous action, for love and for adventure.

Elric's dreams had not dulled his taste for life. They had taught him sorcery more than teaching him conventional manners. Though he had the courtliness and grace taught to all Melnibonéan aristocrats, though his own stock of irony was not small and his own powers of observation not minor, yet he was still an untried creature, whose vast sorcerous power was balanced by his own moral uncertainties.

Elric's dream-quests were recalled as nightmares, the vaguest of disturbing memories, interruptions of the sleeping mind. But what he had learned on those quests remained—sorcerous and military arts of complex depth and variety. Arts which something in him feared to use, for he instinctively understood their destructive power.

When one day Elric's father died suddenly, brought low by deep melancholy and too many disappointments, having failed to reinvigorate an empire which had grown lazy with its own great might, Elric was forced to consider his inheritance.

He was now natural successor to the throne of ancient Imrryr. A responsibility he was not sure he could fulfill.

And Elric was not the only one to doubt his own abilities. Some said he was not suited for the task, that he had deficient blood, impaired strength, weak eyes and an unstable mind, such as marked earlier, so-called 'Silver Emperors', the white-haired, crimson-eyed albinos whose strange condition marked them out in the long line of sorcerer emperors and empresses.

Some, who supported another contender for the throne, said this 'Silver Emperor' who conversed with humans as if they were equals, who had human friends as well as alliances with demons, would bring the Empire down. It was predicted, they said (though these predications, when challenged, proved to be somewhat numinous). Elric's succession would cause the defenses of Imrryr to tumble, they said. He would allow the human hordes to flood in. These hordes had grown powerful and longed to sack the city of the Dragon Lords. They hated these lords, who had ruled them for so many millennia. They longed to loot, to destroy, to rape. These voices warned that Elric was fated to be the very last of his ancient line, a prince of ruins and desolation.

Even Melniboné's greatest power, the Phoorn, asleep in the dragon caves far below the Dreaming City, dragons who dripped fiery venom upon their enemies, even these would not defend the Bright Empire against the threat of those nations they called the Young Kingdoms, the upstart nations of a new and changing world.

Some of Elric's own party, often the wisest, argued that Melniboné had grown too certain of herself, too proud to make alliances with those who refused vassalage, too arrogant to call upon the emergent nations and respect them as brothers, rather than clients. In her lofty pride lay the seeds of her own doom. Even as she rose to her greatest power, Melniboné was already facing destruction. But this was not talk Elric's enemies cared to hear. Rather, they blamed him alone for any dangers Melniboné might face. And they championed his cousin, the swaggering warrior prince Yyrkoon, who promised them glory, who promised them new wealth, who promised them a kind of immortality.

Yyrkoon, too, had learned his sorcerous craft upon the dream couches, though not with Elric's patience. He saw that his power lay not in wisdom but in strength. He placed all his ambitions in the blade of his sword.

And so they schemed, these various parties—some for Elric, some for Yyrkoon, some for themselves. There were those who loved their strange country as passionately as any patriot loved their country, there were some who cared little for Melniboné, but sought personal advancement. There were others who calculated the security of their nation and saw Elric as too weak to defend them, while loving the man himself. Some hated him and his dependence on drugs to survive at all, yet revered his lineage as the true blood of ancient Melniboné. They would support him no matter what arguments were brought against him. Still others spoke of ridding Melniboné of kings and aristocrats and founding a fresh republic, as had once ruled the Dreaming City.

And all of these and more gathered at the great Court of Emperors, to scheme behind their hands, to whisper of betrayal and support, of wisdom and folly, and plot the dominance of this party or that. Over all of them, the young Emperor must preside, with due ceremony and pride. Over all of them he must appear dispassionate and distant, as his blood demanded. Over all he must exert his enormous power, a power he did not even understand as yet.

Soon he would begin to learn of that power. But meanwhile, a great Masque must be played out, for the entertainment of the fresh-crowned Emperor, for the satisfaction of tradition. A masque which, some would later say, predicted much that was to occur to bring about the doom of Elric's long line and the destruction of the Dreaming City . . .

ELRIC OF MELNIBONÉ

ELRIC OF MELNIBONÉ
(1972)

To Poul Anderson for *The Broken Sword* and *Three Hearts and Three Lions*. To the late Fletcher Pratt for *The Well of the Unicorn*. To the late Bertolt Brecht for *The Threepenny Opera,* which, for obscure reasons, I link with the other books as being one of the chief influences on the first Elric stories.

PROLOGUE

This is the tale of Elric before he was called Womanslayer, before the final collapse of Melniboné. This is the tale of his rivalry with his cousin Yyrkoon and his love for his cousin Cymoril, before that rivalry and that love brought Imrryr, the Dreaming City, crashing in flames, raped by the reavers from the Young Kingdoms. This is the tale of the two black swords, Stormbringer and Mournblade, and how they were discovered and what part they played in the destiny of Elric and Melniboné—a destiny which was to shape a larger destiny: that of the world itself. This is the tale of when Elric was a king, the commander of dragons, fleets and all the folk of that half-human race which had ruled the world for ten thousand years.

This is a tale of tragedy, this tale of Melniboné, the Dragon Isle. This is a tale of monstrous emotions and high ambitions. This is a tale of sorceries and treacheries and worthy ideals, of agonies and fearful pleasures, of bitter love and sweet hatred. This is the tale of Elric of Melniboné. Much of it Elric himself was to remember only in his nightmares.

—*The Chronicle of the Black Sword*

BOOK ONE

On the island kingdom of Melniboné all the old rituals are still observed, though the nation's power has waned for five hundred years, and now her way of life is maintained only by her trade with the Young Kingdoms and by the fact that the city of Imrryr has become the meeting place of merchants. Are those rituals no longer useful; can the rituals be denied and doom avoided? One who would rule in Emperor Elric's stead prefers to think not. He says that Elric will bring destruction to Melniboné by his refusal to honour all the rituals (Elric honours many). And now opens the tragedy which will close many years from now and precipitate the destruction of this world.

CHAPTER ONE

A Melancholy King: A Court Strives to Honour Him

I T IS THE colour of a bleached skull, his flesh; and the long hair which flows below his shoulders is milk-white. From the tapering, beautiful head stare two slanting eyes, crimson and moody, and from the loose sleeves of his yellow gown emerge two slender hands, also the colour of bone, resting on each arm of a seat which has been carved from a single, massive ruby.

The crimson eyes are troubled and sometimes one hand will rise to finger the light helm which sits upon the white locks: a helm made from some dark, greenish alloy and exquisitely moulded into the likeness of a dragon about to take wing. And on the hand which absently caresses the crown there is a ring in which is set a single rare Actorios stone whose core sometimes shifts sluggishly and reshapes itself, as if it were sentient smoke and as restless in its jeweled prison as the young albino on his Ruby Throne.

He looks down the long flight of quartz steps to where his court disports itself, dancing with such delicacy and whispering grace that it might be a court of ghosts. Mentally he debates moral issues and in itself this activity divides him from the great majority of his subjects, for these people are not human.

These are the people of Melniboné, the Dragon Isle, which ruled the world for ten thousand years and has ceased to rule it for less than five hundred years. And they are cruel and clever and to them 'morality' means little more than a proper respect for the traditions of a hundred centuries.

To the young man, four hundred and twenty-eighth in direct line of descent from the first Sorcerer Emperor of Melniboné, their assumptions seem not only arrogant but foolish; it is plain that the Dragon Isle has lost most of her power and will soon be threatened, in another century or two, by a direct conflict with the emerging human nations whom they call, somewhat patronizingly, the Young Kingdoms. Already pirate fleets have made unsuccessful attacks on Imrryr the Beautiful, the Dreaming City, capital of the Dragon Isle of Melniboné.

Yet even the emperor's closest friends refuse to discuss the prospect of Melniboné's fall. They are not pleased when he mentions the idea, considering his remarks not only unthinkable, but also a singular breach of good taste.

So, alone, the emperor broods. He mourns that his father, Sadric the Eighty-Sixth, did not sire more children, for then a more suitable monarch might have been available to take his place on the Ruby Throne. Sadric has been dead a year; seeming to whisper glad welcome to that which came to claim his soul. Through most of his life Sadric had never known another woman than his wife, for the empress had died bringing her sole thin-blooded issue into the world. But, with Melnibonéan emotions (oddly different from those of the human newcomers), Sadric had loved his wife and had been unable to find pleasure in any other company, even that of the son who had killed her and who was all that was left of her. By magic potions and the chanting of runes, by rare herbs had her son been nurtured, his strength sustained artificially by every art known to the Sorcerer Kings of Melniboné. And he had lived—still lives—thanks to sorcery alone, for he is naturally lassitudinous and, without his drugs, would barely be able to raise his hand from his side through most of a normal day.

If the young emperor has found any advantage in his lifelong weakness it must be in that, perforce, he has read much. Before he was fifteen he had read every book in his father's library, some more than once. His sorcerous powers, learned initially from Sadric, are now greater than any possessed by his ancestors for many a generation. His knowledge of the world beyond the shores of Melniboné is profound, though he has as yet had little direct experience of it. If he wished he could resurrect the Dragon Isle's former might and rule both his own land and the Young Kingdoms as an invulnerable tyrant. But his reading has also taught him to question the uses to which power is put, to question his motives, to question whether his own power should be used at all, in any cause. His reading has led him to this 'morality', which, still, he barely understands. Thus, to his subjects, he is an enigma and, to some, he is a threat, for he neither thinks nor acts in accordance with their conception of how a true Melnibonéan (and a Melnibonéan emperor, at that) should think and act. His cousin Yyrkoon, for instance, has been heard more than once to voice strong doubts concerning the emperor's right to rule the people of Melniboné. "This feeble scholar will bring doom to us all," he said one night to Dyvim Tvar, Lord of the Dragon Caves.

Dyvim Tvar is one of the emperor's few friends and he had duly reported the conversation, but the youth had dismissed the remarks as "only a trivial treason", whereas any of his ancestors would have rewarded such sentiments with a very slow and exquisite public execution.

The emperor's attitude is further complicated by the fact that

Yyrkoon, who is even now making precious little secret of his feelings that he should be emperor, is the brother of Cymoril, a girl whom the albino considers the closest of his friends, and who will one day become his empress.

Down on the mosaic floor of the court Prince Yyrkoon can be seen in all his finest silks and furs, his jewels and his brocades, dancing with a hundred women, all of whom are rumoured to have been mistresses of his at one time or another. His dark features, at once handsome and saturnine, are framed by long black hair, waved and oiled, and his expression, as ever, is sardonic while his bearing is arrogant. The heavy brocade cloak swings this way and that, striking other dancers with some force. He wears it almost as if it is armour or, perhaps, a weapon. Amongst many of the courtiers there is more than a little respect for Prince Yyrkoon. Few resent his arrogance and those who do keep silent, for Yyrkoon is known to be a considerable sorcerer himself. Also his behaviour is what the court expects and welcomes in a Melnibonéan noble; it is what they would welcome in their emperor.

The emperor knows this. He wishes he could please his court as it strives to honour him with its dancing and its wit, but he cannot bring himself to take part in what he privately considers a wearisome and irritating sequence of ritual posturings. In this he is, perhaps, somewhat more arrogant than Yyrkoon who is, at least, a conventional boor.

From the galleries, the music grows louder and more complex as the slaves, specially trained and surgically operated upon to sing but one perfect note each, are stimulated to more passionate efforts. Even the young emperor is moved by the sinister harmony of their song which in few ways resembles anything previously uttered by the human voice. Why should their pain produce such marvelous beauty? he wonders. Or is all beauty created through pain? Is that the secret of great art, both human and Melnibonéan?

The Emperor Elric closes his eyes.

There is a stir in the hall below. The gates have opened and the dancing courtiers cease their motion, drawing back and bowing low as soldiers enter. The soldiers are clad all in light blue, their ornamental helms cast in fantastic shapes, their long, broad-bladed lances decorated with jeweled ribbons. They surround a young woman whose blue dress matches their uniforms and whose bare arms are encircled by five or six bracelets of diamonds, sapphires and gold. Strings of diamonds and sapphires are wound into her hair. Unlike most of the women of the court, her face has no designs painted upon the eyelids or cheekbones. Elric smiles. This is Cymoril. The soldiers are her personal ceremonial guard who, according to tradition, must escort her into the court. They ascend the steps leading to the Ruby Throne. Slowly Elric rises and stretches out his hands.

"Cymoril. I thought you had decided not to grace the court tonight."

She returns his smile. "My emperor, I found that I was in the mood for conversation, after all."

Elric is grateful. She knows that he is bored and she knows, too, that she is one of the few people of Melniboné whose conversation interests him. If protocol allowed, he would offer her the throne, but as it is she must sit on the topmost step at his feet.

"Please sit, sweet Cymoril." He resumes his place upon the throne and leans forward as she seats herself and looks into his eyes with a mixed expression of humour and tenderness. She speaks softly as her guard withdraws to mingle at the sides of the steps with Elric's own guard. Her voice can be heard only by Elric.

"Would you ride out to the wild region of the island with me tomorrow, my lord?"

"There are matters to which I must give my attention . . ." He is attracted by the idea. It is weeks since he left the city and rode with her, their escort keeping a discreet distance away.

"Are they urgent?"

He shrugs. "What matters are urgent in Melniboné? After ten thousand years, most problems may be seen in a certain perspective." His smile is almost a grin, rather like that of a young scholar who plans to play truant from his tutor. "Very well—early in the morning, we'll leave, before the others are up."

"The air beyond Imrryr will be clear and sharp. The sun will be warm for the season. The sky will be blue and unclouded."

Elric laughs. "Such sorcery you must have worked!"

Cymoril lowers her eyes and traces a pattern on the marble of the dais. "Well, perhaps a little. I am not without friends among the weakest of the elementals . . ."

Elric stretches down to touch her fine, dark hair. "Does Yyrkoon know?"

"No."

Prince Yyrkoon has forbidden his sister to meddle in magical matters. Prince Yyrkoon's friends are only amongst the darker of the supernatural beings and he knows that they are dangerous to deal with; thus he assumes that all sorcerous dealings bear a similar element of danger. Besides this, he hates to think that others possess the power that he possesses. Perhaps this is what, in Elric, he hates most of all.

"Let us hope that all Melniboné needs fine weather for tomorrow," says Elric. Cymoril stares curiously at him. She is still a Melnibonéan. It has not occurred to her that her sorcery might prove unwelcome to some. Then she shrugs her lovely shoulders and touches her lord lightly upon the hand.

"This 'guilt'," she says. "This searching of the conscience. Its purpose is beyond my simple brain."

"And mine, I must admit. It seems to have no practical function. Yet more than one of our ancestors predicted a change in the nature of our earth. A spiritual as well as a physical change. Perhaps I have glimmerings of this change when I think my stranger, un-Melnibonéan, thoughts?"

The music swells. The music fades. The courtiers dance on, though many eyes are upon Elric and Cymoril as they talk at the top of the dais. There is speculation. When will Elric announce Cymoril as his empress-to-be? Will Elric revive the custom that Sadric dismissed, of sacrificing twelve brides and their bridegrooms to the Lords of Chaos in order to ensure a good marriage for the rulers of Melniboné?

It was obvious that Sadric's refusal to allow the custom to continue brought misery upon him and death upon his wife; brought him a sickly son and threatened the very continuity of the monarchy. Elric must revive the custom. Even Elric must fear a repetition of the doom which visited his father. But some say that Elric will do nothing in accordance with tradition and that he threatens not only his own life, but the existence of Melniboné itself and all it stands for. And those who speak thus are often seen to be on good terms with Prince Yyrkoon who dances on, seemingly unaware of their conversation or, indeed, unaware that his sister talks quietly with the cousin who sits on the Ruby Throne; who sits on the edge of the seat, forgetful of his dignity, who exhibits none of the ferocious and disdainful pride which has, in the past, marked virtually every other emperor of Melniboné; who chats animatedly, forgetful that the court is supposed to be dancing for his entertainment.

And then suddenly Prince Yyrkoon freezes in mid-pirouette and raises his dark eyes to look up at his emperor. In one corner of the hall, Dyvim Tvar's attention is attracted by Yyrkoon's calculated and dramatic posture and the Lord of the Dragon Caves frowns. His hand falls to where his sword would normally be, but no swords are worn at a court ball. Dyvim Tvar looks warily and intently at Prince Yyrkoon as the tall nobleman begins to ascend the stairs to the Ruby Throne. Many eyes follow the emperor's cousin and now hardly anyone dances, though the music grows wilder as the masters of the music slaves goad their charges to even greater exertions.

Elric looks up to see Yyrkoon standing one step below that on which Cymoril sits. Yyrkoon makes a bow which is subtly insulting.

"I present myself to my emperor," he says.

CHAPTER TWO

An Upstart Prince: He Confronts His Cousin

"And how do you enjoy the ball, cousin?" Elric asked, aware that Yyrkoon's melodramatic presentation had been designed to catch him off-guard and, if possible, humiliate him. "Is the music to your taste?"

Yyrkoon lowered his eyes and let his lips form a secret little smile. "Everything is to my taste, my liege. But what of yourself? Does something displease you? You do not join the dance."

Elric raised one pale finger to his chin and stared at Yyrkoon's hidden eyes. "I enjoy the dance, cousin, nonetheless. Surely it is possible to take pleasure in the pleasure of others?"

Yyrkoon seemed genuinely astonished. His eyes opened fully and met Elric's. Elric felt a slight shock and then turned his own gaze away, indicating the music galleries with a languid hand. "Or perhaps it is the pain of others which brings me pleasure. Fear not, for my sake, cousin. I am pleased. I am pleased. You may dance on, assured that your emperor enjoys the ball."

But Yyrkoon was not to be diverted from his object. "Surely, if his subjects are not to go away saddened and troubled that they have not pleased their ruler, the emperor should demonstrate his enjoyment . . . ?"

"I would remind you, cousin," said Elric quietly, "that the emperor has no duty to his subjects at all, save to rule them. Their duty is to him. That is the tradition of Melniboné."

Yyrkoon had not expected Elric to use such arguments against him, but he rallied with his next retort. "I agree, my lord. The emperor's duty is to rule his subjects. Perhaps that is why so many of them do not, themselves, enjoy the ball as much as they might."

"I do not follow you, cousin."

Cymoril had risen and stood with her hands clenched on the step above her brother. She was tense and anxious, worried by her brother's bantering tone, his disdainful bearing.

"Yyrkoon . . ." she said.

He acknowledged her presence. "Sister. I see you share our emperor's reluctance to dance."

"Yyrkoon," she murmured, "you are going too far. The emperor is tolerant, but . . ."

"Tolerant? Or is he careless? Is he careless of the traditions of our great race? Is he contemptuous of that race's pride?"

Dyvim Tvar was now mounting the steps. It was plain that he, too, sensed that Yyrkoon had chosen this moment to test Elric's power.

Cymoril was aghast. She said urgently: "Yyrkoon. If you would live . . ."

"I would not care to live if the soul of Melniboné perished. And the guardianship of our nation's soul is the responsibility of the emperor. And what if we should have an emperor who failed in that responsibility? An emperor who was weak? An emperor who cared nothing for the greatness of the Dragon Isle and its folk?"

"A hypothetical question, cousin." Elric had recovered his composure and his voice was an icy drawl. "For such an emperor has never sat upon the Ruby Throne and such an emperor never shall."

Dyvim Tvar came up, touching Yyrkoon on the shoulder. "Prince, if you value your dignity and your life . . ."

Elric raised his hand. "There is no need for that, Dyvim Tvar. Prince Yyrkoon merely entertains us with an intellectual debate. Fearing that I was bored by the music and the dance—which I am not—he thought he would provide the subject for a stimulating discourse. I am certain that we are most stimulated, Prince Yyrkoon." Elric allowed a patronizing warmth to colour his last sentence.

Yyrkoon flushed with anger and bit his lips.

"But go on, dear cousin Yyrkoon," Elric said. "I am interested. Enlarge further on your argument."

Yyrkoon looked around him, as if for support. But all his supporters were on the floor of the hall. Only Elric's friends, Dyvim Tvar and Cymoril, were nearby. Yet Yyrkoon knew that his supporters were hearing every word and that he would lose face if he did not retaliate. Elric could tell that Yyrkoon would have preferred to have retired from this confrontation and choose another day and another ground on which to continue the battle, but that was not possible. Elric, himself, had no wish to continue the foolish banter which was, no matter how disguised, little better than the quarreling of two little girls over who should play with the slaves first. He decided to make an end of it.

Yyrkoon began: "Then let me suggest that an emperor who was physically weak might also be weak in his will to rule as befitted . . ."

And Elric raised his hand. "You have done enough, dear cousin. More than enough. You have wearied yourself with this conversation when you would have preferred to dance. I am touched by your concern. But now I, too, feel weariness steal upon me." Elric signaled for his old servant Tanglebones who stood on the far side of the throne dais, amongst the soldiers. "Tanglebones! My cloak."

Elric stood up. "I thank you again for your thoughtfulness, cousin." He addressed the court in general. "I was entertained. Now I retire."

Tanglebones brought the cloak of white fox fur and placed it around his master's shoulders. Tanglebones was very old and much taller than Elric, though his back was stooped and all his limbs seemed knotted and twisted back on themselves, like the limbs of a strong, old tree.

Elric walked across the dais and through the door which opened onto a corridor which led to his private apartments.

Yyrkoon was left fuming. He whirled round on the dais and opened his mouth as if to address the watching courtiers. Some, who did not support him, were smiling quite openly. Yyrkoon clenched his fists at his sides and glowered. He glared at Dyvim Tvar and opened his thin lips to speak. Dyvim Tvar coolly returned the glare, daring Yyrkoon to say more.

Then Yyrkoon flung back his head so that the locks of his hair, all curled and oiled, swayed against his back. And Yyrkoon laughed.

The harsh sound filled the hall. The music stopped. The laughter continued.

Yyrkoon stepped up so that he stood on the dais. He dragged his heavy cloak round him so that it engulfed his body.

Cymoril came forward. "Yyrkoon, please do not . . ." He pushed her back with a motion of his shoulder.

Yyrkoon walked stiffly towards the Ruby Throne. It became plain that he was about to seat himself in it and thus perform one of the most traitorous actions possible in the code of Melniboné. Cymoril ran the few steps to him and pulled at his arm.

Yyrkoon's laughter grew. "It is Yyrkoon they would wish to see on the Ruby Throne," he told his sister. She gasped and looked in horror at Dyvim Tvar whose face was grim and angry.

Dyvim Tvar signed to the guards and suddenly there were two ranks of armoured men between Yyrkoon and the throne.

Yyrkoon glared back at the Lord of the Dragon Caves. "You had best hope you perish with your master," he hissed.

"This guard of honour will escort you from the hall," Dyvim Tvar said evenly. "We were all stimulated by your conversation this evening, Prince Yyrkoon."

Yyrkoon paused, looked about him, then relaxed. He shrugged. "There's time enough. If Elric will not abdicate, then he must be deposed."

Cymoril's slender body was rigid. Her eyes blazed. She said to her brother:

"If you harm Elric in any way, I will slay you myself, Yyrkoon."

He raised his tapering eyebrows and smiled. At that moment he seemed to hate his sister even more than he hated his cousin. "Your loyalty to that creature has ensured your own doom, Cymoril. I would rather you died than that you should give birth to any progeny of his. I will not have the blood of our house diluted, tainted—even touched— by his blood. Look to your own life, sister, before you threaten mine."

And he stormed down the steps, pushing through those who came up to congratulate him. He knew that he had lost and the murmurs of his sycophants only irritated him further.

The great doors of the hall crashed together and closed. Yyrkoon was gone from the hall.

Dyvim Tvar raised both his arms. "Dance on, courtiers. Pleasure yourselves with all that the hall provides. It is what will please the emperor most."

But it was plain there would be little more dancing done tonight. Courtiers were already deep in conversation as, excitedly, they debated the events.

Dyvim Tvar turned to Cymoril. "Elric refuses to understand the danger, Princess Cymoril. Yyrkoon's ambition could bring disaster to all of us."

"Including Yyrkoon." Cymoril sighed.

"Aye, including Yyrkoon. But how can we avoid this, Cymoril, if Elric will not give orders for your brother's arrest?"

"He believes that such as Yyrkoon should be allowed to say what they please. It is part of his philosophy. I can barely understand it, but it seems integral to his whole belief. If he destroys Yyrkoon, he destroys the basis on which his logic works. That at any rate, Dragon Master, is what he has tried to explain to me."

Dyvim Tvar sighed and he frowned. Unable to understand Elric, he was afraid that he could sometimes sympathize with Yyrkoon's viewpoint. At least Yyrkoon's motives and arguments were relatively straightforward. He knew Elric's character too well, however, to believe that Elric acted from weakness or lassitude. The paradox was that Elric tolerated Yyrkoon's treachery because he was strong, because he had the power to destroy Yyrkoon whenever he cared. And Yyrkoon's own character was such that he must constantly be testing that strength of Elric's, for he knew instinctively that if Elric did weaken and order him slain, then he would have won. It was a complicated situation and Dyvim Tvar dearly wished that he was not embroiled in it. But his loyalty to the royal line of Melniboné was strong and his personal loyalty to Elric was great. He considered the idea of having Yyrkoon secretly assassinated, but he knew that such a plan would almost certainly come to nothing. Yyrkoon was a sorcerer of immense power and doubtless would be forewarned of any attempt on his life.

"Princess Cymoril," said Dyvim Tvar, "I can only pray that your brother swallows so much of his rage that it eventually poisons him."

"I will join you in that prayer, Lord of the Dragon Caves."
Together, they left the hall.

CHAPTER THREE

Riding Through the Morning: A Moment of Tranquility

The light of the early morning touched the tall towers of Imrryr and
made them scintillate. Each tower was of a different hue; there were a
thousand soft colours. There were rose pinks and pollen yellows, there
were purples and pale greens, mauves and browns and oranges, hazy
blues, whites and powdery golds, all lovely in the sunlight. Two riders
left the Dreaming City behind them and rode away from the walls,
over the green turf towards a pine forest where, amongst the shadowy
trunks, a little of the night seemed to remain. Squirrels were stirring
and foxes crept homeward; birds were singing and forest flowers
opened their petals and filled the air with delicate scent. A few insects
wandered sluggishly aloft. The contrast between life in the nearby city
and this lazy rusticity was very great and seemed to mirror some of the
contrasts existing in the mind of at least one of the riders who now dismounted and led his horse, walking knee-deep through a mass of blue
flowers. The other rider, a girl, brought her own horse to a halt but did
not dismount. Instead, she leaned casually on her high Melnibonéan
pommel and smiled at the man, her lover.

"Elric? Would you stop so near to Imrryr?"

He smiled back at her, over his shoulder. "For the moment. Our
flight was hasty. I would collect my thoughts before we ride on."

"How did you sleep last night?"

"Well enough, Cymoril, though I must have dreamed without
knowing it, for there were—there were little intimations in my head
when I awoke. But then, the meeting with Yyrkoon was not pleasant . . ."

"Do you think he plots to use sorcery against you?"

Elric shrugged. "I would know if he brought a large sorcery against me. And he knows my power. I doubt if he would dare employ wizardry."

"He has reason to believe you might not use your power. He has worried at your personality for so long—is there not a danger he will begin to worry at your skills? Testing your sorcery as he has tested your patience?"

Elric frowned. "Yes, I suppose there is that danger. But not yet, I should have thought."

"He will not be happy until you are destroyed, Elric."

"Or is destroyed himself, Cymoril." Elric stooped and picked one of the flowers. He smiled. "Your brother is inclined to absolutes, is he not? How the weak hate weakness."

Cymoril took his meaning. She dismounted and came towards him. Her thin gown matched, almost perfectly, the colour of the flowers through which she moved. He handed her the flower and she accepted it, touching its petals with her perfect lips. "And how the strong hate strength, my love. Yyrkoon is my kin and yet I give you this advice—use your strength against him."

"I could not slay him. I have not the right." Elric's face fell into familiar, brooding lines.

"You could exile him."

"Is not exile the same as death to a Melnibonéan?"

"You, yourself, have talked of traveling in the lands of the Young Kingdoms."

Elric laughed somewhat bitterly. "But perhaps I am not a true Melnibonéan. Yyrkoon has said as much—and others echo his thoughts."

"He hates you because you are contemplative. Your father was contemplative and no-one denied that he was a fitting emperor."

"My father chose not to put the results of his contemplation into his personal actions. He ruled as an emperor should. Yyrkoon, I must admit, would also rule as an emperor should. He, too, has the opportunity to make Melniboné great again. If he were emperor, he would embark on a campaign of conquest to restore our trade to its former volume, to extend our power across the earth. And that is what the majority of our folk would wish. Is it my right to deny that wish?"

"It is your right to do what you think, for you are the emperor. All who are loyal to you think as I do."

"Perhaps their loyalty is misguided. Perhaps Yyrkoon is right and I will betray that loyalty, bring doom to the Dragon Isle." His moody, crimson eyes looked directly into hers. "Perhaps I should have died as I left my mother's womb. Then Yyrkoon would have become emperor. Has Fate been thwarted?"

"Fate is never thwarted. What has happened has happened because Fate willed it thus—if, indeed, there is such a thing as Fate and if men's actions are not merely a response to other men's actions."

Elric drew a deep breath and offered her an expression tinged with irony. "Your logic leads you close to heresy, Cymoril, if we are to believe the traditions of Melniboné. Perhaps it would be better if you forgot your friendship with me."

She laughed. "You begin to sound like my brother. Are you testing my love for you, my lord?"

He began to remount his horse. "No, Cymoril, but I would advise you to test your love yourself, for I sense there is tragedy implicit in our love."

As she swung herself back into her saddle she smiled and shook her head. "You see doom in all things. Can you not accept the good gifts granted you? They are few enough, my lord."

"Aye. I'll agree with that."

They turned in their saddles, hearing hoofbeats behind them. Some distance away they saw a company of yellow-clad horsemen riding about in confusion. It was their guard, which they had left behind, wishing to ride alone.

"Come!" cried Elric. "Through the woods and over yonder hill and they'll never find us!"

They spurred their steeds through the sun-speared wood and up the steep sides of the hill beyond, racing down the other side and away across a plain where *noidel* bushes grew, their lush, poison fruit glimmering a purplish blue, a night-colour which even the light of day could not disperse. There were many such peculiar berries and herbs on Melniboné and it was to some of them that Elric owed his life. Others were used for sorcerous potions and had been sown generations before by Elric's ancestors. Now few Melnibonéans left Imrryr even to collect these harvests. Only slaves visited the greater part of the island, seeking the roots and the shrubs which made men dream monstrous and magnificent dreams, for it was in their dreams that the nobles of Melniboné found most of their pleasures; they had ever been a moody, inward-looking race and it was for this quality that Imrryr had come to be named the Dreaming City. There, even the meanest slaves chewed berries to bring them oblivion and thus were easily controlled, for they came to depend on their dreams. Only Elric himself refused such drugs, perhaps because he required so many others simply to ensure his remaining alive.

The yellow-clad guards were lost behind them and once across the plain where the *noidel* bushes grew they slowed their flight and came at length to cliffs and then the sea.

The sea shone brightly and languidly washed the white beaches below the cliffs. Seabirds wheeled in the clear sky and their cries were distant, serving only to emphasize the sense of peace which both Elric and Cymoril now had. In silence the lovers guided their horses down steep paths to the shore and there they tethered the steeds and began to walk across the sand, their hair—his white, hers jet black—waving in the wind which blew from the east.

They found a great, dry cave which caught the sounds the sea made and replied in a whispering echo. They removed their silken garments and made love tenderly in the shadows of the cave. They lay in each other's arms as the day warmed and the wind dropped. Then they went to bathe in the waters, filling the empty sky with their laughter.

When they were dry and were dressing themselves they noticed a darkening of the horizon and Elric said: "We shall be wet again before we return to Imrryr. No matter how fast we ride, the storm will catch us."

"Perhaps we should remain in the cave until it is past?" she suggested, coming close and holding her soft body against him.

"No," he said. "I must return soon, for there are potions in Imrryr I must take if my body is to retain its strength. An hour or two longer and I shall begin to weaken. You have seen me weak before, Cymoril."

She stroked his face and her eyes were sympathetic. "Aye. I've seen you weak before, Elric. Come, let's find the horses."

By the time they reached the horses the sky was grey overhead and full of boiling blackness not far away in the east. They heard the grumble of thunder and the crash of lightning. The sea was threshing as if infected by the sky's hysteria. The horses snorted and pawed at the sand, anxious to return. Even as Elric and Cymoril climbed into their saddles large spots of rain began to fall on their heads and spread over their cloaks.

Then, suddenly, they were riding at full tilt back to Imrryr while the lightning flashed around them and the thunder roared like a furious giant, like some great old Lord of Chaos attempting to break through, unbidden, into the Realm of Earth.

Cymoril glanced at Elric's pale face, illuminated for a moment by a flash of sky-fire, and she felt a chill come upon her then and the chill had nothing to do with the wind or the rain, for it seemed to her in that second that the gentle scholar she loved had been transformed by the elements into a hell-driven demon, into a monster with barely a semblance of humanity. His crimson eyes had flared from the whiteness of his skull like the very flames of the Higher Hell; his hair had been whipped upward so that it had become the crest of a sinister war-helm and, by a trick of the stormlight, his mouth had seemed twisted in a mixture of rage and agony.

And suddenly Cymoril knew.

She knew, profoundly, that their morning's ride was the last moment of peace the two of them would ever experience again.

The storm was a sign from the gods themselves—a warning of storms to come.

She looked again at her lover. Elric was laughing. He had turned his face upward so that the warm rain fell upon it, so that the water splashed into his open mouth. The laughter was the easy, unsophisticated laughter of a happy child.

Cymoril tried to laugh back, but then she had to turn her face away so that he should not see it. For Cymoril had begun to weep.

She was weeping still when Imrryr came in sight—a black and grotesque silhouette against a line of brightness which was the as yet untainted western horizon.

CHAPTER FOUR

Prisoners: Their Secrets Are Taken from Them

The men in yellow armour saw Elric and Cymoril as the two approached the smallest of the eastern gates.

"They have found us at last," smiled Elric through the rain, "but somewhat belatedly, eh, Cymoril?"

Cymoril, still embattled with her sense of doom, merely nodded and tried to smile in reply.

Elric took this as an expression of disappointment, nothing more, and called to his guards: "Ho, men! Soon we shall all be dry again!"

But the captain of the guard rode up urgently, crying: "My lord emperor is needed at Monshanjik Tower where spies are held."

"Spies?"

"Aye, my lord." The man's face was pale. Water cascaded from his helm and darkened his thin cloak. His horse was hard to control and kept sidestepping through pools of water, which had gathered wherever the road was in disrepair. "Caught in the maze this morning. Southern barbarians, by their chequered dress. We are holding them until the emperor himself can question them."

Elric waved his hand. "Then lead on, captain. Let's see the brave fools who dare Melniboné's sea-maze."

The Tower of Monshanjik had been named for the wizard-architect who had designed the sea-maze millennia before. The maze was the only means of reaching the great harbour of Imrryr and its secrets had been carefully guarded, for it was their greatest protection against sudden attack. The maze was complicated and pilots had to be specially trained to steer ships through it. Before the maze had been built, the harbour had been a kind of inland lagoon, fed by the sea which swept in through a system of natural caverns in the towering cliff which rose between lagoon and ocean. There were five separate routes through the

sea-maze and any individual pilot knew but one. In the outer wall of
the cliff there were five entrances. Here Young Kingdom ships waited
until a pilot came aboard. Then one of the gates to one of the entrances
would be lifted; all aboard the ship would be blindfolded and sent
below save for the oar-master and the steersman who would also be
masked in heavy steel helms so that they could see nothing, do nothing
but obey the complicated instructions of the pilot. And if a Young
Kingdom ship should fail to obey any of those instructions and should
crush itself against the rock walls, Melniboné did not mourn for it and
any survivors from the crew would be taken as slaves. All who sought
to trade with the Dreaming City understood the risks, but scores of
merchants came every month to dare the dangers of the maze and
trade their own poor goods for the splendid riches of Melniboné.

The Tower of Monshanjik stood overlooking the harbour and the
massive mole which jutted out into the middle of the lagoon. It was a
sea-green tower and was squat compared with most of those in Imrryr,
though still a beautiful and tapering construction, with wide windows
so that the whole of the harbour could be seen from it. From Monshanjik Tower most of the business of the harbour was done and in its lower
cellars were kept any prisoners who had broken any of the myriad rules
governing the functioning of the harbour. Leaving Cymoril to return
to the palace with a guard, Elric entered the tower, riding through the
great archway at the base, scattering not a few merchants who were
waiting for permission to begin their bartering, for the whole of the
ground floor was full of sailors, merchants and Melnibonéan officials
engaged in the business of trade, though it was not here that the actual
wares were displayed. The great echoing babble of a thousand voices
engaged in a thousand separate aspects of bargaining slowly stilled as
Elric and his guard rode arrogantly through to another dark arch at the
far end of the hall. This arch opened onto a ramp which sloped and
curved down into the bowels of the tower.

Down this ramp clattered the horsemen, passing slaves, servants
and officials who stepped hastily aside, bowing low as they recognized
the emperor. Great brands illuminated the tunnel, guttering and

smoking and casting distorted shadows onto the smooth obsidian walls. A chill was in the air now, and a dampness, for water washed about the outer walls below the quays of Imrryr. And still the emperor rode on and still the ramp struck lower through the glassy rock. And then a wave of heat rose to meet them and shifting light could be seen ahead and they passed into a chamber that was full of smoke and the scent of fear. From the low ceiling hung chains and from eight of the chains, swinging by their feet, hung four people. Their clothes had been torn from them, but their bodies were clothed in blood from tiny wounds, precise but severe, made by the artist who stood, scalpel in hand, surveying his handiwork.

The artist was tall and very thin, almost like a skeleton in his stained, white garments. His lips were thin, his eyes were slits, his fingers were thin, his hair was thin and the scalpel he held was thin, too, almost invisible save when it flashed in the light from the fire which erupted from a pit on the far side of the cavern. The artist was named Doctor Jest and the art he practised was a performing art rather than a creative one (though he could argue otherwise with some conviction): the art of drawing secrets from those who kept them. Doctor Jest was the Chief Interrogator of Melniboné. He turned sinuously as Elric entered, the scalpel held between the thin thumb and the thin forefinger of his right hand; he stood poised and expectant, almost like a dancer, and then bowed from the waist.

"My sweet emperor!" His voice was thin. It rushed from his thin throat as if bent on escape and one was inclined to wonder if one had heard the words at all, so quickly had they come and gone.

"Doctor. Are these the southlanders caught this morning?"

"Indeed they are, my lord." Another sinuous bow. "For your pleasure."

Coldly Elric inspected the prisoners. He felt no sympathy for them. They were spies. Their actions had led them to this pass. They had known what would happen to them if caught. But one of them was a boy and another a woman, it appeared, though they writhed so in their chains it was quite difficult to tell at first. It seemed a shame. Then the woman snapped what remained of her teeth at him and hissed: "Demon!" And Elric stepped back, saying:

"Have they informed you of what they were doing in our maze, doctor?"

"They still tantalize me with hints. They have a fine sense of drama. I appreciate that. They are here, I would say, to map a route through the maze which a force of raiders might then follow. But they have so far withheld the details. That is the game. We all understand how it must be played."

"And when will they tell you, Doctor Jest?"

"Oh, very soon, my lord."

"It would be best to know if we are to expect attackers. The sooner we know, the less time we shall lose dealing with the attack when it comes. Do you not agree, doctor?"

"I do, my lord."

"Very well." Elric was irritated by this break in his day. It had spoiled the pleasure of the ride, it had brought him face to face with his duties too quickly.

Doctor Jest returned to his charges and, reaching out with his free hand, expertly seized the genitals of one of the male prisoners. The scalpel flashed. There was a groan. Doctor Jest tossed something onto the fire. Elric sat in the chair prepared for him. He was bored rather than disgusted by the rituals attendant upon the gathering of information and the discordant screams, the clash of the chains, the thin whisperings of Doctor Jest, all served to ruin the feeling of well-being he had retained even as he reached the chamber. But it was one of his kingly duties to attend such rituals and attend this one he must until the information was presented to him and he could congratulate his Chief Interrogator and issue orders as to the means of dealing with any attack and even when that was over he must confer with admirals and with generals, probably through the rest of the night, choosing between arguments, deciding on the deposition of men and ships. With a poorly disguised yawn he leaned back and watched as Doctor Jest ran fingers and scalpel, tongue, tongs and pincers over the bodies. He was soon thinking of other matters: philosophical problems which he had still failed to resolve.

It was not that Elric was inhumane; it was that he was, still, a Melnibonéan. He had been used to such sights since childhood. He could not have saved the prisoners, even if he had desired, without going against every tradition of the Dragon Isle. And in this case it was a simple matter of a threat being met by the best methods available. He had become used to shutting off those feelings which conflicted with his duties as emperor. If there had been any point in freeing the four who danced now at Doctor Jest's pleasure he would have freed them, but there was no point and the four would have been astonished if they had received any other treatment than this. Where moral decisions were concerned Imrryr was, by and large, practical. He would make his decision in the context of what action he could take. In this case, he could take no action. Such a reaction had become second nature to him. His desire was not to reform Melniboné but to reform himself, not to initiate action but to know the best way of responding to the actions of others. Here, the decision was easy to make. A spy was an aggressor. One defended oneself against aggressors in the best possible way. The methods employed by Doctor Jest were the best methods.

"My lord?"

Absently, Elric looked up.

"We have the information now, my lord." Doctor Jest's thin voice whispered across the chamber. Two sets of chains were now empty and slaves were gathering things up from the floor and flinging them on the fire. The two remaining shapeless lumps reminded Elric of meat carefully prepared by a chef. One of the lumps still quivered a little, but the other was still.

Doctor Jest slid his instruments into a thin case he carried in a pouch at his belt. His white garments were almost completely covered in stains.

"It seems there have been other spies before these," Doctor Jest told his master. "These came merely to confirm the route. If they do not return in time, the barbarians will still sail."

"But surely they will know that we expect them?" Elric said.

"Probably not, my lord. Rumours have been spread amongst the Young Kingdom merchants and sailors that four spies were seen in the maze and were speared—slain whilst trying to escape."

"I see." Elric frowned. "Then our best plan will be to lay a trap for the raiders."

"Aye, my lord."

"You know the route they have chosen?"

"Aye, my lord."

Elric turned to one of his guards. "Have messages sent to all our generals and admirals. What's the hour?"

"The hour of sunset is just past, my liege."

"Tell them to assemble before the Ruby Throne at two hours past sunset."

Wearily, Elric rose. "You have done well, as usual, Doctor Jest."

The thin artist bowed low, seeming to fold himself in two. A thin and somewhat unctuous sigh was his reply.

CHAPTER FIVE

A Battle: The King Proves His War-Skill

Yyrkoon was the first to arrive, all clad in martial finery, accompanied by two massive guards, each holding one of the prince's ornate war-banners.

"My emperor!" Yyrkoon's shout was proud and disdainful. "Would you let me command the warriors? It will relieve you of that care when, doubtless, you have many other concerns with which to occupy your time."

Elric replied impatiently: "You are most thoughtful, Prince Yyrkoon, but fear not for me. I shall command the armies and the navies of Melniboné, for that is the duty of the emperor."

Yyrkoon glowered and stepped to one side as Dyvim Tvar, Lord of the Dragon Caves, entered. He had no guard whatsoever with him and it seemed he had dressed hastily. He carried his helmet under his arm.

"My emperor—I bring news of the dragons . . ."

"I thank you, Dyvim Tvar, but wait until all my commanders are assembled and impart that news to them, too."

Dyvim Tvar bowed and went to stand on the opposite side of the hall to that on which Prince Yyrkoon stood.

Gradually the warriors arrived until a score of great captains waited at the foot of the steps which led to the Ruby Throne where Elric sat. Elric himself still wore the clothes in which he had gone riding that morning. He had not had time to change and had until a little while before been consulting maps of the mazes—maps which only he could read and which, at normal times, were hidden by magical means from any who might attempt to find them.

"Southlanders would steal Imrryr's wealth and slay us all," Elric began. "They believe they have found a way through our sea-maze. A fleet of a hundred warships sails on Melniboné even now. Tomorrow it will wait below the horizon until dusk, then it will sail to the maze and enter. By midnight it expects to reach the harbour and to have taken the Dreaming City before dawn. Is that possible, I wonder?"

"No!" Many spoke the single word.

"No." Elric smiled. "But how shall we best enjoy this little war they offer us?"

Yyrkoon, as ever, was first to shout. "Let us go to meet them now, with dragons and with battle-barges. Let us pursue them to their own land and take their war to them. Let us attack their nations and burn their cities! Let us conquer them and thus ensure our own security!"

Dyvim Tvar spoke up again:

"No dragons," he said.

"What?" Yyrkoon whirled. "What?"

"No dragons, prince. They will not be awakened. The dragons sleep in their caverns, exhausted by their last engagement on your behalf."

"Mine?"

"You would use them in our conflict with the Vilmirian pirates. I told you that I would prefer to save them for a larger engagement. But you flew them against the pirates and you burned their little boats and now the dragons sleep."

Yyrkoon glowered. He looked up at Elric. "I did not expect . . ."

Elric raised his hand. "We need not use our dragons until such a time as we really need them. This attack from the southlander fleet is nothing. But we will conserve our strength if we bide our time. Let them think we are unready. Let them enter the maze. Once the whole hundred are through, we close in, blocking off all routes in or out of the maze. Trapped, they will be crushed by us."

Yyrkoon looked pettishly at his feet, evidently wishing he could think of some flaw in the plan. Tall, old Admiral Magum Colim in his sea-green armour stepped forward and bowed. "The golden battle-barges of Imrryr are ready to defend their city, my liege. It will take time, however, to manoeuvre them into position. It is doubtful if all will fit into the maze at once."

"Then sail some of them out now and hide them around the coast, so that they can wait for any survivors that may escape our attack," Elric instructed him.

"A useful plan, my liege." Magum Colim bowed and sank back into the crowd of his peers.

The debate continued for some time and then they were ready and about to leave. But then Prince Yyrkoon bellowed once more:

"I repeat my offer to the emperor. His person is too valuable to risk in battle. My person—it is worthless. Let me command the warriors of both land and sea while the emperor may remain at the palace, untroubled by the battle, confident that it will be won and the southlanders trounced—perhaps there is a book he wishes to finish?"

Elric smiled. "Again I thank you for your concern, Prince Yyrkoon. But an emperor must exercise his body as well as his mind. I will command the warriors tomorrow."

When Elric arrived back at his apartments it was to discover that Tanglebones had already laid out his heavy, black war-gear. Here was the armour which had served a hundred Melnibonéan emperors; an armour which was forged by sorcery to give it a strength unequaled on the Realm of Earth, which could, so rumour went, even withstand the bite of the mythical runeblades, Stormbringer and Mournblade, which had been wielded by the wickedest of Melniboné's many wicked rulers before being seized by the Lords of the Higher Worlds and hidden for ever in a realm where even those lords might rarely venture.

The face of the tangled man was full of joy as he touched each piece of armour, each finely balanced weapon, with his long, gnarled fingers. His seamed face looked up to regard Elric's care-ravaged features. "Oh, my lord! Oh, my king! Soon you will know the joy of the fight!"

"Aye, Tanglebones—and let us hope it will be a joy."

"I taught you all the skills—the art of the sword and the poignard—the art of the bow—the art of the spear, both mounted and on foot. And you learned well, for all they say you are weak. Save one, there's no better swordsman in Melniboné."

"Prince Yyrkoon could be better than me," Elric said reflectively. "Could he not?"

"I said 'save one,' my lord."

"And Yyrkoon is that one. Well, one day perhaps we'll be able to test the matter. I'll bathe before I don all that metal."

"Best make speed, master. From what I hear, there is much to do."

"And I'll sleep after I've bathed." Elric smiled at his old friend's consternation. "It will be better thus, for I cannot personally direct the barges into position. I am needed to command the fray—and that I will do better when I've rested."

"If you think it good, lord king, then it is good."

"And you are astonished. You are too eager, Tanglebones, to get me into all that stuff and see me strut about in it as if I were Arioch himself . . ."

Tanglebones's hand flew to his mouth as if he had spoken the words, not his master, and he was trying to block them. His eyes widened.

Elric laughed. "You think I speak bold heresies, eh? Well, I've spoken worse without any ill befalling me. On Melniboné, Tanglebones, the emperors control the demons, not the reverse."

"So you say, my liege."

"It is the truth." Elric swept from the room, calling for his slaves. The war-fever filled him and he was jubilant.

Now he was in all his black gear: the massive breastplate, the padded jerkin, the long greaves, the mail gauntlets. At his side was a five-foot broadsword which, it was said, had belonged to a human hero called Aubec. Resting on the deck against the golden rail of the bridge was the great round war-board, his shield, bearing the sign of the swooping dragon. And a helm was on his head; a black helm, with a dragon's head craning over the peak, and dragon's wings flaring backward above it, and a dragon's tail curling down the back. All the helm was black, but within the helm there was a white shadow from which glared two crimson orbs, and from the sides of the helm strayed wisps of milk-white hair, almost like smoke escaping from a burning building. And, as the helm turned in what little light came from the lantern hanging at the base of the mainmast, the white shadow sharpened to reveal features— fine, handsome features—a straight nose, curved lips, up-slanting eyes. The face of Emperor Elric of Melniboné peered into the gloom of the maze as he listened for the first sounds of the sea-raiders' approach.

He stood on the high bridge of the great golden battle-barge which, like all its kind, resembled a floating ziggurat equipped with masts and sails and oars and catapults. The ship was called *The Son of the Pyaray* and it was the flagship of the fleet. The Grand Admiral Magum Colim stood beside Elric. Like Dyvim Tvar, the admiral was one of Elric's few close friends. He had known Elric all his life and had encouraged him to learn all he could concerning the running of fighting ships and fighting fleets. Privately Magum Colim might fear that Elric was too scholarly and introspective to rule Melniboné, but he accepted Elric's right to rule and was made angry and impatient by the talk of the likes of Yyrkoon. Prince Yyrkoon was also aboard the flagship, though at this moment he was below, inspecting the war-engines.

The Son of the Pyaray lay at anchor in a huge grotto, one of hundreds built into the walls of the maze when the maze itself was built, and designed for just this purpose—to hide a battle-barge. There was just enough height for the masts and enough width for the oars to move freely. Each of the golden battle-barges was equipped with banks of oars, each bank containing between twenty and thirty oars on either side. The banks were four, five or six decks high and, as in the case of *The Son of the Pyaray*, might have three independent steering systems, fore and aft. Being armoured all in gold, the ships were virtually indestructible, and, for all their massive size, they could move swiftly and manoeuvre delicately when occasion demanded. It was not the first time they had waited for their enemies in these grottoes. It would not be the last (though when next they waited it would be in greatly different circumstances).

The battle-barges of Melniboné were rarely seen on the open seas these days, but once they had sailed the oceans of the world like fearsome floating mountains of gold and they had brought terror whenever they were sighted. The fleet had been larger then, comprising hundreds of craft. Now there were less than forty ships. But forty would suffice. Now, in damp darkness, they awaited their enemies.

Listening to the hollow slap of the water against the sides of the ship, Elric wished that he had been able to conceive a better plan than this. He was sure that this one would work, but he regretted the waste of lives, both Melnibonéan and barbarian. It would have been better if some way could have been devised of frightening the barbarians away rather than trapping them in the sea-maze. The southlander fleet was not the first to have been attracted by Imrryr's fabulous wealth. The southlander crews were not the first to entertain the belief that the Melnibonéans, because they never now ventured far from the Dreaming City, had become decadent and unable to defend their treasures. And so the southlanders must be destroyed in order to make the lesson clear. Melniboné was still strong. She was strong enough, in Yyrkoon's view, to resume her former dominance of the world—strong in sorcery if not in soldiery.

"Hist!" Admiral Magum Colim craned forward. "Was that the sound of an oar?"

Elric nodded. "I think so."

Now they heard regular splashes, as of rows of oars dipping in and out of the water, and they heard the creak of timbers. The southlanders were coming. *The Son of the Pyaray* was the ship nearest to the entrance and it would be the first to move out, but only when the last of the southlanders' ships had passed them. Admiral Magum Colim bent and extinguished the lantern, then, quickly, quietly, he descended to inform his crew of the raiders' coming.

Not long before, Yyrkoon had used his sorcery to summon a peculiar mist, which hid the golden barges from view, but through which those on the Melnibonéan ships could peer. Now Elric saw torches burning in the channel ahead as carefully the reavers negotiated the maze. Within the space of a few minutes ten of the galleys had passed the grotto. Admiral Magum Colim rejoined Elric on the bridge and now Prince Yyrkoon was with him. Yyrkoon, too, wore a dragon helm, though less magnificent than Elric's, for Elric was chief of the few surviving Dragon Princes of Melniboné. Yyrkoon was grinning through the gloom and his eyes gleamed in anticipation of the bloodletting to come. Elric wished that Prince Yyrkoon had chosen another ship than this, but it was Yyrkoon's right to be aboard the flagship and he could not deny it.

Now half the hundred vessels had gone past.

Yyrkoon's armour creaked as, impatiently, he waited, pacing the bridge, his gauntleted hand on the hilt of his broadsword. "Soon," he kept saying to himself. "Soon."

And then their anchor was groaning upwards and their oars were plunging into the water as the last southland ship went by and they shot from the grotto into the channel ramming the enemy galley amidships and smashing it in two.

A great yell went up from the barbarian crew. Men were flung in all directions. Torches danced erratically on the remains of the deck as men tried to save themselves from slipping into the dark, chill waters of the channel. A few brave spears rattled against the sides of the Melnibonéan flag-galley as it began to turn amongst the debris it had created. But Imrryrian archers returned the shots and the few survivors went down.

The sound of this swift conflict was the signal to the other battle-barges. In perfect order they came from both sides of the high rock walls and it must have seemed to the astonished barbarians that the great golden ships had actually emerged from solid stone—ghost ships filled with demons who rained spears, arrows and brands upon them. Now the whole of the twisting channel was confusion and a medley of war-shouts echoed and boomed and the clash of steel upon steel was like the savage hissing of some monstrous snake, and the raiding fleet itself resembled a snake which had been broken into a hundred pieces by the tall, implacable golden ships of Melniboné. These ships seemed almost serene as they moved against their enemies, their grappling irons flashing out to catch wooden decks and rails and draw the galleys nearer so that they might be destroyed.

But the southlanders were brave and they kept their heads after their initial astonishment. Three of their galleys headed directly for *The Son of the Pyaray*, recognizing it as the flagship. Fire arrows sailed high and dropped down into the decks which were wooden and not protected by the golden armour, starting fires wherever they fell, or else bringing blazing death to the men they struck.

Elric raised his shield above his head and two arrows struck it, bouncing, still flaring, to a lower deck. He leapt over the rail, following the arrows, jumping down to the widest and most exposed deck where his warriors were grouping, ready to deal with the attacking galleys. Catapults thudded and balls of blue fire swished through the blackness, narrowly missing all three galleys. Another volley followed and one mass of fire struck the far galley's mast and then burst upon the deck, scattering huge flames wherever it touched. Grapples snaked out and seized the first galley, dragging it close and Elric was amongst the first to leap down onto the deck, rushing forward to where he saw the southland captain, dressed all in crude, chequered armour, a chequered surcoat over that, a big sword in both his huge hands, bellowing at his men to resist the Melnibonéan dogs.

As Elric approached the bridge three barbarians armed with curved swords and small, oblong shields ran at him. Their faces were full of fear, but there was determination there as well, as if they knew they must die but planned to wreak as much destruction as they could before their souls were taken.

Shifting his war-board onto his arm, Elric took his own broadsword in both hands and charged the sailors, knocking one off his feet with the lip of the shield and smashing the collar-bone of another. The remaining barbarian skipped aside and thrust his curved sword at Elric's face. Elric barely escaped the thrust and the sharp edge of the sword grazed his cheek, bringing out a drop or two of blood. Elric swung the broadsword like a scythe and it bit deep into the barbarian's waist, almost cutting him in two. He struggled for a moment, unable to believe that he was dead but then, as Elric yanked the sword free, he closed his eyes and dropped. The man who had been struck by Elric's shield was staggering to his feet as Elric whirled, saw him, and smashed the broadsword into his skull. Now the way was clear to the bridge. Elric began to climb the ladder, noting that the captain had seen him and was waiting for him at the top.

Elric raised his shield to take the captain's first blow. Through all the noise he thought he heard the man shouting at him.

"Die, you white-faced demon! Die! You have no place on this earth any longer!"

Elric was almost diverted from defending himself by these words. They rang true to him. Perhaps he really had no place on the earth. Perhaps that was why Melniboné was slowly collapsing, why fewer children were born every year, why the dragons themselves were no longer breeding. He let the captain strike another blow at the shield, then he reached under it and swung at the man's legs. But the captain had anticipated the move and jumped backwards. This, however, gave Elric time to run up the few remaining steps and stand on the deck, facing the captain.

The man's face was almost as pale as Elric's. He was sweating and he was panting and his eyes had misery in them as well as a wild fear.

"You should leave us alone," Elric heard himself saying. "We offer you no harm, barbarian. When did Melniboné last sail against the Young Kingdoms?"

"You offer us harm by your very presence, Whiteface. There is your sorcery. There are your customs. And there is your arrogance."

"Is that why you came here? Was your attack motivated by disgust for us? Or would you help yourselves to our wealth? Admit it, captain—greed brought you to Melniboné."

"At least greed is an honest quality, an understandable one. But you creatures are not human. Worse—you are not gods, though you behave as if you were. Your day is over and you must be wiped out, your city destroyed, your sorceries forgotten."

Elric nodded. "Perhaps you are right, captain."

"I am right. Our holy men say so. Our seers predict your downfall. The Chaos Lords whom you serve will themselves bring about that downfall."

"The Chaos Lords no longer have any interest in the affairs of Melniboné. They took away their power nearly a thousand years since." Elric watched the captain carefully, judging the distance between them. "Perhaps that is why our own power waned. Or perhaps we merely became tired of power."

"Be that as it may," the captain said, wiping his sweating brow, "your time is over. You must be destroyed once and for all." And then he groaned, for Elric's broadsword had come under his chequered breastplate and gone up through his stomach and into his lungs.

One knee bent, one leg stretched behind him, Elric began to withdraw the long sword, looking up into the barbarian's face which had now assumed an expression of reconciliation. "That was unfair, Whiteface. We had barely begun to talk and you cut the conversation short. You are most skillful. May you writhe for ever in the Higher Hell. Farewell."

Elric hardly knew why, after the captain had fallen face down on the deck, he hacked twice at the neck until the head rolled off the body, rolled to the side of the bridge and was then kicked over the side so that it sank into the cold, deep water.

And then Yyrkoon came up behind Elric and he was still grinning.

"You fight fiercely and well, my lord emperor. That dead man was right."

"Right?" Elric glared at his cousin. "Right?"

"Aye—in his assessment of your prowess." And, chuckling, Yyrkoon went to supervise his men who were finishing off the few remaining raiders.

Elric did not know why he had refused to hate Yyrkoon before. But now he did hate Yyrkoon. At that moment he would gladly have slain him. It was as if Yyrkoon had looked deeply into Elric's soul and expressed contempt for what he had seen there.

Suddenly Elric was overwhelmed by an angry misery and he wished with all his heart that he was not a Melnibonéan, that he was not an emperor and that Yyrkoon had never been born.

CHAPTER SIX

Pursuit: A Deliberate Treachery

Like haughty leviathans the great golden battle-barges swam through the wreckage of the reaver fleet. A few ships burned and a few were still sinking, but most had sunk into the unplumbable depths of the channel. The burning ships sent strange shadows dancing against the dank walls of the sea-caverns, as if the ghosts of the slain offered a last salute before departing to the sea-depths where, it was said, a Chaos king still ruled, crewing his eerie fleets with the souls of all who died in conflict upon the oceans of the world. Or perhaps they went to a gentler doom, serving Straasha, Lord of the Water Elementals, who ruled the upper reaches of the sea.

But a few had escaped. Somehow the southland sailors had got past the massive battle-barges, sailed back through the channel and must even now have reached the open sea. This was reported to the flagship where Elric, Magum Colim and Prince Yyrkoon now stood together again on the bridge, surveying the destruction they had wreaked.

"Then we must pursue them and finish them," said Yyrkoon. He was sweating and his dark face glistened; his eyes were alight with fever. "We must follow them."

Elric shrugged. He was weak. He had brought no extra drugs with him to replenish his strength. He wished to go back to Imrryr and rest. He was tired of bloodletting, tired of Yyrkoon and tired, most of all, of himself. The hatred he felt for his cousin was draining him still further—and he hated the hatred; that was the worst part. "No," he said. "Let them go."

"Let them go? Unpunished? Come now, my lord king! That is not our way!" Prince Yyrkoon turned to the aging admiral. "Is that our way, Admiral Magum Colim?"

Magum Colim shrugged. He, too, was tired, but privately he agreed with Prince Yyrkoon. An enemy of Melniboné should be punished for daring even to think of attacking the Dreaming City. Yet he said: "The emperor must decide."

"Let them go," said Elric again. He leant heavily against the rail. "Let them carry the news back to their own barbarian land. Let them say how the Dragon Princes defeated them. The news will spread. I believe we shall not be troubled by raiders again for some time."

"The Young Kingdoms are full of fools," Yyrkoon replied. "They will not believe the news. There will always be raiders. The best way to warn them will be to make sure that not one southlander remains alive or uncaptured."

Elric drew a deep breath and tried to fight the faintness which threatened to overwhelm him. "Prince Yyrkoon, you are trying my patience . . ."

"But, my emperor, I think only of the good of Melniboné. Surely you do not want your people to say that you are weak, that you fear a fight with but five southland galleys?"

This time Elric's anger brought him strength. "Who will say that Elric is weak? Will it be you, Yyrkoon?" He knew that his next statement was senseless, but there was nothing he could do to stop it. "Very well, let us pursue these poor little boats and sink them. And let us make haste. I am weary of it all."

There was a mysterious light in Yyrkoon's eyes as he turned away to relay the orders.

The sky was turning from black to grey when the Melnibonéan fleet reached the open sea and turned its prows south towards the Boiling Sea and the Southern Continent beyond. The barbarian ships would not sail through the Boiling Sea—no mortal ship could do that, it was said—but would sail around it. Not that the barbarian ships would even reach the edges of the Boiling Sea, for the huge battle-barges were fast-sailing vessels. The slaves who pulled the oars were full of a drug which increased their speed and their strength for a score or so of hours, before it slew them. And now the sails billowed out, catching the breeze. Golden mountains, skimming rapidly over the sea, these ships; their method of construction was a secret lost even to the Melnibonéans (who had forgotten so much of their lore). It was easy to imagine how men of the Young Kingdoms hated Melniboné and its inventions, for it did seem that the battle-barges belonged to an older, alien age, as they bore down upon the fleeing galleys now sighted on the horizon.

The Son of the Pyaray was in the lead of the rest of the fleet and was priming its catapults well before any of its fellows had seen the enemy. Perspiring slaves gingerly manhandled the viscous stuff of the fireballs, getting them into the bronze cups of the catapults by means of long, spoon-ended tongs. It flickered in the pre-dawn gloom.

Now slaves climbed the steps to the bridge and brought wine and food on platinum platters for the three Dragon Princes who had remained there since the pursuit had begun. Elric could not summon the strength to eat, but he seized a tall cup of yellow wine and drained it. The stuff was strong and revived him a trifle. He had another cup poured and drank that as swiftly as the other. He peered ahead. It was almost dawn. There was a line of purple light on the horizon. "At the first sign of the sun's disc," Elric said, "let loose the fireballs."

"I will give the order," said Magum Colim, wiping his lips and putting down the meat bone on which he had been chewing. He left the bridge. Elric heard his feet striking the steps heavily. All at once the albino felt surrounded by enemies. There had been something strange in Magum Colim's manner during the argument with Prince Yyrkoon. Elric tried to shake off such foolish thoughts. But the weariness, the self-doubt, the open mockery of his cousin, all succeeded in increasing the feeling that he was alone and without friends in the world. Even Cymoril and Dyvim Tvar were, finally, Melnibonéans and could not understand the peculiar concerns which moved him and dictated his actions. Perhaps it would be wise to renounce everything Melnibonéan and wander the world as an anonymous soldier of fortune, serving whoever needed his aid?

The dull red semi-circle of the sun showed above the black line of the distant water. There came a series of booming sounds from the forward decks of the flagship as the catapults released their fiery shot; there was a whistling scream, fading away, and it seemed that a dozen meteors leapt through the sky, hurtling towards the five galleys which were now little more than thirty ship-lengths away.

Elric saw two galleys flare, but the remaining three began to sail a zig-zag course and avoided the fireballs which landed on the water and burned fitfully for a while before sinking (still burning) into the depths.

More fireballs were prepared and Elric heard Yyrkoon shout from the other side of the bridge, ordering the slaves to greater exertions. Then the fleeing vessels changed their tactics, evidently realizing that they could not save themselves for long, and, spreading out, sailed towards *The Son of the Pyaray*, just as the other ships had done in the sea-maze. It was not merely their courage that Elric admired but their manoeuvring skill and the speed at which they had arrived at this logical, if hopeless, decision.

The sun was behind the southland ships as they turned. Three brave silhouettes drew nearer to the Melnibonéan flagship as scarlet stained the sea, as if in anticipation of the bloodletting to come.

Another volley of fireballs was flung from the flagship and the leading galley tried to tack round and avoid it, but two of the fiery globes spattered directly on its deck and soon the whole ship was alive with flame. Burning men leapt into the water. Burning men shot arrows at the flagship. Burning men fell slowly from their positions in the

rigging. The burning men died, but the burning ship came on; someone had lashed the steering arm and directed the galley at *The Son of
the Pyaray*. It crashed into the golden side of the battle-barge and some
of the fire splashed on the deck where the main catapults were in position. A cauldron containing the fire-stuff caught and immediately men
were running from all quarters of the ship to try to douse the flame.
Elric grinned as he saw what the barbarians had done. Perhaps that
ship had deliberately allowed itself to be fired. Now the majority of the
flagship's complement was engaged with putting out the blaze—while
the southland ships drew alongside, threw up their own grapples, and
began to board.

"'Ware boarders!" Elric shouted, long after he might have warned
his crew. "Barbarians attack."

He saw Yyrkoon whirl round, see the situation, and rush down the
steps from the bridge. "You stay there, my lord king," he flung at Elric
as he disappeared. "You are plainly too weary to fight."

And Elric summoned all that was left of his strength and stumbled
after his cousin, to help in the defense of the ship.

The barbarians were not fighting for their lives—they knew those
to be taken already. They were fighting for their pride. They wanted to
take one Melnibonéan ship down with them and that ship must be the
flagship itself. It was hard to be contemptuous of such men. They knew
that even if they took the flagship the other ships of the golden fleet
would soon overwhelm them.

But the other ships were still some distance away. Many lives
would be lost before they reached the flagship.

On the lowest deck Elric found himself facing a pair of tall barbarians, each armed with a curved blade and a small, oblong shield. He
lunged forward, but his armour seemed to drag at his limbs, his own
shield and sword were so heavy that he could barely lift them. Two
swords struck his helm, almost simultaneously. He lunged back and
caught a man in the arm, rammed the other with his shield. A curved
blade clanged on his backplate and he all but lost his footing. There
was choking smoke everywhere, and heat, and the tumult of battle.
Desperately he swung about him and felt his broadsword bite deep into

flesh. One of his opponents fell, gurgling, with blood spouting from his mouth and nose. The other lunged. Elric stepped backwards, fell over the corpse of the man he had slain, and went down, his broadsword held out before him in one hand. And as the triumphant barbarian leapt forward to finish the albino, Elric caught him on the point of the broadsword, running him through. The dead man fell towards Elric who did not feel the impact, for he had already fainted. Not for the first time had his deficient blood, no longer enriched by drugs, betrayed him.

He tasted salt and thought at first it was blood. But it was sea water. A wave had risen over the deck and momentarily revived him. He struggled to crawl from under the dead man and then he heard a voice he recognized. He twisted his head and looked up.

Prince Yyrkoon stood there. He was grinning. He was full of glee at Elric's plight. Black, oily smoke still drifted everywhere, but the sounds of the fight had died.

"Are—are we victorious, cousin?" Elric spoke painfully.

"Aye. The barbarians are all dead now. We are about to sail for Imrryr."

Elric was relieved. He would begin to die soon if he could not get to his store of potions.

His relief must have been evident, for Yyrkoon laughed. "It is as well the battle did not last longer, my lord, or we should have been without our leader."

"Help me up, cousin." Elric hated to ask Prince Yyrkoon any favour, but he had no choice. He stretched out his empty hand. "I am fit enough to inspect the ship."

Yyrkoon came forward as if to take the hand, but then he hesitated, still grinning. "But, my lord, I disagree. You will be dead by the time this ship turns eastward again."

"Nonsense. Even without the drugs I can live for a considerable time, though movement is difficult. Help me up, Yyrkoon, I command you."

"You cannot command me, Elric. I am emperor now, you see."

"Be wary, cousin. I can overlook such treachery, but others will not. I shall be forced to . . ."

Yyrkoon swung his legs over Elric's body and went to the rail. Here were bolts which fixed one section of the rail in place when it was not used for the gangplank. Yyrkoon slowly released the bolts and kicked the section of rail into the water.

Now Elric's efforts to free himself became more desperate. But he could hardly move at all.

Yyrkoon, on the other hand, seemed possessed of unnatural strength. He bent and easily flung the corpse away from Elric.

"Yyrkoon," said Elric, "this is unwise of you."

"I was never a cautious man, cousin, as well you know." Yyrkoon placed a booted foot against Elric's ribs and began to shove. Elric slid towards the gap in the rail. He could see the black sea heaving below. "Farewell, Elric. Now a true Melnibonéan shall sit upon the Ruby Throne. And, who knows, might even make Cymoril his queen? It has not been unheard of . . ."

And Elric felt himself rolling, felt himself fall, felt himself strike the water, felt his armour pulling him below the surface. And Yyrkoon's last words drummed in Elric's ears like the persistent booming of the waves against the sides of the golden battle-barge.

BOOK TWO

Less certain of himself or his destiny than ever, the albino
king must perforce bring his powers of sorcery into play,
conscious of embarking on actions which will make of his
life something other than he might have wished it to be.
And now matters must be settled. He must begin to
rule. He must become cruel. But even in this
he will find himself thwarted.

CHAPTER ONE

The Caverns of the Sea-King

ELRIC SANK RAPIDLY, desperately trying to keep the last of
his breath in his body. He had no strength to swim and the
weight of the armour denied any hope of his rising to the surface and
being sighted by Magum Colim or one of the others still loyal to him.

The roaring in his ears gradually faded to a whisper so that it
sounded as if little voices were speaking to him, the voices of the water
elementals with whom, in his youth, he had had a kind of friendship,
and the pain in his lungs faded; the red mist cleared from his eyes and
he thought he saw the face of his father, Sadric, of Cymoril and, fleet-
ingly, of Yyrkoon. Stupid Yyrkoon: for all that he prided himself that
he was a Melnibonéan, he lacked the Melnibonéan subtlety. He was as
brutal and direct as some of the Young Kingdom barbarians he so
much despised. And now Elric began to feel almost grateful to his
cousin. His life was over. The conflicts which tore his mind would no
longer trouble him. His fears, his torments, his loves and his hatreds

all lay in the past and only oblivion lay before him. As the last of his breath left his body, he gave himself wholly to the sea; to Straasha, Lord of all the Water Elementals, once the comrade of the Melnibonéan folk. And as he did this he remembered the old spell which his ancestors had used to summon Straasha. The spell came unbidden into his dying brain.

> Waters of the sea, thou gave us birth
> And were our milk and mother both
> In days when skies were overcast
> You who were first shall be the last.
>
> Sea-rulers, fathers of our blood,
> Thine aid is sought, thine aid is sought,
> Your salt is blood, our blood your salt,
> Your blood the blood of Man.
>
> Straasha, eternal king, eternal sea
> Thine aid is sought by me;
> For enemies of thine and mine
> Seek to defeat our destiny, and drain away our sea.

Either the words had an old, symbolic meaning or they referred to some incident in Melnibonéan history which even Elric had not read about. The words meant very little to him and yet they continued to repeat themselves as his body sank deeper and deeper into the green waters. Even when blackness overwhelmed him and his lungs filled with water, the words continued to whisper through the corridors of his brain. It was strange that he should be dead and still hear the incantation.

It seemed a long while later that his eyes opened and revealed swirling water and, through it, huge, indistinct figures gliding towards him. Death, it appeared, took a long time to come and, while he died, he dreamed. The leading figure had a turquoise beard and hair, pale green skin that seemed made of the sea itself and, when he spoke, a voice that was like a rushing tide. He smiled at Elric.

"Straasha answers thy summons, mortal. Our destinies are bound together. How may I aid thee, and, in aiding thee, aid myself?"

Elric's mouth was filled with water and yet he still seemed capable of speech (thus proving he dreamed).

He said:

"King Straasha. The paintings in the Tower of D'a'rputna—in the library. When I was a boy I saw them, King Straasha."

The sea-king stretched out his sea-green hands. *"Aye. You sent the summons. You need our aid. We honour our ancient pact with your folk."*

"No. I did not mean to summon you. The summons came unbidden to my dying mind. I am happy to drown, King Straasha."

"That cannot be. If your mind summoned us it means you wish to live. We will aid you." King Straasha's beard streamed in the tide and his deep, green eyes were gentle, almost tender, as they regarded the albino.

Elric closed his own eyes again. "I dream," he said. "I deceive myself with fantasies of hope." He felt the water in his lungs and he knew he no longer breathed. It stood to reason, therefore, that he was dead. "But if you were real, old friend, and you wished to aid me, you would return me to Melniboné so that I might deal with the usurper, Yyrkoon, and save Cymoril, before it is too late. That is my only regret—the torment which Cymoril will suffer if her brother becomes Emperor of Melniboné."

"Is that all you ask of the water elementals?" King Straasha seemed almost disappointed.

"I do not even ask that of you. I only voice what I would have wished, had this been reality and I was speaking, which I know is impossible. Now I shall die."

"That cannot be, Lord Elric, for our destinies are truly intertwined and I know that it is not yet your destiny to perish. Therefore I will aid you as you have suggested."

Elric was surprised at the sharpness of detail of this fantasy. He said to himself, "What a cruel torment I subject myself to. Now I must set about admitting my death . . ."

"*You cannot die. Not yet.*"

Now it was as if the sea-king's gentle hands had picked him up and bore him through twisting corridors of a delicate coral pink texture, slightly shadowed, no longer in water. And Elric felt the water vanish from his lungs and stomach and he breathed. Could it be that he had actually been brought to the legendary plane of the elemental folk—a plane which intersected that of the earth and in which they dwelled, for the most part?

In a huge, circular cavern, which shone with pink and blue mother-of-pearl, they came to rest at last. The sea-king laid Elric down upon the floor of the cavern, which seemed to be covered with fine, white sand which was yet not sand for it yielded and then sprang back when he moved.

When King Straasha moved, it was with a sound like the tide drawing itself back over shingle. The sea-king crossed the white sand, walking towards a large throne of milky jade. He seated himself upon this throne and placed his green head on his green fist, regarding Elric with puzzled, yet compassionate, eyes.

Elric was still physically weak, but he could breathe. It was as if the sea water had filled him and then cleansed him when it was driven out. He felt clear-headed. And now he was much less sure that he dreamed.

"I still find it hard to know why you saved me, King Straasha," he murmured from where he lay on the sand.

"*The rune. We heard it on this plane and we came. That is all.*"

"Aye. But there is more to sorcery-working than that. There are chants, symbols, rituals of all sorts. Previously that has always been true."

"*Perhaps the rituals take the place of urgent need of the kind which sent out your summons to us. Though you say you wished to die, it was evident that this was not your true desire or the Summoning would not have been so clear nor reached us so swiftly. Forget all this now. When you have rested, we shall do what you have requested of us.*"

Painfully, Elric raised himself into a sitting position. "You spoke earlier of 'intertwined destinies'. Do you, then, know something of my destiny?"

"A little, I think. Our world grows old. Once the elementals were powerful on your plane and the people of Melniboné all shared that power. But now our power wanes, as does yours. Something is changing. There are intimations that the Lords of the Higher Worlds are again taking an interest in your world. Perhaps they fear that the folk of the Young Kingdoms have forgotten them. Perhaps the folk of the Young Kingdoms threaten to bring in a new age, where gods and beings such as myself no longer shall have a place. I suspect there is a certain unease upon the planes of the Higher Worlds."

"You know no more?"

King Straasha raised his head and looked directly into Elric's eyes. *"There is no more I can tell you, son of my old friends, save that you would be happier if you gave yourself up entirely to your destiny when you understand it."*

Elric sighed. "I think I know of what you speak, King Straasha. I shall try to follow your advice."

"And now that you have rested, it is time to return."

The sea-king rose from his throne of milky jade and flowed towards Elric, lifting him up in strong, green arms.

"We shall meet again before your life ends, Elric. I hope that I shall be able to aid you once more. And remember that our brothers of the air and of fire will try to aid you also. And remember the beasts—they, too, can be of service to you. There is no need to suspect their help. But beware of gods, Elric. Beware of the Lords of the Higher Worlds and remember that their aid and their gifts must always be paid for."

These were the last words Elric heard the sea-king speak before they rushed again through the sinuous tunnels of this other plane, moving at such a speed that Elric could distinguish no details and, at times, did not know whether they remained in King Straasha's kingdom or had returned to the depths of his own world's sea.

CHAPTER TWO

A New Emperor and an Emperor Renewed

Strange clouds filled the sky and the sun hung heavy and huge and red behind them and the ocean was black as the golden galleys swept homeward before their battered flagship *The Son of the Pyaray* which moved slowly with dead slaves at her oars and her tattered sails limp at their masts and smoke-begrimed men on her decks and a new emperor upon her war-wrecked bridge. The new emperor was the only jubilant man in the fleet and he was jubilant indeed. It was his banner now, not Elric's, which took pride of place on the flagmast, for he had lost no time in proclaiming Elric slain and himself ruler of Melniboné.

To Yyrkoon, the peculiar sky was an omen of change, of a return to the old ways and the old power of the Dragon Isle. When he issued orders, his voice was a veritable croon of pleasure, and Admiral Magum Colim, who had ever been wary of Elric but who now had to obey Yyrkoon's orders, wondered if, perhaps, it would not have been preferable to have dealt with Yyrkoon in the manner in which (he suspected) Yyrkoon had dealt with Elric.

Dyvim Tvar leaned on the rail of his own ship, *Terhali's Particular Satisfaction*, and he also paid attention to the sky, though he saw omens of doom, for he mourned for Elric and considered how he might take vengeance on Prince Yyrkoon, should it emerge that Yyrkoon had murdered his cousin for possession of the Ruby Throne.

Melniboné appeared on the horizon, a brooding silhouette of crags, a dark monster squatting in the sea, calling her own back to the heated pleasures of her womb, the Dreaming City of Imrryr. The great cliffs loomed, the central gate to the sea-maze opened, water slapped and gasped as the golden prows disturbed it and the golden ships were swallowed into the murky dankness of the tunnels where bits of wreckage still floated from the previous night's encounter; where white, bloated corpses could still be seen when the brandlight touched them. The prows nosed arrogantly through the remains of their prey, but there was no joy aboard the golden battle-barges, for they brought news of their old emperor's death in battle (Yyrkoon had told them what had happened). Next night and for seven nights in all the Wild Dance of Melniboné would fill the streets. Potions and petty spells would ensure that no-one slept, for sleep was forbidden to any Melnibonéan, old or young, while a dead emperor was mourned. Naked, the Dragon Princes would prowl the city, taking any young woman they found and filling her with their seed for it was traditional that if an emperor died then the nobles of Melniboné must create as many children of aristocratic blood as was possible. Music-slaves would howl from the top of every tower. Other slaves would be slain and some eaten. It was a dreadful dance, the Dance of Misery, and it took as many lives as it created. A tower would be pulled down and a new one erected during those seven days and the tower would be called for Elric VIII, the Albino Emperor, slain upon the sea, defending Melniboné against the southland pirates.

Slain upon the sea and his body taken by the waves. That was not a good portent, for it meant that Elric had gone to serve Pyaray, the Tentacled Whisperer of Impossible Secrets, the Chaos Lord who commanded the Chaos Fleet—dead ships, dead sailors, forever in his thrall—and it was not fitting that such a fate should befall one of the Royal Line of Melniboné. Ah, but the mourning would be long, thought Dyvim Tvar. He had loved Elric, for all that he had sometimes disapproved of his methods of ruling the Dragon Isle. Secretly he would go to the Dragon Caves that night and spend the period of mourning with the sleeping dragons who, now that Elric was dead, were all he had left to love. And Dyvim Tvar then thought of Cymoril, awaiting Elric's return.

The ships began to emerge into the half-light of the evening. Torches and braziers already burned on the quays of Imrryr which were deserted save for a small group of figures who stood around a chariot which had been driven out to the end of the central mole. A cold wind blew. Dyvim Tvar knew that it was the Princess Cymoril who waited, with her guards, for the fleet.

Though the flagship was the last to pass through the maze, the rest of the ships had to wait until it could be towed into position and dock first. If this had not been the required tradition, Dyvim Tvar would have left his ship and gone to speak to Cymoril, escort her from the quay and tell her what he knew of the circumstances of Elric's death. But it was impossible. Even before *Terhali's Particular Satisfaction* had dropped anchor, the main gangplank of *The Son of the Pyaray* had been lowered and the Emperor Yyrkoon, all swaggering pride, had stepped down it, his arms raised in triumphant salute to his sister who could be seen, even now, searching the decks of the ships for a sign of her beloved albino.

Suddenly Cymoril knew that Elric was dead and she suspected that Yyrkoon had, in some way, been responsible for Elric's death. Either Yyrkoon had allowed Elric to be borne down by a group of southland reavers or else he had managed to slay Elric himself. She knew her brother and she recognized his expression. He was pleased with himself as he always had been when successful in some form of treachery or another. Anger flashed in her tear-filled eyes and she threw back her head and shouted at the shifting, ominous sky:

"Oh! Yyrkoon has destroyed him!"

Her guards were startled. The captain spoke solicitously. "Madam?"

"He is dead—and that brother slew him. Take Prince Yyrkoon, captain. Kill Prince Yyrkoon, captain."

Unhappily, the captain put his right hand on the hilt of his sword. A young warrior, more impetuous, drew his blade, murmuring: "I will slay him, princess, if that is your desire." The young warrior loved Cymoril with considerable and unthinking intensity.

The captain offered the warrior a cautionary glance, but the warrior was blind to it. Now two others slid swords from scabbards as Yyrkoon, a red cloak wound about him, his dragon crest catching the light from the brands guttering in the wind, stalked forward and cried:

"Yyrkoon is emperor now!"

"No!" shrieked Yyrkoon's sister. "Elric! Elric! Where are you?"

"Serving his new master, Pyaray of Chaos. His dead hands pull at the sweep of a Chaos ship, sister. His dead eyes see nothing at all. His dead ears hear only the crack of Pyaray's whips and his dead flesh cringes, feeling nought but that unearthly scourge. Elric sank in his armour to the bottom of the sea."

"Murderer! Traitor!" Cymoril began to sob.

The captain, who was a practical man, said to his warriors in a low voice: "Sheathe your weapons and salute your new emperor."

Only the young guardsman who loved Cymoril disobeyed. "But he slew the emperor! My lady Cymoril said so!"

"What of it? He is emperor now. Kneel or you'll be dead within the minute."

The young warrior gave a wild shout and leapt towards Yyrkoon, who stepped back, trying to free his arms from the folds of his cloak. He had not expected this.

But it was the captain who leapt forward, his own sword drawn, and hacked down the youngster so that he gasped, half-turned, then fell at Yyrkoon's feet.

This demonstration of the captain's was confirmation of his real power and Yyrkoon almost smirked with satisfaction as he looked down at the corpse. The captain fell to one knee, the bloody sword still in his hand. "My emperor," he said.

"You show a proper loyalty, captain."

"My loyalty is to the Ruby Throne."

"Quite so."

Cymoril shook with grief and rage, but her rage was impotent. She knew now that she had no friends.

Leering, the Emperor Yyrkoon presented himself before her. He reached out his hand and he caressed her neck, her cheek, her mouth. He let his hand fall so that it grazed her breast. "Sister," he said, "thou art mine entirely now."

And Cymoril was the second to fall at his feet, for she had fainted.

"Pick her up," Yyrkoon said to the guard. "Take her back to her own tower and there be sure she remains. Two guards will be with her at all times, in even her most private moments they must observe her, for she may plan treachery against the Ruby Throne."

The captain bowed and signed to his men to obey the emperor. "Aye, my lord. It shall be done."

Yyrkoon looked back at the corpse of the young warrior. "And feed that to her slaves tonight, so that he can continue serving her." He smiled.

The captain smiled, too, appreciating the joke. He felt it was good to have a proper emperor in Melniboné again. An emperor who knew how to behave, who knew how to treat his enemies and who accepted unswerving loyalty as his right. The captain fancied that fine, martial times lay ahead for Melniboné. The golden battle-barges and the warriors of Imrryr could go a-spoiling again and instill in the barbarians of the Young Kingdoms a sweet and satisfactory sense of fear. Already, in his mind, the captain helped himself to the treasures of Lormyr, Argimiliar and Pikarayd, of Ilmiora and Jadmar. He might even be made governor, say, of the Isle of the Purple Towns. What luxuries of torment would he bring to those upstart sea-lords, particularly Count Smiorgan Baldhead who was even now beginning to try to make the isle a rival to Melniboné as a trading port! As he escorted the limp body of the Princess Cymoril back to her tower, the captain looked on that body and felt the swellings of lust within him. Yyrkoon would reward his loyalty, there was no doubt of that. Despite the cold wind, the captain began to sweat in his anticipation. He, himself, would guard the Princess Cymoril. He would relish it.

Marching at the head of his army, Yyrkoon strutted for the Tower of D'a'rputna, the Tower of Emperors, and the Ruby Throne within. He preferred to ignore the litter which had been brought for him and to go on foot, so that he might savour every small moment of his triumph. He approached the tower, tall among its fellows at the very centre of Imrryr, as he might approach a beloved woman. He approached it with a sense of delicacy and without haste, for he knew that it was his.

He looked about him. His army marched behind him. Magum Colim and Dyvim Tvar led the army. People lined the twisting streets and bowed low to him. Slaves prostrated themselves. Even the beasts of burden were made to kneel as he strode by. Yyrkoon could almost taste the power as one might taste a luscious fruit. He drew deep breaths of the air. Even the air was his. All Imrryr was his. All Melniboné. Soon would all the world be his. And he would squander it all. How he would squander it! Such a grand terror would he bring back to the earth; such a munificence of fear! In ecstasy, almost blindly, did the Emperor Yyrkoon enter the tower. He hesitated at the great doors of the throne room. He signed for the doors to be opened and as they opened he deliberately took in the scene tiny bit by tiny bit. The walls, the banners, the trophies, the galleries, all were his. The throne room was empty now, but soon he would fill it with colour and celebration and true, Melnibonéan entertainments. It had been too long since blood had sweetened the air of this hall. Now he let his eyes linger upon the steps leading up to the Ruby Throne itself, but, before he looked at the throne, he heard Dyvim Tvar gasp behind him and his gaze went suddenly to the Ruby Throne and his jaw slackened at what he saw. His eyes widened in incredulity.

"An illusion!"

"An apparition," said Dyvim Tvar with some satisfaction.

"Heresy!" cried the Emperor Yyrkoon, staggering forward, finger pointing at the robed and cowled figure which sat so still upon the Ruby Throne. "Mine! Mine!"

The figure made no reply.

"Mine! Begone! The throne belongs to Yyrkoon. Yyrkoon is emperor now! What are you? Why would you thwart me thus?"

The cowl fell back and a bone-white face was revealed, surrounded by flowing, milk-white hair. Crimson eyes looked coolly down at the shrieking, stumbling thing which came towards them.

"You are dead, Elric! I know that you are dead!"

The apparition made no reply, but a thin smile touched the white lips.

"You *could* not have survived. You drowned. You cannot come back. Pyaray owns your soul!"

"There are others who rule in the sea," said the figure on the Ruby Throne. "Why did you slay me, cousin?"

Yyrkoon's guile had deserted him, making way for terror and con-fusion. "Because it is my right to rule! Because you were not strong enough, nor cruel enough, nor humorous enough . . ."

"Is this not a good joke, cousin?"

"Begone! Begone! Begone! I shall not be ousted by a spectre! A dead emperor cannot rule Melniboné!"

"We shall see," said Elric, signing to Dyvim Tvar and his soldiers.

CHAPTER THREE

A Traditional Justice

"Now indeed I shall rule as you would have had me rule, cousin." Elric watched as Dyvim Tvar's soldiers surrounded the would-be usurper and seized his arms, relieving him of his weapons.

Yyrkoon panted like a captured wolf. He glared around him as if hoping to find support from the assembled warriors, but they stared back at him either neutrally or with open contempt.

"And you, Prince Yyrkoon, will be the first to benefit from this new rule of mine. Are you pleased?"

Yyrkoon lowered his head. He was trembling now. Elric laughed. "Speak up, cousin."

"May Arioch and all the Dukes of Hell torment you for eternity," growled Yyrkoon. He flung back his head, his wild eyes rolling, his lips curling: "Arioch! Arioch! Curse this feeble albino! Arioch! Destroy him or see Melniboné fall!"

Elric continued to laugh. "Arioch does not hear you. Chaos is weak upon the earth now. It needs a greater sorcery than yours to bring the Chaos Lords back to aid you as they aided our ancestors. And now, Yyrkoon, tell me—where is the Lady Cymoril?"

But Yyrkoon had lapsed, again, into a sullen silence.

"She is at her own tower, my emperor," said Magum Colim.

"A creature of Yyrkoon's took her there," said Dyvim Tvar. "The captain of Cymoril's own guard, he slew a warrior who tried to defend his mistress against Yyrkoon. It could be that Princess Cymoril is in danger, my lord."

"Then go quickly to the tower. Take a force of men. Bring both Cymoril and the captain of her guard to me."

"And Yyrkoon, my lord?" asked Dyvim Tvar.

"Let him remain here until his sister returns."

Dyvim Tvar bowed and, selecting a body of warriors, left the throne room. All noticed that Dyvim Tvar's step was lighter and his expression less grim than when he had first approached the throne room at Prince Yyrkoon's back.

Yyrkoon straightened his head and looked about the court. For a moment he seemed like a pathetic and bewildered child. All the lines of hate and anger had disappeared and Elric felt sympathy for his cousin growing again within him. But this time Elric quelled the feeling.

"Be grateful, cousin, that for a few hours you were totally powerful, that you enjoyed domination over all the folk of Melniboné."

Yyrkoon said in a small, puzzled voice: "How did you escape? You had no time for making a sorcery, no strength for it. You could barely move your limbs and your armour must have dragged you deep to the bottom of the sea so that you should have drowned. It is unfair, Elric. You should have drowned."

Elric shrugged, "I have friends in the sea. They recognize my royal blood and my right to rule if you do not."

Yyrkoon tried to disguise the astonishment he felt. Evidently his respect for Elric had increased, as had his hatred for the albino emperor. "Friends."

"Aye," said Elric, with a thin grin.

"I—I thought, too, you had vowed not to use your powers of sorcery."

"But you thought that a vow which was unbefitting for a Melnibonéan monarch to make, did you not? Well, I agree with you. You see, Yyrkoon, you have won a victory, after all."

Yyrkoon stared narrowly at Elric, as if trying to divine a secret meaning behind Elric's words. "You will bring back the Chaos Lords?"

"No sorcerer, however powerful, can summon the Chaos Lords or, for that matter, the Lords of Law, if they do not wish to be summoned. That you know. You must know it, Yyrkoon. Have you not, yourself, tried? And Arioch did not come, did he? Did he bring you the gift you sought—the gift of the two black swords?"

"You know that?"

"I did not. I guessed. Now I know."

Yyrkoon tried to speak but his voice would not form words, so angry was he. Instead, a strangled growl escaped his throat and for a few moments he struggled in the grip of his guards.

Dyvim Tvar returned with Cymoril. The girl was pale but she was smiling. She ran into the throne room. "Elric!"

"Cymoril! Are you harmed?"

Cymoril glanced at the crestfallen captain of her guard who had been brought with her. A look of disgust crossed her fine face. Then she shook her head. "No. I am not harmed."

The captain of Cymoril's guard was shaking with terror. He looked pleadingly at Yyrkoon as if hoping that his fellow prisoner could help him. But Yyrkoon continued to stare at the floor.

"Have that one brought closer." Elric pointed at the captain of the guard. The man was dragged to the foot of the steps leading to the Ruby Throne. He moaned. "What a petty traitor you are," said Elric. "At least Yyrkoon had the courage to attempt to slay me. And his ambitions were high. Your ambition was merely to become one of his pet curs. So you betrayed your mistress and slew one of your own men. What is your name?"

The man had difficulty speaking, but at last he murmured, "It is Valharik, my name. What could I do? I serve the Ruby Throne, whoever sits upon it."

"So the traitor claims that loyalty motivated him. I think not."

"It was, my lord. It was." The captain began to whine. He fell to his knees. "Slay me swiftly. Do not punish me more."

Elric's impulse was to heed the man's request, but he looked at Yyrkoon and then remembered the expression on Cymoril's face when she had looked at the guard. He knew that he must make a point now, whilst making an example of Captain Valharik. So he shook his head. "No. I will punish you more. Tonight you will die here according to the traditions of Melniboné, while my nobles feast to celebrate this new era of my rule."

Valharik began to sob. Then he stopped himself and got slowly to his feet, a Melnibonéan again. He bowed low and stepped backward, giving himself into the grip of his guards.

"I must consider a way in which your fate may be shared with the one you wished to serve," Elric went on. "How did you slay the young warrior who sought to obey Cymoril?"

"With my sword. I cut him down. It was a clean stroke. But one."

"And what became of the corpse."

"Prince Yyrkoon told me to feed it to Princess Cymoril's slaves."

"I understand. Very well, Prince Yyrkoon, you may join us at the feast tonight while Captain Valharik entertains us with his dying."

Yyrkoon's face was almost as pale as Elric's. "What do you mean?"

"The little pieces of Captain Valharik's flesh which our Doctor Jest will carve from his limbs will be the meat on which you feast. You may give instructions as to how you wish the captain's flesh prepared. We should not expect you to eat it raw, cousin."

Even Dyvim Tvar looked astonished at Elric's decision. Certainly it was in the spirit of Melniboné and a clever irony improving on Prince Yyrkoon's own idea, but it was unlike Elric—or at least, it was unlike the Elric he had known up until a day earlier.

As he heard his fate, Captain Valharik gave a great scream of terror and glared at Prince Yyrkoon as if the would-be usurper were already tasting his flesh. Yyrkoon tried to turn away, his shoulders shaking.

"And that will be the beginning of it," said Elric. "The feast will start at midnight. Until that time, confine Yyrkoon to his own tower."

After Prince Yyrkoon and Captain Valharik had been led away, Dyvim Tvar and Princess Cymoril came and stood beside Elric who had sunk back in his great throne and was staring bitterly into the middle-distance.

"That was a clever cruelty," Dyvim Tvar said.

Cymoril said: "It is what they both deserve."

"Aye," murmured Elric. "It is what my father would have done. It is what Yyrkoon would have done had our positions been reversed. I but follow the traditions. I no longer pretend that I am my own man. Here I shall stay until I die, trapped upon the Ruby Throne—serving the Ruby Throne as Valharik claimed to serve it."

"Could you not kill them both quickly?" Cymoril asked. "You know that I do not plead for my brother because he is my brother. I hate him most of all. But it might destroy you, Elric, to follow through with your plan."

"What if it does? Let me be destroyed. Let me merely become an unthinking extension of my ancestors. The puppet of ghosts and memories, dancing to strings which extend back through time for ten thousand years."

"Perhaps if you slept . . ." Dyvim Tvar suggested.

"I shall not sleep, I feel, for many nights after this. But your brother is not going to die, Cymoril. After his punishment—after he has eaten the flesh of Captain Valharik—I intend to send him into exile. He will go alone into the Young Kingdoms and he will not be allowed to take his grimoires with him. He must make his way as best he can in the lands of the barbarian. That is not too severe a punishment, I think."

"It is too lenient," said Cymoril. "You would be best advised to slay him. Send soldiers now. Give him no time to consider counterplots."

"I do not fear his counterplots." Elric rose wearily. "Now I should like it if you would both leave me, until an hour or so before the feasting begins. I must think."

"I will return to my tower and prepare myself for tonight," said Cymoril. She kissed Elric lightly upon his pale forehead. He looked up, filled with love and tenderness for her. He reached out and touched her hair and her cheek. "Remember that I love you, Elric," she said.

"I will see that you are safely escorted homeward," Dyvim Tvar said to her. "And you must choose a new commander of your guard. Can I assist in that?"

"I should be grateful, Dyvim Tvar."

They left Elric still upon the Ruby Throne, still staring into space. The hand that he lifted from time to time to his pale head shook a little and now the torment showed in his strange, crimson eyes.

Later, he rose up from the Ruby Throne and walked slowly, head

bowed, to his own apartments, followed by his guards. He hesitated at
the door which led onto the steps going up to the library. Instinctively
he sought the consolation and forgetfulness of a certain kind of knowledge, but at that moment he suddenly hated his scrolls and his books.
He blamed them for his ridiculous concerns regarding 'morality' and
'justice'; he blamed them for the feelings of guilt and despair which
now filled him as a result of his decision to behave as a Melnibonéan
monarch was expected to behave. So he passed the door to the library
and went on to his apartments, but even his apartments displeased him
now. They were austere. They were not furnished according to the lux-
urious tastes of all Melnibonéans (save for his father) with their delight
in lush mixtures of colour and bizarre design. He would have them
changed as soon as possible. He would give himself up to those ghosts
who ruled him. For some time he stalked from room to room, trying to
push back that part of him which demanded he be merciful to Valharik
and to Yyrkoon—at very least to slay them and be done with it or, better, to send them both into exile. But it was impossible to reverse his decision now.

At last he lowered himself to a couch which rested beside a window looking out over the whole of the city. The sky was still full of tur-
bulent cloud, but now the moon shone through, like the yellow eye of
an unhealthy beast. It seemed to stare with a certain triumphant irony
at him, as if relishing the defeat of his conscience. Elric sank his head
into his arms.

Later the servants came to tell him that the courtiers were assembling for the celebration feast. He allowed them to dress him in his yellow robes of state and to place the dragon crown upon his head and
then he returned to the throne room to be greeted by a mighty cheer,
more wholehearted than any he had ever received before. He acknowledged the greeting and then seated himself in the Ruby Throne, looking out over the banqueting tables which now filled the hall. A table
was brought and set before him and two extra seats were brought, for
Dyvim Tvar and Cymoril would sit beside him. But Dyvim Tvar and
Cymoril were not yet here and neither had the renegade Valharik been
brought. And where was Yyrkoon? They should, even now, be at the

centre of the hall—Valharik in chains and Yyrkoon seated beneath him. Doctor Jest was there, heating his brazier on which rested his cooking pans, testing and sharpening his knives. The hall was filled with excited talk as the court waited to be entertained. Already the food was being brought in, though no-one might eat until the emperor ate first.

Elric signed to the commander of his own guard. "Has the Princess Cymoril or Lord Dyvim Tvar arrived at the tower yet?"

"No, my lord."

Cymoril was rarely late and Dyvim Tvar never. Elric frowned. Perhaps they did not relish the entertainment.

"And what of the prisoners?"

"They have been sent for, my lord."

Doctor Jest looked up expectantly, his thin body tensed in anticipation.

And then Elric heard a sound above the din of the conversation. A groaning sound which seemed to come from all around the tower. He bent his head and listened closely.

Others were hearing it now. They stopped talking and also listened intently. Soon the whole hall was in silence and the groaning increased.

Then, all at once, the doors of the throne room burst open and there was Dyvim Tvar, gasping and bloody, his clothes slashed and his flesh gashed. And following him in came a mist—a swirling mist of dark purples and unpleasant blues and it was this mist that groaned.

Elric sprang from his throne and knocked the table aside. He leapt down the steps towards his friend. The groaning mist began to creep further into the throne room, as if reaching out for Dyvim Tvar.

Elric took his friend in his arms. "Dyvim Tvar! What is this sorcery?"

Dyvim Tvar's face was full of horror and his lips seemed frozen until at last he said:

"It is Yyrkoon's sorcery. He conjured the groaning mist to aid him in his escape. I tried to follow him from the city but the mist engulfed me and I lost my senses. I went to his tower to bring him and his accessory here, but the sorcery had already been accomplished."

"Cymoril? Where is she?"

"He took her, Elric. She is with him. Valharik is with him and so are a hundred warriors who remained secretly loyal to him."

"Then we must pursue him. We shall soon capture him."

"You can do nothing against the groaning mist. Ah! It comes!"

And sure enough the mist was beginning to surround them. Elric tried to disperse it by waving his arms, but then it had gathered thickly around him and its melancholy groaning filled his ears, its hideous colours blinded his eyes. He tried to rush through it, but it remained with him. And now he thought he heard words amongst the groans. "Elric is weak. Elric is foolish. Elric must die!"

"Stop this!" he cried. He bumped into another body and fell to his knees. He began to crawl, desperately trying to peer through the mist. Now faces formed in the mist—frightful faces, more terrifying than any he had ever seen, even in his worst nightmares.

"Cymoril!" he cried. "Cymoril!"

And one of the faces became the face of Cymoril—a Cymoril who leered at him and mocked him and whose face slowly aged until he saw a filthy crone and, ultimately, a skull on which the flesh rotted. He closed his eyes, but the image remained.

"*Cymoril*," whispered the voices. "*Cymoril.*"

And Elric grew weaker as he became more desperate. He cried out for Dyvim Tvar, but heard only a mocking echo of the name, as he had heard Cymoril's. He shut his lips and he shut his eyes and, still crawling, tried to free himself from the groaning mist. But hours seemed to pass before the groans became whines and the whines became faint strands of sound and he tried to rise, opening his eyes to see the mist fading, but then his legs buckled and he fell down against the first step which led to the Ruby Throne. Again he had ignored Cymoril's advice concerning her brother—and again she was in danger. Elric's last thought was a simple one:

"I am not fit to live," he thought.

CHAPTER FOUR

To Call the Chaos Lord

As soon as he recovered from the blow which had knocked him unconscious and thus wasted even more time, Elric sent for Dyvim Tvar. He was eager for news. But Dyvim Tvar could report nothing. Yyrkoon had summoned sorcerous aid to free him, sorcerous aid to effect his escape. "He must have had some magical means of leaving the island, for he could not have gone by ship," said Dyvim Tvar.

"You must send out expeditions," said Elric. "Send a thousand detachments if you must. Send every man in Melniboné. Strive to wake the dragons that they might be used. Equip the golden battle-barges. Cover the world with our men if you must, but find Cymoril."

"All those things I have already done," said Dyvim Tvar, "save that I have not yet found Cymoril."

A month passed and Imrryrian warriors marched and rode through the Young Kingdoms seeking news of their renegade countrymen.

"I worried more for myself than for Cymoril and I called that 'morality'," thought the albino. "I tested my sensibilities, not my conscience."

A second month passed and Imrryrian dragons sailed the skies to South and East, West and North, but though they flew across mountains and seas and forests and plains and, unwittingly, brought terror to many a city, they found no sign of Yyrkoon and his band.

"For, finally, one can only judge oneself by one's actions," thought Elric. "I have looked at what I have done, not at what I meant to do or thought I would like to do, and what I have done has, in the main, been foolish, destructive and with little point. Yyrkoon was right to despise me and that was why I hated him so."

A fourth month came and Imrryrian ships stopped in remote ports and Imrryrian sailors questioned other travelers and explorers for news of Yyrkoon. But Yyrkoon's sorcery had been strong and none had seen him (or remembered seeing him).

"I must now consider the implications of all these thoughts," said Elric to himself.

Wearily, the swiftest of the soldiers began to return to Melniboné, bearing their useless news. And as faith disappeared and hope faded, Elric's determination increased. He made himself strong, both physically and mentally. He experimented with new drugs which would increase his energy. He read much in the library, though this time he read only certain grimoires and he read those over and over again.

These grimoires were written in the High Speech of Melniboné— the ancient language of sorcery with which Elric's ancestors had been able to communicate with the supernatural beings they had summoned. And at last Elric was satisfied that he understood them fully, though what he read sometimes threatened to stop him in his present course of action.

And when he was satisfied—for the dangers of misunderstanding the implications of the things described in the grimoires were catastrophic—he slept for three nights in a drugged slumber.

And then Elric was ready. He ordered all slaves and servants from his quarters. He placed guards at the doors with instructions to admit no-one, no matter how urgent their business. He cleared one great chamber of all furniture so that it was completely empty save for one grimoire which he had placed in the very centre of the room. Then he seated himself beside the book and began to think.

When he had meditated for more than five hours Elric took a brush and a jar of ink and began to paint both walls and floor with complicated symbols, some of which were so intricate that they seemed to disappear at an angle to the surface on which they had been laid. At last this was done and Elric spreadeagled himself in the very centre of his huge rune, face down, one hand upon his grimoire, the other (with the Actorios upon it) stretched palm down. The moon was full. A shaft of its light fell directly upon Elric's head, turning the hair to silver. And then the Summoning began.

Elric sent his mind into twisting tunnels of logic, across endless plains of ideas, through mountains of symbolism and endless universes of alternate truths; he sent his mind out further and further and as it went he sent with it the words which issued from his writhing lips— words that few of his contemporaries would understand, though their very sound would chill the blood of any listener. And his body heaved as he forced it to remain in its original position and from time to time a groan would escape him. And through all this a few words came again and again.

One of these words was a name. "Arioch".

Arioch, the patron demon of Elric's ancestors; one of the most powerful of all the Dukes of Hell, who was called Knight of the Swords, Lord of the Seven Darks, Lord of the Higher Hell and many more names besides.

"Arioch!"

It was on Arioch whom Yyrkoon had called, asking the Lord of Chaos to curse Elric. It was Arioch whom Yyrkoon had sought to summon to aid him in his attempt upon the Ruby Throne. It was Arioch who was known as the Keeper of the Two Black Swords—the swords of unearthly manufacture and infinite power which had once been wielded by emperors of Melniboné.

"Arioch! I summon thee."

Runes, both rhythmic and fragmented, howled now from Elric's throat. His brain had reached the plane on which Arioch dwelt. Now it sought Arioch himself.

"Arioch! It is Elric of Melniboné who summons thee."

Elric glimpsed an eye staring down at him. The eye floated, joined another. The two eyes regarded him.

"Arioch! My Lord of Chaos! Aid me!"

The eyes blinked—and vanished.

"Oh, Arioch! Come to me! Come to me! Aid me and I will serve you."

A silhouette that was not a human form turned slowly until a black, faceless head looked down upon Elric. A halo of red light gleamed behind the head.

Then that, too, vanished.

Exhausted, Elric let the image fade. His mind raced back through plane upon plane. His lips no longer chanted the runes and the names. He lay exhausted upon the floor of his chamber, unable to move, in silence.

He was certain that he had failed.

There was a small sound. Painfully he raised his weary head.

A fly had come into the chamber. It buzzed about erratically, seeming almost to follow the lines of the runes Elric had so recently painted.

The fly settled first upon one rune and then on another.

It must have come in through the window, thought Elric. He was annoyed by the distraction but still fascinated by it.

The fly settled on Elric's forehead. It was a large, black fly and its buzz was loud, obscene. It rubbed its forelegs together, and it seemed to be taking a particular interest in Elric's face as it moved over it. Elric shuddered, but he did not have the strength to swat it. When it came into his field of vision, he watched it. When it was not visible he felt its legs covering every inch of his face. Then it flew up and, still buzzing loudly, hovered a short distance from Elric's nose. And then Elric could see the fly's eyes and recognize something in them. They were the eyes—and yet not the eyes—he had seen on that other plane.

It began to dawn on him that this fly was no ordinary creature. It had features that were in some way faintly human.

The fly smiled at him.

From his hoarse throat and through his parched lips Elric was able to utter but one word:

"Arioch?"

And a beautiful youth stood where the fly had hovered. The beautiful youth spoke in a beautiful voice—soft and sympathetic and yet manly. He was clad in a robe that was like a liquid jewel and yet which did not dazzle Elric, for in some way no light seemed to come from it. There was a slender sword at the youth's belt and he wore no helm, but a circlet of red fire. His eyes were wise and his eyes were old and when they were looked at closely they could be seen to contain an ancient and confident evil.

"Elric."

That was all the youth said, but it revived the albino so that he could raise himself to his knees.

"Elric."

And Elric could now stand. He was filled with energy.

The youth was taller, now, than Elric. He looked down at the Emperor of Melniboné and he smiled the smile that the fly had smiled. "You alone are fit to serve Arioch. It is long since I was invited to this plane, but now that I am here I shall aid you, Elric. I shall become your patron. I shall protect you and give you strength and the source of strength, though master I be and slave you be."

"How must I serve you, Duke Arioch?" Elric asked, having made a monstrous effort of self-control, for he was filled with terror by the implications of Arioch's words.

"You will serve me by serving yourself for the moment. Later a time will come when I shall call upon you to serve me in specific ways, but (for the moment) I ask little of you, save that you swear to serve me."

Elric hesitated.

"You must swear that," said Arioch reasonably, "or I cannot help you in the matter of your cousin Yyrkoon or his sister Cymoril."

"I swear to serve you," said Elric. And his body was flooded with ecstatic fire and he trembled with joy and he fell to his knees.

"Then I can tell you that, from time to time, you can call on my aid and I will come if your need is truly desperate. I will come in whichever form is appropriate, or no form at all if that should prove appropriate. And now you may ask me one question before I depart."

"I need the answers to two questions."

"Your first question I cannot answer. I will not answer. You must accept that you have now sworn to serve me. I will not tell you what the future holds. But you need not fear, if you serve me well."

"Then my second question is this: Where is Prince Yyrkoon?"

"Prince Yyrkoon is in the South, in a land of barbarians. By sorcery and by superior weapons and intelligence he has effected the conquest of two mean nations, one of which is called Oin and the other of which is called Yu. Even now he trains the men of Oin and the men of Yu to march upon Melniboné, for he knows that your forces are spread thinly across the earth, searching for him. Ask a third."

"How has he hidden?"

"He has not. But he has gained possession of the Mirror of Memory—a magical device whose hiding place he discovered by his sorceries. Those who look into this mirror have their memories taken. The mirror contains a million memories: the memories of all who have looked into it. Thus anyone who ventures into Oin or Yu or travels by sea to the capital which serves both is confronted by the mirror and forgets that he has seen Prince Yyrkoon and his Imrryrians in those lands. It is the best way of remaining undiscovered."

"It is." Elric drew his brows together. "Therefore it might be wise to consider destroying the mirror. But what would happen then, I wonder?"

Arioch raised his beautiful hand. "Although I have answered further questions which are, one could argue, part of the same question, I will answer no more. It could be in your interest to destroy the mirror, but it might be better to consider other means of countering its effects, for it does, I remind you, contain many memories, some of which have been imprisoned for thousands of years. Now I must go. And you must go—to the lands of Oin and Yu which lie several months' journey from here, to the South and well beyond Lormyr. They are best reached by the Ship Which Sails Over Land and Sea. Farewell, Elric."

And a fly buzzed for a moment upon the wall before vanishing.

Elric rushed from the room, shouting for his slaves.

CHAPTER FIVE

The Ship Which Sails Over Land and Sea

"And how many dragons still sleep in the caverns?" Elric paced the gallery overlooking the city. It was morning, but no sun came through the dull clouds which hung low upon the towers of the Dreaming City. Imrryr's life continued unchanged in the streets below, save for the absence of the majority of her soldiers who had not yet returned home from their fruitless quests and would not be home for many months to come.

Dyvim Tvar leaned on the parapet of the gallery and stared unseeingly into the streets. His face was tired and his arms were folded on his chest as if he sought to contain what was left of his strength.

"Two perhaps. It would take a great deal to wake them and even then I doubt if they'd be useful to us. What is this 'Ship Which Sails Over Land and Sea' which Arioch spoke of?"

"I've read of it before—in the Silver Grimoire and in other tomes. A magic ship. Used by a Melnibonéan hero even before there was Melniboné and the empire. But where it exists, and if it exists, I do not know."

"Who would know?" Dyvim Tvar straightened his back and turned it on the scene below.

"Arioch?" Elric shrugged. "But he would not tell me."

"What of your friends the water elementals? Have they not promised you aid? And would they not be knowledgable in the matter of ships?"

Elric frowned, deepening the lines which now marked his face. "Aye—Straasha might know. But I'm loath to call on his aid again. The water elementals are not the powerful creatures that the Lords of Chaos are. Their strength is limited and, moreover, they are inclined to be capricious, in the manner of the elements. What is more, Dyvim Tvar, I hesitate to use sorcery, save where absolutely imperative . . ."

"You are a sorcerer, Elric. You have but lately proved your greatness in that respect, involving the most powerful of all sorceries, the summoning of a Chaos Lord—and you still hold back? I would suggest, my lord king, that you consider such logic and that you judge it unsound. You decided to use sorcery in your pursuit of Prince Yyrkoon. The die is already cast. It would be wise to use sorcery now."

"You cannot conceive of the mental and physical effort involved . . ."

"I can conceive of it, my lord. I am your friend. I do not wish to see you pained—and yet . . ."

"There is also the difficulty, Dyvim Tvar, of my physical weakness," Elric reminded his friend. "How long can I continue in the use of these overstrong potions that now sustain me? They supply me with energy, aye—but they do so by using up my few resources. I might die before I find Cymoril."

"I stand rebuked."

But Elric came forward and put his white hand on Dyvim Tvar's butter-coloured cloak. "But what have I to lose, eh? No. You are right. I am a coward to hesitate when Cymoril's life is at stake. I repeat my stupidities—the stupidities which first brought this pass upon us all. I'll do it. Will you come with me to the ocean?"

"Aye."

Dyvim Tvar began to feel the burden of Elric's conscience settling upon him also. It was a peculiar feeling to come to a Melnibonéan and Dyvim Tvar knew very well that he liked it not at all.

Elric had last ridden these paths when he and Cymoril were happy. It seemed a long age ago. He had been a fool to trust that happiness. He turned his white stallion's head towards the cliffs and the sea beyond them. A light rain fell. Winter was descending swiftly on Melniboné.

They left their horses on the cliffs, lest they be disturbed by Elric's sorcery-working, and clambered down to the shore. The rain fell into the sea. A mist hung over the water little more than five ship lengths from the beach. It was deathly still and, with the tall, dark cliffs behind them and the wall of mist before them, it seemed to Dyvim Tvar that they had entered a silent netherworld where might easily be encountered the melancholy souls of those who, in legend, had committed suicide by a process of slow self-mutilation. The sound of the two men's boots on shingle was loud and yet was at once muffled by the mist which seemed to suck at noise and swallow it greedily as if it sustained its life on sound.

"Now," Elric murmured. He seemed not to notice the brooding and depressive surroundings. "Now I must recall the rune which came so easily, unsummoned, to my brain not many months since." He left Dyvim Tvar's side and went down to the place where the chill water lapped the land and there, carefully, he seated himself, cross-legged. His eyes stared, unseeingly, into the mist.

To Dyvim Tvar the tall albino appeared to shrink as he sat down. He seemed to become like a vulnerable child and Dyvim Tvar's heart went out to Elric as it might go out to a brave, nervous boy, and he had it in mind to suggest that the sorcery be done with and they seek the lands of Oin and Yu by ordinary means.

But Elric was already lifting his head as a dog lifts its head to the moon. And strange, thrilling words began to tumble from his lips and it became plain that, even if Dyvim Tvar did speak now, Elric would not hear him.

Dyvim Tvar was no stranger to the High Speech—as a Melnibonéan noble he had been taught it as a matter of course—but the
words seemed nonetheless strange to him, for Elric used peculiar inflections and emphases, giving the words a special and secret weight
and chanting them in a voice which ranged from bass groan to falsetto
shriek. It was not pleasant to listen to such noises coming from a mortal throat and now Dyvim Tvar had some clear understanding of why
Elric was reluctant to use sorcery. The Lord of the Dragon Caves, Melnibonéan though he was, found himself inclined to step backward a
pace or two, even to retire to the cliff-tops and watch over Elric from
there, and he had to force himself to hold his ground as the Summoning continued.

For a good space of time the rune-chanting went on. The rain beat
harder upon the pebbles of the shore and made them glisten. It dashed
most ferociously into the still, dark sea, lashed about the fragile head of
the chanting, pale-haired figure, and caused Dyvim Tvar to shiver and
draw his cloak more closely about his shoulders.

"Straasha—Straasha—Straasha . . ."

The words mingled with the sound of the rain. They were now
barely words at all but sounds which the wind might make or a language which the sea might speak.

"*Straasha . . .*"

Again Dyvim Tvar had the impulse to move, but this time he desired to go to Elric and tell him to stop, to consider some other means
of reaching the lands of Oin and Yu.

"*Straasha!*"

There was a cryptic agony in the shout.

"*Straasha!*"

Elric's name formed on Dyvim Tvar's lips, but he found that he
could not speak it.

"*Straasha!*"

The cross-legged figure swayed. The word became the calling of
the wind through the Caverns of Time.

"*Straasha!*"

It was plain to Dyvim Tvar that the rune was, for some reason, not working and that Elric was using up all his strength to no effect. And yet there was nothing the Lord of the Dragon Caves could do. His tongue was frozen. His feet seemed frozen to the ground.

He looked at the mist. Had it crept closer to the shore? Had it taken on a strange, almost luminous, green tinge? He peered closely.

There was a massive disturbance of the water. The sea rushed up the beach. The shingle crackled. The mist retreated. Vague lights flickered in the air and Dyvim Tvar thought he saw the shining silhouette of a gigantic figure emerging from the sea and he realized that Elric's chant had ceased.

"King Straasha," Elric was saying in something approaching his normal tone. "You have come. I thank you."

The silhouette spoke and the voice reminded Dyvim Tvar of slow, heavy waves rolling beneath a friendly sun.

"We elementals are concerned, Elric, for there are rumours that you have invited Chaos Lords back to your plane and the elementals have never loved the Lords of Chaos. Yet I know that if you have done this it is because you are fated to do it and therefore we hold no enmity against you."

"The decision was forced upon me, King Straasha. There was no other decision I could make. If you are therefore reluctant to aid me, I shall understand that and call on you no more."

"I will help you, though helping you is harder now, not for what happens in the immediate future but what is hinted will happen in years to come. Now you must tell me quickly how we of the water can be of service to you."

"Do you know ought of the Ship Which Sails Over Land and Sea? I need to find that ship if I am to fulfill my vow to find my love, Cymoril."

"I know much of that ship, for it is mine. Grome also lays claim to it. But it is mine. Fairly, it is mine."

"Grome of the Earth?"

"Grome of the Land Below the Roots. Grome of the Ground and all that lives under it. My brother. Grome. Long since, even as we elementals count time, Grome and I built that ship so that we could travel between the realms of Earth and Water whenever we chose. But we quarreled (may we

be cursed for such foolishness) and we fought. There were earthquakes, tidal waves, volcanic eruptions, typhoons and battles in which all the elementals joined, with the result that new continents were flung up and old ones drowned. It was not the first time we had fought each other, but it was the last. And finally, lest we destroy each other completely, we made a peace. I gave Grome part of my domain and he gave me the Ship Which Sails Over Land and Sea. But he gave it somewhat unwillingly and thus it sails the sea better than it sails the land, for Grome thwarts its progress whenever he can. Still, if the ship is of use to you, you shall have it."

"I thank you, King Straasha. Where shall I find it?"

"It will come. And now I grow weary, for the further from my own realm I venture, the harder it is to sustain my mortal form. Farewell, Elric—and be cautious. You have a greater power than you know and many would make use of it to their own ends."

"Shall I wait here for the Ship Which Sails Over Land and Sea?"

"No . . ." the sea-king's voice was fading as his form faded. Grey mist drifted back where the silhouette and the green lights had been. The sea again was still. *"Wait. Wait in your tower . . . It will come . . ."*

A few wavelets lapped the shore and then it was as if the king of the water elementals had never been there at all. Dyvim Tvar rubbed his eyes. Slowly at first he began to move to where Elric still sat. Gently he bent down and offered the albino his hand. Elric looked up in some surprise. "Ah, Dyvim Tvar. How much time has passed?"

"Some hours, Elric. It will soon be night. What little light there is begins to wane. We had best ride back for Imrryr."

Stiffly Elric rose to his feet, with Dyvim Tvar's assistance. "Aye . . ." he murmured absently. "The sea-king said . . ."

"I heard the sea-king, Elric. I heard his advice and I heard his warning. You must remember to heed both. I like too little the sound of this magic boat. Like most things of sorcerous origin, the ship appears to have vices as well as virtues, like a double-bladed knife which you raise to stab your enemy and which, instead, stabs you . . ."

"That must be expected where sorcery is concerned. It was you who urged me on, my friend."

"Aye," said Dyvim Tvar almost to himself as he led the way up the cliff-path towards the horses. "Aye. I have not forgotten that, my lord king."

Elric smiled wanly and touched Dyvim Tvar's arm. "Worry not. The Summoning is over and now we have the vessel we need to take us swiftly to Prince Yyrkoon and the lands of Oin and Yu."

"Let us hope so." Dyvim Tvar was privately skeptical about the benefits they would gain from the Ship Which Sails Over Land and Sea. They reached the horses and he began to wipe the water off the flanks of his own roan. "I regret," he said, "that we have once again allowed the dragons to expend their energy on a useless endeavour. With a squadron of my beasts, we could do much against Prince Yyrkoon. And it would be fine and wild, my friend, to ride the skies again, side by side, as we used to."

"When all this is done and Princess Cymoril brought home, we shall do that," said Elric, hauling himself wearily into the saddle of his white stallion. "You shall blow the Dragon Horn and our dragon brothers will hear it and you and I shall sing the Song of the Dragon Masters and our goads shall flash as we straddle Flamefang and his mate Sweetclaw. Ah, that will be like the days of old Melniboné, when we no longer equate freedom with power, but let the Young Kingdoms go their own way and be certain that they let us go ours!"

Dyvim Tvar pulled on his horse's reins. His brow was clouded. "Let us pray that day will come, my lord. But I cannot help this nagging thought which tells me that Imrryr's days are numbered and that my own life nears its close . . ."

"Nonsense, Dyvim Tvar. You'll survive me. There's little doubt of that, though you be my elder."

Dyvim Tvar said, as they galloped back through the closing day: "I have two sons. Did you know that, Elric?"

"You have never mentioned them."

"They are by old mistresses."

"I am happy for you."

"They are fine Melnibonéans."

"Why do you mention this, Dyvim Tvar?" Elric tried to read his friend's expression.

"It is that I love them and would have them enjoy the pleasures of the Dragon Isle."

"And why should they not?"

"I do not know." Dyvim Tvar looked hard at Elric. "I could suggest that it is your responsibility, the fate of my sons, Elric."

"Mine?"

"It seems to me, from what I gathered from the water elemental's words, that your decisions could decide the fate of the Dragon Isle. I ask you to remember my sons, Elric."

"I shall, Dyvim Tvar. I am certain they shall grow into superb Dragon Masters and that one of them shall succeed you as Lord of the Dragon Caves."

"I think you miss my meaning, my lord emperor."

And Elric looked solemnly at his friend and shook his head. "I do not miss your meaning, old friend. But I think you judge me harshly if you fear I'll do ought to threaten Melniboné and all she is."

"Forgive me, then." Dyvim Tvar lowered his head. But the expression in his eyes did not change.

In Imrryr they changed their clothes and drank hot wine and had spiced food brought. Elric, for all his weariness, was in better spirits than he had been for many a month. And yet there was still a tinge of something behind his surface mood which suggested he encouraged himself to speak gaily and put vitality into his movements. Admittedly, thought Dyvim Tvar, the prospects had improved and soon they would be confronting Prince Yyrkoon. But the dangers ahead of them were unknown, the pitfalls probably considerable. Still, he did not, out of sympathy for his friend, want to dispel Elric's mood. He was glad, in fact, that Elric seemed in a more positive frame of mind. There was talk of the equipment they would need in their expedition to the mysterious lands of Yu and Oin, speculation concerning the capacity of the Ship Which Sails Over Land and Sea—how many men it would take, what provisions they should put aboard and so on.

When Elric went to his bed, he did not walk with the dragging tiredness which had previously accompanied his step and again, bidding him goodnight, Dyvim Tvar was struck by the same emotion which had filled him on the beach, watching Elric begin his rune. Perhaps it was not by chance that he had used the example of his sons when speaking to Elric earlier that day, for he had a feeling that was almost protective, as if Elric were a boy looking forward to some treat which might not bring him the joy he expected.

Dyvim Tvar dismissed the thoughts, as best he could, and went to his own bed. Elric might blame himself for all that had occurred in the question of Yyrkoon and Cymoril, but Dyvim Tvar wondered if he, too, were not to blame in some part. Perhaps he should have offered his advice more cogently—more vehemently, even—earlier and made a stronger attempt to influence the young emperor. And then, in the Melnibonéan manner, he dismissed such doubts and questions as pointless. There was only one rule—seek pleasure however you would. But had that always been the Melnibonéan way? Dyvim Tvar wondered suddenly if Elric might not have regressive rather than deficient blood. Could Elric be a reincarnation of one of their most distant ancestors? Had it always been in the Melnibonéan character to think only of oneself and one's own gratification?

And again Dyvim Tvar dismissed the questions. What use was there in questions, after all? The world was the world. A man was a man. Before he sought his own bed he went to visit both his old mistresses, waking them up and insisting that he see his sons, Dyvim Slorm and Dyvim Mav and when his sons, sleepy-eyed, bewildered, had been brought to him, he stared at them for a long while before sending them back. He had said nothing to either, but he had brought his brows together frequently and rubbed at his face and shaken his head and, when they had gone, had said to Niopal and Saramal, his mistresses, who were as bewildered as their offspring, "Let them be taken to the Dragon Caves tomorrow and begin their learning."

"So soon, Dyvim Tvar?" said Niopal.

"Aye. There's little time left, I fear."

He would not amplify on this remark because he could not. It was

merely a feeling he had. But it was a feeling that was fast becoming an
obsession with him.

In the morning Dyvim Tvar returned to Elric's tower and found the
emperor pacing the gallery above the city, asking eagerly for any news
of a ship sighted off the coast of the island. But no such ship had been
seen. Servants answered earnestly that if their emperor could describe
the ship, it would be easier for them to know for what to look, but he
could not describe the ship, and could only hint that it might not be
seen on water at all, but might appear on land. He was all dressed up in
his black war-gear and it was plain to Dyvim Tvar that Elric was in-
dulging in even larger quantities of the potions which replenished his
blood. The crimson eyes gleamed with a hot vitality, the speech was
rapid and the bone-white hands moved with unnatural speed when
Elric made even the lightest gesture.

"Are you well this morning, my lord?" asked the Dragon Master.

"In excellent spirits, thank you, Dyvim Tvar." Elric grinned.
"Though I'd feel even better if the Ship Which Sails Over Land and
Sea were here now." He went to the balustrade and leaned upon it,
peering over the towers and beyond the city walls, looking first to the
sea and then to the land. "Where can it be? I wish that King Straasha
had been able to be more specific."

"I'll agree with that." Dyvim Tvar, who had not breakfasted,
helped himself from the variety of succulent foods laid upon the table.
It was evident that Elric had eaten nothing.

Dyvim Tvar began to wonder if the volume of potions had not affected his old friend's brain; perhaps madness, brought about by his in-
volvement with complicated sorcery, his anxiety for Cymoril, his
hatred of Yyrkoon, had begun to overwhelm Elric.

"Would it not be better to rest and to wait until the ship is
sighted?" he suggested quietly as he wiped his lips.

"Aye—there's reason in that," Elric agreed. "But I cannot. I have
an urge to be off, Dyvim Tvar, to come face to face with Yyrkoon, to
have my revenge on him, to be united with Cymoril again."

"I understand that. Yet, still . . ."

Elric's laugh was loud and ragged. "You fret like Tanglebones over my well-being. I do not need two nursemaids, Lord of the Dragon Caves."

With an effort Dyvim Tvar smiled. "You are right. Well, I pray that this magical vessel—what is that?" He pointed out across the island. "A movement in yonder forest. As if the wind passes through it. But there is no sign of wind elsewhere."

Elric followed his gaze. "You are right. I wonder . . ."

And then they saw something emerge from the forest and the land itself seemed to ripple. It was something which glinted white and blue and black. It came closer.

"A sail," said Dyvim Tvar. "It is your ship, I think, my lord."

"Aye," Elric whispered, craning forward. "My ship. Make yourself ready, Dyvim Tvar. By midday we shall be gone from Imrryr."

CHAPTER SIX

What the Earth God Desired

The ship was tall and slender and she was delicate. Her rails, masts and bulwarks were exquisitely carved and obviously not the work of a mortal craftsman. Though built of wood, the wood was not painted but naturally shone blue and black and green and a kind of deep smoky red; and her rigging was the colour of sea-weed and there were veins in the planks of her polished deck, like the roots of trees, and the sails on her three tapering masts were as fat and white and light as clouds on a fine summer day. The ship was everything that was lovely in nature; few could look upon her and not feel a delight like that which comes from sighting a perfect view. In a word, the ship radiated harmony, and Elric could think of no finer vessel in which to sail against Prince Yyrkoon and the dangers of the lands of Oin and Yu.

The ship sailed gently in the ground as if upon the surface of a river and the earth beneath the keel rippled as if turned momentarily to water. Wherever the keel of the ship touched, and a few feet around it, this effect became evident, though, after the ship had passed, the ground would return to its usual stable state. This was why the trees of the forest had swayed as the ship passed through them, parting before the keel as the ship sailed towards Imrryr.

The Ship Which Sails Over Land and Sea was not particularly large. Certainly she was considerably smaller than a Melnibonéan battle-barge and only a little bigger than a southern galley. But the grace of her; the curve of her line; the pride of her bearing—in these, she had no rival at all.

Already her gangplanks had been lowered to the ground and she was being made ready for her journey. Elric, hands on his slim hips, stood looking up at King Straasha's gift. From the gates of the city wall slaves were bearing provisions and arms and carrying them up the gangways. Meanwhile Dyvim Tvar was assembling the Imrryrian warriors and assigning them their ranks and duties while on the expedition. There were not many warriors. Only half the available strength could come with the ship, for the other half must remain behind under the command of Admiral Magum Colim and protect the city. It was unlikely that there would be any large attack on Melniboné after the punishment meted out to the barbarian fleet, but it was wise to take precautions, particularly since Prince Yyrkoon had vowed to conquer Imrryr. Also, for some strange reason that none of the onlookers could divine, Dyvim Tvar had called for volunteers—veterans who shared a common disability—and made up a special detachment of these men who, so the onlookers thought, could be of no use at all on the expedition. Still, neither were they of use when it came to defending the city, so they might as well go. These veterans were led aboard first.

Last to climb the gangway was Elric himself. He walked slowly, heavily, a proud figure in his black armour, until he reached the deck. Then he turned, saluted his city, and ordered the gangplank raised.

Dyvim Tvar was waiting for him on the poop deck. The Lord of the Dragon Caves had stripped off one of his gauntlets and was running his naked hand over the oddly coloured wood of the rail. "This is not a ship made for war, Elric," he said. "I should not like to see it harmed."

"How can it be harmed?" Elric asked lightly as Imrryrians began to climb the rigging and adjust the sails. "Would Straasha let it be destroyed? Would Grome? Fear not for the Ship Which Sails Over Land and Sea, Dyvim Tvar. Fear only for our own safety and the success of our expedition. Now, let us consult the charts. Remembering Straasha's warning concerning his brother Grome, I suggest we travel by sea for as far as possible, calling in here ..." he pointed to a sea-port on the western coast of Lormyr—"to get our bearings and learn what we can of the lands of Oin and Yu and how those lands are defended."

"Few travelers have ever ventured beyond Lormyr. It is said that the edge of the world lies not far from that country's most southerly borders." Dyvim Tvar frowned. "Could not this whole mission be a trap, I wonder? Arioch's trap? What if he is in league with Prince Yyrkoon and we have been completely deceived into embarking upon an expedition which will destroy us?"

"I have considered that," said Elric. "But there is no other choice. We must trust Arioch."

"I suppose we must." Dyvim Tvar smiled ironically. "Another matter now occurs to me. How does the ship move? I saw no anchors we could raise and there are no tides that I know of that sweep across the land. The wind fills the sails—see." It was true. The sails were billowing and the masts creaked slightly as they took the strain.

Elric shrugged and spread his hands. "I suppose we must tell the ship," he suggested. "Ship—we are ready to sail."

Elric took some pleasure in Dyvim Tvar's expression of astonishment as, with a lurch, the ship began to move. It sailed smoothly, as over a calm sea, and Dyvim Tvar instinctively clutched the rail, shouting: "But we are heading directly for the city wall!"

Elric crossed quickly to the centre of the poop deck where a large lever lay, horizontally attached to a ratchet which in turn was attached to a spindle. This was almost certainly the steering gear. Elric grasped the lever as one might grasp an oar and pushed it round a notch or two. Immediately the ship responded—and turned towards another part of the wall! Elric hauled back on the lever and the ship leaned, protesting a little as she yawed around and began to head out across the island. Elric laughed in delight. "You see, Dyvim Tvar, it is easy. A slight effort of logic was all it took!"

"Nonetheless," said Dyvim Tvar suspiciously, "I'd rather we rode dragons. At least they are beasts and may be understood. But this sorcery, it troubles me."

"Those are not fitting words for a noble of Melniboné!" Elric shouted above the sound of the wind in the rigging, the creaking of the ship's timbers, the slap of the great white sails.

"Perhaps not," said Dyvim Tvar. "Perhaps that explains why I stand beside you now, my lord."

Elric darted his friend a puzzled look before he went below to find a helmsman whom he could teach how to steer the ship.

The ship sped swiftly over rocky slopes and up gorse-covered hills; she cut her way through forests and sailed grandly over grassy plains. She moved like a low-flying hawk which keeps close to the ground but progresses with incredible speed and accuracy as it searches for its prey, altering its course with an imperceptible flick of a wing. The soldiers of Imrryr crowded her decks, gasping in amazement at the ship's progress over the land, and many of the men had to be clouted back to their positions at the sails or elsewhere about the ship. The huge warrior who acted as bosun seemed the only member of the crew unaffected by the miracle of the ship. He was behaving as he would normally behave aboard one of the golden battle-barges; going solidly about his duties and seeing to it that all was done in a proper seamanly manner. The helmsman Elric had selected was, on the other hand, wide-eyed and somewhat nervous of the ship he handled. You could see that he felt he was, at any moment, going to be dashed against a slab of rock or smash the ship apart in a tangle of thick-trunked pines. He was forever wetting his lips and wiping sweat from his brow, even though the air was sharp and his breath steamed as it left his throat. Yet he was a good helmsman and gradually he became used to handling the ship, though his movements were, perforce, more rapid, for there was little time to deliberate upon a decision, the ship traveled with such speed over the land. The speed was breathtaking; they sped more swiftly than any horse—were swifter, even, than Dyvim Tvar's beloved dragons. Yet the motion was exhilarating, too, as the expressions on the faces of all the Imrryrians told.

Elric's delighted laughter rang through the ship and infected many another member of the crew.

"Well, if Grome of the Roots is trying to block our progress, I hesitate to guess how fast we shall travel when we reach water!" he called to Dyvim Tvar.

Dyvim Tvar had lost some of his earlier mood. His long, fine hair streamed around his face as he smiled at his friend. "Aye—we shall all be whisked off the deck and into the sea!"

And then, as if in answer to their words, the ship began suddenly to buck and at the same time sway from side to side, like a ship caught in powerful cross-currents. The helmsman went white and clung to his lever, trying to get the ship back under control. There came a brief, terrified yell and a sailor fell from the highest crosstree in the main mast and crashed onto the deck, breaking every bone in his body. And then the ship swayed once or twice and the turbulence was behind them and they continued on their course.

Elric stared at the body of the fallen sailor. Suddenly the mood of gaiety left him completely and he gripped the rail in his black gauntleted hands and he gritted his strong teeth and his crimson eyes glowed and his lips curled in self-mockery. "What a fool I am. What a fool I am to tempt the gods so!"

Still, though the ship moved almost as swiftly as it had done, there seemed to be something dragging at it, as if Grome's minions clung on to the bottom as barnacles might cling in the sea. And Elric sensed something around him in the air, something in the rustling of the trees through which they passed, something in the movement of the grass and the bushes and the flowers over which they crossed, something in the weight of the rocks, of the angle of the hills. And he knew that what he sensed was the presence of Grome of the Ground—Grome of the Land Below the Roots—Grome, who desired to own what he and his brother Straasha had once owned jointly, what they had made as a sign

of the unity between them and over which they had then fought.
Grome wanted very much to take back the Ship Which Sails Over
Land and Sea. And Elric, staring down at the black earth, became
afraid.

CHAPTER SEVEN

King Grome

But at last, with the land tugging at their keel, they reached the sea,
sliding into the water and gathering speed with every moment, until
Melniboné was gone behind them and they were sighting the thick
clouds of steam which hung for ever over the Boiling Sea. Elric
thought it unwise to risk even this magic vessel in those peculiar waters, so the vessel was turned and headed for the coast of Lormyr,
sweetest and most tranquil of the Young Kingdom nations, and the
port of Ramasaz on Lormyr's western shore. If the southern barbarians
with whom they had so recently fought had been from Lormyr, Elric
would have considered making for some other port, but the barbarians
had almost certainly been from the south-east on the far side of the continent, beyond Pikarayd. The Lormyrians, under their fat, cautious
King Fadan, were not likely to join a raid unless its success was completely assured. Sailing slowly into Ramasaz, Elric gave instructions
that their ship be moored in a conventional way and treated like any ordinary ship. It attracted attention, nonetheless, for its beauty, and the
inhabitants of the port were astonished to find Melnibonéans crewing
the vessel. Though Melnibonéans were disliked throughout the Young
Kingdoms, they were also feared. Thus, outwardly at any rate, Elric
and his men were treated with respect and were served reasonably
good food and wine in the hostelries they entered.

In the largest of the waterfront inns, a place called Heading Outward and Coming Safely Home Again, Elric found a garrulous host
who had, until he bought the inn, been a prosperous fisherman and

who knew the southernmost shores reasonably well. He certainly knew the lands of Oin and Yu, but he had no respect for them at all.

"You think they could be massing for war, my lord." He raised his eyebrows at Elric before hiding his face in his wine-mug. Wiping his lips, he shook his red head. "Then they must war against sparrows. Oin and Yu are barely nations at all. Their only halfway decent city is Dhoz-Kam—and that is shared between them, half being on one side of the River Ar and half being on the other. As for the rest of Oin and Yu—it is inhabited by peasants who are for the most part so ill-educated and superstition-ridden that they are poverty stricken. Not a potential soldier among 'em."

"You've heard nothing of a Melnibonéan renegade who has conquered Oin and Yu and set about training these peasants to make war?" Dyvim Tvar leaned on the bar next to Elric. He sipped fastidiously from a thick cup of wine. "Prince Yyrkoon is the renegade's name."

"Is that whom you seek?" The innkeeper became more interested. "A dispute between the Dragon Princes, eh?"

"That's our business," said Elric haughtily.

"Of course, my lords."

"You know nothing of a great mirror which steals men's memories?" Dyvim Tvar asked.

"A magical mirror!" The innkeeper threw back his head and laughed heartily. "I doubt if there's one decent mirror in the whole of Oin or Yu! No, my lords, I think you are misled if you fear danger from those lands!"

"Doubtless you are right," said Elric, staring down into his own untasted wine. "But it would be wise if we were to check for ourselves—and it would be in Lormyr's interests, too, if we were to find what we seek and warn you accordingly."

"Fear not for Lormyr. We can deal easily with any silly attempt to make war from that quarter. But if you'd see for yourselves, you must follow the coast for three days until you come to a great bay. The River Ar runs into that bay and on the shores of the river lies Dhoz-Kam—a seedy sort of city, particularly for a capital serving two nations. The inhabitants are corrupt, dirty and disease-ridden, but fortunately they are also lazy and thus afford little trouble, especially if you keep a sword by you. When you have spent an hour in Dhoz-Kam, you will realize the impossibility of such folk becoming a menace to anyone else, unless they should get close enough to you to infect you with one of their several plagues!" Again the innkeeper laughed hugely at his own wit. As he ceased shaking, he added: "Or unless you fear their navy. It consists of a dozen or so filthy fishing boats, most of which are so unseaworthy they dare only fish the shallows of the estuary."

Elric pushed his wine-cup aside. "We thank you, landlord." He placed a Melnibonéan silver piece upon the counter.

"This will be hard to change," said the innkeeper craftily.

"There is no need to change it on our account," Elric told him.

"I thank you, masters. Would you stay the night at my establishment? I can offer you the finest beds in Ramasaz."

"I think not," Elric told him. "We shall sleep aboard our ship tonight, that we might be ready to sail at dawn."

The landlord watched the Melnibonéans depart. Instinctively he bit at the silver piece and then, suspecting he tasted something odd about it, removed it from his mouth. He stared at the coin, turning it this way and that. Could Melnibonéan silver be poisonous to an ordinary mortal? he wondered. It was best not to take risks. He tucked the coin into his purse and collected up the two wine-cups they had left behind. Though he hated waste, he decided it would be wiser to throw the cups out lest they should have become tainted in some way.

The Ship Which Sails Over Land and Sea reached the bay at noon on the following day and now it lay close inshore, hidden from the distant city by a short isthmus on which grew thick, near-tropical foliage. Elric and Dyvim Tvar waded through the clear, shallow water to the beach and entered the forest. They had decided to be cautious and not make their presence known until they had determined the truth of the innkeeper's contemptuous description of Dhoz-Kam. Near the tip of the isthmus was a reasonably high hill and growing on the hill were several good-sized trees. Elric and Dyvim Tvar used their swords to clear a path through the undergrowth and made their way up the hill until they stood under the trees, picking out the one most easily climbed. Elric selected a tree whose trunk bent and then straightened out again. He sheathed his sword, got his hands onto the trunk and hauled himself up, clambering along until he reached a succession of thick branches which would bear his weight. In the meantime Dyvim Tvar climbed another nearby tree until at last both men could get a good view across the bay where the city of Dhoz-Kam could be clearly seen. Certainly the city itself deserved the innkeeper's description. It was squat and grimy and evidently poor. Doubtless this was why Yyrkoon had chosen it, for the lands of Oin and Yu could not have been hard to conquer with the help of a handful of well-trained Imr-ryrians and some of Yyrkoon's sorcerous allies. Indeed, few would have bothered to conquer such a place, since its wealth was plainly virtually non-existent and its geographical position of no strategic importance. Yyrkoon had chosen well, for purposes of secrecy if nothing else. But the landlord had been wrong about Dhoz-Kam's fleet. Even from here Elric and Dyvim Tvar could make out at least thirty good-sized war-ships in the harbour and there seemed to be more anchored up-river. But the ships did not interest them as much as the thing which flashed and glittered above the city—something which had been mounted on huge pillars which supported an axle which, in turn, supported a vast, circular mirror set in a frame whose workmanship was as plainly non-mortal as that of the ship which had brought the Melnibonéans here. There was no doubt that they looked upon the Mirror of Memory and that any who had sailed into the harbour after it had been erected must have had their memory of what they had seen stolen from them in-stantly.

"It seems to me, my lord," said Dyvim Tvar from his perch a yard or two away from Elric, "that it would be unwise of us to sail directly into the harbour of Dhoz-Kam. Indeed, we could be in danger if we entered the bay. I think that we look upon the mirror, even now, only because it is not pointed directly at us. But you notice there is machinery to turn it in any direction its user chooses—save one. It cannot be turned inland, behind the city. There is no need for it, for who would approach Oin and Yu from the wastelands beyond their borders and who but the inhabitants of Oin or Yu would need to come overland to their capital?"

"I think I take your meaning, Dyvim Tvar. You suggest that we would be wise to make use of the special properties of our ship and . . ."

". . . and go overland to Dhoz-Kam, striking suddenly and making full use of those veterans we brought with us, moving swiftly and ignoring Prince Yyrkoon's new allies—seeking the prince himself, and his renegades. Could we do that, Elric? Dash into the city—seize Yyrkoon, rescue Cymoril—then speed out again and away?"

"Since we have too few men to make a direct assault, it is all we can do, though it's dangerous. The advantage of surprise would be lost, of course, once we had made the attempt. If we failed in our first attempt it would become much harder to attack a second time. The alternative is to sneak into the city at night and hope to locate Yyrkoon and Cymoril alone, but then we should not be making use of our one important weapon, the Ship Which Sails Over Land and Sea. I think your plan is the best one, Dyvim Tvar. Let us turn the ship inland, now, and hope that Grome takes his time in finding us—for I still worry lest he try seriously to wrest the ship from our possession." Elric began to climb down towards the ground.

Standing once more upon the poop deck of the lovely ship, Elric ordered the helmsman to turn the vessel once again towards the land. Under half-sail the ship moved gracefully through the water and up the curve of the bank and the flowering shrubs of the forest parted before its prow and then they were sailing through the green dark of the jungle, while startled birds cawed and shrilled and little animals paused in astonishment and peered down from the trees at the Ship Which Sails Over Land and Sea and some almost lost their balance as the graceful boat progressed calmly over the floor of the forest, turning aside for only the thickest of the trees.

And thus they made their way to the interior of the land called Oin, which lay to the north of the River Ar, which marked the border between Oin and the land called Yu with which Oin shared a single capital.

Oin was a country consisting largely of unforested jungle and infertile plains where the inhabitants farmed, for they feared the forest and would not go into it, even though that was where Oin's wealth might be found.

The ship sailed well enough through the forest and out over the plain and soon they could see a large river glinting ahead of them and Dyvim Tvar, glancing at the crude map with which he had furnished himself in Ramasaz, suggested that they begin to turn towards the south again and approach Dhoz Kam by means of a wide semi-circle. Elric agreed and the ship began to tack round.

It was then that the land began to heave again and huge waves of grassy earth this time rolled around the ship and blotted out the surrounding view. The ship pitched wildly up and down and from side to side. Two more Imrryrians fell from the rigging and were killed on the deck below. The bosun was shouting loudly—though in fact all this upheaval was happening in silence—and the silence made the situation seem that much more menacing. The bosun yelled to his men to tie themselves to their positions. "And all those not doing anything—get below at once!" he added.

Elric had wound a scarf around the rail and tied the other end to his wrist. Dyvim Tvar had used a long belt for the same purpose. But still they were flung in all directions, often losing their footing as the ship bucked this way and that, and every bone in Elric's body seemed about to crack and every inch of his flesh seemed bruised. And the ship was creaking and protesting and threatening to break up under the awful strain of riding the heaving land.

"Is this Grome's work, Elric?" Dyvim Tvar panted. "Or is it some sorcery of Yyrkoon's?"

Elric shook his head. "Not Yyrkoon. It is Grome. And I know no way to placate him. Not Grome, who thinks least of all the kings of the elements, yet, perhaps, is the most powerful."

"But surely he breaks his bargain with his brother by doing this to us?"

"No. I think not. King Straasha warned us this might happen. We can only hope that Grome expends all his energy and that the ship survives, as it might survive a natural storm at sea."

"This is worse than a sea-storm, Elric!"

Elric nodded his agreement but could say nothing, for the deck was tilting at a crazy angle and he had to cling to the rails with both hands in order to retain any kind of footing.

And now the silence stopped.

Instead they heard a rumbling and a roaring that seemed to have something of the character of laugher.

"King Grome!" Elric shouted. "King Grome! Let us be! We have done you no harm!"

But the laughter increased and it made the whole ship quiver as the land rose and fell around it, as trees and hills and rocks rushed towards the ship and then fell away again, never quite engulfing them, for Grome doubtless wanted his ship intact.

"Grome! You have no quarrel with mortals!" Elric cried again. "Let us be! Ask a favour of us if you must, but grant us this favour in return!"

Elric was shouting almost anything that came into his head. Really, he had no hope of being heard by the earth god and he did not expect King Grome to bother to listen even if the elemental did hear. But there was nothing else to do.

"*Grome! Grome! Grome!* Listen to me!"

Elric's only response was in the louder laughter which made every nerve in him tremble. And the earth heaved higher and dropped lower and the ship spun round and round until Elric was sure he would lose his senses entirely.

"*King Grome! King Grome!* Is it just to slay those who have never done you harm?"

And then, slowly, the heaving earth subsided and the ship was still and a huge, brown figure stood looking down at the ship. The figure was the colour of earth and looked like a vast, old oak. His hair and his beard were the colour of leaves and his eyes were the colour of gold ore and his teeth were the colour of granite and his feet were like roots and his skin seemed covered in tiny green shoots in place of hair and he smelled rich and musty and good and he was King Grome of the Earth Elementals. He sniffed and he frowned and he said in a soft, mighty voice that was yet coarse and grumpy: "I want my ship."

"It is not our ship to give, King Grome," said Elric.

Grome's tone of petulance increased. "I want my ship," he said slowly. "I want the thing. It is mine."

"Of what use is it to you, King Grome?"

"Use? It is mine."

Grome stamped and the land rippled.

Elric said desperately: "It is your brother's ship, King Grome. It is King Straasha's ship. He gave you part of his domain and you allowed him to keep the ship. That was the bargain."

"I know nothing of a bargain. The ship is mine."

"You know that if you take the ship then King Straasha will have to take back the land he gave you."

"I want my ship." The huge figure shifted its position and bits of earth fell from it, landing with distinctly heard thuds on the ground below and on the deck of the ship.

"Then you must kill us to obtain it," Elric said.

"Kill? Grome does not kill mortals. He kills nothing. Grome builds. Grome brings to life."

"You have already killed three of our company," Elric pointed out. "Three are dead, King Grome, because you made the land-storm."

Grome's great brows drew together and he scratched his great head, causing an immense rustling noise to sound. "Grome does not kill," he said again.

"King Grome has killed," said Elric reasonably. "Three lives lost."

Grome grunted. "But I want my ship."

"The ship is lent to us by your brother. We cannot give it to you. Besides, we sail in it for a purpose—a noble purpose, I think. We . . ."

"I know nothing of 'purposes'—and care nothing for you. I want my ship. My brother should not have lent it to you. I had almost forgotten it. But now that I remember it, I want it."

"Will you not accept something else in place of the ship, King Grome?" said Dyvim Tvar suddenly. "Some other gift."

Grome shook his monstrous head. "How could a mortal give me something? It is mortals who take from me all the time. They steal my bones and my blood and my flesh. Could you give me back all that your kind has taken?"

"Is there not one thing?" Elric said.

Grome closed his eyes.

"Precious metals? Jewels?" suggested Dyvim Tvar. "We have many such in Melniboné."

"I have plenty," said King Grome.

Elric shrugged in despair. "How can we bargain with a god, Dyvim Tvar?" He gave a bitter smile. "What can the Lord of the Soil desire? More sun, more rain? These are not ours to give."

"I am a rough sort of god," said Grome, "if indeed god I am. But I did not mean to kill your comrades. I have an idea. Give me the bodies of the slain. Bury them in my earth."

Elric's heart leapt. "That is all you wish of us?"

"It would seem much to me."

"And for that you will let us sail on?"

"On water, aye," growled Grome. "But I do not see why I should allow you to sail over my land. It is too much to expect of me. You can go to yonder river, but from now this ship will only possess the properties bestowed upon it by my brother Straasha. No longer shall it cross my domain."

"But, King Grome, we need this ship. We are upon urgent business. We need to sail to the city yonder." Elric pointed in the direction of Dhoz-Kam.

"You may go to the river, but after that the ship will sail only on water. Now give me what I ask."

Elric called down to the bosun who, for the first time, seemed amazed by what he was witnessing. "Bring up the bodies of the three dead men."

The bodies were brought up from below. Grome stretched out one of his great, earthy hands and picked them up.

"I thank you," he growled. "Farewell."

And slowly Grome began to descend into the ground, his whole huge frame becoming, atom by atom, absorbed with the earth until he was gone.

And then the ship was moving again, slowly towards the river, on the last short voyage it would ever make upon the land.

"And thus our plans are thwarted," said Elric.

Dyvim Tvar looked miserably towards the shining river. "Aye. So much for that scheme. I hesitate to suggest this to you, Elric, but I fear we must resort to sorcery again if we are to stand any chance of achieving our goal."

Elric sighed.

"I fear we must," he said.

CHAPTER EIGHT

The City and the Mirror

Prince Yyrkoon was pleased. His plans went well. He peered through the high fence which enclosed the flat roof of his house (three storeys high and the finest in Dhoz-Kam); he looked out towards the harbour at his splendid, captured fleet. Every ship which had come to Dhoz-Kam and which had not flown the standard of a powerful nation had been easily taken after its crew had looked upon the great mirror which squatted on its pillars above the city. Demons had built those pillars and Prince Yyrkoon had paid them for their work with the souls of all those in Oin and Yu who had resisted him. Now there was one last ambition to fulfill and then he and his new followers would be on their way to Melniboné . . .

He turned and spoke to his sister. Cymoril lay on a wooden bench, staring unseeingly at the sky, clad in the filthy tatters of the dress she had been wearing when Yyrkoon abducted her from her tower.

"See our fleet, Cymoril! While the golden barges are scattered we shall sail unhampered into Imrryr and declare the city ours. Elric cannot defend himself against us now. He fell so easily into my trap. He is a fool! And you were a fool to give him your affection!"

Cymoril made no response. Through all the months she had been away, Yyrkoon had drugged her food and drink and produced in her a lassitude which rivaled Elric's undrugged condition. Yyrkoon's own experiments with his sorcerous powers had turned him gaunt, wild-eyed and somewhat mangy; he ceased to take any pains with his physical appearance. But Cymoril had a wasted, haunted look to her, for all that beauty remained. It was as if Dhoz-Kam's rundown seediness had infected them both in different ways.

"Fear not for your own future, however, my sister," Yyrkoon continued. He chuckled. "You shall still be empress and sit beside the emperor on his Ruby Throne. Only I shall be emperor and Elric shall die for many days and the manner of his death will be more inventive than anything he thought to do to me."

Cymoril's voice was hollow and distant. She did not turn her head when she spoke. "You are insane, Yyrkoon."

"Insane? Come now, sister, is that a word that a true Melnibonéan should use? We Melnibonéans judge nothing sane or insane. What a man is—he is. What he does—he does. Perhaps you have stayed too long in the Young Kingdoms and its judgments are becoming yours. But that shall soon be righted. We shall return to the Dragon Isle in triumph and you will forget all this, just as if you yourself had looked into the Mirror of Memory." He darted a nervous glance upwards, as if he half-expected the mirror to be turned on him.

Cymoril closed her eyes. Her breathing was heavy and very slow; she was bearing this nightmare with fortitude, certain that Elric must eventually rescue her from it. That hope was all that had stopped her from destroying herself. If the hope went altogether, then she would bring about her own death and be done with Yyrkoon and all his horrors.

"Did I tell you that last night I was successful? I raised demons, Cymoril. Such powerful, dark demons. I learned from them all that was left for me to learn. And I opened the Shade Gate at last. Soon I shall pass through it and there I shall find what I seek. I shall become the most powerful mortal on earth. Did I tell you all this, Cymoril?"

He had, in fact, repeated himself several times that morning, but Cymoril had paid no more attention to him then than she did now. She felt so tired. She tried to sleep. She said slowly, as if to remind herself of something: "I hate you, Yyrkoon."

"Ah, but you shall love me soon, Cymoril. Soon."

"Elric will come . . ."

"Elric! Ha! He sits twiddling his thumbs in his tower, waiting for news that will never come—save when I bring it to him!"

"Elric will come," she said.

Yyrkoon snarled. A brute-faced Oinish girl brought him his morning wine. Yyrkoon seized the cup and sipped the stuff. Then he spat it at the girl who, trembling, ducked away. Yyrkoon took the jug and emptied it onto the white dust of the roof. "This is Elric's thin blood. This is how it will flow away!"

But again Cymoril was not listening. She was trying to remember her albino lover and the few sweet days they had spent together since they were children.

Yyrkoon hurled the empty jug at the girl's head, but she was adept at dodging him. As she dodged, she murmured her standard response to all his attacks and insults. "Thank you, Demon Lord," she said. "Thank you, Demon Lord."

Yyrkoon laughed. "Aye. Demon Lord. Your folk are right to call me that, for I rule more demons than I rule men. My power increases every day!"

The Oinish girl hurried away to fetch more wine, for she knew he would be calling for it in a moment. Yyrkoon crossed the roof to stare through the slats in the fence at the proof of his power, but as he looked upon his ships he heard sounds of confusion from the other side of the roof. Could the Yurits and the Oinish be fighting amongst themselves? Where were their Imrryrian centurions? Where was Captain Valharik?

He almost ran across the roof, passing Cymoril who appeared to be sleeping, and peered down into the streets.

"Fire?" he murmured. "Fire?"

It was true that the streets appeared to be on fire. And yet it was not an ordinary fire. Balls of fire seemed to drift about, igniting rush-thatched roofs, doors, anything which would easily burn—as an invading army might put a village to the torch.

Yyrkoon scowled, thinking at first that he had been careless and some spell of his had turned against him, but then he looked over the burning houses at the river and he saw a strange ship sailing there, a ship of great grace and beauty, that somehow seemed more a creation of nature than of man—and he knew they were under attack. But who would attack Dhoz-Kam? There was no loot worth the effort. It could not be Imrryrians . . .

It could not be Elric.

"It must not be Elric," he growled. "The mirror. It must be turned upon the invaders."

"And upon yourself, brother?" Cymoril had risen unsteadily and leaned against a table. She was smiling. "You were too confident, Yyrkoon. Elric comes."

"Elric! Nonsense! Merely a few barbarian raiders from the interior. Once they are in the centre of the city, we shall be able to use the Mirror of Memory upon them." He ran to the trapdoor which led down into his house. "Captain Valharik! Valharik where are you?"

Valharik appeared in the room below. He was sweating. There was a blade in his gloved hand, though he did not seem to have been in any fighting as yet.

"Make the mirror ready, Valharik. Turn it upon the attackers."

"But, my lord, we might . . ."

"Hurry! Do as I say. We'll soon have these barbarians added to our own strength—along with their ships."

"Barbarians, my lord? Can barbarians command the fire elementals? These things we fight are flame spirits. They cannot be slain any more than fire itself can be slain."

"Fire can be slain by water," Prince Yyrkoon reminded his lieutenant. "By water, Captain Valharik. Have you forgotten?"

"But, Prince Yyrkoon, we have tried to quench the spirits with water—and the water will not move from our buckets. Some powerful sorcerer commands the invaders. He has the aid of the spirits of fire *and* water."

"You are mad, Captain Valharik," said Yyrkoon firmly. "Mad. Prepare the mirror and let us have no more of these stupidities."

Valharik wetted his dry lips. "Aye, my lord." He bowed his head and went to do his master's bidding.

Again Yyrkoon went to the fence and looked through. There were men in the streets now, fighting his own warriors, but smoke obscured his view, he could not make out the identities of any of the invaders. "Enjoy your petty victory," Yyrkoon chuckled, "for soon the mirror will take away your minds and you will become my slaves."

"It is Elric," said Cymoril quietly. She smiled. "Elric comes to take vengeance on you, brother."

Yyrkoon sniggered. "Think you? Think you? Well, should that be the case, he'll find me gone, for I still have a means of evading him— and he'll find you in a condition which will not please him (though it will cause him considerable anguish). But it is not Elric. It is some crude shaman from the steppes to the east of here. He will soon be in my power."

Cymoril, too, was peering through the fence.

"Elric," she said. "I can see his helm."

"What?" Yyrkoon pushed her aside. There, in the streets, Imrryrian fought Imrryrian, there was no longer any doubt of that. Yyrkoon's men—Imrryrian, Oinish and Yurit—were being pushed back. And at the head of the attacking Imrryrians could be seen a black dragon helm such as only one Melnibonéan wore. It was Elric's helm. And Elric's sword, that had once belonged to Earl Aubec of Malador, rose and fell and was bright with blood which glistened in the morning sunshine.

For a moment Yyrkoon was overwhelmed with despair. He groaned. "Elric. Elric. Elric. Ah, how we continue to underestimate each other! What curse is on us?"

Cymoril had flung back her head and her face had come to life again. "I said he would come, brother!"

Yyrkoon whirled on her. "Aye—he has come—and the mirror will rob him of his brain and he will turn into my slave, believing anything I care to put in his skull. This is even sweeter than I planned, sister. Ha!" He looked up and then flung his arms across his eyes as he realized what he had done. "Quickly—below—into the house—the mirror begins to turn." There came a great creaking of gears and pulleys and chains as the terrible Mirror of Memory began to focus on the streets below. "It will be only a little while before Elric has added himself and his men to my strength. What a splendid irony!" Yyrkoon hurried his sister down the steps leading from the roof and he closed the trapdoor behind him. "Elric himself will help in the attack on Imrryr. He will destroy his own kind. He will oust himself from the Ruby Throne!"

"Do you not think that Elric has anticipated the threat of the Mirror of Memory, brother?" Cymoril said with relish.

"Anticipate it, aye—but resist it he cannot. He must see to fight. He must either be cut down or open his eyes. No man with eyes can be safe from the power of the mirror." He glanced around the crudely furnished room. "Where is Valharik? Where is the cur?"

Valharik came running in. "The mirror is being turned, my lord, but it will affect our own men, too. I fear . . ."

"Then cease to fear. What if our own men are drawn under its influence? We can soon feed what they need to know back into their brains—at the same time as we feed our defeated foes. You are too nervous, Captain Valharik."

"But Elric leads them . . ."

"And Elric's eyes *are* eyes—though they look like crimson stones. He will fare no better than his men."

In the streets around Prince Yyrkoon's house Elric, Dyvim Tvar and their Imrryrians pushed on, forcing back their demoralized opponents. The attackers had lost barely a man, whereas many Oinish and Yurits lay dead in the streets, beside a few of their renegade Imrryrian commanders. The flame elementals, whom Elric had summoned with some effort, were beginning to disperse, for it cost them dear to spend so much time entirely within Elric's plane, but the necessary advantage had been gained and there was now little question of who would win as a hundred or more houses blazed throughout the city, igniting others and requiring attention from the defenders lest the whole squalid place burn down about their ears. In the harbour, too, ships were burning.

Dyvim Tvar was the first to notice the mirror beginning to swing into focus on the streets. He pointed a warning finger, then turned, blowing on his war-horn and ordering forward the troops who, up to now, had played no part in the fighting. "Now you must lead us!" he cried, and he lowered his helm over his face. The eye-holes of the helm had been blocked so that he could not see through.

Slowly Elric lowered his own helm until he was in darkness. The sound of fighting continued however, as the veterans who had sailed with them from

Melniboné set to work in their place and the other troops fell back. The leading Imrryrians had not blocked their eye-holes.

Elric prayed that the scheme would work.

Yyrkoon, peeking cautiously through a chink in a heavy curtain, said querulously: "Valharik? They fight on. Why is that? Is not the mirror focused?"

"It should be, my lord."

"Then, see for yourself, the Imrryrians continue to forge through our defenders—and our men are beginning to come under the influence of the mirror. What is wrong, Valharik? What is wrong?"

Valharik drew air between his teeth and there was a certain admiration in his expression as he looked upon the fighting Imrryrians.

"They are blind," he said. "They fight by sound and touch and smell. They are blind, my lord emperor—and they lead Elric and his men whose helms are so designed they can see nothing."

"Blind?" Yyrkoon spoke almost pathetically, refusing to understand. "Blind?"

"Aye. Blind warriors—men wounded in earlier wars, but good fighters nonetheless. That is how Elric defeats our mirror, my lord."

"Agh! No! No!" Yyrkoon beat heavily on his captain's back and the man shrank away. "Elric is not cunning. He is not cunning. Some powerful demon gives him these ideas."

"Perhaps, my lord. But are there demons more powerful than those who have aided you?"

"No," said Yyrkoon. "There are none. Oh, that I could summon some of them now! But I have expended my powers in opening the Shade Gate. I should have anticipated ... I could not anticipate ... Oh Elric! I shall yet destroy you, when the runeblades are mine!" Then Yyrkoon frowned. "But how could he have been prepared? What demon ...? Unless he summoned Arioch himself? But he has not the power to summon Arioch. I could not summon him ..."

And then, as if in reply, Yyrkoon heard Elric's battle song sounding from the nearby streets. And that song answered the question.

"Arioch! Arioch! Blood and souls for my lord Arioch!"

"Then I must have the runeblades. I must pass through the Shade Gate. There I still have allies—supernatural allies who shall deal easily with Elric, if need be. But I need time . . ." Yyrkoon mumbled to himself as he paced about the room. Valharik continued to watch the fighting.

"They come closer," said the captain.

Cymoril smiled. "Closer, Yyrkoon? Who is the fool now? Elric? Or you?"

"Be still! I think. I think . . ." Yyrkoon fingered his lips.

Then a light came into his eye and he looked cunningly at Cymoril for a second before turning his attention to Captain Valharik.

"Valharik, you must destroy the Mirror of Memory."

"Destroy it? But it is our only weapon, my lord?"

"Exactly—but is it not useless now?"

"Aye."

"Destroy it and it will serve us again." Yyrkoon flicked a long finger in the direction of the door. "Go. Destroy the mirror."

"But, Prince Yyrkoon—emperor, I mean—will that not have the effect of robbing us of our only weapon?"

"Do as I say, Valharik! Or perish!"

"But how shall I destroy it, my lord?"

"Your sword. You must climb the column *behind* the face of the mirror. Then, without looking into the mirror itself, you must swing your sword against it and smash it. It will break easily. You know the precautions I have had to take to make sure that it was not harmed."

"Is that all I must do?"

"Aye. Then you are free from my service—you may escape or do whatever else you wish to do."

"Do we not sail against Melniboné?"

"Of course not. I have devised another method of taking the Dragon Isle."

Valharik shrugged. His expression showed that he had never really believed Yyrkoon's assurances. But what else had he to do but follow Yyrkoon, when fearful torture awaited him at Elric's hands? With shoulders bowed, the captain slunk away to do his prince's work.

"And now, Cymoril..." Yyrkoon grinned like a ferret as he reached out to grab his sister's soft shoulders. "Now to prepare you for your lover, Elric."

One of the blind warriors cried: "They no longer resist us, my lord. They are limp and allow themselves to be cut down where they stand. Why is this?"

"The mirror has robbed them of their memories," Elric called, turning his own blind head towards the sound of the warrior's voice. "You can lead us into a building now—where, with luck, we shall not glimpse the mirror."

At last they stood within what appeared to Elric, as he lifted his helm, to be a warehouse of some kind. Luckily it was large enough to hold their entire force and when they were all inside Elric had the doors shut while they debated their next action.

"We should find Yyrkoon," Dyvim Tvar said. "Let us interrogate one of those warriors..."

"There'll be little point in that, my friend," Elric reminded him. "Their minds are gone. They'll remember nothing at all. They do not at present remember even what they are, let alone who. Go to the shutters yonder, where the mirror's influence cannot reach, and see if you can see the building most likely to be occupied by my cousin."

Dyvim Tvar crossed swiftly to the shutters and looked cautiously out. "Aye—there's a building larger than the rest and I see some movement within, as if the surviving warriors were regrouping. It's likely that's Yyrkoon's stronghold. It should be easily taken."

Elric joined him. "Aye. I agree with you. We'll find Yyrkoon there. But we must hurry, lest he decides to slay Cymoril. We must work out the best means of reaching the place and instruct our blind warriors as to how many streets, how many houses and so forth, we must pass."

"What is that strange sound?" One of the blind warriors raised his head. "Like the distant ringing of a gong."

"I hear it too," said another blind man.

And now Elric heard it. A sinister noise. It came from the air above them. It shivered through the atmosphere.

"The mirror!" Dyvim Tvar looked up. "Has the mirror some property we did not anticipate?"

"Possibly . . ." Elric tried to remember what Arioch had told him. But Arioch had been vague. He had said nothing of this dreadful, mighty sound, this shattering clangour as if . . . "He is breaking the mirror!" he said. "But why?" There was something more now, something brushing at his brain. As if the sound were, itself, sentient.

"Perhaps Yyrkoon is dead and his magic dies with him," Dyvim Tvar began. And then he broke off with a groan.

The noise was louder, more intense, bringing sharp pain to his ears.

And now Elric knew. He blocked his ears with his gauntleted hands. The memories in the mirror. They were flooding into his mind. The mirror had been smashed and was releasing all the memories it had stolen over the centuries—the aeons, perhaps. Many of those memories were not mortal. Many were the memories of beasts and intelligent creatures which had existed even before Melniboné. And the memories warred for a place in Elric's skull—in the skulls of all the Imrryrians—in the poor, tortured skulls of the men outside whose pitiful screams could be heard rising from the streets—and in the skull of Captain Valharik, the turncoat, as he lost his footing on the great column and fell with the shards from the mirror to the ground far below.

But Elric did not hear Captain Valharik scream and he did not hear Valharik's body crash first to a roof-top and then into the street where it lay all broken beneath the broken mirror.

Elric lay upon the stone floor of the warehouse and he writhed, as his comrades writhed, trying to clear his head of a million memories that were not his own—of loves, of hatreds, of strange experiences and ordinary experiences, of wars and journeys, of the faces of relatives who were not his relatives, of men and women and children, of animals, of ships and cities, of fights, of love-making, of fears and desires—and the memories fought each other for possession of his crowded skull, threatening to drive his own memories (and thus his own character) from his head. And as Elric writhed upon the ground, clutching at his ears, he spoke a word over and over again in an effort to cling to his own identity.

"Elric. Elric. Elric."

And gradually, by an effort which he had experienced only once before when he had summoned Arioch to the plane of the Earth, he managed to extinguish all those alien memories and assert his own until, shaken and feeble, he lowered his hands from his ears and no longer shouted his own name. And then he stood up and looked about him.

More than two thirds of his men were dead, blind or otherwise. The big bosun was dead, his eyes wide and staring, his lips frozen in a scream, his right eye-socket raw and bleeding from where he had tried to drag his eye from it. All the corpses lay in unnatural positions, all had their eyes open (if they had eyes) and many bore the marks of self-mutilation, while others had vomited and others had dashed their brains against a wall. Dyvim Tvar was alive, but curled up in a corner, mumbling to himself and Elric thought he might be mad. Some of the other survivors were, indeed, mad, but they were quiet, they afforded no danger. Only five, including Elric, seemed to have resisted the alien memories and retained their own sanity. It seemed to Elric, as he stumbled from corpse to corpse, that most of the men had had their hearts fail.

"Dyvim Tvar?" Elric put his hand on his friend's shoulder. "Dyvim Tvar?"

Dyvim Tvar took his head from his arm and looked into Elric's eyes. In Dyvim Tvar's own eyes was the experience of a score of millennia and there was irony there, too. "I live, Elric."

"Few of us live now."

A little later they left the warehouse, no longer needing to fear the mirror, and found that all the streets were full of the dead who had received the mirror's memories. Stiff bodies reached out hands to them. Dead lips formed silent pleas for help. Elric tried not to look at them as he pressed through them, but his desire for vengeance upon his cousin was even stronger now.

They reached the house. The door was open and the ground floor was crammed with corpses. There was no sign of Prince Yyrkoon.

Elric and Dyvim Tvar led the few Imrryrians who were still sane up the steps, past more imploring corpses, until they reached the top floor of the house.

And here they found Cymoril.

She was lying upon a couch and she was naked. There were runes painted on her flesh and the runes were, in themselves, obscene. Her eyelids were heavy and she did not at first recognize them. Elric rushed to her side and cradled her body in his arms. The body was oddly cold.

"He—he makes me—sleep..." said Cymoril. "A sorcerous sleep—from which—only he can wake me..." She gave a great yawn. "I have stayed awake—this long—by an effort of—will—for Elric comes..."

"Elric is here," said her lover, softly. "I am Elric, Cymoril."

"Elric?" She relaxed in his arms. "You—you must find Yyrkoon—for only he can wake me..."

"Where has he gone?" Elric's face had hardened. His crimson eyes were fierce. "Where?"

"To find the two black swords—the runeswords—of—our ancestors—Mournblade..."

"And Stormbringer," said Elric grimly. "Those swords are cursed. But where has he gone, Cymoril? How has he escaped us?"

"Through—through—through the—Shade Gate—he conjured it—he made the most fearful pacts with demons to go through . . . The—other—room . . ."

Now Cymoril slept, but there seemed to be a certain peace on her face.

Elric watched as Dyvim Tvar crossed the room, sword in hand, and flung the door open. A dreadful stench came from the next room, which was in darkness. Something flickered on the far side.

"Aye—that's sorcery, right enough," said Elric. "And Yyrkoon has thwarted me. He conjured the Shade Gate and passed through it into some netherworld. Which one, I'll never know, for there is an infinity of them. Oh, Arioch, I would give much to follow my cousin!"

"*Then follow him you shall,*" said a sweet, sardonic voice in Elric's head.

At first the albino thought it was a vestige of a memory still fighting for possession of his head, but then he knew that Arioch spoke to him.

"*Dismiss your followers that I may speak with thee,*" said Arioch.

Elric hesitated. He wished to be alone—but not with Arioch. He wished to be with Cymoril, for Cymoril was making him weep. Tears already flowed from his crimson eyes.

"*What I have to say could result in Cymoril being restored to her normal state,*" said the voice. "*And, moreover, it will help you defeat Yyrkoon and be revenged upon him. Indeed, it could make you the most powerful mortal there has ever been.*"

Elric looked up at Dyvim Tvar. "Would you and your men leave me alone for a few moments?"

"Of course." Dyvim Tvar led his men away and shut the door behind him.

Arioch stood leaning against the same door. Again he had assumed the shape and poise of a handsome youth. His smile was friendly and open and only the ancient eyes belied his appearance.

"It is time to seek the black swords yourself, Elric," said Arioch. "Lest Yyrkoon reach them first. I warn you of this—with the runeblades Yyrkoon will be so powerful he will be able to destroy half the world without thinking of it. That is why your cousin risks the dangers of the world beyond the Shade Gate. If Yyrkoon possesses those swords before you find them, it will mean the end of you, of Cymoril, of the Young Kingdoms and, quite possibly, the destruction of Melniboné, too. I will help you enter the netherworld to seek for the twin runeswords."

Elric said musingly: "I have often been warned of the dangers of seeking the swords—and the worse dangers of owning them. I think I must consider another plan, my lord Arioch."

"There is no other plan. Yyrkoon desires the swords if you do not. With Mournblade in one hand and Stormbringer in the other, he will be invincible, for the swords give their user power. Immense power." Arioch paused.

"You must do as I say. It is to your advantage."

"And to yours, Lord Arioch?"

"Aye—to mine. I am not entirely selfless."

Elric shook his head. "I am confused. There has been too much of the supernatural about this affair. I suspect the gods of manipulating us . . ."

"The gods serve only those who are willing to serve them. And the gods serve destiny, also."

"I like it not. To stop Yyrkoon is one thing, to assume his ambitions and take the swords myself—that is another thing."

"It is your destiny."

"Cannot I change my destiny?"

Arioch shook his head. "No more than can I."

Elric stroked sleeping Cymoril's hair. "I love her. She is all I desire."

"You shall not wake her if Yyrkoon finds the blades before you do."

"And how shall I find the blades?"

"Enter the Shade Gate—I have kept it open, though Yyrkoon thinks it closed—then you must seek the Tunnel Under the Marsh which leads to the Pulsing Cavern. In that chamber the runeswords are

kept. They have been kept there ever since your ancestors relinquished them . . ."

"Why were they relinquished?"

"Your ancestors lacked courage."

"Courage to face what?"

"Themselves."

"You are cryptic, my lord Arioch."

"That is the way of the Lords of the Higher Worlds. Hurry. Even I cannot keep the Shade Gate open long."

"Very well. I will go."

And Arioch vanished immediately.

Elric called in a hoarse, cracking voice for Dyvim Tvar who entered at once.

"Elric? What has happened in here? Is it Cymoril? You look . . ."

"I am going to follow Yyrkoon—alone, Dyvim Tvar. You must make your way back to Melniboné with those of our men who remain. Take Cymoril with you. If I do not return in reasonable time, you must declare her empress. If she still sleeps, then you must rule as regent until she wakes."

Dyvim Tvar said softly, "Do you know what you do, Elric?"

Elric shook his head.

"No, Dyvim Tvar, I do not."

He got to his feet and staggered towards the other room where the Shade Gate waited for him.

BOOK THREE

And now there is no turning back at all. Elric's destiny has
been forged and fixed as surely as the hellswords were
forged and fixed aeons before. Was there ever a point where
he might have turned off this road to despair, damnation
and destruction? Or has he been doomed since before his
birth? Doomed through a thousand incarnations to know
little else but sadness and struggle, loneliness and remorse—
eternally the champion of some unknown cause?

CHAPTER ONE

Through the Shade Gate

AND ELRIC STEPPED into a shadow and found himself in a
world of shadows. He turned, but the shadow through which he
had entered now faded and was gone. Old Aubec's sword was in Elric's
hand, the black helm and the black armour were upon his body and
only these were familiar, for the land was dark and gloomy as if contained in a vast cave whose walls, though invisible, were oppressive and
tangible. And Elric regretted the hysteria, the weariness of brain,
which had given him the impulse to obey his patron demon Arioch and
plunge through the Shade Gate. But regret was useless now, so he forgot it.

Yyrkoon was nowhere to be seen. Either Elric's cousin had had a
steed awaiting him or else, more likely, he had entered this world at a
slightly different angle (for all the planes were said to turn about each
other) and was thus either nearer or farther from their mutual goal.

The air was rich with brine—so rich that Elric's nostrils felt as if they had been packed with salt—it was almost like walking under water and just being able to breathe the water itself. Perhaps this explained why it was so difficult to see any great distance in any direction, why there were so many shadows, why the sky was like a veil which hid the roof of a cavern. Elric sheathed his sword, there being no evident danger present at that moment, and turned slowly, trying to get some kind of bearing.

It was possible that there were jagged mountains in what he judged the east, and perhaps a forest to the west. Without sun, or stars, or moon, it was hard to gauge distance or direction. He stood on a rocky plain over which whistled a cold and sluggish wind, which tugged at his cloak as if it wished to possess it. There were a few stunted, leafless trees standing in a clump about a hundred paces away. It was all that relieved the bleak plain, save for a large, shapeless slab of rock which stood a fair way beyond the trees. It was a world which seemed to have been drained of all life, where Law and Chaos had once battled and, in their conflict, destroyed all. Were there many planes such as this one? Elric wondered. And for a moment he was filled with a dreadful presentiment concerning the fate of his own rich world. He shook this mood off at once and began to walk towards the trees and the rock beyond.

He reached the trees and passed them, and the touch of his cloak on a branch broke the brittle thing which turned almost at once to ash which was scattered on the wind. Elric drew the cloak closer about his body.

As he approached the rock he became conscious of a sound which seemed to emanate from it. He slowed his pace and put his hand upon the pommel of his sword.

The noise continued—a small, rhythmic noise. Through the gloom Elric peered carefully at the rock, trying to locate the source of the sound.

And then the noise stopped and was replaced by another—a soft scuffle, a padding footfall, and then silence. Elric took a pace backward and drew Aubec's sword. The first sound had been that of a man sleeping. The second sound was that of a man waking and preparing himself either for attack or to defend himself.

Elric said: "I am Elric of Melniboné. I am a stranger here."

And an arrow slid past his helm almost at the same moment as a bowstring sounded. Elric flung himself to one side and sought about for cover, but there was no cover save the rock behind which the archer hid.

And now a voice came from behind the rock. It was a firm, rather bleak voice. It said:

"That was not meant to harm you but to display my skill in case you considered harming me. I have had my fill of demons in this world and you look like the most dangerous demon of all, Whiteface."

"I am mortal," said Elric, straightening up and deciding that if he must die it would be best to die with some sort of dignity.

"You spoke of Melniboné. I have heard of the place. An isle of demons."

"Then you have not heard enough of Melniboné. I am mortal as are all my folk. Only the ignorant think us demons."

"I am not ignorant, my friend. I am a Warrior Priest of Phum, born to that caste and the inheritor of all its knowledge and, until recently, the Lords of Chaos themselves were my patrons. Then I refused to serve them any longer and was exiled to this plane by them. Perhaps the same fate befell you, for the folk of Melniboné serve Chaos, do they not?"

"Aye. And I know of Phum—it lies in the Unmapped East—beyond the Weeping Waste, beyond the Sighing Desert, beyond even Elwher. It is one of the oldest of the Young Kingdoms."

"All that is so—though I dispute that the East is unmapped, save by the savages of the West. So you are, indeed, to share my exile, it seems."

"I am not exiled. I am upon a quest. When the quest is done, I shall return to my own world."

"Return, say you? That interests me, my pale friend. I had thought return impossible."

"Perhaps it is and I have been tricked. And if your own powers have not found you a way to another plane, perhaps mine will not save me either."

"Powers? I have none since I relinquished my servitude to Chaos. Well, friend, do you intend to fight me?"

"There is only one upon this plane I would fight and it is not you, Warrior Priest of Phum." Elric sheathed his sword and at the same moment the speaker rose from behind the rock, replacing a scarlet-fletched arrow in a scarlet quiver.

"I am Rackhir," said the man. "Called the Red Archer for, as you see, I affect scarlet dress. It is a habit of the Warrior Priests of Phum to choose but a single colour to wear. It is the only loyalty to tradition I still possess." He had on a scarlet jerkin, scarlet breeks, scarlet shoes and a scarlet cap with a scarlet feather in it. His bow was scarlet and the pommel of his sword glowed ruby-red. His face, which was aquiline and gaunt, as if carved from fleshless bone, was weather-beaten, and that was brown. He was tall and he was thin, but muscles rippled on his arms and torso. There was irony in his eyes and something of a smile upon his thin lips, though the face showed that it had been through much experience, little of it pleasant.

"An odd place to choose for a quest," said the Red Archer, standing with hands on hips and looking Elric up and down. "But I'll strike a bargain with you if you're interested."

"If the bargain suits me, archer, I'll agree to it, for you seem to know more of this world than do I."

"Well—you must find something here and then leave, whereas I have nothing at all to do here and wish to leave. If I help you in your quest, will you take me with you when you return to our own plane?"

"That seems a fair bargain, but I cannot promise what I have no power to give. I will say only this—if it is possible for me to take you back with me to our own plane, either before or after I have finished my quest, I will do it."

"That is reasonable," said Rackhir the Red Archer. "Now—tell me what you seek."

"I seek two swords, forged millennia ago by immortals, used by my ancestors but then relinquished by them and placed upon this plane.

The swords are large and heavy and black and they have cryptic runes carved into their blades. I was told that I would find them in the Pulsing Cavern which is reached through the Tunnel Under the Marsh. Have you heard of either of these places?"

"I have not. Nor have I heard of the two black swords." Rackhir rubbed his bony chin. "Though I remember reading something in one of the Books of Phum and what I read disturbed me . . ."

"The swords are legendary. Many books make some small reference to them—almost always mysterious. There is said to be one tome which records the history of the swords and all who have used them— and all who will use them in the future—a timeless book which contains all time. Some call it the Chronicle of the Black Sword and in it, it is said, men may read their whole destinies."

"I know nothing of that, either. It is not one of the Books of Phum. I fear, Comrade Elric, that we shall have to venture to the City of Ameeron and ask your questions of the inhabitants there."

"There is a city upon this plane?"

"Aye—a city. I stayed but a short time in it, preferring the wilderness. But with a friend, it might be possible to bear the place a little longer."

"Why is Ameeron unsuited to your taste?"

"Its citizens are not happy. Indeed, they are a most depressed and depressing group, for they are all, you see, exiles or refugees or travelers between the worlds who lost their way and never found it again. No-one lives in Ameeron by choice."

"A veritable City of the Damned."

"As the poet might remark, aye." Rackhir offered Elric a sardonic wink. "But I sometimes think all cities are that."

"What is the nature of this plane where there are, as far as I can tell, no planets, no moon, no sun? It has something of the air of a great cavern."

"There is, indeed, a theory that it is a sphere buried in an infinity of rock. Others say that it lies in the future of our own Earth—a future where the universe has died. I heard a thousand theories during the short space of time I spent in the City of Ameeron. All, it seemed to me, were of equal value. All, it seemed to me, could be correct. Why not? There are some who believe that everything is a Lie. Conversely, everything could be the Truth."

It was Elric's turn to remark ironically: "You are a philosopher, then, as well as an archer, friend Rackhir of Phum?"

Rackhir laughed. "If you like! It is such thinking that weakened my loyalty to Chaos and led me to this pass. I have heard that there is a city called Tanelorn which may sometimes be found on the shifting shores of the Sighing Desert. If I ever return to our own world, Comrade Elric, I shall seek that city, for I have heard that peace may be found there—that such debates as the nature of Truth are considered meaningless. That men are content merely to exist in Tanelorn."

"I envy those who dwell in Tanelorn," said Elric.

Rackhir sniffed. "Aye. But it would probably prove a disappointment, if found. Legends are best left as legends and attempts to make them real are rarely successful. Come—yonder lies Ameeron and that, sad to say, is more typical of most cities one comes across—on any plane."

The two tall men, both outcasts in their different ways, began to trudge through the gloom of that desolate wasteland.

CHAPTER TWO

In the City of Ameeron

The city of Ameeron came in sight and Elric had never seen such a place before. Ameeron made Dhoz-Kam seem like the cleanest and most well-run settlement there could be. The city lay below the plain of rocks, in a shallow valley over which hung perpetual smoke: a filthy, tattered cloak meant to hide the place from the sight of men and gods.

The buildings were mostly in a state of semi-ruin or else were wholly ruined and shacks and tents erected in their place. The mixture of architectural styles—some familiar, some most alien—was such that Elric was hard put to see one building which resembled another. There were shanties and castles, cottages, towers and forts, plain, square villas and wooden huts heavy with carved ornamentation. Others seemed merely piles of rock with a jagged opening at one end for a door. But none looked well—could not have looked well in that landscape under that perpetually gloomy sky.

Here and there red fires sputtered, adding to the smoke, and the smell as Elric and Rackhir reached the outskirts was rich with a great variety of stinks.

"Arrogance, rather than pride, is the paramount quality of most of Ameeron's residents," said Rackhir, wrinkling his hawklike nose. "Where they have any qualities of character left at all."

Elric trudged through filth. Shadows scuttled amongst the close-packed buildings. "Is there an inn, perhaps, where we can enquire after the Tunnel Under the Marsh and its whereabouts?"

"No inn. By and large the inhabitants keep themselves to themselves . . ."

"A city square where folk meet?"

"This city has no centre. Each resident or group of residents built their own dwelling where they felt like it, or where there was space, and they come from all planes and all ages, thus the confusion, the decay and the oldness of many of the places. Thus the filth, the hopelessness, the decadence of the majority."

"How do they live?"

"They live off each other, by and large. They trade with demons who occasionally visit Ameeron from time to time . . ."

"Demons?"

"Aye. And the bravest hunt the rats which dwell in the caverns below the city."

"What demons are these?"

"Just creatures, mainly minor minions of Chaos, who want something that the Ameeronese can supply—a stolen soul or two, a baby, perhaps (though few are born here)—you can imagine what else, if you've knowledge of what demons normally demand from sorcerers."

"Aye. I can imagine. So Chaos can come and go on this plane as it pleases?"

"I'm not sure it's quite as easy. But it is certainly easier for the demons to travel back and forth here than it would be for them to travel back and forth in our plane."

"Have you seen any of these demons?"

"Aye. The usual bestial sort. Coarse, stupid and powerful—many of them were once human before electing to bargain with Chaos. Now they are mentally and physically warped into foul, demon shapes."

Elric found Rackhir's words not to his taste. "Is that ever the fate of those who bargain with Chaos?" he said.

"You should know, if you come from Melniboné. I know that in Phum it is rarely the case. But it seems that the higher the stakes the subtler are the changes a man undergoes when Chaos agrees to trade with him."

Elric sighed. "Where shall we enquire of our Tunnel Under the Marsh?"

"There was an old man . . ." Rackhir began, and then a grunt behind him made him pause.

Another grunt.

A face with tusks in it emerged from a patch of darkness formed by a fallen slab of masonry. The face grunted again.

"Who are you?" said Elric, his sword-hand ready.

"Pig," said the face with tusks in it. Elric was not certain whether he was being insulted or whether the creature was describing himself. "Pig."

Two more faces with tusks in them came out of the patch of darkness. "Pig," said one.

"Pig," said another.

"Snake," said a voice behind Elric and Rackhir. Elric turned while Rackhir continued to watch the pigs. A tall youth stood there. Where his head would have been sprouted the bodies of about fifteen good-sized snakes. The head of each snake glared at Elric. The tongues flickered and they all opened their mouths at exactly the same moment to say again:

"Snake."

"Thing," said another voice. Elric glanced in that direction, gasped, drew his sword and felt nausea sweep through him.

Then Pigs, Snake and Thing were upon them.

Rackhir took one Pig before it could move three paces. His bow was off his back and strung and a red-fletched arrow nocked and shot, all in a second. He had time to shoot one more Pig and then drop his bow to draw his sword. Back to back he and Elric prepared to defend themselves against the demons' attack. Snake was bad enough, with its fifteen darting heads hissing and snapping with teeth which dripped venom, but Thing kept changing its form—first an arm would emerge, then a face would appear from the shapeless, heaving flesh which shuffled implacably closer.

"Thing!" it shouted. Two swords slashed at Elric who was dealing with the last Pig and missed his stroke so that instead of running the Pig through the heart, he took him in a lung. Pig staggered backward and slumped to the ground in a pool of muck. He crawled for a moment, but then collapsed. Thing had produced a spear and Elric barely managed to deflect the cast with the flat of his sword. Now Rackhir was engaged with Snake and the two demons closed on the men, eager to make a finish of them. Half the heads of Snake lay writhing on the ground and Elric had managed to slice one hand off Thing, but the demon still seemed to have three other hands ready. It seemed to be created not from one creature but from several. Elric wondered if, through his bargaining with Arioch, this would ultimately be his fate, to be turned into a demon—a formless monster. But wasn't he already something of a monster? Didn't folk already mistake him for a demon?

These thoughts gave him strength. He yelled as he fought. "Elric!"

And: "Thing!" replied his adversary, also eager to assert what he regarded as the essence of his being.

Another hand flew off as Aubec's sword bit into it. Another javelin jabbed out and was knocked aside; another sword appeared and came down on Elric's helm with a force which dazed him and sent him reeling back against Rackhir who missed his thrust at Snake and was almost bitten by four of the heads. Elric chopped at the arm and the tentacle which held the sword and saw them part from the body but then become reabsorbed again. The nausea returned. Elric thrust his sword into the mass and the mass screamed: "Thing! Thing! Thing!"

Elric thrust again and four swords and two spears waved and clashed and tried to deflect Aubec's blade.

"Thing!"

"This is Yyrkoon's work," said Elric, "without a doubt. He has heard that I have followed him and seeks to stop us with his demon allies." He gritted his teeth and spoke through them. "Unless one of these is Yyrkoon himself! Are you my cousin Yyrkoon, Thing?"

"Thing . . ." The voice was almost pathetic. The weapons waved and clashed but they no longer darted so fiercely at Elric.

"Or are you some other old, familiar friend?"

"Thing . . ."

Elric stabbed again and again into the mass. Thick, reeking blood spurted and fell upon his armour. Elric could not understand why it had become so easy to take the attack to the demon.

"Now!" shouted a voice from above Elric's head. "Quickly!"

Elric glanced up and saw a red face, a white beard, a waving arm. "Don't look at me you fool! Now—strike!"

And Elric put his two hands above his sword hilt and drove the blade deep into the shapeless creature which moaned and wept and said in a small whisper "Frank . . ." before it died.

Rackhir thrust at the same moment and his blade went under the remaining snake heads and plunged into the chest and thence into the heart of the youth-body and his demon died, too.

The white-haired man came clambering down from the ruined archway on which he had been perched. He was laughing. "Niun's sorcery still has some effect, even here, eh? I heard the tall one call his demon friends and instruct them to set upon you. It did not seem fair to me that five should attack two—so I sat upon that wall and I drew the many-armed demon's strength out of it. I still can. I still can. And now I have his strength (or a fair part of it) and feel considerably better than I have done for many a moon (if such a thing exists)."

"It said 'Frank'," said Elric frowning. "Was that a name, do you think? Its name before?"

"Perhaps," said old Niun, "perhaps. Poor creature. But still, it is dead now. You are not of Ameeron, you two—though I've seen you here before, red one."

"And I've seen you," said Rackhir with a smile. He wiped Snake's blood from his blade, using one of Snake's heads for the purpose. "You are Niun Who Knew All."

"Aye. Who Knew All but who now knows very little. Soon it will

be over, when I have forgotten everything. Then I may return from
this awful exile. It is the pact I made with Orland of the Staff. I was a
fool who wished to know everything and my curiosity led me into an
adventure concerning this Orland. Orland showed me the error of my
ways and sent me here to forget. Sadly, as you noticed, I still remember
some of my powers and my knowledge from time to time. I know you
seek the black swords. I know you are Elric of Melniboné. I know what
will become of you."

"You know my destiny?" said Elric eagerly. "Tell me what it is,
Niun Who Knew All."

Niun opened his mouth as if to speak but then firmly shut it again.
"No," he said. "I have forgotten."

"No!" Elric made as if to seize the old man. "No! You remember!
I can see that you remember!"

"I have forgotten." Niun lowered his head.

Rackhir took hold of Elric's arm. "He has forgotten, Elric."

Elric nodded. "Very well." Then he said, "But have you remembered where lies the Tunnel Under the Marsh?" ·

"Yes. It is only a short distance from Ameeron, the marsh itself.
You go that way. Then you look for a monument in the shape of an
eagle carved in black marble. At the base of the monument is the entrance to the tunnel." Niun repeated this information parrot-fashion
and when he looked up his face was clearer. "What did I just tell you?"

Elric said: "You gave us instructions on how to reach the entrance
to the Tunnel Under the Marsh."

"Did I?" Niun clapped his old hands. "Splendid. I have forgotten
that now, too. Who are you?"

"We are best forgotten," said Rackhir with a gentle smile. "Farewell,
Niun and thanks."

"Thanks for what?"

"Both for remembering and for forgetting."

They walked on through the miserable City of Ameeron, away
from the happy old sorcerer, sighting the odd face staring at them from
a doorway or a window, doing their best to breathe as little of the foul
air as possible.

"I think perhaps that I envy Niun alone of all the inhabitants of this desolate place," said Rackhir.

"I pity him," said Elric.

"Why so?"

"It occurs to me that when he has forgotten everything, he may well forget that he is allowed to leave Ameeron."

Rackhir laughed and slapped the albino upon his black armoured back. "You are a gloomy comrade, friend Elric. Are all your thoughts so hopeless?"

"They tend in that direction, I fear," said Elric with a shadow of a smile.

CHAPTER THREE

The Tunnel Under the Marsh

And on they traveled through that sad and murky world until at last they came to the marsh.

The marsh was black. Black spiky vegetation grew in clumps here and there upon it. It was cold and it was dank; a dark mist swirled close to the surface and through the mist sometimes darted low shapes. From the mist rose a solid black object which could only be the monument described by Niun.

"The monument," said Rackhir, stopping and leaning on his bow. "It's well out into the marsh and there's no evident pathway leading to it. Is this a problem, do you think, Comrade Elric?"

Elric waded cautiously into the edge of the marsh. He felt the cold ooze drag at his feet. He stepped back with some difficulty.

"There must be a path," said Rackhir, fingering his bony nose. "Else how would your cousin cross?"

Elric looked over his shoulder at the Red Archer and he shrugged. "Who knows? He could be traveling with sorcerous companions who have no difficulty where marshes are concerned."

Suddenly Elric found himself sitting down upon the damp rock. The stink of brine from the marsh seemed for a moment to have overwhelmed him. He was feeling weak. The effectiveness of his drugs, last taken just as he stepped through the Shade Gate, was beginning to fade.

Rackhir came and stood by the albino. He smiled with a certain amount of bantering sympathy. "Well, Sir Sorcerer, cannot you summon similar aid?"

Elric shook his head. "I know little that is practical concerning the raising of small demons. Yyrkoon has all his grimoires, his favourite spells, his introductions to the demon worlds. We shall have to find a path of the ordinary kind if we wish to reach yonder monument, Warrior Priest of Phum."

The Warrior Priest of Phum drew a red kerchief from within his tunic and blew his nose for some time. When he had finished he put down a hand, helped Elric to his feet, and began to walk along the rim of the marsh, keeping the black monument ever in sight.

It was some time later that they found a path at last and it was not a natural path but a slab of black marble extending out into the gloom of the mire, slippery to the feet and itself covered with a film of ooze.

"I would almost suspect this of being a false path—a lure to take us to our death," said Rackhir as he and Elric stood and looked at the long slab, "but what have we to lose now?"

"Come," said Elric, setting foot on the slab and beginning to make his cautious way along it. In his hand he now held a torch of sorts, a bundle of sputtering reeds which gave off an unpleasant yellow light and a considerable amount of greenish smoke. It was better than nothing.

Rackhir, testing each footstep with his unstrung bow-stave, followed behind, whistling a small, complicated tune as he went along. Another of his race would have recognized the tune as the *Song of the Son of the Hero of the High Hell Who Is About to Sacrifice his Life*, a popular melody in Phum, particularly amongst the caste of the Warrior Priest.

Elric found the tune irritating and distracting, but he said nothing, for he concentrated every fragment of his attention on keeping his balance upon the slippery surface of the slab, which now appeared to rock slightly, as if it floated on the surface of the marsh.

And now they were halfway to the monument whose shape could be clearly distinguished: a great eagle with spread wings and a savage beak and claws extended for the kill. An eagle in the same black marble as the slab on which they tried to keep their balance. And Elric was reminded of a tomb. Had some ancient hero been buried here? Or had the tomb been built to house the black swords—imprison them so that they might never enter the world of men again and steal men's souls?

The slab rocked more violently. Elric tried to remain upright but swayed first on one foot and then the other, the brand waving crazily. Both feet slid from under him and he went flying into the marsh and was instantly buried up to his knees.

He began to sink.

Somehow he had managed to keep his grip on the brand and by its light he could see the red-clad archer peering forward.

"Elric?"

"I'm here, Rackhir."

"You're sinking?"

"The marsh seems intent on swallowing me, aye."

"Can you lie flat?"

"I can lie forward, but my legs are trapped." Elric tried to move his body in the ooze which pressed against it. Something rushed past him in front of his face, giving voice to a kind of muted gibbering. Elric did his best to control the fear which welled up in him. "I think you must give me up, friend Rackhir."

"What? And lose my means of getting out of this world? You must think me more selfless than I am, Comrade Elric. Here . . ." Rackhir carefully lowered himself to the slab and reached out his arm towards Elric. Both men were now covered in clinging slime; both shivered with cold. Rackhir stretched and stretched and Elric leaned forward as far as he could and tried to reach the hand, but it was impossible. And every second dragged him deeper into the stinking filth of the marsh.

Then Rackhir took up his bow-stave and pushed that out.

"Grab the bow, Elric. Can you?"

Leaning forward and stretching every bone and muscle in his body, Elric just managed to get a grip on the bow-stave.

"Now, I must—Ah!" Rackhir, pulling at the bow, found his own feet slipping and the slab beginning to rock quite wildly. He flung out one arm to grab the far lip of the slab and with his other hand kept a grip on the bow. "Hurry, Elric! Hurry!"

Elric began painfully to pull himself from the ooze. The slab still rocked crazily and Rackhir's hawklike face was almost as pale as Elric's own as he desperately strove to keep his hold on both slab and bow. And then Elric, all soaked in mire, managed to reach the slab and crawl onto it, the brand still sputtering in his hand, and lie there gasping.

Rackhir, too, was short of breath, but he laughed. "What a fish I've caught!" he said. "The biggest yet, I'd wager!"

"I am grateful to you, Rackhir the Red Archer. I am grateful, Warrior Priest of Phum. I owe you my life," said Elric after a while. "And I swear that whether I'm successful in my quest or not I'll use all my powers to see you through the Shade Gate and back into the world from which we have both come."

Rackhir shrugged and grinned. "Now I suggest we continue towards yonder monument on our knees. Undignified it might be, but safer it is also. And it is but a short way to crawl."

Elric agreed.

Not much more time had passed in that timeless darkness before they had reached a little moss-grown island on which stood the Monument of the Eagle, huge and heavy and towering above them into the greater gloom which was either the sky or the roof of the cavern. And at the base of the plinth they saw a low doorway. And the doorway was open.

"A trap?" mused Rackhir.

"Or does Yyrkoon assume us perished in Ameeron?" said Elric, wiping himself free of slime as best he could. He sighed. "Let's enter and be done with it."

And so they entered.

They found themselves in a small room. Elric cast the faint light of the brand about the place and saw another doorway. The rest of the room was featureless—each wall made of the same faintly glistening black marble. The room was filled with silence.

Neither man spoke. Both walked unfalteringly towards the next doorway and, when they found steps, began to descend the steps, which wound down and down into total darkness.

For a long time they descended, still without speaking, until eventually they reached the bottom and saw before them the entrance to a narrow tunnel which was irregularly shaped so that it seemed more the work of nature than of some intelligence. Moisture dripped from the roof of the tunnel and fell with the regularity of heartbeats to the floor, seeming to echo a deeper sound, far away, emanating from somewhere in the tunnel itself.

"This is without doubt a tunnel," said the Red Archer, "and it, unquestionably, leads under the marsh."

Elric felt that Rackhir shared his reluctance to enter the tunnel. He stood with the guttering brand held high, listening to the sound of the drops falling to the floor of the tunnel, trying to recognize that other sound which came so faintly from the depths.

And then he forced himself forward, almost running into the tunnel, his ears filled with a sudden roaring which might have come from within his head or from some other source in the tunnel. He heard Rackhir's footfalls behind him. He drew his sword, the sword of the dead hero Aubec, and he heard the hissing of his own breath echo from the walls of the tunnel which was now alive with sounds of every sort.

Elric shuddered, but he did not pause.

The tunnel was warm. The floor felt spongy beneath his feet, the smell of brine persisted. And now he could see that the walls of the tunnel were smoother, that they seemed to shiver with quick, regular movement. He heard Rackhir gasp behind him as the archer, too, noted the peculiar nature of the tunnel.

"It's like flesh," murmured the Warrior Priest of Phum. "Like flesh."

Elric could not bring himself to reply. All his attention was required to force himself forward. He was consumed by terror. His whole body shook. He sweated and his legs threatened to buckle under him. His grip was so weak that he could barely keep his sword from falling to the floor. And there were hints of something in his memory, something which his brain refused to consider. Had he been here before? His trembling increased. His stomach turned. But he still stumbled on, the brand held before him.

And now the soft, steady thrumming sound grew louder and he saw ahead a small, almost circular aperture at the very end of the tunnel. He stopped, swaying.

"The tunnel ends," whispered Rackhir. "There is no way through."

The small aperture was pulsing with a swift, strong beat.

"The Pulsing Cavern," Elric whispered. "That is what we should find at the end of the Tunnel Under the Marsh. That must be the entrance, Rackhir."

"It is too small for a man to enter, Elric," said Rackhir reasonably.

"No . . ."

Elric stumbled forward until he stood close to the opening. He sheathed his sword. He handed the brand to Rackhir and then, before the Warrior Priest of Phum could stop him, he had flung himself head-first through the gap, wriggling his body through—and the walls of the aperture parted for him and then closed behind him, leaving Rackhir on the other side.

Elric got slowly to his feet. A faint, pinkish light now came from the walls and ahead of him was another entrance, slightly larger than the one through which he had just come. The air was warm and thick and salty. It almost stifled him. His head throbbed and his body ached and he could barely act or think, save to force himself onward. On faltering legs he flung himself towards the next entrance as the great, muffled pulsing sounded louder and louder in his ears.

"Elric!"

Rackhir stood behind him, pale and sweating. He had abandoned the brand and followed Elric through.

Elric licked dry lips and tried to speak.

Rackhir came closer.

Elric said thickly: "Rackhir. You should not be here."

"I said I would help."

"Aye, but . . ."

"Then help I shall."

Elric had no strength for arguing, so he nodded and with his hands forced back the soft walls of the second aperture and saw that it led into a cavern whose round wall quivered to a steady pulsing. And in the centre of the cavern, hanging in the air without any support at all were two swords. Two identical swords, huge and fine and black.

And standing beneath the swords, his expression gloating and greedy, stood Prince Yyrkoon of Melniboné, reaching up for them, his lips moving but no words escaping from him. And Elric himself was able to voice but one word as he climbed through and stood upon that shuddering floor. "No," he said.

Yyrkoon heard the word. He turned with terror in his face. He snarled when he saw Elric and then he, too, voiced a word which was at once a scream of outrage.

"No!"

With an effort Elric dragged Aubec's blade from its scabbard. But it seemed too heavy to hold upright, it tugged his arm so that it rested on the floor, his arm hanging straight at his side. Elric drew deep breaths of heavy air into his lungs. His vision was dimming. Yyrkoon had become a shadow. Only the two black swords, standing still and cool in the very centre of the circular chamber, were in focus. Elric sensed Rackhir enter the chamber and stand beside him.

"Yyrkoon," said Elric at last, "those swords are mine."

Yyrkoon smiled and reached up towards the blades. A peculiar moaning sound seemed to issue from them. A faint, black radiance seemed to emanate from them. Elric saw the runes carved into them and he was afraid.

Rackhir fitted an arrow to his bow. He drew the string back to his shoulder, sighting along the arrow at Prince Yyrkoon. "If he must die, Elric, tell me."

"Slay him," said Elric.

And Rackhir released the string.

But the arrow moved very slowly through the air and then hung halfway between the archer and his intended target.

Yyrkoon turned, a ghastly grin on his face. "Mortal weapons are useless here," he said.

Elric said to Rackhir. "He must be right. And your life is in danger, Rackhir. Go . . ."

Rackhir gave him a puzzled look. "No, I must stay here and help you . . ."

Elric shook his head. "You cannot help, you will only die if you stay. Go."

Reluctantly the Red Archer unstrung his bow, glanced suspiciously up at the two black swords, then squeezed his way through the doorway and was gone.

"Now, Yyrkoon," said Elric, letting Aubec's sword fall to the floor. "We must settle this, you and I."

Chapter Four

Two Black Swords

And then the runeblades Stormbringer and Mournblade were gone from where they had hung so long.

And Stormbringer had settled into Elric's right hand. And Mournblade lay in Prince Yyrkoon's right hand.

And the two men stood on opposite sides of the Pulsing Cavern and regarded first each other and then the swords they held.

The swords were singing. Their voices were faint but could be heard quite plainly. Elric lifted the huge blade easily and turned it this way and that, admiring its alien beauty.

"Stormbringer," he said.

And then he felt afraid.

It was suddenly as if he had been born again and that this runesword was born with him. It was as if they had never been separate.

"Stormbringer."

And the sword moaned sweetly and settled even more smoothly into his grasp.

"Stormbringer!" yelled Elric and he leapt at his cousin.

"Stormbringer!"

And he was full of fear—so full of fear. And the fear brought a wild kind of delight—a demonic need to fight and kill his cousin, to sink the blade deep into Yyrkoon's heart. To take vengeance. To spill blood. To send a soul to hell.

And now Prince Yyrkoon's cry could be heard above the thrum of the sword-voices, the drumming of the pulse of the cavern.

"Mournblade!"

And Mournblade came up to meet Stormbringer's blow and turn that blow and thrust back at Elric who swayed aside and brought Stormbringer round and down in a side-stroke which knocked Yyrkoon and Mournblade backward for an instant. But Stormbringer's next thrust was met again. And the next thrust was met. And the next. If the swordsmen were evenly matched, then so were the blades, which seemed possessed of their own wills.

And the clang of the metal upon metal turned into a wild, metallic song which the swords sang. A joyful song as if they were glad at last to be back to battling, though they battled each other.

And Elric barely saw his cousin, Prince Yyrkoon, at all, save for an occasional flash of his dark, wild face. Elric's attention was given entirely to the two black swords, for it seemed that the swords fought with the life of one of the swordsmen as a prize (or perhaps the lives of both, thought Elric) and that the rivalry between Elric and Yyrkoon was nothing compared with the brotherly rivalry between the swords who seemed full of pleasure at the chance to engage again after many millennia.

And this observation, as he fought—and fought for his soul as well as his life—gave Elric pause to consider his hatred of Yyrkoon.

Kill Yyrkoon he would, but not at the will of another power. Not to give sport to these alien swords.

Mournblade's point darted at his eyes and Stormbringer rose to deflect the thrust once more.

Elric no longer fought his cousin. He fought the will of the two black swords.

Stormbringer dashed for Yyrkoon's momentarily undefended

throat. Elric clung to the sword and dragged it back, sparing his cousin's life. Stormbringer whined almost petulantly, like a dog stopped from biting an intruder.

And Elric spoke through clenched teeth. "I'll not be your puppet, runeblade. If we must be united, let it be upon a proper understanding."

The sword seemed to hesitate, to drop its guard, and Elric was hard put to defend himself against the whirling attack of Mournblade which, in turn, seemed to sense its advantage.

Elric felt fresh energy pour up his right arm and into his body. This was what the sword could do. With it, he needed no drugs, would never be weak again. In battle he would triumph. At peace, he could rule with pride. When he traveled, it could be alone and without fear. It was as if the sword reminded him of all these things, even as it returned Mournblade's attack.

And what must the sword have in return?

Elric knew. The sword told him, without words of any sort. Stormbringer needed to fight, for that was its reason for existence. Stormbringer needed to kill, for that was its source of energy, the lives and the souls of men, demons—even gods.

And Elric hesitated, even as his cousin gave a huge, cackling yell and dashed at him so that Mournblade glanced off his helm and he was flung backwards and down and saw Yyrkoon gripping his moaning black sword in both hands to plunge the runeblade into Elric's body.

And Elric knew he would do anything to resist that fate—for his soul to be drawn into Mournblade and his strength to feed Prince Yyrkoon's strength. And he rolled aside, very quickly, and got to one knee and turned and lifted Stormbringer with one gauntleted hand upon the blade and the other upon the hilt to take the great blow Prince Yyrkoon brought upon it. And the two black swords shrieked as if in pain, and they shivered, and black radiance poured from them as blood might pour from a man pierced by many arrows. And Elric was driven, still on his knees, away from the radiance, gasping and sighing and peering here and there for sight of Yyrkoon who had disappeared.

And Elric knew that Stormbringer spoke to him again. If Elric did not wish to die by Mournblade, then Elric must accept the bargain which the Black Sword offered.

"He must not die!" said Elric. "I will not slay him to make sport for you!"

And through the black radiance ran Yyrkoon, snarling and snapping and whirling his runesword.

Again Stormbringer darted through an opening, and again Elric made the blade pull back and Yyrkoon was only grazed.

Stormbringer writhed in Elric's hands.

Elric said: "You shall not be my master."

And Stormbringer seemed to understand and become quieter, as if reconciled. And Elric laughed, thinking that he now controlled the runesword and that from now on the blade would do his bidding.

"We shall disarm Yyrkoon," said Elric. "We shall not kill him."

Elric rose to his feet.

Stormbringer moved with all the speed of a needle-thin rapier. It feinted, it parried, it thrust. Yyrkoon, who had been grinning in triumph, snarled and staggered back, the grin dropping from his sullen features.

Stormbringer now worked for Elric. It made the moves that Elric wished to make. Both Yyrkoon and Mournblade seemed disconcerted by this turn of events. Mournblade shouted as if in astonishment at its brother's behaviour. Elric struck at Yyrkoon's sword-arm, pierced cloth—pierced flesh—pierced sinew—pierced bone. Blood came, soaking Yyrkoon's arm and dripping down onto the hilt of the sword. The blood was slippery. It weakened Yyrkoon's grip on his runesword. He took it in both hands, but he was unable to hold it firmly.

Elric, too, took Stormbringer in both hands. Unearthly strength surged through him. With a gigantic blow he dashed Stormbringer against Mournblade where blade met hilt. The runesword flew from Yyrkoon's grasp. It sped across the Pulsing Cavern.

Elric smiled. He had defeated his own sword's will and, in turn, had defeated the brother sword.

Mournblade fell against the wall of the Pulsing Cavern and for a moment was still.

A groan then seemed to escape the defeated runesword. A high-pitched shriek filled the Pulsing Cavern. Blackness flooded over the eerie pink light and extinguished it.

When the light returned Elric saw that a scabbard lay at his feet. The scabbard was black and of the same alien craftsmanship as the runesword. Elric saw Yyrkoon. The prince was on his knees and he was sobbing, his eyes darting about the Pulsing Cavern seeking Mournblade, looking at Elric with fright as if he knew he must now be slain.

"Mournblade?" Yyrkoon said hopelessly. He knew he was to die.

Mournblade had vanished from the Pulsing Cavern.

"Your sword is gone," said Elric quietly.

Yyrkoon whimpered and tried to crawl towards the entrance of the cavern. But the entrance had shrunk to the size of a small coin. Yyrkoon wept.

Stormbringer trembled, as if thirsty for Yyrkoon's soul. Elric stooped.

Yyrkoon began to speak rapidly. "Do not slay me, Elric—not with that runeblade. I will do anything you wish. I will die in any other way."

Elric said: "We are victims, cousin, of a conspiracy—a game played by gods, demons and sentient swords. They wish one of us dead. I suspect they wish you dead more than they wish me dead. And that is the reason why I shall not slay you here." He picked up the scabbard. He forced Stormbringer into it and at once the sword was quiet. Elric took off his old scabbard and looked around for Aubec's sword, but that, too, was gone. He dropped the old scabbard and hooked the new one to his belt. He rested his left hand upon the pommel of Stormbringer and he looked not without sympathy upon the creature that was his cousin.

"You are a worm, Yyrkoon. But is that your fault?"

Yyrkoon gave him a puzzled glance.

"I wonder, if you had all you desire, would you cease to be a worm, cousin?"

Yyrkoon raised himself to his knees. A little hope began to show in his eyes.

Elric smiled and drew a deep breath. "We shall see," he said. "You must agree to wake Cymoril from her sorcerous slumber."

"You have humbled me, Elric," said Yyrkoon in a small pitiful voice. "I will wake her. Or would . . ."

"Can you not undo your spell?"

"We cannot escape from the Pulsing Cavern. It is past the time . . ."

"What's this?"

"I did not think you would follow me. And then I thought I would easily finish you. And now it is past the time. One can keep the entrance open for only a little while. It will admit anyone who cares to enter the Pulsing Cavern, but it will let no-one out after the power of the spell dies. I gave much to know that spell."

"You have given too much for everything," said Elric. He went to the entrance and peered through. Rackhir waited on the other side. The Red Archer had an anxious expression. Elric said: "Warrior Priest of Phum, it seems that my cousin and I are trapped in here. The entrance will not part for us." Elric tested the warm, moist stuff of the wall. It would not open more than a tiny fraction. "It seems that you can join us or else go back. If you do join us, you share our fate."

"It is not much of a fate if I go back," said Rackhir. "What chances have you?"

"One," said Elric. "I can invoke my patron."

"A Lord of Chaos?" Rackhir made a wry face.

"Exactly," said Elric. "I speak of Arioch."

"Arioch, eh? Well, he does not care for renegades from Phum."

"What do you choose to do?"

Rackhir stepped forward. Elric stepped back. Through the opening came Rackhir's head, followed by his shoulders, followed by the rest of him. The entrance closed again immediately. Rackhir stood up and untangled the string of his bow from the stave, smoothing it. "I agreed to share your fate—to gamble all on escaping from this plane," said the Red Archer. He looked surprised when he saw Yyrkoon. "Your enemy is still alive?"

"Aye."

"You are merciful indeed."

"Perhaps. Or obstinate. I would not slay him merely because some supernatural agency used him as a pawn, to be killed if I should win. The Lords of the Higher Worlds do not as yet control me completely— nor will they if I have any power at all to resist them."

Rackhir grinned. "I share your view—though I'm not optimistic about its realism. I see you have one of those black swords at your belt. Will that not hack a way through the cavern?"

"No," said Yyrkoon from his place against the wall. "Nothing can harm the stuff of the Pulsing Cavern."

"I'll believe you," said Elric, "for I do not intend to draw this new sword of mine often. I must learn how to control it first."

"So Arioch must be summoned." Rackhir sighed.

"If that is possible," said Elric.

"He will doubtless destroy me," said Rackhir, looking to Elric in the hope that the albino would deny this statement.

Elric looked grave. "I might be able to strike a bargain with him. It will also test something."

Elric turned his back on Rackhir and on Yyrkoon. He adjusted his mind. He sent it out through vast spaces and complicated mazes. And he cried:

"Arioch! Arioch! Aid me, Arioch!"

He had a sense of something listening to him.

"Arioch!"

Something shifted in the places where his mind went.

"Arioch . . ."

And Arioch heard him. He knew it was Arioch.

Rackhir gave a horrified yell. Yyrkoon screamed. Elric turned and saw that something disgusting had appeared near the far wall. It was black and it was foul and it slobbered and its shape was intolerably alien. Was this Arioch? How could it be? Arioch was beautiful. But perhaps, thought Elric, this was Arioch's true shape. Upon this plane, in this peculiar cavern, Arioch could not deceive those who looked upon him.

But then the shape had disappeared and a beautiful youth with an- cient eyes stood looking at the three mortals.

"You have won the sword, Elric," said Arioch, ignoring the others. "I congratulate you. And you have spared your cousin's life. Why so?"

"More than one reason," said Elric. "But let us say he must remain alive in order to wake Cymoril."

Arioch's face bore a little, secret smile for a moment and Elric realized that he had avoided a trap. If he had killed Yyrkoon, Cymoril would never have woken again.

"And what is this little traitor doing with you?" Arioch turned a cold eye on Rackhir who did his best to stare back at the Chaos Lord.

"He is my friend," said Elric. "I made a bargain with him. If he aided me to find the Black Sword, then I would take him back with me to our own plane."

"That is impossible. Rackhir is an exile here. That is his punishment."

"He comes back with me," said Elric. And now he unhooked the scabbard holding Stormbringer from his belt and he held the sword out before him. "Or I do not take the sword with me. Failing that, we all three remain here for eternity."

"That is not sensible, Elric. Consider your responsibilities."

"I have considered them. That is my decision."

Arioch's smooth face had just a tinge of anger. "You must take the sword. It is your destiny."

"So you say. But I now know that the sword may only be borne by me. You cannot bear it, Arioch, or you would. Only I—or another mortal like me—can take it from the Pulsing Cavern. Is that not so?"

"You are clever, Elric of Melniboné." Arioch spoke with sardonic admiration. "And you are a fitting servant of Chaos. Very well—that traitor can go with you. But he would be best warned to tread warily. The Lords of Chaos have been known to bear malice . . ."

Rackhir said hoarsely: "So I have heard, My Lord Arioch."

Arioch ignored the archer. "The man of Phum is not, after all, important. And if you wish to spare your cousin's life, so be it. It matters little. Destiny can contain a few extra threads in her design and still accomplish her original aims."

"Very well then," said Elric. "Take us from this place."

"Where to?"

"Why, to Melniboné, if you please."

With a smile that was almost tender Arioch looked down on Elric and a silky hand stroked Elric's cheek. Arioch had grown to twice his original size. "Oh, you are surely the sweetest of all my slaves," said the Lord of Chaos.

And there was a whirling. There was a sound like the roar of the sea. There was a dreadful sense of nausea. And three weary men stood on the floor of the great throne room in Imrryr. The throne room was deserted, save that in one corner a black shape, like smoke, writhed for a moment and then was gone.

Rackhir crossed the floor and seated himself carefully upon the first step to the Ruby Throne. Yyrkoon and Elric remained where they were, staring into each other's eyes. Then Elric laughed and slapped his scabbarded sword. "Now you must fulfill your promises to me, cousin. Then I have a proposition to put to you."

"It is like a market place," said Rackhir, leaning on one elbow and inspecting the feather in his scarlet hat. "So many bargains!"

CHAPTER FIVE

The Pale King's Mercy

Yyrkoon stepped back from his sister's bed. He was worn and his features were drawn and there was no spirit in him as he said: "It is done." He turned away and looked through the window at the towers of Imrryr, at the harbour where the returned golden battle-barges rode at anchor, together with the ship which had been King Straasha's gift to Elric. "She will wake in a moment," added Yyrkoon absently.

Dyvim Tvar and Rackhir the Red Archer looked enquiringly at Elric who kneeled by the bed, staring into the face of Cymoril. Her face grew peaceful as he watched and for one terrible moment he suspected

Prince Yyrkoon of tricking him and of killing Cymoril. But then the eyelids moved and the eyes opened and she saw him and she smiled. "Elric? The dreams . . . You are safe?"

"I am safe, Cymoril. As you are."

"Yyrkoon . . .?"

"He woke you."

"But you swore to slay him . . ."

"I was as much subject to sorcery as you. My mind was confused. It is still confused where some matters are concerned. But Yyrkoon is changed now. I defeated him. He does not doubt my power. He no longer lusts to usurp me."

"You are merciful, Elric." She brushed hair from her face.

Elric exchanged a glance with Rackhir.

"It might not be mercy which moves me," said Elric. "It might merely be a sense of fellowship with Yyrkoon."

"Fellowship? Surely you cannot feel . . ."

"We are both mortal. We were both victims of a game played between the Lords of the Higher Worlds. My loyalty must, finally, be to my own kind—and that is why I ceased to hate Yyrkoon."

"And that is mercy," said Cymoril.

Yyrkoon walked towards the door. "May I leave, my lord emperor?"

Elric thought he detected a strange light in his defeated cousin's eyes. But perhaps it was only humility or despair. He nodded. Yyrkoon went from the room, closing the door softly.

Dyvim Tvar said: "Trust Yyrkoon not at all, Elric. He will betray you again." The Lord of the Dragon Caves was troubled.

"No," said Elric. "If he does not fear me, he fears the sword I now carry."

"And you should fear that sword," said Dyvim Tvar.

"No," said Elric. "I am the master of the sword."

Dyvim Tvar made to speak again but then shook his head almost sorrowfully, bowed and, together with Rackhir the Red Archer, left Elric and Cymoril alone.

Cymoril took Elric in her arms. They kissed. They wept.

*   *   *

There were celebrations in Melniboné for a week. Now almost all the ships and men and dragons were home. And Elric was home, having proved his right to rule so well that all his strange quirks of character (this 'mercy' of his was perhaps the strangest) were accepted by the populace.

In the throne room there was a ball and it was the most lavish ball any of the courtiers had ever known. Elric danced with Cymoril, taking a full part in the activities. Only Yyrkoon did not dance, preferring to remain in a quiet corner below the gallery of the music-slaves, ignored by the guests. Rackhir the Red Archer danced with several Melnibonéan ladies and made assignations with them all, for he was a hero now in Melniboné. Dyvim Tvar danced, too, though his eyes were often brooding when they fell upon Prince Yyrkoon.

And later, when people ate, Elric spoke to Cymoril as they sat together on the dais of the Ruby Throne.

"Would you be empress, Cymoril?"

"You know I will marry you, Elric. We have both known that for many a year, have we not?"

"So you would be my wife?"

"Aye." She laughed for she thought he joked.

"And not be empress? For a year at least?"

"What mean you, my lord?"

"I must go away from Melniboné, Cymoril, for a year. What I have learned in recent months has made me want to travel the Young Kingdoms—see how other nations conduct their affairs. For I think Melniboné must change if she is to survive. She could become a great force for good in the world, for she still has much power."

"For good?" Cymoril was surprised and there was a little alarm in her voice, too. "Melniboné has never stood for good or for evil, but for herself and the satisfaction of her desires."

"I would see that changed."

"You intend to alter everything?"

"I intend to travel the world and then decide if there is any point to such a decision. The Lords of the Higher Worlds have ambitions in our world. Though they have given me aid, of late, I fear them. I should like to see if it is possible for men to rule their own affairs."

"And you will go?" There were tears in her eyes. "When?"

"Tomorrow—when Rackhir leaves. We will take King Straasha's ship and make for the Isle of the Purple Towns where Rackhir has friends. Will you come?"

"I cannot imagine—I cannot. Oh, Elric, why spoil this happiness we now have?"

"Because I feel that the happiness cannot last unless we know completely what we are."

She frowned. "Then you must discover that, if that is what you wish," she said slowly. "But it is for you to discover alone, Elric, for I have no such desire. You must go by yourself into those barbarian lands."

"You will not accompany me?"

"It is not possible. I—I am Melnibonéan . . ." She sighed. "I love you, Elric."

"And I you, Cymoril."

"Then we shall be married when you return. In a year."

Elric was full of sorrow, but he knew that his decision was correct. If he did not leave, he would grow restless soon enough and if he grew restless he might come to regard Cymoril as an enemy, someone who had trapped him.

"Then you must rule as empress until I return," he sad.

"No, Elric. I cannot take that responsibility."

"Then, who . . .? Dyvim Tvar . . ."

"I know Dyvim Tvar. He will not take such power. Magum Colim, perhaps . . ."

"No."

"Then you must stay, Elric."

But Elric's gaze had traveled through the crowd in the throne room below. It stopped when it reached a lonely figure seated by itself under the gallery of the music-slaves. And Elric smiled ironically and said:

"Then it must be Yyrkoon."

Cymoril was horrified. "No, Elric. He will abuse any power . . ."

"Not now. And it is just. He is the only one who wanted to be emperor. Now he can rule as emperor for a year in my stead. If he rules well, I may consider abdicating in his favour. If he rules badly, it will prove, once and for all, that his ambitions were misguided."

"Elric," said Cymoril. "I love you. But you are a fool—a criminal, if you trust Yyrkoon again."

"No," he said evenly. "I am not a fool. All I am is Elric. I cannot help that, Cymoril."

"It is Elric that I love!" she cried. "But Elric is doomed. We are all doomed unless you remain here now."

"I cannot. Because I love you, Cymoril, I cannot."

She stood up. She was weeping. She was lost.

"And I am Cymoril," she said. "You will destroy us both." Her voice softened and she stroked his hair. "You will destroy us, Elric."

"No," he said. "I will build something that will be better. I will discover things. When I return we shall marry and we shall live long and we shall be happy, Cymoril."

And now, Elric had told three lies. The first concerned his cousin Yyrkoon. The second concerned the Black Sword. The third concerned Cymoril. And upon those three lies was Elric's destiny to be built, for it is only about things which concern us most profoundly that we lie clearly and with profound conviction.

EPILOGUE

There was a port called Menii which was one of the humblest and friendliest of the Purple Towns. Like the others on the isle it was built mainly of the purple stone which gave the towns their name. And there were red roofs on the houses and there were bright-sailed boats of all kinds in the harbour as Elric and Rackhir the Red Archer came ashore in the early morning when just a few sailors were beginning to make their way down to their ships.

King Straasha's lovely ship lay some way out beyond the harbour wall. They had used a small boat to cross the water between it and the town. They turned and looked back at the ship. They had sailed it themselves, without crew, and the ship had sailed well.

"So, I must seek peace and mythic Tanelorn," said Rackhir, with a certain amount of self-mockery. He stretched and yawned and the bow and the quiver danced on his back.

Elric was dressed in simple costume that might have marked any soldier-of-fortune of the Young Kingdoms. He looked fit and relaxed. He smiled into the sun. The only remarkable thing about his garb was the great, black runesword at his side. Since he had donned the sword, he had needed no drugs to sustain him at all.

"And I must seek knowledge in the lands I find marked upon my map," said Elric. "I must learn and I must carry what I learn back to Melniboné at the end of a year. I wish that Cymoril had accompanied me, but I understand her reluctance."

"You will go back?" Rackhir said. "When a year is over?"

"She will draw me back!" Elric laughed. "My only fear is that I will weaken and return before my quest is finished."

"I should like to come with you," said Rackhir, "for I have traveled in most lands and would be as good a guide as I was in the netherworld. But I am sworn to find Tanelorn, for all I know it does not really exist."

"I hope that you find it, Warrior Priest of Phum," said Elric.

"I shall never be that again," said Rackhir. Then his eyes widened a little. "Why, look—your ship!"

And Elric looked and saw the ship that had once been called The Ship Which Sails Over Land and Sea, and he saw that slowly it was sinking. King Straasha was taking it back.

"The elementals are friends, at least," he said. "But I fear their power wanes as the power of Melniboné wanes. For all that we of the Dragon Isle are considered evil by the folk of the Young Kingdoms, we share much in common with the spirits of air, earth, fire and water."

Rackhir said, as the masts of the ship disappeared beneath the waves: "I envy you those friends, Elric. You may trust them."

"Aye."

Rackhir looked at the runesword hanging on Elric's hip. "But you would be wise to trust nothing else," he added.

Elric laughed. "Fear not for me, Rackhir, for I am my own master—for a year at least. And I am master of this sword now!"

The sword seemed to stir at his side and he took firm hold of its grip and slapped Rackhir on the back and he laughed and shook his white hair so that it drifted in the air and he lifted his strange, red eyes to the sky and he said:

"I shall be a new man when I return to Melniboné."

ASPECTS OF FANTASY (1)

This is the first of a series of fascinating and absorbing articles in which Michael Moorcock will diagnose the various aspects of many famous writers and their works as applied to the fantasy field as a whole.

—*John Carnell, SCIENCE FANTASY No. 61, October 1963*

ASPECTS OF FANTASY
(1963)

I. INTRODUCTION

WHAT *IS* "FANTASY fiction"? It is, of course, a broad field but, on the other hand, fairly easy to define. It is fiction which deals in the fantastic, in what is outside of ordinary human experience.

It contains many sub-categories of which science fiction is one; it is written on many levels by writers of varying ability who use it for a great number of purposes. Today it ranges from the ill-written ghoul-operas published in poor-quality paperbacks to the well-written extravaganzas of Peake, Tolkien and others.

A more interesting question, and one which I hope partially to answer in these articles, is *why* is fantasy? Why is it written, why is it read, what is its appeal?

H. P. Lovecraft, that well-known describer of the indescribable, says in his book *Marginalia*:

> Modern Science has, in the end, proved an enemy to art and pleasure; for by revealing to us the whole sordid and prosaic basis of our thoughts, motives, and acts, it has stripped the world of glamour, wonder, and all those illusions of heroism, nobility, and sacrifice which used to sound so impressive when romantically treated. Indeed, it is not too much to say that psychological discovery, and chemical, physical, and psychological research have largely destroyed the element of

> emotion among informed and sophisticated people by
> resolving it into its component parts . . .

That I disagree with this judgment will be obvious, for I believe that dissection of the fantasy story into its component parts does not detract from the story but rather adds a new dimension to it—a dimension which, to me, is far more interesting and rewarding. In an article published in the *Woman Journalist* for Spring 1963, J. G. Ballard writes:

> I feel that the writer of fantasy has a marked tendency
> to select images and ideas which directly reflect the in-
> ternal landscapes of his mind, and the reader of fan-
> tasy must interpret them on this level, distinguishing
> between the manifest content, which may seem ob-
> scure, meaningless or nightmarish, and the latent con-
> tent, the private vocabulary of symbols drawn by the
> narrative from the writer's mind. The dream worlds,
> synthetic landscapes and plasticity of visual forms in-
> vented by the writer of fantasy are external equiva-
> lents of the inner world of the psyche . . .

Lovecraft was writing forty years ago, Ballard is writing now and I feel it is likely that the developments in physics and psychology which have taken place since 1922 would have caused Lovecraft to revise his views if he were living today, for Einstein and Jung between them have, by analysis, broadened rather than destroyed the scope of the artist.

The increasing interest in the fantasy form seems to show that intelligent people are, indeed, looking beyond its purely sensational and romantic aspects and finding it a rewarding literary field. Those critics who still decry it for its usual lack of deep characterization do not see that it completely reverses the "real" world of the social novel—placing its heroes in a landscape directly reflecting the inner landscape of the ordinary man. The hero ranges the lands of his own psyche, encountering the various aspects of himself. When we read a good fantasy we are being admitted into the subterranean worlds of our own souls.

Therefore the fascination of the fantasy story may well lie in its concern with direct subconscious symbols. The mingled attraction and revulsion felt by its readers may well express the combined wish to see into themselves and at the same time withdraw into "normal" life when they begin to feel they are probing too deeply.

Generally speaking, fantasy stories can fall into two broad categories. There is the kind that permanently disturbs and the kind that comforts. Part of the purpose of the child's fairy story is to describe the horror and then, by means of an easily identifiable hero, destroy it, thus laying the ghost. The child is full of fears and fancies. Therefore one of the differences between fairy stories and the major proportion of adult fantasy stories is that an adult story rarely produces a comforting end. Whether the hero wins through or not, the reader is left with the suspicion or knowledge that all is not quiet on the supernatural front. For supernatural also read subconscious and you're still with me.

The typical *Unknown Worlds* story is a kind of rational ghost-laying substitute for the child's fairy story—it diminishes that which is described to the level of whimsey and makes it appear harmless—but it avoids the essential nature of the horror story/supernatural romance and is in many ways a corrupt and unproductive form. Most of the Gothic novels, incidentally, tried to tack "rational" explanations of their horrors on to their last chapters, although here the rationality was so totally superficial that it did not, in most cases, convince—whereas the supernatural episodes *did*.

The fantasy which we read today is not really very much different from the fantasy of, say, 2000 B.C. It is the oldest form of storytelling and, essentially, it has not changed much.

We are all familiar with the Greek legends, English folk tales and the stories of King Arthur and his Round Table, even if we haven't read them since our schooldays. One thing is obvious in all of these, and that is the repetition of certain kinds of characters (archetypal characters) and situations (classical situations). They recur constantly and they recur in Chivalric and Gothic romances, in Goethe, Wagner and the Jacobean tragedists, the works of Poe, Hawthorne, Melville, Bierce, Dunsany, Blackwood, Machen, etc.—through the first half of the twentieth century with James Branch Cabell, E. F. Benson, Charles Williams, Lovecraft, Howard and the *Weird Tales* school, to Bloch, Leiber, Bradbury and others in the USA and Peake, Tolkien, Powys, etc., in this country. And, apart from complexities of plot, more sophisticated means of storytelling and the odd change of scenery, the basic form has not changed since Cervantes took the mickey out of it in *Don Quixote*. It is romantic, it is sensational and, at its best, illuminating.

There are writers who go directly to their source of inspiration and write within its context (Thomas Burnett Swann or Treece, for instance), others who remove the whole machinery to an imaginary setting (Merritt, Howard, Leiber, Tolkien) and yet others who specialize in a contemporary setting, contrasting the prosaic with the supernatural to produce their effects (this particular talent seems to have been all but lost since the days of the Edwardian school). There is the kind of story intended only to horrify (the typical *Weird Tales* story) and the kind which seeks to entertain the reader on a wider canvas (the typical Lost Land or Sword-and-Sorcery story). The difference between these is that the one *hints* at entities, worlds and events existing beyond ordinary human ken, whereas the other attempts to describe them in more concrete terms. Other writers go further—they make use of the symbols, archetypes and narrative machinery of the fantasy story—and attempt to weave them into a structure which, in its implications, causes the reader to sense more deeply the nature of his existence. Cabell's Poictesme mythos and, I suppose, Lewis's *Perelandra* trilogy are obvious examples of authors consciously exploiting the form in order to discuss their own ideas about the nature of Man.

　　This use of archetypes and classical situations is, of course, to be discovered in the entire body of literature, but only in fantasy, whether it is intended merely to entertain or to enlighten as well, is it at once apparent. This is one of the reasons why writers like Iris Murdoch, William Golding and John Cowper Powys find a sympathetic audience amongst adherents of fantasy fiction, for all three writers use only a thin disguise to clothe their central characters. Indeed, far from limiting the writer, direct use of mythic material increases the richness and range of the work, whether he's a Realist or a Romantic.

As Lovecraft shows, there is no need for the writer to be aware of his real sources, though, as Ballard's work illustrates, it can be greatly improved if he is.

Having sketched in these few initial ideas about the form, I shall now sketch in its development.

First, if we leave aside the basic mythologies and religions of the world, we come to a body of Western literature which, in the form we know it, emerged from the Dark Ages. This literature, though still disguised as hero legends, was created by men who made it their living to journey from place to place telling stories of mighty deeds and supernatural horrors, usually in verse. *Beowulf* is the best-known of these.

Later we begin to find examples of what are generally called Chivalric Romances, stories of brave knights, doomed hero-villain knights (such as Lancelot), fair maidens, dark sorceresses, mysterious magicians and foul monsters. The legends of King Arthur and his Table Round are probably the best-known in Britain and America, though there are two other important bodies of Chivalric Romance— Charlemagnian and Peninsula. The Charlemagnian cycle involves a set-up similar to the court of King Arthur, with a king uniting his nation and vanquishing the pagan, helped by a group of paladins (usually twelve in number) who are his right-hand men. If Lancelot and Galahad are the best-known Arthurian knights, then Roland and Oliver are the best-known Charlemagnian knights.

The Peninsula Romances are not quite so complex. Many are based on the character of El Cid, the legendary champion of Spain who drove the Moslem invaders from his homeland. It is in the Peninsula Romances that we find the main body of what are termed by the experts "decadent Romances" and it is in the decadent Romance that we find our first real examples of the fantasy story as opposed to the folk-legend for, from about the fourteenth century on, the romance-chronicler ceased hanging his stories onto already existing heroes and began to invent new ones.

Chief of these is *Amadis de Gaul*, probably created by the Portuguese Vasco Lobeira, comprising in the original four long books but, in sequels by a host of imitators, making up some fifty books in all. Whereas the original Chivalric Romances were a mixture of ancient pagan legend, later Christian revision, history and myth, the decadent Romances, though borrowing heavily from the original body, were of definite authorship. They were, in fact, the first novels. The fourteenth, fifteenth and sixteenth centuries produced a vast spate of these with titles like *Palmerin of England* (a four-volume Romance reprinted in 1807, translated by Southey), *Tirante the White*, *Felixmarte of Hyrcania*, *The Mirror of Chivalry* and hundreds more.

It was these Romances that Cervantes satirized in *Don Quixote* and, in rejecting the Romance form, laid the foundations for the modern novel in his pastoral and picaresque stories.

About fifty years after *Don Quixote* debunked the form, the last of its examples was published. It had given way to the novel of country life and the colourful novel of thieves and vagabonds, though, in drama and poetry we still find evidence of its appeal—*The Faerie Queene*, for instance, makes direct use of Romantic imagery, while the Jacobean Tragedy, with its emphasis on gratuitous horror was later to influence the Gothic.

For over a hundred years, as the Age of Reason reigned, the prose romance was unpopular with intellectual and general public alike and it took an aesthetic and antiquarian politician, Sir Horace Walpole, to instigate the return of the romance in Britain with what is generally thought to be the first real Gothic novel—*The Castle of Otranto*. Though there were one or two hints in other works that it was coming, it was Walpole's short novel that launched the Romantic Revival in

English literature. This was published in 1764. It deals with all kinds of sensational supernatural events in and about the grotesque Castle, makes no attempt to rationalize them, from the mysterious appearance one day of a gigantic helmet in the first chapter, to the "awful spectre" who reminds one of the characters of his duty in the last chapter.

Since later articles will deal with examples in detail, I won't bother to describe the best of the Gothics here. These included the works of Mrs. Ann Radcliffe (*Mysteries of Udolpho*), Matthew Gregory Lewis (*Ambrosio; or, The Monk*), Mary Shelley (*Frankenstein*), Charles Maturin (*Melmoth the Wanderer*) and many, many more. For fifty years, from 1770 to 1820, the Gothic novel was the most popular form in England and its influence remained with later writers such as Scott, the Brontës, even Austen, Le Fanu and, of course, Poe and the Victorian/Edwardian school of horror-story writers. In fact it never really died after *The Castle of Otranto*, but continued to develop to the present day (my own early "Elric" stories are written, I feel, in the tradition of the Chivalric and Gothic Romance).

The fantasy story, with its overtones of romance and its undertones of the "inner world of the psyche," has never lost its appeal, though it often goes through periods where serious critics abhor it and a large section of the public disdains it. If we take into consideration folk-epics and religious works such as the Bible, the *Bhagavad Gita*, traditional tales such as *The Arabian Nights* and the Norse *Eddara*, we can see that its development has been continuous since primitive man first began to invent stories. For better or worse, this can hardly be said of any other form.

I should like to finish this introductory article to a series which will deal with specific works of fantasy with a quote from Jung (*Modern Man in Search of a Soul*, Routledge and Kegan Paul, pages 180–181):

> It [the second part of Goethe's *Faust*] is a strange something that derives its existence from the hinterland of man's mind—that suggests the abyss of time separating us from pre-human ages, or evokes a super-human

world of contrasting light and darkness. It is a primordial experience which surpasses man's understanding
and to which he is therefore in danger of succumbing.
The value and the force of the experience are given by
its enormity. It arises from timeless depths; it is foreign
and cold, many-sided, demonic and grotesque. A
grimly ridiculous sample of the eternal chaos ... it
bursts asunder our human standards of value and of
aesthetic form. The disturbing vision of monstrous and
meaningless happenings that in every way exceed the
grasp of human feelings and comprehension makes
quite other demands upon the powers of the artist than
do the experiences of the foreground of life. These
never rend the curtain that veils the cosmos; they never
transcend the bounds of the humanly possible, and for
this reason are readily shaped to the demands of art, no
matter how great a shock to the individual they may
be. But the primordial experiences rend from the top to
bottom the curtain upon which is painted the picture
of an ordered world, and allow a glimpse into the un-
fathomed abyss of what has not yet become. Is it a vision of other worlds, or of the obscuration of the spirit,
or of the beginning of things before the age of man, or
of the unborn generations of the future? We cannot say
that it is any or none of these ... In a more restricted
and specific way, the primordial experience furnishes
material for Rider Haggard in the fiction-cycle that
turns upon *She* ...

It is in this more restricted and specific way that I intend to look at
some of the more important works of fantasy in subsequent articles.

*(Note: Most of this essay was originally written earlier for an unpublished
magazine.)*

ELRIC OF MELNIBONÉ:
INTRODUCTION TO THE
GRAPHIC ADAPTATION

INTRODUCTION

to *Elric of Melniboné*, graphic adaptation
(1986)

R IGHT FROM ELRIC'S earliest appearances (in *Science Fantasy* magazine, 1961) he has attracted the attention of some of the best fantasy illustrators. Indeed, Jim Cawthorn (who depicted him on the covers of *Science Fantasy* and the first edition of *Stormbringer*) was more than a little responsible for my descriptions, since Jim and I worked for years in very close liaison (including a commissioned illustrated serial done for the *Illustrated Weekly of India* in the late '60s) and sometimes were hard put to say who had invented an image first.

I have always placed a high emphasis on illustration, both in my own books and in *New Worlds*, the magazine I edited for a number of years. I'm inclined to plan my books in terms of scenes and images. The fantasies in particular are always very thoroughly worked out in what I like to think of as a coherent pictorial vocabulary. This is singularly important to someone who works, when actually writing, at the kind of speed and intensity which has enabled me to complete the majority of my fantasy books in less than a week and frequently within three days. Everything must be "in tune"—there must be an internal logic of images, just as there is in dreams. This much, I think, I learned from the surrealists. Like the surrealists, too, I found Freud and Jung of great help in maintaining this coherence.

All of which is a roundabout way of reiterating just how much I care about illustration.

Over the years, since Jim Cawthorn's first (and still in many ways the finest) portraits of Elric, there have been a number of interpretations of the albino. The first strip version to be published was actually in French, by Philippe Druillet, in an obscure magazine called *Moi Aussi* in the mid-'60s (reprinted as a portfolio, 1972; in English, 1973) which was given an altogether idiosyncratic cast, since Druillet spoke no English and the stories were *told* to him by a friend, whereupon he drew his interpretation! The second version was Jim Cawthorn's black-and-white, large-format *Stormbringer*, which was published with somewhat limited distribution by Savoy Books in the mid-'70s.

Thereafter, all the other versions have originated in America. One of the best of these was Robert Gould's original Elric tale (with Eric Kimball) published by Star*Reach, 1976. I have always been a huge admirer of Gould's work and am especially delighted that he is now illustrating virtually the entire Eternal Champion cycle on recent paperback editions (chiefly by Berkley). A very odd version of Elric came from the pen of that excellent Conan illustrator, Barry Windsor-Smith, in a Marvel *Conan* comic. Jim Cawthorn and I were responsible for the scenario, Roy Thomas wrote the script, and Barry, having no clear idea of what Elric should look like, based his interpretation on the early U.S. covers of *Stormbringer* and *The Stealer of Souls* by Jack Gaughan, not knowing that I had heartily disliked Gaughan's Elric! This was not Barry's fault, but it meant that the Conan meets Elric story, "A Sword Called Stormbringer" (*Conan the Barbarian* Nos. 14 & 15, March & May 1972), always remained something of a disappointment, visually, for me.

In 1979 Frank Brunner produced a tremendously powerful twenty-page story in *Heavy Metal* magazine (reprinted in *Star*Reach Greatest Hits*, together with the Gould story)—a rendition which almost got Elric into his first movie. I was approached by a film producer to do an Elric movie entirely on the strength of having seen Frank's story. Sadly, the project fell through for a number of reasons. Another Hollywood proposal came from Ralph Bakshi, but I wasn't prepared, in the end, to subject Elric to his kind of trivialization and I pulled out very early. I am also disappointed that although Howard Chaykin and I have worked together on projects (notably *The Swords of Heaven, The Flowers of Hell*) Howard's only Elric work remains the early portfolio he did in the mid-'70s.

It seemed for some time that Elric projects were doomed to founder after one or two enthusiastic attempts. Mike Friedrich, who was offered control of U.S. comic rights to the Eternal Champion in 1976, had worked very hard to get a regular Elric series running in America and at last things began to come together in the 1980s when Roy Thomas and P. Craig Russell first teamed up to produce the Marvel Graphic Novel version of "The Dreaming City" (1982) and then (in *Epic Illustrated* No. 14) "While the Gods Laugh." With Friedrich as editor, Thomas as writer, and Russell and Gilbert as illustrators, a winning team had finally been fielded.

In April 1983 the first regular Elric comic book began to appear, published by Pacific Comics. The fey, eery quality—especially experienced in the large set-piece pages—is like no other version of the Elric stories, and the strangely etiolated figures make the characters seem genuinely of another, more magical and alien world. Some of the work is extraordinary, both in detail and colour, in the originality of imagination which the artists have brought to their interpretation. I was greatly impressed and, in looking through the pages again, continue to be surprised and delighted by subtle touches which I had not taken in at first reading. I have never had the opportunity to congratulate the artists before, but am glad to do so now.

Elric of Melniboné is chronologically the first in the Elric series, although it was written as one of the last (in 1972). With the comic's first publication in paperback form I very much hope it will lead the way to the entire Elric saga being eventually available in illustrated versions. First Comics, who have already produced a further Elric series (*The Sailor on the Seas of Fate* by Thomas, Gilbert and Freeman) and who are, as I write, beginning an excellent interpretation of *The Jewel in the Skull* (featuring Dorian Hawkmoon) by a new team (Gerry Conway, Rafael Kayanan and Rico Rival), continue to prove themselves both reliable and conscientious in their treatment of writers and artists and this, in itself, is fairly unusual in the world of comics.

A long time ago I used to edit and write comics myself. I have lost track of the vast number of science fiction, Western and historical stories I produced in the '50s and '60s, chiefly for Amalgamated Press (later Fleetway Publications), but I well remember how I longed to be able to expand my imaginative range, how I tried to convince conservative editors and publishers to do something a bit different and how frustrated I used to feel when I was refused. Eventually I gave up my attempts to talk people into doing more interesting comics and looked elsewhere for a living. Now, through the new generation of comics publishers, writers and illustrators, I can at last feel encouraged that the old frustrations are ended and enjoy work which expands the medium and actually revels in the possibilities of the form.

My thanks, as ever, to Mike Friedrich, to Roy Thomas, to Messrs. Russell, Gilbert and Freeman and, of course, to Rick Oliver and all at First Comics (who nobly took up Pacific's fallen banner) for these wonderful pages. They have succeeded in making a fairly old man pretty damned happy . . .

EL CID AND ELRIC:
UNDER THE INFLUENCE!

EL CID AND ELRIC:
Under the Influence!
(2007)

ELRIC AND EL Cid! The similarity between the two names is not entirely coincidental, since the legends and romances of El Cid were a huge influence on my juvenile imagination.

I was brought up, like most British boys—I suspect like most boys of my generation everywhere—on stories of idealism, heroism and self-sacrifice. Macaulay's *How Horatius Held the Bridge*, Tennyson's *The Charge of the Light Brigade*, Newbolt's *Vitai Lampada*, Chesterton's *Lepanto* and many, many more were the stirring narrative poems we recited not to please teachers but for our own delight. Much of our history was already mythologized—the cool courage of Francis Drake and the brave death of Nelson were mixed in our minds with the fictional death of Sidney Carton in *A Tale of Two Cities* and a whole army of heroes who, in true Christian tradition, gave their lives for the benefit of others. Usually these heroes were depicted, like Robin Hood, as underdogs, fighting against the rich, the powerful and the thoroughly unjust!

The movies were the same. The stories were often of brave "ordinary" men who sacrificed themselves for the good of the many. *High Noon* represented this theme in Westerns while *Quo Vadis* and *Ben Hur* offered it in what were known as "toga and sandal epics," Humphrey Bogart sacrificed his own desire in *Casablanca* and in the urban thrillers which eventually were given the generic name of "noir" by French critics. These were the popular entertainment of my day, but I had another enthusiasm, not shared by any of my peers. This was for all the books on myth and legend I could find, as well as for the few adult stories which in those days were still to be given the name of "Fantasy," including Lord Dunsany, Edgar Rice Burroughs and, when I came across them, the American pulp magazines with names like *Planet Stories* or *Startling Stories*, specializing in a Burroughs-influenced "sword-and-planet" fiction. Early on I came across a series which told the stories of Greece and Rome, Scandinavia and Britain, most familiar to English children, but also included a volume on Peninsula Romance and it was in that book I first came across the story of Rodrigo Díaz, El Cid Campeador, whose story especially thrilled me.

Perhaps I was impressed by the fact that Díaz was an historical figure living at one of the most colourful and romantic times in Spanish history, when Christians and Moslems were enjoying perhaps the highest level of civilization either had ever known, when chivalric knights on both sides exemplified the highest ideals, irrespective of religion, while on the other hand there were villains amongst both communities, and El Cid fought with Moslem allies against corrupt Christians or with mixed armies of both religions to secure Valencia for himself. I was thrilled when Díaz was named El Campeador—"The Champion"—bearing his sword Tizona in man-to-man combat and I am sure all this went to inspire my own character Elric and the background of his world. When I wrote, at seventeen, the first draft of my story "The Eternal Champion," there is no doubt that El Cid was influencing it. Like Elric, the Champion fights first for one side and then another, turning "traitor" as he learns more about those he fights for and against. He is moved not by loyalty to a certain flag, but by loyalty to a certain ideal. And in the end he perishes as a result of the destiny he sets in motion. But, in perishing, he saves the world for others!

Noble self-sacrifice still brings me to tears to this day, irrespective of the loyalties of the man or woman who performs the deed. Their loyalty is to a higher ideal, to a noble ethic. To this day epic films, like Ridley Scott's recent *Kingdom of Heaven*, have shown the noblest hero to be the one who rises above simplistic loyalties to serve what is best in mankind and what is universal in mankind's religious or political systems. When, long after I first read of his exploits, I saw Charlton Heston as El Cid have the arrow pulled from his body and strap himself to his horse in order to rally his troops against the invader (even though I knew that in real life Díaz had died in his bed) I enjoyed the same sensations. All this went to inspire my own troubled characters who wonder, in the words of E. M. Forster, whether it is best to betray one's country or one's friend—or, indeed, oneself.

To me, no attempt to mirror the great epics of our ancestors can succeed, even marginally, without an understanding of death. My quarrel with many of the fantasy romances written in the past fifty years or so is precisely that they do not understand the issue of mortality. All they do is keep us wondering *whether* the protagonist will live or die. This is scarcely important to us or Malory would not have called his work "Morte d'Arthur." "All death is certain," says the Hospitaler over his shoulder as he goes to certain doom against Saladin in Scott's film. It is the *meaning* that we give our deaths (and, of course, our lives) that is important. This idea is at the root of all our great chivalric epics. How the hero dies is as resonant as how he lives. This is the point I have tried to make in my own stories. El Cid's legendary end at the battle of Valencia reminds us that courage without sacrifice is an empty quality. Elric's death, to herald in a new and better era, must be equally meaningful if I am to do even modest justice to those great epics which meant so much to me when I was a child.

ORIGINS

*Early artwork associated with Elric's first
appearances in magazines and books.*

A page from an aborted graphic adaptation of *Stormbringer*, by James Cawthorn, 1965, previously unpublished.

Front- and back-cover artwork by James Cawthorn, for *The Sleeping Sorceress*, first edition, New English Library, 1971.

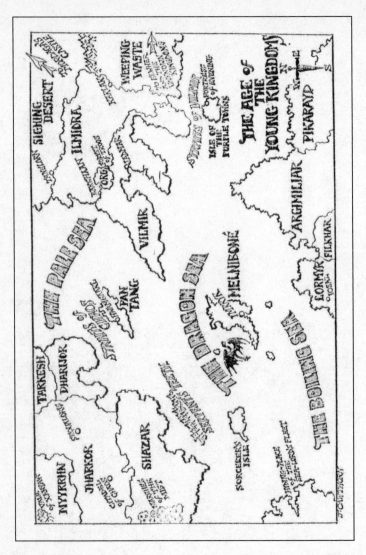

"The Age of the Young Kingdoms" map by James Cawthorn, 1971; first published in *Elric of Melniboné*, first edition.

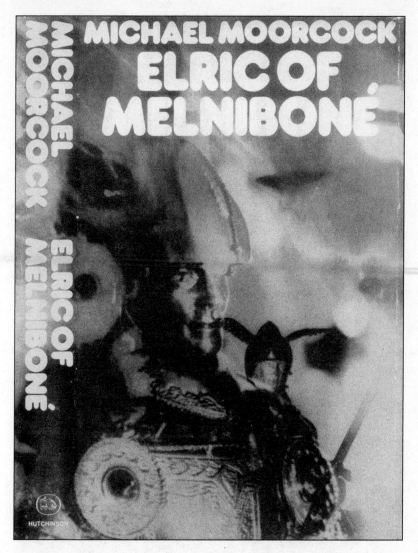

Cover artwork designed by Laurence Cutting, for *Elric of Melniboné*, first edition, Hutchinson, 1972.

UY1304

MICHAEL
MOORCOCK
THE VANISHING
TOWER

DAW sf
BOOKS
No. 245 $1.25

The Fourth Novel of Elric of Melniboné
An earlier version was previously published as
THE SLEEPING SORCERESS

Cover artwork by Michael Whelan, for *The Vanishing Tower*, first retitled edition
of *The Sleeping Sorceress*, DAW Books, 1977.

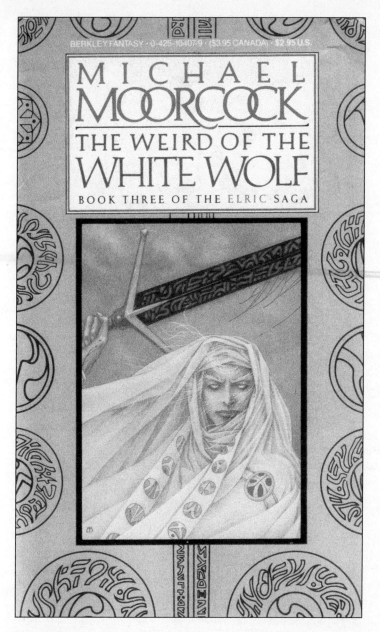

Cover artwork by Robert Gould, for *The Weird of the White Wolf*, book three of the Elric Saga as reconfigured in the mid-1970s, Berkley Books, 1983, comprising "Master of Chaos" (as "The Dream of Earl Aubec") and three stories from *The Stealer of Souls*.

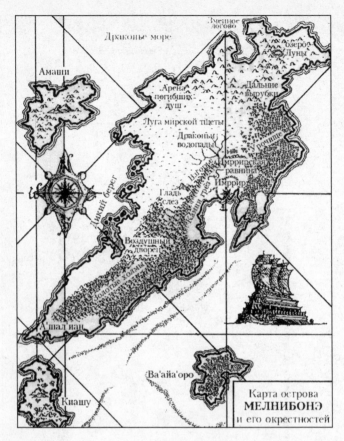

"МеЛнибонэ" ("Melniboné") map by Н. Михайлов, 1992, appeared in *Хроники Элрика/Приэрвчнъии Гороб* (*The Dreaming City/The Sleeping Sorceress*), Terra Fantastica, 2001. Original map drawn by James Cawthorn.

Front- and back-cover artwork by Dalmazio Frau, for *Elric of Melniboné*, first audiobook edition, AudioRealms, 2003.

Cover artwork by Chris Achilleos, for *Elric de Melniboné/La Fortaleza de la Perla*
(*Elric of Melniboné/The Fortress of the Pearl*), Spanish edition, Edhasa, 2007.

For further information about Michael Moorcock and his work, please send a stamped, self-addressed envelope to:

The Nomads of the Time Streams
P.O. Box 385716
Waikoloa, HI 96738

ABOUT THE AUTHOR

Recently voted by the London *Times* one of the fifty greatest English writers since 1945, MICHAEL JOHN MOORCOCK is an SFWA Grand Master and the author of a number of science fiction, fantasy, and literary novels, including the Elric novels, the Cornelius Quartet, *Gloriana, King of the City,* and many more. As editor of the controversial British science fiction magazine *New Worlds,* Moorcock fostered the development of the New Wave in the U.K. and indirectly in the U.S. He won the Nebula Award for his novella *Behold the Man.* He has also won the World Fantasy Award, the British Fantasy Award, and many others. *Mother London* was shortlisted (final three) for the Whitbread Prize.

ABOUT THE ARTIST

A graduate of Syracuse University's School of Art, award-winning artist STEVE ELLIS began his career as a penciller for both Marvel and DC Comics, where he illustrated iconic titles such as *Iron Man, Green Lantern,* and *Lobo,* then moved on to illustrate for Dungeons and Dragons, Magic: The Gathering, and Spectrum. Recently, along with author David Gallaher, Steve cocreated the critically acclaimed werewolf western webcomic series *High Moon* for DC Comics.

Steve is honored to be contributing art to this most recent incarnation of Elric. Michael Moorcock's powerful writing and the fantastic imagery created by Elric's numerous past illustrators have been an inspiration. In executing Elric, Steve draws his influences from the classic illustration work of Gustav Dore and Joseph Clement Cole, as well as that of modern artists.

After several years teaching illustration and drawing at the university he once attended, Steve has moved to Brooklyn, where he lives with his wife and son.

Good

SENTENCES
WITHDRAWN

by Steve Wiesinger

EDUCATIONAL DESIGN, INC.   **EDI 277**

Dedication

To may father, a teacher of English for thirty-seven years, whose honesty and open mind encouraged me to search.

ISBN# 0-87694-321-0   EDI 277

Table of Contents

To The Student

This book is designed to show you some of the basics of writing good sentences and to give you a foundation that will help you write more naturally, confidently, and enjoyably.

Of the three "R's," writing is easily the most complex. Even the best professional writers talk about the difficulty of their craft. But writing also gives you unique opportunities: it increases your ability to communicate, from the simplest letter to the most profound poetry, and it offers you great possibilities for self-expression, a primary need of the human animal.

When we write, we put words and ideas onto paper in the form of sentences and paragraphs. Every sentence is supposed to be constructed so that it is clear and reasonably easy for a reader to understand. To write good sentences, a writer needs a basic understanding of what is called "sentence mechanics." And to help make the sentence structure clear, the writer must know how to use punctuation marks.

Unfortunately, many students find it difficult to write well-constructed, well-punctuated sentences. I remember one vocal student who politely slammed down his pencil and said, "I didn't learn this in the seventh grade, and I didn't learn it in the eighth grade, and I'm not going to learn it now."

I ended up packing away my grammar texts and developing a method of approaching sentence structure that most professional writers use: listening to the rhythm of sentences, hearing the pauses and stops. I used models and examples of the principal sentence patterns in the language—sentence patterns you speak and hear every day. My students were soon writing sentences with no structural errors at all.

This book uses the same method. There are five major sentence patterns explained in the book. The patterns all look and sound familiar, since they derive from the most commonly used sentences in the language. Each pattern is explained in detail, and you concentrate on one pattern at a time. Then you practice writing and punctuating the pattern. The method gains much of its strength from drawing out and systematizing language skills that you have been developing since you learned to speak.

Good Sentences aims at de-frustrating you. It is designed to be self-teaching, so that you can work through the book by yourself. You can also work with a small group, or your teacher might elect to work with your whole class. In any case, make sure you don't skip around among the first eight chapters. The patterns are laid out in a step-by-step sequence from the simple to the most complex. Trying to work with parenthetical sentences before you understand complete ideas would be like attempting long division before you have mastered addition.

After eighteen years of watching the results with my students—and watching students teach other students in my school's writing center—I have every confidence you'll find the method just as clear, helpful, and unfrustrating.

The Basic Sentence

1

COMPLETE IDEAS

A basic sentence expresses a **complete idea**. *Complete* means whole, having all its parts.

> Dwight runs fast.

> The Smiths left for Reno.

These examples stand by themselves as complete ideas. But when ideas are incomplete, they become vague, confusing, or difficult to understand.

> Runs fast.   (Who runs fast?)

> The Smiths.   (What about them?)

These incomplete ideas are definitely confusing. Like blurred photographs, they cause you to guess at what is meant. On the other hand, complete ideas are not only easy to grasp, they also form the foundation for all sentence mechanics. Once you fully understand the concept of completeness, problems with sentence structure will be banished for good.

> Mayling is a troublemaker.

> Delwin made all-county track.

The complete ideas above can be understood independently of other sentences because they are self-contained units. Try picking up a book and reading anywhere. Chances are each independent sentence will make sense by itself. That's because every sentence is a complete thought unit.

> George Washington wore wooden teeth.

> My friend Al can program computers in his sleep.

Each of these examples stands as a thought unit, a complete idea. Now take a look at these incomplete ideas.

> Wore wooden teeth.

> My friend Al computers.

"Wore wooden teeth"—who wore wooden teeth? "My friend Al computers"? Does this mean the man is a computer?

HEADLINES, TITLES, ADS

Sometimes you will see writing that does not express complete ideas. For example, newspaper headlines, titles, and advertising slogans often suggest only part of an idea. Titles and headlines need to be fleshed out in order to carry a whole idea like a sentence.

BOMB TEST (headline, meaning that Tuesday morning the U.S.S.R. and the U.S. cooperated on a nuclear bomb test.)

The car of the century! (from an advertising brochure, trying to persuade you that a particular car is the finest ever built)

Headlines, titles, and advertisements often utilize fragments to suggest meaning.

ECONOMIC SLUMP (The U.S. experienced an economic slump for the third month.)

Insightful! The vet's Vietnam! (The cover of a book is praising it)

Homecoming! (A flyer is announcing homecoming.)

⌕ EXERCISE 1

A. Check over the following examples. Match the phrase in the letter column with its correct partner in the number column. Be sure the sentences make sense. Note: One example is already a complete idea.

___1. study math.	A. I got
___2. Grapes	B. Surfers like
___3. study physics.	C. need sun to ripen.
___4. Have you	D. My cat died.
___5. some fine Reeboks.	E....special keys to the...
___6. David always	F. seen Erin?
___7. giant-sized waves.	G. Luis chose to
___8. Sal got...gym.	H. flirts with Heidi.
	I. Luis also chose to

B. Now, just for fun, try writing 5 headlines, slogans, or titles that are <u>not</u> complete sentences.

1. _____

2. _____

3. _____

4. _____

5. _____

FRAGMENTS

Complete ideas are clear. *Fragments* are only part of an idea, and in writing they're often confusing.

> At camp this summer. (What happened?)
>
> Staying in our house. (Who is staying?)

These fragments or incomplete sentences are anything but clear. Compare the fragments to these complete ideas:

> I nearly got drowned at camp this summer.
>
> My uncle is staying in our house.

Sometimes a writer assumes that an idea from one sentence carries over to another.

> John's camping trip was a complete disaster. He forgot the tent pegs and the food. *Forgot to check the weather.* The rain nearly drowned him.

The fragment in italics neglects to say <u>who</u> forgot to check the weather. Even though John is mentioned in the two previous sentences, you still have to add *He* to have the following thought unit stand by itself.

⌒➔ EXERCISE 2

Turn these next fragments into complete ideas. Include each fragment in a complete sentence that you make up, so it can be understood clearly. (Hint: Some may go best at the beginning of a sentence, and some may go best at the end.)

1. Passed every class_____

2. The last spaceship_____

3. Fun time in the park_____

4. The desk nearby_____

5. My friend Ezra_____

6. The snow turned_____

7. Caught the train_____

8. Lester finished every_____

9. The pencil sharpener_____

SUBJECTS AND PREDICATES

As you've seen from the examples, a single word or two can make the difference between a fragment and a complete idea. Often the word that's missing in fragments is the part of the sentence that is grammatically known as the *subject*. It is either a *noun* (the name of a person, place, or thing) or a *pronoun* (a word like *I, he, she, it, we, you, they,* etc.)

Mary passed every class.
|___|
subject

He caught the train.
|__|
subject

A short side trip into simplified traditional grammar will help you understand this concept and provides another avenue for coming at sentence mechanics.

A complete idea requires only a subject and a *predicate*.

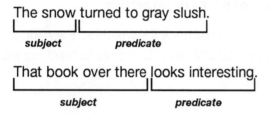

The snow turned to gray slush.
|_____||_____|
   subject   *predicate*

That book over there looks interesting.
|_____||_____|
    subject   *predicate*

A *subject* names <u>who</u> or <u>what</u> is doing the action of the sentence. The *complete subject* of a sentence consists of a noun or a pronoun plus all the words that describe (or "modify") it. In the examples above, *The snow* and *That book over there* are complete subjects built on the nouns *snow* and *book*.

A *predicate* describes the action of a sentence. It consists of a verb plus anything else in the sentence that is not the subject. In the examples above, *turned to gray slush* and *looks interesting* are predicates built around the verbs *turned* and *looks*.

An easy way to describe subject and predicate is: <u>Who</u> is doing <u>what</u>.

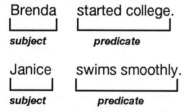

Brenda   started college.
|_____| |_____|
subject   *predicate*

Janice   swims smoothly.
|_____| |_____|
subject   *predicate*

In the last example *Janice* is the subject; notice that the subject is a noun (person, place, or thing). The predicate here is *swims smoothly*, which is built around the verb or action word *swims*. The predicate always contains a verb, just as the complete subject contains a noun or pronoun.

Now look at the expanded versions of these sentences.

Janice, a tall, dark-haired girl, swims smoothly in the relay.

noun

complete subject | predicate

My good friend *Brenda* started college this fall.

noun

complete subject | predicate

In most sentences simple subjects (nouns or pronouns) and verbs are surrounded by numerous other words that describe them or add information about the basic action. The key is simply to recognize the two core elements of sentence structure—the nouns (or pronouns) and the verbs. Nouns are simply persons, places, or things; verbs show action or existence (like *is*—Jim is good; or like *does*—Mack does a good job.) Understanding nouns and verbs insures that you'll write complete sentences.

☞ **EXERCISE 3**

Write out the following sentences. Then label the complete subjects and predicates.

1. Ahmed slowly walked home.

_____

2. Dogs frighten me.

_____

3. The Ozark Mountains are great for vacations.

_____

4. A new Porsche would come in handy.

_____

5. The police car pulled onto campus.

_____

6. My apartment is on the sixth floor.

_____

7. Six people qualified for the scholarship.

_____

8. I am learning computer programming.

_____

9. Sheena acts incredibly polite.

_____

10. The grizzled old man turned out to be quite pleasant.

_____

Remember that fragments frequently occur because of leaving out the noun or subject.

> **Fragment:** Packed all her clothes for the trip.

> **Fragment:** Went to the corner calling for help.

Here the nouns (subjects) are added.

> _Sonia_ packed all her clothes for the trip.

> _Racine_ went to the corner calling for help.

THE SOUND OF COMPLETE IDEAS

Complete ideas sound finished. Fragments often sound peculiar and unfinished.

> Was boring.

> My old jacket with the torn sleeve.

Adding subjects and verbs makes the difference.

> The movie was boring.

> I am missing my old jacket with the torn sleeve.

Over the years you've built up language skills through speaking and listening. Your ears are so acutely trained that you know the best way to make yourself understood is through complete ideas. You knew this long before you knew what "complete idea" meant. A toddler, for instance, progresses within a year from saying "want" or "apple" to "want apple" to "I want an apple."

☞ EXERCISE 4

Look at each of the following sentences and fragments. Use your "ear"—your sense of language—to distinguish between them. Put a check mark before those that are good sentences with complete ideas. After each fragment, write a sentence of your own that includes and completes it. (You don't have to write anything after the sentences that are already complete.)

1. Nadine school.

_____

2. The stupid dogs barked all night.

_____

12

3. Three cheerleaders today.

_____

4. John painted his room black.

_____

5. You have.

_____

6. Loving is more important than thinking.

_____

7. Running for the bus.

_____

8. Has a new locker combination.

_____

WRITING AND SPEAKING

In speaking, we grow so accomplished with language that we complete what would be fragments through gestures, tone of voice, facial expression, and a whole range of non-verbal communication skills. Look at the way you and your friends get across complex ideas with just a shrug or a smile. But all these non-verbal clues that occur naturally in speaking have to be spelled out in writing.

> "Hey, cool"—spoken with a slow nod might mean, yes, I'm thinking it over; it might be a good idea.

> "Wild shoes"—spoken with a surprised smile might mean that the shoes are highly unusual yet still appealing.

In speaking we put together highly complex thoughts with the greatest ease. ("Man, am I getting tired of the way Rachel gossips. Really, did you hear what she said about Lester and me?")

We also know without thinking about it how to make a single point stand out. ("If she doesn't stop gossiping, I swear I'm going to clobber her.")

We instinctively stop before going from one thought to the next. ("I guess I'd better hang on, though. *(stop)* If I smacked her, I'd only bring myself down to her level.")

Structure is second nature—in speaking, that is. But much of this wealth of experience suddenly evaporates with writing.

What has happened? Probably we have made learning to write overly formal and dependent on rules. Indeed, many people think that you can't write correctly unless you know traditional grammar. But that isn't true. What we're doing here, beginning at the most basic level, is developing a foundation for writing correctly by drawing out your hidden language skills.

In carrying over your many speaking and listening skills to writing, you utilize your sense of humor, your sense of drama, your sense of completeness, and your sense of how to make a point. Most certainly you carry over what has been called the sixth sense, your imagination.

☞ EXERCISE 5

A. Use your sense of oral language to place the stops (periods) in the following example. Put in capitals at the beginning of sentences, too.

I saw my friend Claudia the other day she was really in a bad mood her mother grounded her for three weeks the spring dance is coming up Claudia wants me to talk to her mom and tell her that everyone is going I get along with her mother real well maybe she'll listen to me

B. Now experiment with your language skills by turning each of the fragments below into a sentence.

1. Her hat size.

_____

2. Hates those drugs now.

_____

3. Leaped over the stream.

_____

4. At the mall.

_____

5. Dilcy's best characteristic.

_____

6. Shocking to parents.

_____

7. The senator.

_____

8. Olympic highlights.

_____

9. Got me in trouble.

_____

10. So frustrating.

_____

C. Now write out seven complete ideas that you make up yourself. Don't worry about being fancy with your sentences. The important thing here is to nail down the concept of completeness.

1._____

2._____

3._____

4._____

5._____

6._____

7._____

Summary

BASIC SENTENCE

A basic sentence expresses a complete idea.

> Jeanie is a newcomer.

> The roses faded in October.

Complete means whole, having all its parts. The concept of completeness is crucial for understanding sentence mechanics. Each sentence is a unit, complete in itself.

> Sometimes parties are a drag.

> Faith likes cold weather.

Even when sentences are taken out of context, they make sense because they convey a complete thought, a thought unit.

Headlines, titles, and advertisements seldom use complete ideas. Working by inference and suggestion, they require the reader to make associations which stitch together ideas.

PRESIDENT UP IN POLLS (newspaper headline)

The Witches from Marin (book title)

FRAGMENTS

Incomplete ideas are called fragments. Fragments are unclear and often difficult to understand.

Jumped up.

My old car.

Fragments leave the reader guessing because the idea is unfinished.

Patricia jumped up.

My old car *has started making weird noises.*

Each sentence must be able to stand by itself independent of other thought units. Fragments are often caused simply by leaving out the subject or predicate of the sentence. (*Patricia,* and *has started making weird noises.*) Sometimes writers assume that the subject carries over from sentence to sentence. (*John went to the movies. He took his seat. Ate popcorn.*)

SUBJECTS AND PREDICATES

Grammatically, a complete idea requires only a subject and a predicate.

The ratty old truck spewed exhaust.
    subject   *predicate*

Indra first noticed John in her math class.
  subject   *predicate*

A subject usually centers on a noun (or a pronoun, like *I, he, she, it, we, you, they*), while a predicate revolves around a verb.

My friend *Zeke slamdunks* like a pro.
    noun   *verb*

She created a marvelous painting.
pronoun *verb*

Learning to recognize nouns and verbs or subjects and predicates helps you avoid writing sentence fragments. Once again, fragments often occur because the subject or predicate was left out.

Fragment: Went home angry. (Who is angry here?)

Sentence: My good friend Dolores went home angry.

subject

THE SOUND OF COMPLETE IDEAS

Fragments sound incomplete and are often confusing.

Walked for hours.

Left the sweatsocks under the bench.

Even without understanding the concept of complete ideas, your ear is attuned to using complete ideas in order to make yourself understood.

We walked for hours to get to camp.

I left the sweatsocks under the bench.

WRITING AND SPEAKING

Your ear has become highly developed through years of speaking and listening to English. This grasp of language applies directly to writing. You carry over your sense of humor, drama, imagination, and rhythm. Rhythm, for instance, aids with determining punctuation.

It was no good.(stop) I knew it.(stop) Now I had
to rethink my entire approach.(stop)

While speaking draws on slang and non-verbal language to create short cuts, writing needs to be fleshed out to complete the ideas inferred.

"Good, good"—might mean someone found the outcome of the hockey match was exactly what she/he wanted.

"No, please"—might be fleshed out to mean that the young lady would prefer to skip desert.

☞ CHAPTER REVIEW

Put your understanding of complete ideas to work by turning the following fragments into sentences. Capitalize the first letter, and end each of your sentences with a period.

1. went to the amusement park

_____

2. painted the flat

_____

3. helped my brother move

_____

4. the table

_____

5. cloudy all day

_____

6. enough snow

_____

7. we

_____

8. the river outside town

_____

9. michael Jackson

_____

10. left a flood

_____

The List Pattern

2

Ideas in English can be expressed in sentences that have standard patterns. You are already familiar with one such pattern: the basic sentence (subject plus predicate).

Surprisingly, the number of sentence patterns is not very large, though they can be combined in thousands of different ways. In this book you will examine some of the most common patterns. In particular, you will learn how to handle those patterns that give the most trouble to student writers.

Let's start with one of the easiest patterns to recognize: the *List Pattern*. In this pattern a complete idea is expanded with a list of three or more items.

> Lilly found *hope, courage, and purpose*.
> └──────────────┘
>   *list*

> *Hamburger, chicken, and salami* are popular for lunch.
> └──────────────┘
>   *list*

The list works on the same principle as a grocery list: you set down items in a row.

> She likes *apples, oranges, and papayas*.

> My bruised eye turned *black, then green, then yellow*.

The List Pattern only occurs when the items are set down one after the other, like an actual list. This next example doesn't belong to the List Pattern.

> My eye looked terrible as it changed from black to green and then gradually faded to a pale yellow.

THREE ITEMS TO A LIST

It takes three or more items in a row to make a List Pattern.

> Bert seems *bright, curious,* and *knowledgeable*.

> *China, India, Indonesia,* and *Mexico* are all heavily populated.

When there are only two items in a list, leave out commas.

> Bert seems bright and curious.

> China and India are heavily populated.

Some people get confused when they see the word *and*. They start throwing around punctuation. Putting in a comma on two-item lists is definitely an error.

Incorrect: Bert seems bright, and curious.

Incorrect: China, and India are heavily populated.

Only use commas when you list three or more items.

Correct: Bert seems bright, curious, and pleasant.

Correct: China, India, Indonesia, and Pakistan are heavily populated.

☞ EXERCISE 1

Show your understanding of the List Pattern by putting a check mark before each sentence that needs commas. Watch out for those two-item lists that do not need any commas.

1. My locker is full of books paper and clothes.
2. I'm going to the assembly with Maria and Luz.
3. Stop taking all my skirts sweaters and blouses.
4. I'm getting more confident calm and outgoing.
5. Let's get some apples grapes and sodas.
6. My baby sister still hits and bites.
7. Enrique and David made straight A's.
8. Do you know Tamra Lucy and Florence?
9. He bought shoelaces lightbulbs and napkins.
10. She's aiming at a gold bronze or silver medal.

PUNCTUATING THE LIST PATTERN

Commas are placed between the items in a List Pattern.

The motorcyclist was daring, speedy, and alert.

Lacy needs clippers, nail polish, and a comb.

Leaving commas out of the pattern would make the items pile up on each other.

Incorrect: Gangs have become widespread violent and dangerous.

Incorrect: Vicky's three speeds are slow slower and stop.

The eye and ear immediately search for separation. Our sense of language tells us something is wrong with "violent dangerous" and "slow slower." Without separation, confusion quickly follows, as in the next example.

IlikeMarybutMarylikesPhilsothesituationiscrazy.

(Incidentally, this principle of separation is the foundation for all punctuation marks. Every mark is based on giving specific amounts and kinds of separation.)

Most grammar books consider the last comma—the one before the word *and*—to be optional. Some writers put it in. Others leave it out. But to maintain consistency and reinforce the idea of separation, it's best to punctuate each item. This makes it easier to recognize the pattern.

Gangs have become widespread, violent, and dangerous.

Vicky's three speeds are slow, slower, and stop.

However, you don't need to put a comma after the last item in the list.

Incorrect: My brother, my uncle, and my cousins, live in Michigan.

Correct: My brother, my uncle, and my cousins live in Michigan.

☞ EXERCISE 2

Separate the items in the following List Pattern sentences with commas.

1. Parsley sage and rosemary are spices.
2. Jacqueline likes movies school and Freddy.
3. She's taking P.E. Typing III and English.
4. The orphan felt beaten depressed and alone.
5. Indra came saw and conquered John.

COMMAS AS PAUSES

Commas provide the lightest separation of all punctuation marks. In ordinary speech they can be heard as very slight pauses. The pause occurs simultaneously with the comma.

The grapefruit was tart, (pause) juicy, (pause) and cold.

Di bought apples, (pause) oranges, (pause) and ketchup.

Pauses are a natural part of language. You wouldn't run everything together in speaking, because you need to be understood, or you have to take a breath. On top of that, you have a feel for the language. You pause to give separation or sometimes to give effect.

"Yo, Theodor. Come on, say you'll do it."

"No. For the first, last, and definite time, no."

Commas create rhythm and pacing as well as separation. If you draw on your sense of rhythm from years of using the language, it's possible to punctuate by ear. Hearing commas as pauses greatly aids comma usage.

Florence ran the 100, (pause) the 200, (pause) and the 400 yard dashes.

The mountain was cold, (pause) desolate, (pause) and awesome.

☞ EXERCISE 3

Make use of your sense of hearing by punctuating the following examples. Be sure to read the sentences out loud, since this helps make the comma pauses evident to the ear.

1. He was saving for either a jeep a pickup or a mini-van.
2. The hike was long lonely and boring.
3. Ricardo William and Sam made the lacrosse team.
4. My three sisters are Bea Reece and Callie.
5. She hates potatoes bread and macaroni.
6. Cheryl climbed Mt. Whitney Mt. McKinley and Mt. Rainier.
7. She wants to go to a city college a state college or a flight attendant school.
8. Irv wore tights dance shoes and a muscle shirt.
9. The morning broke cold icy and cloudy.
10. Snow black ice and frost covered the roads.
11. He campaigned against crime drugs and waste.

PHRASE LIST

A list can be made from phrases as well as from individual items.

> The new secretary arrived on time, worked hard, and left promptly at five.

> Jessie had to study algebra, fix dinner, and chop the firewood.

A phrase is a group of two or more words which act as a unit in a sentence.

> ...arrived on time

> ...chop the firewood

Phrases arranged in a List Pattern are punctuated exactly the same way that individual items are: commas separate them from each other.

> The soccer team practiced hard, played numerous scrimmages, but had a disappointing season.

> Daniel ate four chicken fajitas, two milkshakes, and three sacks of fries.

As in item lists, commas are not used when there are only two phrases.

Incorrect: Lisa likes *a cup of chocolate*, and *orange juice*.

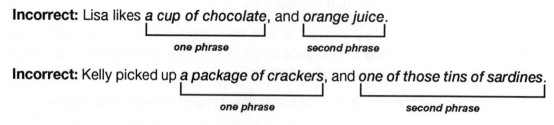
one phrase   second phrase

Incorrect: Kelly picked up *a package of crackers*, and *one of those tins of sardines*.

one phrase   second phrase

Three is the magic number for using commas with a list.

Lisa likes *a cup of chocolate*, *a glass of juice*, and *a muffin with honey*.

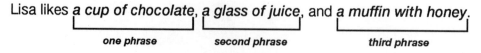
one phrase   second phrase   third phrase

22

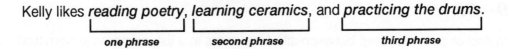

Kelly likes *reading poetry, learning ceramics,* and *practicing the drums.*

one phrase   second phrase   third phrase

EXERCISE 4

Put to use your knowledge of lists and commas by punctuating the following sentences.

1. After delivering the package, Mac ran down the stairs got into his truck and hurried away.
2. For swimming in the ocean you need a wet suit and a pair of booties and a leak-proof squid lid.
3. Matilda got ready for the party by purchasing a new blouse perming her hair and doing her nails.
4. Love gives the world a lot of its joy no small part of its sorrow and a great deal of its excitement.
5. James strolled through the hall sauntered by the library and drifted into class.
6. The Chens took two tents a Coleman stove and an ice chest packed with food.
7. The engaged couple bought a bedroom set a small kitchen table and some silverware.
8. They went to the movies stopped for pizza then cruised the fast food places.
9. I got home and went to bed.
10. My brother is really ambitious and has two jobs.

Did you notice that numbers 9 and 10 had only two items?

LISTS IN THE BEGINNING OR MIDDLE OF SENTENCES

You can use lists anywhere in a sentence—beginning, middle, or end.

Toys, books, and dolls were scattered around the room.

Deer, coyotes, and rabbits often come to drink here.

The older of the two women was *kind, gracious, and intelligent*, which impressed the young people. (NOTE: the comma after the word *intelligent* is not part of the List Pattern. It is there to set off the clause that begins with *which*.)

Darrell *picked up his grades, got his transcript, then caught the train* for his new home.

The car needs to be *washed, vacuumed, and polished*.

Indra likes John's *smile, his brown eyes, and his physique*.

It's especially easy to hear the comma pauses that separate phrase and item lists in the beginning and middle of sentences. Listen to the pauses in these lists.

Toys, (pause) books, (pause) and dolls...

...kind, (pause) gracious, (pause) and intelligent...

...picked up his grades, (pause) got his transcript, (pause) and caught the train...

AND—OR

When *and* or *or* is repeated between all of the items in a list, commas are omitted.

> Taxis and buses and trucks jam Chicago's streets.

> Vida finished practice and took a shower and went out to where his buddies waited.

Sometimes this construction is more effective than the ordinary List Pattern using commas. For instance, you might want to use it to flatten out the rhythm of the sentence and give it an episodic "and then" feeling.

☞ EXERCISE 5

Test your ability with lists in the beginning and middle positions. Write out the sentences and punctuate them as necessary. Notice that some examples use *and* and *or*.

1. A lively interesting and dramatic presidential debate influenced the vote.

_____

_____

2. Davis brought records and drinks and potato chips to the party.

_____

_____

3. Rachel Dawn Jeanie and Alyssa got good grades on their group project.

_____

_____

4. The Rivers brought towels a picnic lunch and sunblock to the beach.

_____

_____

5. Cab driver truck driver heavy equipment operator—these are all jobs I'd like to get.

_____

_____

6. Ramon and I went to the show and met a couple girls and got their phone numbers.

_____

_____

7. Mrs. Petersen says she's feeling tired irritable and stressed out.

_____

_____

8. Doing chores getting to bed early and not talking back are three of my non-habits.

_____

_____

9. The candidate seemed inexperienced immature and easily rattled.

_____

_____

10. Melissa and I hung around at the mall had lunch at the Big T then met our boyfriends.

_____

_____

Did you pick up that numbers 2 and 6 are fine just as they are?

Summary

In a List Pattern a complete idea is expanded with a list of three or more items.

Our P.E. class **walked, jogged, and ran** four miles.

list

Leroy played **soccer, tennis, baseball, and football**.

list

Lists work on the same principle as a grocery list: a number of items are listed in a series.

...walked, jogged, and ran.

...soccer, tennis, baseball, and football.

PUNCTUATING THE LIST PATTERN

Items in a list are separated by commas. (Don't put a comma after the last item.)

...walked**,** jogged**,** and ran

...soccer**,** tennis**,** baseball**,** and football

The commas can be heard as pauses.

The new teacher was tall, (pause) slight, (pause) and funny.

Until she gave up smoking, my friend Josie always had toast, (pause) coffee, (pause) and a cigarette before school.

Hearing the commas as pauses aids in comma placement.

...tall, slight, and funny.

...toast, coffee, and a cigarette...

A list of only two items does not need a comma.

Jack and Jill went up a hill.

I can't read or write without my glasses.

PHRASE LISTS

A list can be made of phrases as well as items.

Emma felt *unsure of herself, out of place,* and *oddly awkward*.

Luke had to *borrow a quarter, call his friends,* and *ask for a ride*.

Each phrase is set off with a comma exactly as in item lists. As in item lists, don't use commas when there are only two phrases.

Emma felt out of place and oddly awkward.

Luke had to call his friends and ask for a ride.

LISTS IN THE BEGINNING OR MIDDLE OF SENTENCES

You can use lists anywhere in a sentence—beginning, middle, or end.

Joe, Frankie, and I rode our bikes like crazy.

Mahalia wants to find *a shirt for her brother, a tie for her father, and a special perfume for her mother* this Christmas.

On their first date, Jean and Sammy *went to the beach, talked for hours, and got home after midnight*.

AND—OR

When *and* or *or* is used between items or phrases in a list, omit any punctuation.

Joe and Frankie and I rode our bikes like crazy.

On their first date Jean and Sammy went to the beach and talked for hours and got home after midnight.

CHAPTER REVIEW:

A. Some of the following sentences are incorrectly punctuated. Some are correctly punctuated. And some have no punctuation at all. Copy each sentence and punctuate it correctly.

1. Dell, and Sue like going to baseball games.

_____

2. Apples bananas and tangerines are wonderful fruits.

_____

3. My uncle is a doctor a skilled magician a skilled amateur astronomer and a whirlwind of energy.

_____

_____

4. Frederic's grandfather worked as a cowboy a soldier a pilot and an investment banker.

_____

_____

5. Natalie found herself thinking more deeply and looking outward with fewer prejudices.

_____

_____

6. Indra was definitely excited, and pleased when John asked her out.

_____

_____

B. Now show your understanding of the List Pattern. On a separate sheet of paper, write out 10 list sentences of your own creation. Don't put all your lists at the end of your sentences. Include at least three or four lists in the beginning and in the middle of your sentences.

The Connective Pattern

3

Many sentences express two or more complete ideas. The next pattern we'll learn puts together two complete ideas in the sme sentence. It can be called the **Connective Pattern**.

The sky turned dark, and *rain began to fall*.

       one idea   second idea

The stapler broke, but *Willy fixed it*.

       one idea   second idea

Notice how the examples can be broken down into two basic sentences.

The sky turned dark. Rain began to fall.

The stapler broke. Willy fixed it.

Connective sentences can always be divided into separate sentences because they contain at least two complete ideas. The complete ideas are called **clauses**.

It rained for a week, and *the ducks were thrilled*.

       clause   clause

The bus was late, so *Althea began to worry*.

       clause   clause

Without the connecting words, the clauses would be separate sentences.

It rained for a week. The ducks were thrilled.

The bus was late. Althea began to worry.

On the other hand, when two sentences are closely related, they can be combined into one sentence containing two clauses:

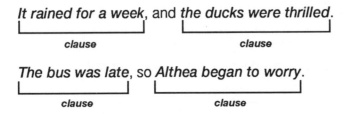

She complained bitterly. Her sister left the house.

              two sentences

She complained bitterly, and *her sister left the house*.

       clause   clause

CONNECTIVES: COORDINATING CONJUNCTIONS

Connectives (also called *coordinating conjunctions*) are the little words—*and, or, but,* and so on—that act as a bridge between complete ideas. They reach between ideas and link them together, as you've seen above.

> I'm terrible in math, *but* I love English.

> It's hard to know Mike, *yet* he's a generous guy.

Connectives are used as a matter of course as you speak and write. In fact, the connective *and* is the second most frequently used word in the language (first is *the*). Other common connectives are: *but, so, yet, or, nor, for* (meaning "because.")

> We had to go home, for we had shot all our money.

PUNCTUATING THE CONNECTIVE PATTERN

Commas are crucial in punctuating the Connective Pattern. The comma goes before the connective.

> The storm washed out the bridge**,** *and* a highway crew was called in.

> The band took a break**,** *and* everyone stopped dancing.

The role of the comma in this pattern is to separate the two parts of the sentence, showing where one complete idea leaves off and the next one begins. Commas, in other words, keep the two complete ideas separated.

> The band took a break   **,**   and everyone stopped dancing.

> The storm washed out the bridge   **,**   so traffic had to be re-routed.

CHECKING FOR COMPLETE IDEAS

If a sentence does not contain two complete ideas, leave out the comma.

To check whether a sentence has two complete ideas, cover the first part and the connective. See if the second half expresses a complete idea by itself.

> Indra likes John, and he feels the same way about her.

> **Check:** ...he feels the same way about her.

> We forgot to leave on the water, and the pipes burst.

> **Check:** ...the pipes burst.

In the next example, the second part doesn't express a complete idea. Putting a comma in is a mistake.

> **Incorrect:** Billy struck out, and walked sadly to the dugout.

> **Check:** walked sadly to the dugout. (not a complete idea)

The second part is only a phrase (a group of words), not a clause (a complete idea). Therefore the sentence should have been punctuated without a comma, like this:

Billy dropped his bat and walked sadly to the dugout.

Think about whether these sentences need commas.

The actor slipped and gave a yelp.

We had to wait for Ezra and got impatient.

No, commas are unnecessary, because the second part of each sentence is a phrase rather than a complete idea.

Cover the first part of the next sentences (including the *and*), and see whether the second halves are phrases or clauses.

My sister went away for the weekend and forgot to call.

Mike yawned but tried to listen to the teacher anyway.

Again, the second part of each of the sentences is a phrase. The sentences thus are correct as written without commas.

However, if a pronoun were inserted into the second part of the sentence, there would be two complete ideas.

My sister went away for the weekend, and *she* forgot to call.

Mike yawned, but *he* tried to listen to the teacher anyway.

Now you have bona-fide connective sentences—two clauses linked by connectives and separated by commas.

COMMAS AS PAUSES

Commas can be heard as pauses.

Tim constantly interrupted Yolanda, (pause) and it drove her stark-raving berserk.

Roscoe's uncle lost his eyesight, (pause) yet he's a remarkable long distance runner.

The pause also gives breathing space before a new idea begins.

Darlene talks a lot, (pause) but she doesn't have a lot to say.
The book was difficult, (pause) so it took a long time to finish.

By listening carefully and hearing the pauses, you can make comma usage natural. The rhythms of sentence structure correspond to the rhythms of speech. You've actually been using connective sentences from the time you were small.

I'll get my puppy, and I'll take him to bed with me. He's sleepy, so I'll give him my pillow.

Your ability with language is highly developed; it built up over numerous years in learning to speak. So when you punctuate, you're putting to work skills that have been deeply ingrained and long practiced. They come from the "deep structure" of the language and make your sentences read the way they sound.

∞ EXERCISE 1

Make 6 sentences by matching the following phrases and clauses. Write the sentences on the lines below. Then put a check mark before the examples that form connective sentences. (Leave blank the sentences that merely contain a phrase at the end.)

Be sure to listen for the comma pauses, and mark the commas correctly.

I'm terrible in math	yet he's a generous guy.
Kids like playing	but it was a struggle.
Deshonne won the match	and got a medal.
I found happiness	but good in English.
Anger is unpleasant	and making messes.
It's hard to know Mike	and so is self-pity.

1._____

2._____

3._____

4._____

5._____

6._____

You should have found that three of the examples are not connective sentences and three are. Keep in mind the difference you see here between a phrase and a clause (complete idea.) It will be crucial as you handle this pattern in your writing.

COMMA SPLICES

If you leave out connectives between two clauses, the result is a major sentence error called a comma splice.

> **Incorrect:** The bus was late, Althea didn't worry.

> **Incorrect:** We called 911, the paramedics quickly arrived.

The clauses here, of course, require a connective.

> **Correct:** The bus was late, *but* Althea didn't worry.

> **Correct:** We called 911, *and* the paramedics quickly arrived.

31

Comma splices are caused by writers assuming that commas are catch-all punctuators. Commas are actually rather weak punctuation marks. They lack the strength to separate complete ideas. Thus, with this pattern, you need commas and connectives working in pairs: the commas separating complete ideas while connectives join them.

> Lester got up late, and he had to rush to school.

> Summer is here, and everyone is excited.

People usually make comma splice errors because they're unsure about sentence mechanics as a whole. They might know that commas separate things, but they don't understand exactly why.

> **Incorrect:** The dog howled outside the classroom, the teacher wouldn't shoo it away.

> **Incorrect:** My friend Ryko is 16, her mother is only thirty-three.

Help from a connective straightens out the comma splices.

> **Correct:** The dog howled outside the classroom, *but* the teacher wouldn't shoo it away.

> **Correct:** My friend Ryko is 16, *and* her mother is only thirty-three.

Comma splices can be totally avoided if you remember that commas need help from connectives or from the pattern of the sentence, as we saw with the List Pattern.

✐ EXERCISE 2

Some of the following sentences are incorrectly punctuated. They contain comma splices, or they put in commas before phrases. Other sentences are punctuated correctly.

Copy each of the sentences, punctuating correctly where necessary and supplying any missing connectives.

1. Wanda walked away, Jim hurried after her.

_____

2. I don't know the answer, but you don't either.

_____

3. We drove home, and parked in back of the house.

_____

4. Selene yelled, and the window finally opened a crack.

_____

5. No one disagreed, or made a fuss.

_____

6. I rather disliked the captain, I'm afraid I showed it.

WARNING: TOO MANY COMMAS!

Phrases sometimes can be heard as slight pauses, but that doesn't mean that you should punctuate them with a comma.

> **Incorrect:** Indra finds John appealing, (slight pause) and really funny.

In this pattern and subsequent patterns, make sure you hear a definite pause before you use a comma. Some people sprinkle around commas like confetti. Commas in the wrong places are a dead giveaway that the writer doesn't know what he or she is doing.

> **Incorrect:** I didn't know, where he was, going and he wouldn't tell me, it was really bad, I had to get off, the phone, after that he disappeared, it just made me, extremely upset, I had to talk with someone.

If the correct pattern for the comma eludes you, or if the sound and rhythm of the sentence fail to help, leave the comma out. The golden rule for commas is: when in doubt, leave it out.

☞ EXERCISE 3

A. Copy the above incorrect comma-flooded paragraph, taking out unnecessary commas and putting in periods and commas where they are needed. Remember to capitalize the first word in each sentence.

_____

_____

_____

_____

_____

B. Now look at the following sentences. Place a check mark before each one that is a bona-fide connective sentence, and add the proper punctuation. Leave the others blank. Then copy the connective sentences on the lines on the next page, putting in commas where they belong.

1. The lights went out and the Franklins found candles.
2. Spelling is easy for me but math drives me nuts.
3. Jeremy likes Christmas because of all the good spirit.
4. The dog bowl needs cleaning but Laurie is too busy.
5. Going to the movies and going to dinner are two of my favorite treats.
6. Danny will bring charcoal and Gregg will bring food.
7. Dana gets home late from practice and collapses.

8. Our class studied *The Great Gatsby* and I felt sorry for Jay Gatsby.

9. The cost of a house is rising each year and I'm afraid I'll never be able to afford one.

10. Our apartment house is getting painted so our apartment is going to look good.

_____

_____

_____

_____

_____

_____

_____

_____

_____

SENTENCES WITH HEAVY CONNECTIVES

In the Connective Pattern sentences you have worked with so far, the two clauses were joined by any of the following words: *and, but, or, nor, for, yet,* or *so.* A comma was put before the connective.

There is another kind of Connective Pattern sentence that you should become familiar with. Look carefully at the following two examples:

Graham was a liar**; *however*,** he saw himself as only practical.

The book was entertaining**; *furthermore*,** it was well written.

In this kind of Connective Pattern, the connecting words (*however, furthermore*) belong to a group called ***heavy connectives.*** (They are also sometimes called ***conjunctive adverbs*.**) A heavy connective is marked off by a semicolon before it and a comma after it. Look back at the two examples and notice how they are punctuated.

The following are common heavy connectives:

however	nevertheless	furthermore
consequently	therefore	moreover
otherwise	besides	in fact

An important thing to note here is that heavy connectives always link two complete ideas. When heavy connectives are used this way, you can hear extended pauses before and after the two punctuation marks. Listen to this.

Studying takes a great deal of discipline; (pause) however, (pause) the payoff in good grades is considerable.

Saretha found that climbing Mount Everest was quite exhilarating; (pause) more-over, (pause) she wanted to do it again.

Heavy connectives modify a complete idea by showing you its relation to the previous idea. This construction is sometimes similar to the way the connective *but* works.

R.J. didn't learn much in the class; however, he did accumulate another credit.

I don't much like the taste of lobster; besides, I'm allergic to shellfish.

The war was poorly planned and poorly executed; nevertheless, it had many supporters.

Blue whales are enormous; in fact, they are the largest animals ever to live on earth.

☞ EXERCISE 4

Listen carefully to the following sentences, and determine where to place the semicolon and the comma. Copy the sentences, and punctuate them correctly.

1. Linda seldom gives herself credit for good work furthermore she simply won't take a compliment.

_____

_____

2. Tragedy can lead to wisdom however it seems a heavy price to pay.

_____

_____

3. People badly want peace moreover they are forcing their governments to listen.

_____

_____

4. Charles hates working at Burger Empire in fact he's looking for another job.

_____

_____

5. I like fooling around with my friends nevertheless I'm serious about learning Spanish.

_____

_____

(Note: Many words like *however*, which you have seen used as heavy connectives, can be used in other ways as well. You will learn more about these usages in a later chapter.)

Summary

CONNECTIVE SENTENCES

Connective sentences express two or more complete ideas.

The sky turned dark, and *rain began to fall*.

          one idea   second idea

Althea is smart, but *she follows every fad*.

          one idea   second idea

Connectives like *and* (also—*but, so, yet, or, for*) act as bridges between complete ideas which otherwise would be punctuated as separate sentences.

> The sky turned dark. Rain began to fall.

> Althea looks good. She follows every fad.

COMMAS

Commas have the opposite function from connectives: instead of linking ideas, commas separate them.

> Neil is a nice guy, but unfortunately he's nicer to his friends than he is to himself.

> Days go slowly when you're bored, and nights are almost impossible.

Commas can be heard as pauses between complete ideas.

> The movie was good, (pause) but the book was better.

> He walked home, (pause) and he found a twenty on the sidewalk.

Commas and connectives work in pairs and must be used together in this pattern.

> The alarm failed to ring, and I was late for school.

> Ginny talked with her friends on the phone all evening, so when she hung up her ear was sore.

Used alone, neither commas nor connectives are strong enough to give the necessary separation or connection needed for this pattern.

> **Incorrect:** The alarm went off, I rolled over.

> **Incorrect:** The alarm buzzed but I only yawned and scratched.

Correct: The alarm went off, and I rolled over.

Correct: The alarm buzzed, but I only yawned and scratched.

COMMON ERRORS

Placing a comma <u>after</u> the connective is incorrect.

> **Incorrect:** He tried three sports but, he was only good at one.

> **Incorrect:** Abe missed the assignment so, he didn't know what to do for homework.

Commas are always placed <u>before</u> the connective.

> **Correct:** He tried three sports**,** *but* he was only good at one.

> **Correct:** Abe missed the assignment**,** *so* he didn't know what to do for homework.

Sometimes you can mistake a complete idea followed by a phrase for a connective sentence.

> **Incorrect:** The baby cried for its bottle, and woke me up.

> **Incorrect:** He barely passed shop, but got an A in P.E.

...and woke me up is a phrase, as well as *...got an A in P.E.* The correct way to write these sentences is:

> **Correct:** The baby cried for its bottle and woke me up.

> **Correct:** He barely passed shop but got an A in P.E.

To check for this error, cover the first part of the sentence and isolate it from the rest. If a comma is necessary, the second part of the sentence must express a complete idea.

COMMA SPLICES

A comma splice is a major structural error. Comma splices occur when a comma is used to join two clauses without help from a connective.

> **Incorrect:** The tree was felled, it was cut up for firewood.

> **Incorrect:** Carl wants to be a heavy equipment operator, he figures on spending a couple of years in trade school.

This error reflects a basic misunderstanding of punctuation and sentence mechanics.

Correct: The tree was felled, and it was cut up for firewood.

Correct: Carl wants to be a heavy equipment operator, so he plans on spending a couple of years in trade school.

HEAVY CONNECTIVES

Heavy connectives like *furthermore* and *however* function in the same manner as lighter connectives, except they modify the second idea and are marked off with a semicolon and a comma.

The car needs a paint job**;** *furthermore***,** it doesn't run.

Mahalia is a good student**;** *however***,** she sometimes outsmarts herself on tests.

LIST OF CONNECTIVES

Coordinating conjunctions:

    and   but   or   nor   for   yet   so

Heavy connectives:

however	nevertheless	furthermore
consequently	therefore	moreover
otherwise	besides	in fact

☞ CHAPTER REVIEW

A. Put your connective sentence skills to work by writing out each of the following examples and punctuating those sentences which express two complete ideas. Draw a line through the examples that only have one complete idea followed by a phrase.

1. The class nearly missed their deadline for putting out the newspaper but they made it by a single hour.

_____

_____

2. The road was long and dusty yet we enjoyed driving along it.

_____

_____

3. On weekends Stacy lives with her dad and during the week she stays with her mom.

_____

_____

4. Karen thought Donny would ask her to the prom moreover she expected Donny to hire a limousine to transport them.

_____

_____

5. Drugs are a concern for young people however each year fewer and fewer teenagers become users.

_____

_____

6. David has cut too many classes so he won't graduate.

_____

_____

7. Jim is an easy-going, sensitive man with a lot of self-doubts that he handles well furthermore he has learned to take his self-doubts as fuel for his courage and integrity.

_____

_____

_____

8. That car is too expensive besides the brakes are shot.

_____

9. Marianne thinks she's hot and the best thing ever to walk the earth.

_____

_____

10. Jewelle wants to take a train or a bus to Las Vegas.

_____

B. On a separate sheet of paper, write 10 connective sentences of your own that contain examples of the connective pattern. Write 5 that use ordinary coordinating conjunctions and 5 that use heavy connectives.

///

The Introductory Pattern

4

The *Introductory Pattern* combines two complete ideas in a different way from a connective sentence. With this pattern, a main clause is preceded by an introductory clause, or *introducer*. (A different kind of introducer, an introductory prepositional phrase, is covered in a later chapter.)

When I saw Bryce Canyon, I was overcome with awe.

      introductory clause   *main clause*

If you don't like my ideas, why do you ask my opinion?

      introductory clause   *main clause*

The introducer raises an expectation:

    If you don't like my ideas,...

This expectation has to be met by the main clause:

    ...why do you ask my opinion?

When the main clause is left out, the sentence sounds strange, as though it's stopping too soon.

    Incorrect: When I get home from school.

    Incorrect: Since I dropped out of the band.

The reader immediately asks, "What happened?" In both cases, the first part of the sentence prepares you for more information which is missing. A main clause cures the confusion.

    When I get home from school, *I'm going to call Brett*.

                           main clause

    Since I dropped out of the band, *they sound awful*.

                           main clause

INTRODUCTORY WORDS

Specific words start the Introductory Pattern. These introductory words must lead off the sentence as the first word.

    After I get into bed, I lie there and daydream.

    Since you asked me, I'd like to skip the homework.

The most common introductory words (mainly *subordinating conjunctions*) are:

if	until	wherever
as	unless	when (whenever)
after	while	since
before	whereas	though (although)
because	when (whenever)	

Whenever one of these introductory words starts a sentence, it automatically shifts the emphasis to the main clause.

Though Desiree has a free evening,...(what will she do?)

While Kathleen was packing,...(what happened?)

☞ EXERCISE 1

Complete the following sentences by supplying main clauses for the following introducers. Put a comma after each introductory clause.

1. If Vinnie misses one more day of math...

_____

2. Because I went to church last Sunday...

_____

3. When Henry finally understood his girl friend...

_____

4. While Beth was laughing with Denise...

_____

5. Since I never understand my feelings...

_____

As you see, introductory sentences are far from unusual. Your ear is accustomed to hearing a main clause follow an introducer. If someone came up to you and said, "When I graduate from school..." you'd be tapping your foot, waiting for more information to follow. As an experiment, try talking to someone using only introducers. Watch how the person reacts. If you can identify how you use the pattern in your speaking life, you'll find it easy to carry it over to your writing.

TIME INTRODUCERS

You might have noticed that many introductory words deal with time (*when, before, as, after, since, while,* etc.)

> *Before* the day was over, he fixed his bike.

> *After* the movies, we drove home in the moonlight.

> *When* I finally got home, my parents massacred me.

Notice how the introductory word shifts the emphasis to the second time sequence, the main clause. Whenever time words start a sentence, look for the Introductory Pattern.

CONDITIONAL INTRODUCERS

Introductory words can also set up conditions.

> *If* you help with the dishes, I'll help with your math.

> *Unless* Buddy gets a date, we won't be able to double.

The outcome of the sentence depends on the condition set up by the introducer. The introducer creates a condition—if this occurs, that will (or won't) follow.

> *If* a drought comes, we will face water shortages.

> *Until* my grades improve, I can't go out on week nights.

Some introducers set up a parallel movement of ideas. *Parallel* means that two separate things are going on at the same time.

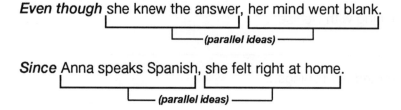

> *Even though* she knew the answer, her mind went blank.
> *(parallel ideas)*

> *Since* Anna speaks Spanish, she felt right at home.
> *(parallel ideas)*

PUNCTUATING INTRODUCTORY CLAUSES

Commas furnish separation after introductory clauses just as they do in other patterns. The break, of course, comes between the introductory clause and the main clause.

> If you like to swim**,** you might try the English Channel.

> Though Jeep liked Sue**,** Sue went for his friend Byron.

The sentence seems to pivot at the comma and take off in a new direction. The comma gives the reader a moment to see where the sentence is heading.

> Since he learned new math**,** he understands computers.

> When I finally finished**,** it was nearly midnight.

Once again the commas can be heard as pauses.

> If you want to excel at tennis, (pause) learn the backhand first.

> During the 1930's depression, (pause) 15 million men were out of work.

Hearing the pauses helps determine comma placement.

> When Doreen went to Hollywood, (pause) she totally expected to become a star.

> Since Tim finally made some friends, (pause) the semester seems to go much faster.

Without commas the ideas tend to pile up on each other.

> **Incorrect:** When it's day time passes quickly.

> **Incorrect:** When Michael watches TV commercials drive him crazy.

Commas immediately clear up the confusion.

> **Correct:** When it's day, time passes quickly.

> **Correct:** When Michael watches TV, commercials drive him crazy.

THE REVERSAL CHECK

A handy feature of this pattern is the reversal check: the position of the introductory clause and the main clause can be switched, and the sentence will still make sense.

> When it's day, time passes quickly.
> **Check:** Time passes quickly when it's day.

> If Don leaves, Julie will soon follow.
> **Check:** Julie will soon follow if Don leaves.

If a sentence doesn't make sense when you reverse it, it doesn't contain the Introductory Pattern.

> When is the turn-off for Highway 9?
> **Check:** The turn-off for Highway 9 when is?

> Since when did you smoke?
> **Check:** Did you smoke since when?

> *As You Like It* is an amusing play.
> **Check:** Is an amusing play *As You Like It*.

PUNCTUATING IN THE "REVERSED" POSITION

Sentences containing the Introductory Pattern can always be reversed. But when you make the reversal, what was introductory now loses its key position.

> Time passes quickly when it's day.

> Judy will soon follow if Don leaves.

In this "reversed" position, you don't always need a comma between the two parts of the sentence. In fact, in most cases you won't need a comma at all.

Correct: Time passes quickly when it's day.

Not so good: Time passes quickly, when it's day.

Correct: Julie will soon follow if Don leaves.

Not so good: Julie will soon follow, if Dan leaves.

You will need a comma, even in the "reversed" position, with the following words:

- although
- though
- while (when it means *whereas*, but not when it means *at the same time that*)
- as (when it means *because*, but not when it means *at the same time that*)
- since (when it means *because*, but not when it means *from the time that*)

For example:

I think the movie was great, though you may disagree.

We were soaking wet, since the rain continued for two hours. (*Since* meaning *because*; use comma)

BUT: We have been soaking wet since the rain started. (*Since* meaning *from the time that*; no comma)

⌕ **EXERCISE 2**

A. Rewrite and correctly punctuate the following examples. Remember to take out unnecessary commas. If an introductory clause has no main clause after it, supply one of your own.

1. We walked to the mall, as slowly as we could.

_____

2. I nearly had heart failure, when he jumped out.

_____

3. Jake got plenty scared, during his father's rages.

_____

4. Since the panther escaped from her cage.

_____

5. When I was your age.

_____

6. If you don't clean your room.

_____

7. Indra holds John's hand, when he walks her to class.

_____

8. Judy's parents allowed her to go to the rock concert since she had already bought tickets.

_____

_____

9. I haven't seen Mary since last summer.

_____

B. Next, write out the following examples, marking off the introductory phrase or clause with a comma—when necessary.

1. If the assignment is too hard people won't learn much.

_____

2. After the camping trip Andrew needed a new tent.

_____

3. The day was unbearable when the heat reached 107 degrees.

_____

_____

4. Before people could react the man escaped.

_____

5. Whys and wherefores are always debated in their family.

_____

6. We will find if there is a way to make a mistake.

_____

7. When I finally make it through this school I'll be eighteen.

_____

-*ING* INTRODUCERS

Words ending in -*ing* (*walking, talking, leaving,* etc.) can introduce phrases before main clauses. The -*ing* word is called a ***participle***, and the phrase is called a ***participial phrase***.

> ***Leaving the dishes for last***, Eli cleaned the house.

> ***Leaping in the air***, the forward captured the rebound.

> ***Experiencing more distaste than pleasure***, LeRoy quit the project.

Sometimes the -ing word can stand alone as an introducer:

> ***Smiling***, the woman extended her hand.

When you start a sentence with an -*ing* word, pay attention to whether a comma is necessary. Not all -*ing* words are participles or begin participial phrases.

> Laughing is good exercise.

> Studying in the morning is better than at night.

Listening for the distinct pause is a good way to figure if you need to use a comma here. The reversal check doesn't work well with introductory participial phrases.

☞ EXERCISE 3

Add commas to the following sentences where necessary. Listen for that definite pause, and use the reversal check for regular introductory <u>clauses</u> (not participial phrases!) if you're unsure about the comma.

1. Going toward school James heard the last bell.
2. Since you're noisy there will be no movie.
3. Getting curious about it he checked for the smell.
4. When that bell rings I'm getting some food.
5. Seeing the right answer she marked her paper.
6. Leaping for the pass I got blindsided.
7. Running like crazy they avoided the rent-a-cop.
8. While Amy ate a bug crawled from her sandwich.

Summary

In an ***Introductory Pattern***, two complete ideas are connected by their introductory relationship.

> When Indra first saw John, she thought he was cute.

46

The first complete idea (clause) introduces the second, which is the main clause.

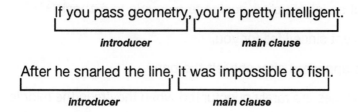

The main clause completes the idea set in motion by the introducer. This intermixed relationship becomes quite clear if you leave the main clause out of the sentence.

Since he was late...(what happened?)

If I don't call work...(what then?)

Because of the heavy snowfall...(yes, go on.)

INTRODUCTORY WORDS (mainly subordinating conjunctions)

Introductory sentences begin with introductory words (e.g., *if, as, until, when,* or *-ing* words). Many introductory words deal with time or set up two time sequences.

As Joanie walked into Spanish, she realized she forgot forgot her homework.

After I get home from school, I go jogging.

Other introductory words set up conditions: if *this* occurs, *that* will follow.

If Dena's late again, her mother will totally erupt.

Unless Dena follows orders, she'll be in hot lava.

COMMAS

The introductory nature of the pattern necessitates a comma.

If you like movies**,** you'll hate commercials.

Even though the exercise was beneficial**,** I got bored.

You need a comma to separate the introducer from the main clause. The commas can be heard as distinct pauses.

Since I fell for you, (pause) I haven't slept.

After she left the party, (pause) the police appeared.

REVERSAL CHECK

Reversing the two parts of an introductory sentence amounts to a check.

> **Check:** I haven't slept since I fell for you.

> **Check:** The police appeared after she left the party.

Introductory phrases or clauses are rarely punctuated when they're in the middle of a sentence as above. Make sure that you don't make this common over-punctuating mistake.

> **Not so good:** The police appeared, after she left the party.

> **Not so good:** I haven't slept, since I fell for you.

In this "reversed" position you don't put a comma between the two parts of the sentence, except with the following words:

- although
- though
- while (when it means *whereas*, but not when it means *at the same time that*)
- as (when it means *because*, but not when it means *at the same time that*)
- since (when it means *because*, but not when it means *from the time that*)

> **Correct:** Time passes quickly when it's day.

> **Not so good:** Time passes quickly, when it's day.

These are examples of where you do use a comma:

> I think the movie was great, though you may disagree.

> We were soaking wet, since the rain continued for two hours. (*Since* meaning *because*; use comma)

> **BUT:** We have been soaking wet since the rain started. (*Since* meaning *from the time that*; no comma)

-ING INTRODUCERS

Words at the beginning of a sentence that end in *-ing* often operate as introducers.

> Doing the heavy work first, Sarah packed the dishes.

> Moving along the hill, the rancher checked for strays.

-ing words used this way need a comma.

> Deciding to be patient, he asked how she was feeling.

> Washing his hands of the project, Leroy found a new job.

The comma divides the introductory *-ing* word (participle or participial phrase) from the main clause.

Be careful of *-ing* words that are not participles, and that do not act as true introducers:

Walking barefoot can be hard on the feet.

CHAPTER REVIEW

A. Try your hand at some more punctuation. Copy the following sentences, putting in punctuation where needed. Remember to use the reversal check to test for regular introductory clauses.

1. Climbing the cliff Ike nearly slipped.

_____

2. When I'm angry I control myself pretty well.

_____

3. As Mara rode home she saw the oddest scene.

_____

4. Unless Bill asks her out she's going to scream.

_____

5. If you ask politely you just might get a yes.

_____

6. Despite Michael's smile he's often moody.

_____

7. Retyping the paper Danielle found numerous errors.

_____

8. Reading the fine print of the contract Marilee found she was being charged nearly 20% interest.

_____

_____

9. When Perry finds himself getting really depressed it's hard for him to figure out what to do.

_____

_____

10. As they rounded the corner they were shocked to discover Les standing there, directing traffic.

_____

_____

11. Because Silvia is so nice to her friends they decided to throw a surprise party for her.

_____

_____

12. Even though it's hard for Tee to actually sit down and study he's decided there's no way he wants to be out on the streets, running around aimlessly, letting his friends think for him.

_____

_____

_____

13. Getting the paper done taking a long shower and feeling utterly relieved Racine finally plopped into bed and fell asleep.

_____

_____

B. On a separate sheet of paper, write 10 sentences of your own that contain introducers. The first 8 should contain introductory clauses. The last 2 should contain participles or participial phrases as introducers.

The Parenthetical Pattern
5

A *parenthetical* comment is one that interrupts an idea already in progress in order to add information or qualification.

> The butcher, *I believe*, stabbed Mr. Doe.
>
> parenthetical comment

> Mr. Muhammed, *the man next door*, tells great stories.
>
> parenthetical comment

After the interruption, the idea continues. So a parenthetical comment breaks into an idea which otherwise would be a single, ongoing complete thought. Without the parenthetical comments, the example sentences would look like this:

> The butcher stabbed Mr. Doe.

> Mr. Muhammed tells great stories.

Since the interrupter divides two parts of a single idea, a pair of commas is used to separate it from the ongoing idea.

> The best answer, it seems to me, is the last one.

> My sister, a redhead, has a sweet nature.

In writing, we often interrupt the flow of a sentence to clarify, qualify, or add information.

> Did you know that Calvin Jones, the quarterback of the football team, is transferring to another school?

> That man, I believe, just fell into the manhole.

> I just saw, or I think I saw, a man fall into a manhole.

The *Parenthetical Pattern* gets its name from the marks known as parentheses—( ). You might write sentences containing a Parenthetical Pattern like this:

> Five new kids (all of them from New York) enrolled in school this semester.

> The San Francisco '49ers (a hot football team) signed their first draft choice.

Years ago, the use of parentheses was much more common, but language continues to change—just as today's conventions will give way to other usages. Today most writers feel that parentheses often stick out too much and make for awkward constructions. They use commas instead.

> Five new kids, all of them from New York, enrolled in school this semester.

> The San Francisco '49ers, a hot football team, signed their first draft choice.

51

Seeing where parentheses might go in the pattern, however, can help you figure where to place the commas. And parentheses are still often used when the information is not closely tied to the main idea or when dates are inserted to identify a person or event.

The Allegheny Mountains (the eroded northwestern portion of the Appalachian Highlands) are beautiful in the spring.

The Nile River (one of the longest rivers in Africa) was the scene of recent conflicts over water rights.

Abraham Lincoln (1809-1865) was the first U.S. president to be assassinated.

◌➤ EXERCISE 1

In the following sentences, insert the correct punctuation and underline the parenthetical comments.

1. My brother the dirty rat tattled on me.

2. Jacob Marley a well-known ghost haunted Ebenezer.

3. Nipper my dog chases rabbits till he drops.

4. *Graceland* an album by Paul Simon has become a classic.

5. Mr. Adler a friend of my dad's has had the most amazing adventures.

COMMAS

The Parenthetical Pattern is the only pattern in the language that must be set off by two punctuation marks. Since the parenthetical comment occurs like an aside or an after-thought that interrupts a thought unit, two commas are needed to keep it from getting mixed up with the separated main idea.

The waitress, *a timid young woman*, suddenly screamed at a customer.

parenthetical comment

Jordan, *the best forward on the team*, hurt his ankle.

parenthetical comment

Without commas, parenthetical comments would become confused with the separated parts of the main clause.

Incorrect: The waitress a timid young woman suddenly screamed at a customer.

Incorrect: Jordan the best forward on the team hurt his ankle.

The comma pauses here are more pronounced here than in any other pattern. Read the examples aloud and listen to the rhythm. The pauses create a definite rhythmic sound.

The dogs, (pause) huge German shepherds, (pause) scared me witless.

The new mechanic, (pause) a big blond guy, (pause) is more interested in women than cars.

In all other patterns, main ideas continue straight through to completion; here the idea is interrupted, information given, then the main idea resumes.

My buddy Henry, *who is really huge*, scares people with his size.

|———————| |———————————| |———————————|
   main . . .   interrupter   . . . clause

Without those rhythm-making commas, you have to stretch to make sense out of parenthetical sentences.

The dogs huge German shepherds scared me silly.

The new mechanic a big blond guy seems more interested in women than cars.

The function of commas for this and all patterns is to make written language clear by separating items, phrases, or clauses within a sentence unit.

⟳ EXERCISE 2

Practice the Parenthetical Pattern by writing out and punctuating the next examples. Remember—two commas go with each parenthetical comment.

1. Mae the woman next door parades around like a queen.

_____

2. Mae I believe thinks that she's related to Elizabeth II.

_____

3. Our street 7th Avenue is roped off for a block party.

_____

4. Five students all of them sharp questioned the speaker.

_____

5. Mr. Markle our beloved teacher had a hair transplant.

_____

6. The principal I presume does not want a student-run school.

_____

QUALIFIERS

You can use parenthetical comments to qualify or limit the strength of your statements.

Sarcasm, *he agrees*, is the refuge of the weak.

Debbie, *they say*, acts like a complete airhead.

Newspapers often use this middle-of-the-sentence structure, and you can use it in your own writing when you want to qualify or limit the strength of your statements.

The president, *it is reported*, has inflamed adenoids.

Alice Walker, *I think*, used a combination of feminism, history, and imagination to create her novel.

APPOSITIVES

The parenthetical comments you have worked with so far in this chapter have been of two types. One type is a clause (complete idea) used parenthetically. The other type is a noun or a phrase built around a noun.

The butcher, *I believe*, stabbed Mr. Doe. (Interrupter is a clause.)

Mr. Muhammed, *the man next door*, tells great stories. (Interrupter is a phrase built on the noun *man*)

This second type of interrupter, the type that is a noun or a phrase built around a noun, is called an **appositive**. Appositives are words or phrases that double back to a preceding noun in order to identify it.

Henry Hinkle, *the inventor*, loves his time machine.

Henry Hinkle, *the inventor of the New Vistas Time Machine*, promises riveting journeys with his invention.

Appositives can be substituted for the words they identify.

The boy, *Jon Jets*, is 7 feet 4 inches tall.

Jon Jets is 7 feet 4 inches tall.

WHICH AND *WHO*

The words *which* and *who* often start Parenthetical Patterns. Newspapers frequently use this construction, too.

The car, *which* is diesel-powered, runs noisily.

President Lincoln, *who* spoke first at the meeting, requested additional funds.

Notice that the pronoun *which* is used with places and things, whereas *who* is only used to refer to people.

The newspaper headlines, *which suggested the starlet was kidnapped by aliens from outer space*, turned out to be somewhat misleading.

Dirk Rainwater, *who is probably the world's most bizarre weather forecaster*, predicted stormy moonlight.

Since they're often used to start a parenthetical comment, *which* and *who* can key you into the entire construction.

The students' unruliness, ***which lasted more than a week***, was reported to be caused by unsatisfied yearnings for a vacation.

Mr. Sanchez, ***who writes novels***, works only at night.

⌘ EXERCISE 3:

A. Copy and punctuate the following examples.

1. Laughter I feel is good for the soul.

_____

2. Mr. Lassiter the substitute cannot be fooled easily.

_____

3. Al a good sport didn't mind getting wet.

_____

4. General Spardon who called for an investigation was rumored to be under suspicion himself.

_____

_____

5. Indra's best friend who is usually sharp about people warned Indra to look out for John.

_____

_____

6. The report which was cited by authorities as unique and thoughtful used only a few statistics.

_____

_____

7. The report cited by authorities as unique and thoughtful used only limited statistics.

_____

_____

Expressions like *who is* or *which was* are sometimes dropped (as in numbers 3 and 6) with parenthetical comments. Of course, the basic construction—and the use of two commas— remains absolutely the same.

B. Now write 5 sentences that contain examples of the Parenthetical Pattern. Try to include both appositives and sentences with *which* and *who*.

1._____

2._____

3._____

4._____

5._____

NON-RESTRICTIVE AND RESTRICTIVE CLAUSES

All the *who* and *which* clauses we have gone over so far belong to the type known as ***non-restrictive*** clauses. Non-restrictive clauses function as expanders. They expand on, or tell you something new about, a noun that comes just before them.

> Tanya, ***who is a bully***, finally got what she deserved.
> └─────────────┘
> **non-restrictive clause**

In this sentence, the clause *who is a bully* is non-restrictive. It adds information about Tanya.

Another kind of *who* or *which* clause, on the other hand, restricts the identification of the noun it describes. This kind of who or which clause is called a ***restrictive*** clause.

> Any person ***who is a bully*** deserves whatever he or she gets.
> └─────────────┘
> **restrictive clause**

In the foregoing sentence, the clause *who is a bully* is restrictive.

Unlike a non-restrictive clause, a restrictive clause is necessary to the meaning of a sentence. Look at the example of the restrictive clause above. The sentence does not mean that any person deserves what he or she gets—only a person who is a bully. This clause cannot be dropped from the sentence without changing the meaning.

WHO, WHICH, AND *THAT*

The pronouns *who* and *which* can introduce either non-restrictive or restrictive clauses. The pronoun *that* only introduces restrictive elements.

> The problem ***that we've encountered*** is not easily solved.

> The wild horses ***that roam the Nevada deserts*** are usually not very large.

Unlike nonrestrictive clauses beginning with *which* and *who*, *that* clauses don't interrupt a complete idea; instead, *that* clauses are limiters that narrow down the terms they are talking about.

The big thing to remember here is not so much to follow the grammatical explanation as to leave *that* clauses unpunctuated.

> The theory that worked best still needed to be checked.

> The hedge that grows near the road needs trimming.

> Indra discovered that John had a roving eye.

THE *THAT* TEST

You know that a clause introduced by *that* is always restrictive. It is not set off by commas.

There's a simple test you can make to find out if a clause introduced by *who* or *which* is restrictive. Simply substitute the word *that* for *which* or *who*. If the new sentence means the same thing as the old, the clause is restrictive and needs no punctuation. If the new sentence makes no sense or means something different, then the clause was non-restrictive. It needs commas to set it off.

For example:

> The Mississippi River, *which* begins in Minnesota, empties into the Gulf of Mexico.

Do the test. Substitute *that* and see if the sentence makes sense:

> The Mississippi River *that* begins in Minnesota empties into the Gulf of Mexico.

Something is wrong here. "The Mississippi River that begins in Minnesota"? What other Mississippi River is there? The word *that* is wrong here. The *which* clause is therefore non-restrictive, and should be set off by commas.

Another example:

> The rivers *which* flow fastest carry the most dirt.

Do the test:

> The rivers *that* flow fastest carry the most dirt.

The two sentences mean the same. The *which* clause is restrictive, and should not be set off by commas.

OPTIONAL PUNCTUATION

When a parenthetical comment is lengthy, it can be punctuated in two ways. One way, of course, is with commas.

> The journey**,** *which was arduous and crossed several mountain ranges and numerous deserts,* lasted a year.

Another option is to make the parenthetical comment easy to spot with a dash at the beginning and the end.

> The journey—*which was arduous and crossed several mountain ranges, numer ous deserts, and large rivers*—took well over a year.

Dashes can give real clarity when used like this, especially if there is additional punctuation within the parenthetical comment.

> Our ingenuity—*collecting lion hairs from the zoo, a letterhead from the mayor's office, and a used police whistle from Jerry*—won the scavenger hunt for us.

✏ EXERCISE 4

Display your ability by punctuating (or not punctuating) the following examples.

1. Sal who is the number one nerd in Missouri follows me around.

2. The one time that I really tried to be cool I spilled soup all over myself.

3. The apartment which we rent is definitely dinky.

4. Li found that popularity was overrated.

5. Ella who invented the exercises improved her posture.

6. Anybody else who tried them couldn't bend over for a week.

7. The sunset which was a remarkable blaze of deep orange, hot pink, and lines of scarlet made it look like the sky had caught fire.

Summary

A parenthetical comment interrupts the flow of a sentence to expand some part of the interrupted idea. After that, the idea resumes.

> The vines, *a nasty variety of ivy*, ripped the shingles off the side of our house.

> The best suggestion, *it seems to me*, is Mary's.

PARENTHESES

Parenthetical comments historically come from parentheses. Parentheses are now used for dates or for information that is not closely tied to the main idea.

> Ben Franklin *(1706-1790)* invented a great stove.

> The house *(a Victorian)* is being used for a group home.

COMMAS

Since a parenthetical comment interrupts a complete idea, two commas are needed to mark it off.

> Daniel**,** *my cousin***,** is a terrible tease.

> Mr. Jones**,** *the man next door***,** bakes great apple pies.

The comma pauses are unmistakable in this pattern since they create twin pauses before and after the comment. You can use your sense of hearing for how the comments should be punctuated.

> Zack, (pause) the stingy jerk, (pause) wouldn't loan me $900.

> That balloon, (pause) the red one, (pause) looks good enough to eat.

> Ellen, (pause) I would say, (pause) likes to be the big boss.

HOW PARENTHETICAL COMMENTS WORK

Parenthetical comments interrupt the flow of a sentence, often referring back to the preceding word or phrase.

> Dionne, *my sister*, has great-looking corn rows.

> The trees, *huge redwoods*, swayed in the wind.

Sometimes the main idea is interrupted to add qualification.

> The game—*I think it's called Twiddle Toes*—is actually quite complicated.

> She's the one, *I believe*, who ripped off my shoelaces.

CLAUSES WITH *WHICH*, *WHO*, AND *THAT*

The pronouns *which* and *who* often introduce these interrupting parenthetical comments (non-restrictive clauses.)

> My piano, *which* is named Wolfgang, is my good friend.

> Doc Waters, *who* listens to the Red Sox, is a total fan.

The pronoun *that* introduces elements that don't interrupt and don't require commas (restrictive clauses.)

> The cat *that* jumped on my face nearly got de-furred.

> The way *that* Celeste looks at Jim makes him wobbly.

The pronouns *which* and *who* can also introduce restrictive clauses as well as non-restrictive ones. The test is to substitute the word *that* for the *which* or *who*.

If the sentence still makes sense or means the same thing, the clause is restrictive and doesn't need to be set off by commas.

If the sentence doesn't make sense, the clause is non- restrictive and must be set off by commas.

> A car *which* needs new tires is unsafe.
> **Test:** A car *that* needs new tires is unsafe. (Sounds OK; clause is restrictive)
>
> Bill, *who* seemed strangely quiet, spoke up.
> **Test:** Bill, *that* seemed strangely quiet, spoke up. (Sounds wrong; clause is non-restrictive.)

☞ CHAPTER REVIEW:

A. Now use your knowledge of parenthetical comments as you punctuate the following sentences. Copy the sentences, and use those paired commas when needed.

1. Summer vacation which should be the most fun time of the year can still get boring.

_____

_____

2. Naomi who is my oldest sister graduated from college.

_____

3. The baby's toys which are scattered through the house need to be picked up.

_____

_____

4. The only jacket which I like seems really expensive.

_____

5. The brain which is a highly complicated organ seems totally unused by some people.

_____

_____

6. Dana my best friend helped me break the habit of thinking negatively.

_____

_____

7. The cow that jumped over the moon landed awkwardly.

_____

8. Anyone who likes teenagers can't be all bad.

_____

9. Once there lived two sisters who were champion dancers and expert jump-rope teachers.

_____

_____

10. Jory Baba who comes from Lebanon has an great sense of humor despite everything he's lived through.

_____

_____

11. Bali which is an island off the southeast of Java with terraced rice fields, a complex system of irrigation, and a fascinating culture is so rich in agriculture that it exports more than thirty varieties of foodstuffs.

_____

_____

_____

Did you catch on with 4, 7, 8, and 9? (restrictive clauses that can't be dropped without ruining the idea.)

B. Now test your skills with this pattern. On a separate sheet of paper, write 5 sentences yourself which contain parenthetical comments.

C. Finally, on the same separate sheet of paper, write two sentences containing _who_ or _which_ clauses used restrictively.

Semicolons

6

Only two rules dictate the use of semicolons in sentences: first, you have to have complete ideas on both sides of the semicolon; and second, the two ideas must be closely related.

The day was hot and humid**;** my clothes stuck to my body.

first clause   *second clause*

Dinner was nearly ready**;** my mother took out the stew.

first clause   *second clause*

Notice the similarity here to connective sentences (e.g., *The day was muggy, and my clothes stuck to my body.*) Semicolons provide alternative punctuation where separate complete ideas seem to flow into one another.

I like iced coffee**;** it tastes great with cream.

The Mercs are hot**;** they're playing tonight at Birds.

Semicolons are stronger than commas and make longer pauses.

Macbeth is an anti-hero; (pause) he's the bad guy.

My sister pitches fits; (pause) she gets her way, too.

Commas by themselves lack the strength to separate complete ideas. Semicolons are strong enough to fix comma splices.

Incorrect (comma splice): Mike is so sweet, I love his manner.

Correct: Mike is so sweet; I love his manner.

Incorrect (comma splice): He sneezes really hard, it sounds like an explosion.

Correct: He sneezes really hard; it sounds like an explosion.

Generally, it's not a good idea to use semicolons and connectives together unless the sentence is long.

Not so good: The party started; and cars pulled up in front.

Better: The party started; cars pulled up in front.

☞ EXERCISE 1

Add a semicolon and a complete, closely related idea to the first clauses here. Make sure to leave out connectives.

1. Two girls got in a fight today at school _____

2. John's car broke down _____

3. My locker is clean now _____

4. Lennae's self-esteem is much better now _____

5. This desk is uncomfortable to work at _____

SEMICOLONS CONTINUED

Semicolons shouldn't be overused: usually no more than a couple a page. But the most glaring mistake with semicolons is using them without complete ideas on both sides.

Incorrect: Dinah went to the chicken coop; to gather some eggs.

Incorrect: The sidewalk is so torn up; that I nearly fell.

Cover the first part of these examples—are the second parts complete ideas or only phrases? Try these examples:

Incorrect: She saved her food stamps; carefully.

Incorrect: Indra began to be suspicious; and watched.

All the above incorrect examples require absolutely no mark. It's even worse to throw around semicolons than commas—if you're in doubt, leave them out.

Semicolons can also be used to separate phrases or clauses in a list (Remember—clauses equal complete ideas.)

Three possible explanations for the late night flat tire occurred to Willy: first, his friends had fooled around with the car; second, his old girlfriend was getting revenge; and third, his luck had just run out.

As we saw in Chapter 3 on the Connective Pattern, semicolons are also used to punctuate complete ideas when they're linked by heavy connectives (adverbial conjunctions.)

The fog was thick; *however*, we continued to drive.

Gael is graceful; *moreover*, she is a great dancer.

The way she feels about him is really complicated and even distressing because of the way he is into drugs; *furthermore*, she doesn't know how to handle his temper.

The heavy connective tells you the relation between the complete ideas, while the semicolons again separate the clauses.

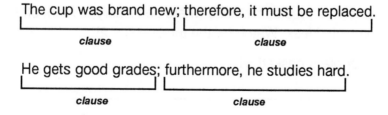

The cup was brand new; therefore, it must be replaced.

     clause   *clause*

He gets good grades; furthermore, he studies hard.

     clause   *clause*

As soon as you have two or more complete ideas in the same sentence, numerous options for punctuation arise. Check out these different ways to handle the same sentence with two complete ideas.

Nancy plays in a band; she thrives on performing. (Semicolon)

Nancy plays in a band. She thrives on performing. (Two sentences)

Nancy plays in a band, and she thrives on performing. (Comma plus *and*)

At the point we've reached, sentence structure becomes creative and a lot more fun—less a matter of rules than choices about what sounds best and works best for you.

Summary

Two rules exist for using semicolons: there must be two complete ideas in a sentence; the ideas must be closely related.

Carmela is super bright; she hardly needs to study.

Kim just came from Korea; he's adjusting quickly.

Generally, don't use semicolons and lighter connectives together.

Not so good: We celebrated New Year's; but it was a headache.

Better: We celebrated New Year's, but it was a headache.

You can hear semicolons as extended pauses.

Christmas was great; (pause) the whole family came.

The stool needs replacing; (pause) the leg is broken.

Heavy connectives are marked off by semicolons and commas.

I failed to understand; *however,* I will study harder.

Jesse fought in Vietnam; *moreover,* he was wounded there.

∝ CHAPTER REVIEW

A. Rewrite the following sentences. Use semicolons where necessary to mark off two or more closely related, complete ideas. Watch for the trick on No. 2!

1. Myra plays tennis her sister plays basketball.

_____

2. The man went to the creek and found a comfortable spot.

_____

3. The pigeons made nests in the eaves the janitor had to climb on a ladder to knock the nests loose.

_____

_____

4. The classes' sculptures are fired in a kiln the heat in there gets so intense, no one is allowed nearby.

_____

_____

5. Craig finished his painting he set it out to dry.

_____

6. The TV conked out I don't miss it at all.

_____

7. Marta started the year with great intentions however she quickly fell into her old habits.

_____

_____

8. Most week days Tito does two hours of homework moreover he still has time to visit his friends.

_____

_____

9. Bucky has to leave school and move he's really stressed.

_____

10. I'm going to pass Chemistry I also plan to get through English literature however typing is a horse of a totally different stripe.

_____

_____

B. Now demonstrate what you know about semicolons. On a separate sheet of paper, write 6 sentences that use semicolons to separate two complete, closely related ideas in the same sentence.

Colons

7

Colons prepare the reader for lists, for examples that explain the previous statement, or for longer quotations.

List: Please bring the following to the party: a dish to share, something to drink, and a game to play.

Example: Few people supported the government's philosophy about nuclear weapons: only three people out of one hundred claimed they supported current policy.

Quote: The critic Seymor Hearse summed up William Faulkner's attitude toward death: "Death seems to draw some characters like a suction, pulling them toward the damp black of the grave with relentless certainty."

You already know about using commas with items in a list. So the only tricky part here is making sure you use a signal word like *follows* or *as follows* when you're first learning colons. Otherwise, there can be confusion with simple list sentences.

List: Mel likes dancing, singing, and Soul Train.
Error: Mel likes: dancing, singing, and Soul Train.
Colon: Mel likes the following: dancing, singing, and acting.

Error: I need: nails, hammer, and saw.
Colon: I need the items in order as follows: first the nails, then the hammer, and then the saw.

As you continue using colons for lists, you'll see that the words *this* and *these* in colon constructions can also be signal words.

I need to get *these* things at the store: honey, insect repellent, and sunblock.

He found *this* to be true: there are more women and children in poverty than men.

Colons are also useful for setting up examples or illustrations that explain the previous statement. Watch how the second statement illustrates or gives an example of the first statement.

Fella came to understand her father: learning about his war experiences and his poverty-stricken childhood explained many things.

Grandma was a strong woman: she supported the family and raised three children.

If you introduce formal or longer quotations from speeches, research, or books, you should definitely set off the quote with a colon.

> Here are Mr. Micawber's words: "Get more sleep, my boy. Push yourself, and you will become quite ill."

> The president was quoted as speaking these words by TIME Magazine: "We must reach for the spirit and goodness in our fellow man, not only react to his possible hostility."

A colon also is used in the salutation of a formal or business letter, in separating hours from minutes, and in showing equality between statements.

> To Whom It May Concern:

> Dear Ms. Quarles:

> 8:10

> 12:40

> hand: an appendage at the end of an arm

Colons also precede the minutes of meetings.

> The Ad Hoc School Committee recommends these changes: dances every lunch, no attendance policy, and no grade lower than an A.

☞ EXERCISE 1

Copy the following sentences. Put in colons where necessary with lists, longer quotes, and examples which explain the previous statement.

1. Every Christmas Theresa has to do the following shop for presents, cook dinner, and care for her cousins.

_____

_____

2. Please buy the following bread, butter, and rutabagas.

_____

3. Our plan is strong it is intelligent and flexible.

_____

4. The driveway is old it has begun to crack.

_____

5. The test was easy only two questions needed thought.

_____

6. I think you'd be silly to elope you would miss graduation and alienate your family.

_____

_____

Notice that the words *for example* can be inserted directly after the colon in the last four sentences. A good way to check whether to use a colon is to see if you can put in *for example* or *that is* after the colon. These words imply equalness.

I liked most of the novel. **For example**, I thought the characters were interesting.
I liked most of the novel: I thought the characters were interesting.

The weather is unpredictable. **That is**, it's rainy one day and sunny the next.
The weather is unpredictable: rainy one day and sunny the next.

Notice that you leave a space after a colon—the same as with semicolons and commas. Also, you don't have to have a complete sentence before or after a colon.

Summary

Colons prepare the reader for lists or examples.

For a great party get these things: good food, lots of friends, and dancing music.

Katy Chin and I are best friends: we have been close one way or another since we were infants.

Colons also set off salutations, separate hours from minutes, and show equality between statements. You don't need a complete idea before or after a colon.

Dear Sir:

5:02

scalpel: a surgical instrument

Colons prepare you for minutes of a meeting or longer quotes:

The following agenda was discussed: bicycle locks, tardiness, and the goldfish in the biology lab.

My mother is fond of giving me this admonition: "If you fail to learn it from me, the world will teach you, and the world is far more harsh than I am."

CHAPTER REVIEW

A. Rewrite the following sentences, putting in colons (and any other punctuation) wherever they are needed.

1. Answer me this do you like to eat dry spaghetti?

_____

2. Her parents grounded her for three reasons she was late her grades dropped and she dented the car.

_____

_____

3. Two things are totally clear I need new pants and I need to run faster from strange bulldogs.

_____

_____

4. The chase left me in a strange position up a tree and hollering for help.

_____

5. Most of my friends want the following from life meaningful work a good marriage and several children.

_____

_____

6. The philosophy known as Existentialism is also a value system it is concerned with the meaning and purpose of existence.

_____

_____

7. Shakespeare's words are widely quoted "To be or not to be, that is the question."

_____

_____

B. Next, on a separate sheet of paper, write 5 original sentences using colons. Be sure to employ signal words like _the following_ or _as follows_ with lists. _This, these,_ and _includes_ can also work.

Dashes

Dashes set off exclamations and abrupt breaks in a sentence.

> The answer was wrong—catastrophe!

> Arrgh—my sister just came in with her hair in a purple Mohawk.

As you can hear, dashes create longer pauses than commas.

> The day was hot—(pause) too hot.

> I got an A on my final—(pause) a total shock!

Notice that dashes don't require a complete idea on both sides. A dash can also substitute for commas, colons, semicolons, and parentheses.

> My car needs repairs—only minor ones, though.

You should use dashes to set off a parenthetical comment when there is punctuation within the comment.

> The entire state of California—an amazing array of mountains, deserts, coastline, water ways, forests, farmlands, industrial centers, cities, and suburbs— will not fall into the ocean during the next earthquake.

> The new governor—a man with proven compassion, high ideals, and large amounts of courage—managed to raise the issue above party politics.

Many people consider overuse of dashes to be lazy punctuation. So if you're tempted to use dashes frequently, take another look at what you've written, and see if a dash really does fit into the flow of the words. If it does, go ahead and use it.

☞ EXERCISE 1

A. Write out the following sentences and season them with dashes.

1. The dam gave way look out!

_____

2. John is a total clown really funny.

_____

3. Her idea of a good time comes down to one word surfing.

_____

4. The trip was exciting almost too exciting.

_____

5. We returned via the unimproved road a mistake if there ever was one.

_____

_____

6. Sometimes school is fun don't you think so?

_____

7. Indra promises to break all her bad habits fat chance.

_____

8. He has a lot of ego too much, I think.

_____

B. Now write five sentences that use dashes to set off exclamations or to indicate abrupt breaks in a sentence.

1._____

2._____

3._____

4._____

5._____

KEEPING PUNCTUATION STRAIGHT

Knowing the relative weight of the various grammatical symbols can help you figure which mark to use in a sentence.

Commas are the lightest of all punctuation symbols. They always needs help from a connective or the pattern of the sentence to provide separation.

Semicolons come next. They can be used to separate two complete, closely related ideas in the same sentence.

Colons follow semicolons in strength. They prepare readers for lists and examples that illustrate the previous statement.

Dashes are the most flexible mark. They work well with abrupt sentence breaks and exclamations.

Periods, question marks, and *exclamation points* are ending marks, the strongest grammatical symbols. Each creates a full stop that marks the end of at least one complete idea.

KEY REVIEW COMMENTS

Now is a good time to review several key points, since they are the basis for all mechanics:

1. First and most obviously, sentences must express at least one complete thought.

2. When there are two or more complete ideas in the same sentence, some form of punctuation is necessary.

3. Listen for definite pauses and stops; they indicate where marks are needed and even which marks.

4. Last, you have to pay attention to your punctuation in whatever you write. Many times students will write far worse in science, for instance, than in English. Writing well takes concentration and practice.

At this point in your learning, it would also be good to explain what you now know to someone else—someone who needs help with sentence mechanics. Teaching skills has a way of printing the skills in your deepest gray matter.

Summary

Dashes set off exclamations and abrupt breaks in ideas.

> The lake was cold—freezing!

> The novel *Beloved* was unusual—very moving.

Dashes are the preferred marks to set off longer parenthetical comments.

> Dan went to dinner at the Trang's house and had an interesting evening—the Trangs escaped from Vietnam by boat, were chased by pirates, and lived at a camp in Thailand—so it was a night with exotic food and fascinating stories.

↪ CHAPTER REVIEW

A. Use dashes to mark off the following examples. Some sentences will need more than one dash.

1. This broken ankle really aches I mean pain.

2. The computer is a handy tool terrific, in fact.

3. Alice finally finished and let out a cheer yes!

4. J.C. finds newspapers great for information depth of thought is another matter, though.

5. They found it hard nearly impossible to agree with the candidate.

6. The piece sounds like funeral music downright spooky.

7. My brother watches too much TV his mistake.

8. The snow is thick this year too thick, people say.

9. Jena is letting her feelings out more just saying what she feels.

10. Nothing is worse than that inner censor the way it tells you that you're wrong or stupid.

B. Now, on a separate sheet of paper, write 5 sentences that contain dashes.

Capitals
9

The rules of capitalization are a little tricky. Here are the main ones for you to remember.

BEGINNING OF SENTENCES

The first letter of every sentence is capitalized.

Indra phoned John.

He answered brusquely.

She replaced the receiver.

He heard the dial tone.

PROPER NOUNS: SPECIFIC PERSONS, PLACES, AND THINGS

In addition to the first letter in every sentence, you need to capitalize the first letter of all proper nouns. A proper noun names a specific person, place, or thing.

Susan **S**chumann is a close friend of **F**red's.

The old movie **C**asablanca is a classic from **W**orld **W**ar II.

Susan Schumann, Fred, Casablanca and *World War II* are all specific things—specific persons, a specific movie, and a specific war.

Now look at the next example. It shows a common error.

Incorrect: The Movie is still exciting to watch.

The word movie shouldn't begin with a capital. It is not the name of a specific movie (e.g., *Casablanca*). It's a common noun—one that doesn't get capitalized.

Look at the next set of examples of common and proper nouns:

Incorrect: The closest City is ten miles.

Correct: The closest city is **S**an **F**rancisco. (a specific city)

Incorrect: That Man should watch his parking meter.

Correct: A ticket was just handed to **H**ank. (a specific person)

Incorrect: Don't turn on the one-way Street.

Correct: A sign directs you to **B**roadway. (a specific street)

PROPER ADJECTIVES

Here's another important capitalization rule. Proper adjectives—descriptive words formed from proper nouns—are capitalized, too.

American (from *America*)

Spanish (from *Spain*)

Shakespearean (from *Shakespeare*)

You'll find that most proper adjectives are from place names: *French, Bostonian, British, Japanese, New Mexican,* etc.

☞ EXERCISE 1

Rewrite the following sentences, removing capitals from all unspecified (common) nouns and capitalizing specific (proper) nouns.

1. She loves to walk the Dog on the beach.

_____

2. indra and john made up at the Movies.

_____

3. The matsons found themselves near the Wharf.

_____

4. dolores went out to walk her poodle, rover.

_____

5. lilly Chen met us on state street near fifth avenue.

_____

6. We hiked near mount ranier.

_____

Did you notice in the last two examples that three of the specific names had more than one word? In other words, *state street* becomes *State Street*, and so on. You can check this or any other capitalization question in the dictionary—and questions will arise because of the number of proper nouns in the language that need capitals. (Remember: specific nouns get capitalized; general nouns don't.)

DOGS, CATS, TREES, AND SCHOOL

Animal and plant names are not capitalized unless you refer to them by a specific name (e.g., *Spot, Rover, Bandit*). Therefore, *redwood tree, cougar, shepherd, calico cat, fern, daisy,* and all those general tree, plant, and animal names should begin with lower case letters.

Certain animal breeds can cause confusion: *Dalmatian*, for instance, is capitalized, as are *German* shepherd and *Irish* wolfhound. You capitalize here because the first word in the breed is a proper noun, the name of a specific place: *Dalmatia* (the coast of Yugoslavia), *Germany*, *Ireland*.

On the other hand, breed names like shepherd, collie, hound, and even dachshund are general. And terrier would be in lower case while the *Y* in *Yorkshire* terrier would be specific (a place) and capitalized.

With classes in school, you need to capitalize for titles of specific classes. Leave in lower case the names of general subjects (except for languages, e.g., *Spanish*.)

Get Mr. Nunes for **F**rench and for **I**ndividualized **R**eading. Take **s**peech, but forget **s**cience and **m**ath.

reading

home ec

social science

Latin

Speech I

But Home Ec or Social Science or any other class is capitalized if it's also the title of your specific class.

Dr. Smith's class, **S**ocial **S**cience, is dynamite.

Mrs. Johns teaches **A**dvanced **H**ome **E**c each year.

☞ EXERCISE 2

Rewrite each sentence, correcting capitals where need be.

1. He likes Bull terriers better than german Shepherds.

_____

2. Darrell did a report on Sparrows for biology I.

_____

3. i saw a Greyhound running in the Park.

_____

4. Eloise decided to take french instead of Math.

_____

5. leaving home early, marcus went to home ec.

_____

6. The york rose is at least six hundred years old.

DAYS AND MONTHS

Days of the week and holidays take a capital—likewise months. However, seasons are left in lower case.

> Zeke's birthday is **M**onday, the twentieth of **M**arch, the first day of **s**pring.

> Sara and Alec met on **C**hristmas **E**ve, a **F**riday, the snowiest **D**ecember of the snowiest **w**inter in memory.

RELATIVES

Relatives like father, mother, sister, grandfather, and wife stay in lower case unless they're in direct address. Direct address means you use the word like a person's name.

> "Hey, **D**ad, let's go to **g**randma's house."

The word *Dad* here is like saying his name—Herbert.

> Eddie met his **s**ister and **b**rother downtown. Eddie said, "Hi, **S**is. What's up, **B**ro?"

Saying *Bro* here is like saying, "What's up, Daniel?"

Titles of relatives used like names are also usually capitalized.

> We asked **F**ather for permission to go out, but he answered by saying to go ask **M**other.

Again, saying *Father* and *Mother* is like saying Al and Flo.

HE, HIS, AND *HIM*

When talking about God or Jesus, the first letters of the pronouns he, his and him are capitalized.

> They say **H**is works are great.

> If you ask, **H**e will answer.

> On Calvary **H**e found **H**imself crucified.

All other pronouns in any usage (except *I*) stay uncapitalized unless they're the first word in a sentence.

> Sy went to the pool. Almost immediately he dove in the water, and then **I** saw that **h**e resurfaced with **h**is eyes squinched.

COURTESY TITLES

Courtesy titles like *Mr., Mrs., and Miss* are capitalized:

> **M**r. Sarducci
>
> **M**rs. Gomez
>
> **M**iss Lucia di Lammermoor

Use this simple trick with capitalization for the titles of people: when the title comes before a name, capitalize it. When the title comes after a name or any other time, leave it in lower case.

> As a young man, **P**resident Theodore Roosevelt played a number of sports. Theodore Roosevelt, the **p**resident, liked sports.
>
> **P**rincipal Manuel Ibarra and his wife, **D**r. Luisa Ibarra, both graduated from Yale. Manuel Ibarra, the **p**rincipal, and his wife Luisa, the **d**octor, both graduated from Yale.
>
> **R**egistered **N**urse Lauren Terry does a great job.
> Lauren Terry, the **r**egistered **n**urse on duty last night, does a fine job.

In many texts, newspapers, and periodicals, the title of the president of the United States (and often his wife) is capitalized in any usage. Capitals are sometimes used to show respect this way.

> The **P**resident gave his first press conference.
>
> The **F**irst **L**ady, on the arm of the President, greeted the crowd.

Many newspapers and magazines, however, as well as dictionaries and stylebooks disagree about this use of capitals. To remain consistent, I would say capitalize the title when it precedes the name and leave it in lower case otherwise.

> George Bush, the forty-third **p**resident....
>
> Arriving in a helicopter, **P**resident George Bush....

TITLES OF STORIES, BOOKS, ETC.

With titles of short stories, articles, poems, and songs, you capitalize first letters. You also put the titles in quotation marks.

> Robert Frost's most popular poem is **"B**irches.**"**
>
> **"G**oodbye, **C**olumbus**"** is a short story by Philip Roth.
>
> Indra's favorite song is **"A**mazing **G**race.**"**
>
> We read the story **"F**or **E**smé—**W**ith **L**ove and **S**qualor.**"**

Notice that the following kinds of short words go in lower case unless they're the first word in the title.

> articles (the words *the, a,* and *an*)
>
> short connectors (*and, or, nor, for, yet, but*)
>
> short prepositions (*of, in, at, on, off,* etc.)

Here are some examples of this.

> Did you like the story "**T**he **C**ow **a**nd **t**he **D**oughnut"?
>
> Can you sing "**T**he **F**armer **i**n **t**he **D**ell"?

As to longer works—movies, whole books, TV programs, magazines, and newspapers—you capitalize those first letters and underline all the words.

> I hid under my chair at the movie <u>**H**alloween II</u>.
>
> <u>**T**he **R**ed **a**nd **t**he **B**lack</u> is a French novel.
>
> I used <u>**L**ife</u> and <u>**T**ime</u> magazines for research.
>
> <u>**T**he **D**enver **P**ost</u> ran a series of articles.
>
> The book <u>**T**he **C**olor **P**urple</u> is set in Georgia.
>
> <u>**M**other **J**ones</u> is a strange title for a magazine.
>
> <u>**S**esame **S**treet</u> has been running for years now.

In printed matter—like this book—these are customarily printed in italics.

> *Halloween II*
>
> *The Red and the Black*

Buy you can't do this, and neither can your typewriter or word processor. You have to underline.

Summary

Along with the first word in a sentence, capitalize nouns which name a specific person, place, or thing.

> The man called for the dog.
>
> The man called Jack whistled for his dog, **T**error.

PLANTS, ANIMALS, SCHOOL

The general names of animals and plants are seldom capitalized. So you write *fern, fox, oak tree,* and *spaniel*, for example, in lower case. Only when these names include a place name do you capitalize that first letter: *German* shepherd; *Boston* terrier; *Irish* setter.

You capitalize the specific classes in a school but not general subjects (except languages.)

| **A**lgebra II | **S**panish | **B**iology I | **B**asic **C**omposition | |
| **m**ath | **r**eading | **h**ealth | **b**iology | **w**riting |

DAYS, SEASONS, AND RELATIONS

Days of the week and months take a capital, while seasons and remain in lower case.

> On **T**hursdays during **w**inter she visits her aunt.

> This **F**ebruary 1, a **M**onday, her sister will call.

Leave general names of family relations in lower case unless you use one like a specific name (e.g., Dad = Bill).

> I told my **m**om, "**M**other, you have to understand."

> He called to his **f**ather, "Hit me a line drive, **D**ad."

TITLES, UNDERLINES, AND QUOTES

Capitalize courtesy titles that immediately precede a name, but leave titles that come after the name in lower case.

> **P**rime **M**inister Margaret Thatcher

> Margaret Thatcher, **p**rime **m**inister of England

> **D**r. Harris, the **d**octor in charge of the case

Capitalize the first letter of each word in titles of poems, short stories, and songs. Put the entire title of these works in quotation marks:

> "**D**addy" is a poem by Sylvia Plath.

> Many people have read the story "**C**harles."

Use capitals for the first letters of each word and also underline the titles of major (i.e. long) works: books, magazines, newspapers, TV programs, and movies.

| <u>**S**oul on **I**ce</u> | <u>**O**f **M**ice and **M**en</u> | <u>**W**ord **P**ower</u> |
| <u>**R**eader's **D**igest</u> | <u>**E**bony</u> | <u>**T**he **D**enver **P**ost</u> |

One Flew Over the Cuckoo's Nest won a slew of Academy Awards.
The Cosby Show has become a classic.

All articles, short connectors, and short prepositions in any title go in lower case unless they're the first word in the title: "The Masque of the Red Death"; *From Here to Eternity.*

∞ CHAPTER REVIEW

A. Fix the capitals as you rewrite these examples. Make sure you remove the incorrect capitals. Underline or quote titles when necessary.

1. Three friends read the novel the great gatsby.

_____

2. The Delicatessen on the corner is open sundays.

_____

3. Cheryl and her Sister went hiking in the adirondacks.

_____

4. The old television program i love lucy is still funny after all these years.

_____

5. I shouted in my loudest voice, "Hey, grandpa!"

_____

6. My Brother and I argued about which Video to rent.

_____

7. The chicago cubs play at wrigley field.

_____

8. Tremaine wants to sing in Carnegie hall.

_____

9. To Simone, Math is easier than spanish.

_____

10. Darrin never misses an issue of rolling stone.

_____

11. indra and john talked intently while the president passed in a Motorcade.

_____

B. Now, on a separate sheet of paper, write 10 sentences with at least two capitals in each sentence. Try to include all of the following:

names of people
titles of people
names of places
the name of a day or month (Remember—seasons are not capitalized.)
the name of a relationship (Be careful—sometimes they're capitalized, sometimes not.)
the title of a book
the title of a movie
the name of a TV program

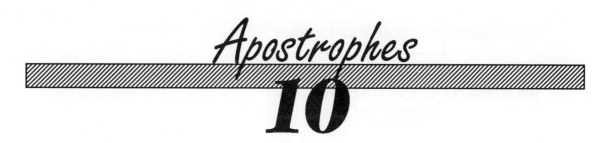

Apostrophes

10

Apostrophes show possession or contraction.

Possession means having something or owning it.

> a dog's life
>
> Sue-Ellen's hair

Contraction means shortening words by dropping letters. For example:

> do not *contracts to* don't
>
> I am *contracts to* I'm

POSSESSIVES

Apostrophes for possessives show that something is owned:

> Jan's hand—the hand is owned by Jan
>
> Manfred's tennis racket—the racket is owned by Manfred

One way of stating ownership is to substitute the word *belongs*.

> Cheryl's job—the job *belongs* to Cheryl
>
> Andre's friend—the friend *belongs* to Andre
>
> the flower's petals—the petals *belong* to the flower

When a question of apostrophes comes up, ask yourself whether a state of belonging exists. *Jason's car*—does the car belong to Jason? *Cecile's tool*—does the tool belong to Cecile?

POSSESSIVES: WHERE THE APOSTROPHE GOES

With possession, apostrophes go before the -s except in a few cases which will be explained shortly. Place the apostrophe between the last letter in the word and the -s: *Susan's house; Otto's car; Rich's coat; Fred's head; Conrad's gerbil; Stephanie's tattoo; Mike's Diner*.

The person, place, or thing which is possessed follows directly after the word which takes the apostrophe unless adjectives come between:

> The seagull's broken, flapping wing...
>
> └──────────┘
> *adjectives in between*

The Midwest's latest spell of bad weather...

adjective

The hurricane's dark, swirling vortex...

adjectives

☞ EXERCISE 1

Write out the following sentences, putting in apostrophes where necessary.

1. Indras weird belief is that she can make John dance like a star in a dance movie.

_____

2. Marcias messy, hacked-up folder looks horrible.

_____

3. This suspension has hurt the teams record.

_____

4. Being left out was a blow to Jasons self-esteem.

_____

5. Supermans latest adventure made me laugh.

_____

6. Can you help me look for Leroys new baseball glove?

_____

APOSTROPHE CHECK

A simple way to check whether a word requires an apostrophe for a possessive is to substitute a possessive pronoun for the word or words in question. (Possessive pronouns: *his, her, its, their,* etc.) If the word in question is possessive, the substitution will make sense.

> *Mark's* wallet is missing.
> *His* wallet is missing.
>
> Someone snatched *Heather's* book.
> Someone snatched *her* book.
>
> *Mai's* cat had its shots.
> *Her* cat had its shots

When you make the substitution check, the possessive pronoun takes the place of the noun plus any words modifying it. As you might guess, it also substitutes for someone's full name.

84

This writer's words have reached millions.
Her words have reached millions.

The earth's crust is only a few feet thick.
Its crust is only a few feet thick.

The old red leather book's cover was cracked and torn.
Its cover was cracked and torn.

Brenda read all of *James Baldwin's* novels.
Brenda read all of *his* novels.

CONFUSING POSSESSIVES WITH OTHER WORD FORMS

Some people are in the habit of putting in an apostrophe before any *-s* at the end of a word. This leads to errors like the following:

Incorrect: The tree's have lost their leaves.

Incorrect: Tomorrow Eric leave's for the army.

Most of the confusion with possession comes from mixing up plurals with possessives. This is the mistake in the first example above. (Remember: *plural* means more than one—*river, rivers; son, sons; potato chip, potato chips*.) Added to that, some verb forms also require an *-s* ending (*play, plays; run, runs; live, lives*). Putting in an apostrophe here is the mistake in the second example above.

Remember: An *-s* ending certainly doesn't mean the word needs an apostrophe! In fact, most words ending in an -s don't require an apostrophe at all.

Use the possessive pronoun check to determine whether to use apostrophes here:

The planes lined up for takeoff.

She goes to kindergarten.

The three boys raced to the far end of the field.

As you see, apostrophes would be wrong. Most apostrophe errors come from mistaking verb endings or plurals for possessives. You don't need an apostrophe with plurals or verb endings, as the check shows:

The plane's lined up—*Their* lined up?

She goe's to kindergarten—She *her* to kindergarten?

The three boy's raced—Three *his* raced?

☞ EXERCISE 2

See if you can use the possessive pronoun check in the following examples. Copy the sentences, putting in apostrophes when needed. Leave out any incorrect apostrophes. If an apostrophe is correctly used, of course, don't change it.

1. This years prom was so crowded that everyone was sweating.

_____

2. Emily envied everyone elses camera.

_____

3. The work's of William Faulkner are intriguing.

_____

4. Sues favorite color is electric blue.

_____

5. The first trimester's are alway's the hardest.

_____

6. The day's are long during July.

_____

7. The staplers base is broken.

_____

8. We crossed five street's to get to the professor's house.

_____

9. The ragweed is in bloom now, giving me horrible sneeze's.

_____

10. Matildas hat got blown off in the wind.

_____

PLURAL POSSESSIVES

Now we'll look at the less common cases where apostrophes follow an -s. The most important is in writing plural possessives. When you write the possessive of a plural noun, you have to put the apostrophe after the -s of the plural.

> The dance will be held in the girls' gym.

Here, *girls'* is both plural (it means more than one girl) and possessive (the gym belongs to the girls.) Since the word has to be written as plural, the apostrophe follows the -s.

> The dancers' tryout is tomorrow night.

The same principle applies here. *Dancers* is plural, and the tryouts belong to the dancers.

> The trees' foliage is thick.

Here *trees* is plural, and the foliage belongs to them.

The boys' voices were finally silent.

The students' complaints were loud and long.

The Screen Actors' Guild is a union.

In each case we're talking about more than one (plural) and also a state of belonging or ownership.

Possessive plurals are not really rare. However, they are not as common as ordinary singular possessives. Most often a word is either plural or possessive, only occasionally both at once.

☞ EXERCISE 3

Practice these plural possessives. Rewrite the following sentences, putting in apostrophes where needed. Be careful— there's one singular possessive thrown in to keep you alert.

1. The truckers strike ended Tuesday.

_____

2. The golfers matches will get underway at 8:00 A.M.

_____

3. The dogs tail wagged furiously.

_____

4. The boys treehouse stands between their houses.

_____

5. I'll meet you outside the boys gym.

_____

6. The meeting will be held in the teachers lounge.

_____

EXTRA TIPS ON POSSESSIVES

Speech patterns effect the way apostrophes are used. A sentence like this is common in speaking:

> We're going to grandma's. Or, Let's go to Jack's.

What has happened here is that the name of the place—grandma's house, Jack's apartment—is understood. The speaker has made a shortcut and left out the word. The same is true in the following:

> After school I go to the dentist's.

> Tomorrow I go to the doctor's.

In both cases the word *office* is understood.

87

CONTRACTIONS

The second major use of apostrophes is in forming contractions. In a contraction two words are contracted together and become one word. In addition, part of one of the original words—usually a vowel—is dropped in pronouncing it. In writing, an apostrophe is put in its place.

Many contractions involve the words *not, is, has, am,* and *are.*

>didn't (contraction of *did not*)
>
>he's (contraction of *he is* or he *has*)
>
>I'm (contraction of *I am*)

Here the most common error is putting the apostrophe in the wrong place. Remember, the apostrophe takes the place of the letter or letters that are omitted. Do not put an apostrophe between the two words that are contracted! Put it in place of whatever is left out.

>**Incorrect:** did'nt
>
>**Correct:** didn't
>
>**Incorrect:** could'nt
>
>**Correct:** couldn't

IT'S AND *ITS*

Two words that are frequently mixed up are *it's* and *its.* One has an apostrophe; the other has none. Here's the rule:

- *It's* (with an apostrophe) is always a contraction. It stands for *it is.*

- *Its* (no apostrophe) is always a possessive. It is a possessive pronoun, like *his* and *her.* Possessive pronouns do not have apostrophes.

For example: *It's* hard to stand a coin on *its* edge.

➲ EXERCISE 4

Rewrite the following sentences. Put in any missing apostrophes, and make sure all apostrophes are correctly placed.

1. Its my problem; Im perfectly able to deal with its complications.

_____

2. His arm isn't healed yet.

_____

3. The tiger did'nt move its head for at least five minute's.

_____

4. You called us, and we're all here.

_____

5. Thats a nasty-looking gash; shouldnt you go to the doctors?

_____

Summary

Apostrophes are used in writing possessives and in writing contractions.

Another way of stating possession is belonging. Something belongs to something else: _Diane's feelings of inferiority_ (the feelings belong to her); _Lennae's talent_ (her talent definitely belongs to her); _J.J.'s stomach muscles_ (the stomach muscles belong to J.J.).

Used this way, apostophes ordinarily precede the -s: _Leo's score_.

CHECK IT OUT

A sure-fire check to determine apostophes for possession is to substitute a possessive pronoun (_his, her, their, its, our_) for the word in question: _Raenna's_ woes: _her_ woes; _Jud's_ Nikes: _his_ Nikes; _a dog's_ life: _its_ life.

Most possessive errors come from confusing plurals (_tree-trees_) or verb endings (_run-runs_) with possessives. The pronoun check corrects this simple error.

PLURAL POSSESSIVES

The apostrophe follows the -s when a word is both plural and possessive: _the girls' gym; the boys' new game; the senators' pay raise; the baseball players' strike._

CONTRACTIONS

An apostrophe substitutes for a missing letter in a contraction: _isn't (is not); I'm (I am); she's (she is or she has)._ Don't make the mistake of putting the apostrophe between the two contracted words.

_IT'S_ AND _ITS_

_It's_ is a contraction (_it is_). _Its_ is a possessive. Don't confuse the two!

☞ CHAPTER REVIEW

A. Check your expertise with apostrophes. Copy the following sentences and provide apostrophes when needed. Leave out incorrect apostrophes, and use the possessive pronouns *his, her, their,* and *its* as checks. Make sure all contractions contain apostrophes in the right place.

1. The lamp's are damaged.

_____

2. Dellas friend is visiting class.

_____

3. The babys bib is stained with strange green stuff.

_____

4. Regardless of Franks grade on the project, he's satisfied with his efforts.

_____

_____

5. As we've seen with nuclear power, todays solutions can become tomorrows problems.

_____

_____

6. Before they realized it, the truck's picked up speed.

_____

7. The dance will be held in Delta High School boys gym.

_____

8. Buddys coat is'nt ready for the cleaners; it's still wet.

_____

9. Indras new dress got a footprint on the hem, but she loved the way Johns dancing improved.

_____

_____

B. On a separate sheet of paper, write 6 sentences that use apostrophes. Include at least one plural possessive and at least three contractions.

90

Quotes 11

Writing dialogue is probably more fun than any other kind of writing. Using quotation marks to set off someone's words is easy, and it requires learning only a few conventions.

Quotation marks look like this: **" "**. You use a set of these marks at either end of the actual words a person speaks.

"I'd like a ham and cheese on rye," said the man.
           quote   *identification of speaker*

You put in a set of marks when someone starts to speak, and another set when he or she finishes. The narrative—anything that is not dialogue—remains outside the quotation marks.

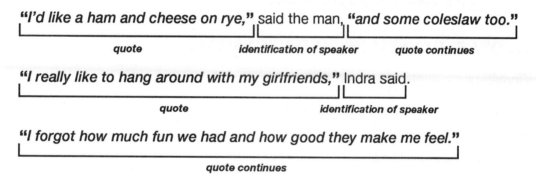

"I'd like a ham and cheese on rye," said the man, *"and some coleslaw too."*
    quote   *identification of speaker*   *quote continues*

"I really like to hang around with my girlfriends," Indra said.
        quote   *identification of speaker*

"I forgot how much fun we had and how good they make me feel."
                    quote continues

Notice here that the words identifying the speaker (*said the man* and *Indra said*) occur between two sets of quotation marks. Again, only the exact words a person speaks are quoted, while the identification of the speaker is outside the quotation.

COMMAS AND IDENTIFYING THE SPEAKER

You often need to identify the speaker when you are writing dialogue.

"Don't bug me now," *Dedra said.*

Bill looked up and said, "It's important."

The important thing to note here is that you usually put a comma between the quotation and the words that identify the speaker.

"I hate all the fuss of birthdays**,**" David declared.

91

Here *David* is the speaker, and *declared* tells that he is speaking. Any word that connotes speaking (*said, shouted, spoke, whispered, screamed, yelled, cheered, clucked*, etc.) can go along with the the identification of the speaker.

"Let's go to the game**,**" Raul suggested.

"What a great day**,**" Shawna crowed.

Rudy commented**,** "It seems like a long way to go for an ice cream."

When action or narrative follows the quote instead of words like *he said* or *she asked*, then a period terminates the quote instead of a comma.

"Get over the fence **.**" Ron paused, gauging the height. "They're right behind us."

narrative

"I love rap**.**" Elmer sang along with the words.

narrative

Whatever the form, the punctuation goes <u>inside</u> the end quotation mark:

"Let's stop**."** Ray gasped for breath. "Enough**."**

QUOTES, QUESTIONS, AND EXCLAMATIONS

Sometimes a quote will be a question. Look carefully at how this is punctuated.

"Did you call me**?**" Denise asked.

First, notice that the question mark goes inside the closing quotation marks just as commas and periods do.

Second, notice that when a quotation ends with a question mark, you don't need to put a comma or a period in also. The question mark alone is enough.

The same rule holds true when you are punctuating an exclamation.

"Help**!**" we shouted.

☞ EXERCISE 1

Copy the following sentences, putting in quotation marks. Again, use commas to separate a quotation from the identification of speaker and use periods to separate it from narrative. Watch where you put the commas and periods.

1. Great work, you really excelled Mr. Roberts stated.

_____

2. I had a so-so time Reed pensively walked to the door.

_____

3. Oh, bug off Indra shouted. (Use an exclamation point after the quote)

_____

4. I got all A's Rodney waved his report card.

_____

5. I hate asking for help Ty confessed. It's a pain.

_____

6. Do you know Bo Jill asked. Willy, this is Bo.

_____

LONGER QUOTATIONS

When dialogue continues after narrative or after the identification of the speaker, you simply carry on the same formula of quoting and unquoting. Quotes can be interspersed with narrative any amount of times in dialogue.

> "We're such a funny family," Dedee said in the living room. "Such different types." She raised her glass to her lips. "Jo, she's the quiet one, always thinking, always with her secrets. And me, I'm the dramatic one. I always have to create a scene."

Notice that you don't quote and unquote each sentence.

Another way to understand the marks for getting in and out of dialogue is that the identification of the speaker completes the idea started in the quote. The whole thing is a sentence.

> "Don't bother me now," Mr. Acre said.
>
> one complete idea

When you have narrative after a quote, the quote itself is a complete idea, as is the narrative. Both are complete sentences and end with periods.

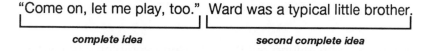

> "Come on, let me play, too." Ward was a typical little brother.
>
> complete idea   second complete idea

WRITING DIALOGUE

In writing dialogue where more than one person speaks, each change of speakers requires a new set of quotes.

> "Man, there's nothing like Friday and getting out of school," Jamal said. "What do you want to do tonight?"
>
> "Stay over at my house," Chad said, "then we can go to the mall. Lani's going to be there."

Besides the new set of quotes, there has to be an entirely new paragraph for each change of speakers.

> "Lani?" Jamal asked, "I thought she was grounded for the next two months."
>
> "No way," Chad answered. "Her mom thought it over, and she's off the hook."
>
> "This keeps getting better," Jamal said.

Notice that when a complete idea continues through the identification of speaker ("Stay over at my house," Chad said, "then we can go to the mall" ...), you punctuate just the same way that you do for regular connective sentences.

SETTING UP QUOTES

There are several basic ways to set up quotes. The first way is to simply start the quote.

> "Let's take another look at that problem."

Another way is to use a comma and identification of speaker to precede the dialogue.

> *Kate reached out and said,* "I'm glad to meet you."

If the narrative doesn't lead directly into the speech as part of the same grammatical idea, you have two complete ideas and revert to model one above.

> Kate reached out. "I'm glad to meet you."

QUOTATIONS AND COLONS

The last basic way to set up dialogue is with a colon.

> The secretary of state's tone was frosty as he delivered the rebuke: "We simply will not tolerate this kind of action. We are breaking off diplomatic relations."

As we covered in Chapter 7, colons set up quotes for formal statements, for lengthy dialogue, and for longer or formal quoted material from books or magazines.

☞ EXERCISE 2

Practice what you've learned so far by writing out the following examples, supplying the quotes and necessary punctuation.

1. Listen to me Jack said. There's no other way to do this.

_____

2. I really have to get home Sukie declared. If someone doesn't help I'm going to scream.

_____

_____

3. The Braves lead 55 to 51 the announcer cried they are three seconds away from the championship.

_____

_____

4. Mel said, I don't think we should get into this. He shook his head. It looks like trouble to me.

_____

_____

5. I wish school was out Benny complained. I'm bored. If you're bored, it's your fault answered his sister.

_____

_____

6. Man, do I like turkey Adam said. I could eat a ton.

_____

7. Give me a break Tom said. I'll have the money soon.

_____

8. The book Megathought claims We need new forms of thinking. People must see interconnectedness.

_____

_____

QUOTING FROM BOOKS AND OTHER SOURCES

Materials from written sources—books, magazines, newspapers—are often quoted in essays. Here is a passage quoted from the short story "The Sire de Malétroit's Door" by Robert Louis Stevenson:

> "It was September, 1429; the weather had fallen sharp; a flighty piping wind, laden with showers, beat around the township; and the dead leaves ran riot along the streets. Here and there a window was already lighted up; and the noise of the men-at-arms, making merry over supper within, came forth in fits and was swallowed up and carried away by the wind."

Notice how the quotation marks enclose all the quoted material. One set goes at the beginning of the paragraph, and the other set goes at the end. You use commas and periods as usual within quotes.

QUOTES WITHIN QUOTES

If dialogue or a quotation occurs in material you are already quoting, then you enclose them in what are called **single quotes**. Single quotes are marks like this: ' '.

The following paragraphs contain dialogue and narrative from the book *Tom Sawyer*, by Mark Twain. Since the complete passage is enclosed in ordinary double quotes, single quotes must be used for the dialogue.

> "Ben stared a moment and then said, 'Hi-yi! You're a stump, aint you!'
>
> No answer. Tom surveyed the last touch with the eye of an artist, then he gave his brush another gentle sweep and surveyed the result as before.
>
> 'Hello, old chap, you got to work, hey?'
>
> 'Why, it's you, Ben! I warn't noticing.' "

Notice two things about this passage.

> As a quotation from a book, it begins and ends with ordinary quotation marks.
>
> Next, each of the speeches in it is enclosed within single quotes.

Single quotes like this occur when you're quoting an entire passage that has dialogue or other quotations in it.

The important points to remember are:

> • The <u>double</u> quotes enclose the passage as a whole.
>
> • The <u>single</u> quotes enclose dialogue or other quotations within that passage.

LONGER QUOTATIONS

Quotations can continue for many pages. When dialogue or quoted material continues past a paragraph, you let the reader know by leaving the end of the paragraph unquoted, and requoting the start of the next paragraph to show the reader the quote is continuing.

> "It was a frightening journey," the captain said. "The swells were so high that when you looked over the bridge all you could see was green, underwater green, fish sometimes over our heads, and seaweed. [no closing quotes]
>
> "One man went out on deck to tie down a crate, and even though we held him with ropes, he nearly drowned."

⌗ EXERCISE 3

Now pretend you are quoting the following material from a magazine story. For each example, insert the proper punctuation to show that you are quoting an entire passage. Be sure you use the proper form of quotation marks for the quotes in the passage.

1. Serena found a really good book. It made a big impression on her. It had a quote: If you look for darkness, you will find darkness. If you look for light, you will find light. But if you look with open eyes, you will find both and know truth.

_____

_____

_____

2. Gregory didn't know what to do. The stranger came up to him and said, I'm going to bust you in the face. I don't like your looks.

_____

_____

INDIRECT QUOTES

There is one kind of quote that is never set off by quotation marks. This is the kind called an *indirect quote*.

My sister said *that I could borrow her jeans*.

If a quotation is introduced by the word *that*, it's an indirect quote. It is not put in quotation marks because it is not in the speaker's exact words. Note the difference:

Ordinary, direct quote: My sister said, "You can borrow my jeans."

Indirect quote: My sister said that I could borrow her jeans.

Sometimes an indirect quote leaves out the word *that*.

Russell says *no one will beat his record*.

In this example, the *that* is "understood." The sentence means the same as

Russell says *that* no one will beat his record.

Either way, it is an indirect quote and does not get put in quotation marks.

PARAPHRASES

When you write in your own words what someone else said, it is called *paraphrasing*. Paraphrasing is like an indirect quote. Quotation marks should not be used.

Paraphrasing: The president said the enemy was strong.
Quoting: "The enemy is powerful," the president said. "We must arm ourselves."

Paraphrasing: I heard Jim say he'd like to date Lyn.
Quoting: "I wouldn't mind going out with Lyn," Jim said. "She's a great person."

Paraphrasing: The police chief suggested real caution.
Quoting: "Say nothing," the police chief advised, "You'll be better off."

COMMON ERRORS

A frequent error made with quotes is punctuating outside the quote.

Incorrect: "We did fine", Bill said.

Incorrect: "Did you like the pie"? Jacy asked.

Punctuation goes inside the quote symbol.

Correct: "We did great**,"** Bill said.

Correct: "Did you like the cake**?"** Jacy asked.

Sometimes writers simply use the wrong punctuation for quotes.

Incorrect: "Get off my case, Draino face   " John said.

comma missing

Incorrect: "You started it." Indra replied.

period used instead of comma

Correct: "Get off my case, Draino face," John said.

Correct: "You started it," Indra replied.

After reading lots of one-line quotes for dialogue, writers sometimes assume that you must unquote with every sentence.

Incorrect: "I love my new dress." "It's fresh." "The color is the brightest pink ever." "Do you like it?"

Correct: "I love my new dress. It's fresh. The color is the brightest pink ever. Do you like it?"

Again, notice that the unquote comes only when the speaker is finished, not with each line or sentence.

☞ EXERCISE 4

All of the following sentences have something wrong with them. Rewrite the sentences, making all the necessary corrections.

1. Lola said that, "She could easily climb the mountain."

_____

2. "No one calls me any more." said Bill.

_____

3. What time is it? "asked the teacher."

_____

4. "It's easy to get to my house." said Teresa, "first go down Green Street." "Then turn left at Orchard Place." "That's all there is to it."

_____

_____

5. "We could try," Dr. Inagaki stroked his chin thoughtfully.

_____

Summary

QUOTATION MARKS, COMMAS, PERIODS, AND COLONS

Quotes enclose dialogue, the actual words a person speaks:

"It was so sweet," Matt said. "We just romped like kids."

A comma is placed inside the quotation marks at the end of the quote when it is followed by identification of speaker or source.

"You are so nutty," Danielle laughed.

"I like the way you smile," said McCoy.

"The president predicted victory," reported *Time*.

"Row, row, row your boat," the song begins.

Be certain you use periods instead of commas when quotes are followed by narration instead of identification of speaker.

"Whew, I thought I'd missed." John ran upcourt.

"Let me fix it." Maude took out her sewing kit.

Quoted words may also end with a question mark or an exclamation point placed inside the quotation marks.

"Ready, set, go!" he shouted.

She replied, "Why do I have to go?"

Quotes from formal sources may be introduced by a colon:

The Constitution begins with these words: "We, the people of the United States..."

QUOTING DIALOGUE

When you write dialogue, each change of speakers requires a new set of quotes and a new paragraph.

> "Why don't we just go?" Vanessa asked.
>
> Allen answered, "I don't think it's a good idea."
>
> "You're such a party pooper," Vanessa rejoined.
>
> Allen replied, "If that's what you want to think, go ahead without me."

QUOTING OUTSIDE SOURCES

When you take material from another source (books, magazines, newspapers), quotation marks must enclose the exact words you copy from the source.

If the quotation is more than one paragraph long, quotation marks are placed at the beginning of every paragraph. However, quotation marks are not placed at the end of each paragraph. They go only at the end of the last paragraph, at the conclusion of the passage as a whole.

> "Three developments changed the course of the election," the article said. "Those developments determined the presidency and history.
>
> "We can only hope that such a combination of circumstances will not occur again in our lifetime."

QUOTES INSIDE QUOTES

Quotes inside quotes are set off by single quotation marks.

> The speech ended: "In the immortal words of Patrick Henry, 'Give me liberty or give me death!'"

INDIRECT QUOTES AND PARAPHRASES

Indirect quotes are quotes that do not reproduce the exact words of the speaker. Paraphrasing means approximating the words of a person or a source. Quotation marks should not be used with either indirect quotes or paraphrasing.

> **Direct quote:** "Let's get out of here," Ian said, "it's boring."
>
> **Paraphrase:** Ian said that he was bored and wanted to leave.

CHAPTER REVIEW

A. Practice writing quotes by writing out the following sentences and supplying quotes or quotes within quotes. Make sure you don't quote material that's only paraphrased. When necessary, take out quotation marks. Be sure to punctuate within quotes when necessary.

1. Old Jake said the trout are going crazy Time to get out the poles.

_____

_____

2. Check out the people down on 38th Street, David said. They do some wild things.

_____

_____

3. Let's not make mountains out of molehills the teacher warned. There's no real problem.

_____

_____

4. The manager agreed that "he would try to find a way to improve morale."

_____

_____

5. I've got four hours of homework tonight, Matt said, I can't believe it.

_____

_____

6. English is my best subject Dawn said. Then she admitted "that she hated math."

_____

_____

7. I didn't know what to do, Marnie said. Then he asked me to meet him that night. Come on, he kept saying. You don't need to worry. I'll talk to your mom. Marnie shook her head. He didn't realize he's exactly the kind of guy my mother would die about.

_____

_____

_____

_____

B. Now try it yourself. On a separate sheet of paper, write a conversation between two people.

Paragraphs

12

Paragraphs indicate where new ideas begin. Indentation, or adding extra space between lines, makes the new paragraph easy to recognize.

Each time there is a significant shift in the direction of an idea, you need a new paragraph. In dialogue, we've seen how paragraphs shift when speakers change. Watch the shifts in the tale below.

There was once a wise woman. People traveled great distances seeking her advice. But she was an aged woman who only emerged from her small, stone house when the crowd was too large to be ignored. Then she appeared with her cane and a plate of small cakes.

"Well, what have you come for?" she asked, moving among the assembled people.

"We have decided together," said a handsome merchant whose soul was troubled, "to bother you with only this one question: How can we find wisdom?"

"Good," the old woman said there in the golden September sunshine. "So here is the secret: wisdom is near you always. It's in the hand you raise in front of your face. It's in the trees of this forest. It's in the sky, blue as the dress of a young girl.

"You," she spoke to the handsome merchant, "who did you leave behind to come here?"

"My wife," he answered immediately, "our children, my workers, and our prosperous drayage business. Because I know now that riches count nothing without wisdom."

"In each of these people's faces, find wisdom," spoke the woman. "In their words and fears find wisdom. And then be sure to tell them what you've found."

The crowd murmured in wonder. Some even clapped, but respectfully, as befitting an old woman. The merchant frowned. He had come a great distance and brought many gifts. "But what do we do with these?" Gifts with ribbon lay on the path. The merchant's agitation made his jacket, adorned with braid, bind his chest. The old woman retreated to her stone house.

"All people desire gifts. Give these to the people you come upon during your journey home. With each of these people you see, no matter what their state, you're seeing part of yourself."

The merchant sighed and dropped to the ground where he touched his forehead to the earth. He slept the night in a hay loft where the straw smelled sweet as a baby.

Reviewing this story demonstrates the two basic uses of paragraphs: 1) Paragraphs mark off large thought units, and 2) they show changes of speaker.

In fulfilling these functions, they make the material easier for the reader to follow.

Let's examine exactly how paragraphs work in the above story. The beginning of the fable, "There was once...", is indented to show the start of the paragraph and the story. The first paragraph amounts to a thought unit about the background of the wise woman. When she begins to speak, the first paragraph ends. After she has spoken, the merchant begins to speak. This change of speakers is marked off with a paragraph. Another change of paragraphs occurs when the merchant finishes speaking. These paragraph changes continue, with shifts marking either change of large thought units, or change of speakers to the conclusion.

Paragraph changes make it easier for the reader to follow the thought of the writer. The eye quickly registers the "non-verbal" communication that something different is going to follow. Generally, the eye finds it easier to absorb information in small chunks. Large paragraphs, therefore, are found in material that is fairly easy to absorb. More difficult material usually requires shorter paragraphs.

Paragraph study doesn't end here. Like most of the material in this book, this chapter is meant to establish a foundation or rectify existing problems. From here, you and your teacher will probably explore broader, more complex areas like paragraph development.

☞ CHAPTER REVIEW

A. Copy the following passage and set up paragraphs where you see the need.

Martin lifted the phone carefully from the cradle where he was downstairs below his sister's room. His sister Katie and Jana talked every night for hours. "I swear," Katie whined, "Martin's listening on the other phone; I can hear him breathing." "You think so?" Jana asked. "I thought he was more mature than that." Now that grabbed Martin's interest. Jana was sleek and petite, an auburn-haired knockout who made even juniors and seniors take notice. "Really, Martin." Jana zeroed in on him there on the extension with her radar. "I used to think you were cute. But Katie is your sister. You bug her all the time." Martin listened, totally unrepentant. He loved his sister but guilt wasn't part of the bargain. "Martin," Jana said, "come on. We know you're listening." "He could care less how anyone feels!" his sister burst in. "You can talk to us," Jana persisted. Then softer, crooning, she said, "Please say something." Her voice made Martin think of full moons and starry nights and the scent of roses in summer.

B. Now, on a separate sheet of paper, write a full page of mixed dialogue and narrative. Make sure paragraph breaks show the shifts when a speaker changes or when the direction of an idea changes.

Other Patterns & Beyond
13

The five sentence patterns covered in the book are the most commonly used patterns in the language. But they are certainly not the only ones. For instance, the patterns covered so far can be combined in numerous ways.

> The apple tree, a sapling, needs to be watered, fertilized, and pruned if it's to produce healthy apples.
> *(mixture of List and Parenthetical Patterns)*

> When Elsa gets home from school, she has to do her chores, help prepare dinner, and look after the baby before she can sit down to her homework.
> *(combination of Introductory and List Patterns)*

> I went to school, and I met my friend—a girl named Jill—and we walked all the way downtown.
> *(mix of Parenthetical and Connective Patterns.)*

> The maid of honor, the best man, and the best man's brother went out on the town after the rehearsal, and they partied so thoroughly they nearly missed the wedding.
> *(blend of List and Connective Patterns)*

☞ EXERCISE 1

A. Copy over and punctuate the following combination sentences, labeling the patterns you see.

1. Doris Curt and I went to the mall and on a lark Curt and I pretended we were newlyweds.

_____

_____

2. When I write a paper first I concentrate on getting my ideas and feelings down and then I look over my paper to see if I made sense.

_____

_____

3. The tree outside the classroom an old oak has two hundred pairs of eyes a day staring at it because the owners are daydreaming away in math or English class.

_____

_____

4. When I picked up my brother which was a good idea since he didn't want to sit at pre-school all day I had to check for his boots coat sweaters and anything else he might have forgotten.

_____

_____

_____

B. Now put together five combination sentences. After each one, list what the combination is. Don't be afraid to experiment. At this stage, an important element of writing is experimenting.

1._____

_____

2._____

_____

3._____

_____

4._____

_____

5._____

_____

VERBALS (participals)

In Chapter 4, we covered an introductory element we termed *verbals*. Verbals are words that are formed from verbs but that are used more like adjectives or nouns in a sentence. in different positions in a sentence they often need punctuation.

There are three kinds of verbals to look out for:

Verbals ending in *-ing*: walking, talking, seeing, being, etc.
Example: *Walking* on the cliffs one day, I noticed a flower I had never seen before.

Verbals ending in *-ed* or *-en*: lifted, dropped; taken, been, etc.
Example: *Taken* by surprise, I stared blankly at my questioner. (There are other possible endings for verbals of this kind, but we won't go into them here.)

Verbals beginning with the word *to*: to go, to dance, to be, etc.
Example: *To make* an omelet, you have to break eggs.

In each case, for purposes of learning how to employ commas, the different kinds of verbals often act similarly in a sentence. Verbals or verbal phrases sometimes start a sentence as an introducer, and they sometimes come in a strategic position where the sentence turns. When they are used in either of these ways, a comma customarily separates them from the rest of the sentence.

Recovering from his slip, the cornerback knocked down the pass.
  verbal introducer   *main clause*

Finding the store closed, she kicked at the door in frustration.
   introducer   *main clause*

Carved and steaming, the turkey would soon enter our eagerly waiting stomachs.
  verbal introducer   *main clause*

To go to college, she'll need to focus better.
  verbal introducer   *main clause*

To find someone truly nice, you often have to look far.
  verbal introducer   *main clause*

Verbals also appear in the middle or end of sentences where the sentence takes a sharp turn. Notice the comma pause.

Diane told her joke, *roaring with laughter.*
       verbal

John waited near the phone, *expecting Indra to call.*
       verbal

There Indra found her purse, *dumped on the ground.*
       verbal

Marie constantly interrupted the class, *talking and fooling around with her friends.*
       verbal

The burglar alarm went off, *startling us all.*
       verbal

Bart ran all over town, *checking the libraries.*
       verbal

Notice again the construction, how the use of the comma remains consistent with both *-ed/-en* or *-ing* verbals.

Tired of John's indecision, Indra decided to forget him and find a new boyfriend.

Tiring of the way he treated her, Indra sadly gave up on John and hoped she could find someone new.

Forced into the streets, Carlyle quickly turned cynical, trusting no one.

Being forced into the streets, Carlyle quickly grew hard and trusted no one.

Patterns involving *-ed/-en* verbals are less common than their *-ing* brothers. Both patterns, however, are keyed by their sound—distinct pauses that signal the position of the comma.

He left the school, (pause) frightened by the gangs.

The period lasted over an hour, (pause) making the students fidget in their seats.

It is important to realize that not all verbals are set off by commas. In many uses verbals are closely tied to the rest of the sentence, and commas should not set them off:

Breaking up is hard to do.

I watched Bill walking down the street.

Dogs abused by people may become savage.

If you listen to these sentences, however, you will notice that they do not contain any of the pauses that signal a comma.

☞ EXERCISE 2

A. Test your skills with verbals by punctuating the following sentences. You don't need to copy them; just put the punctuation in place.

1. Going home to check the mail Grant found the letter from his father.

2. Tired from the long hike Cheryl yawned and slept.

3. Writing carefully he completed his exam book.

4. Michelle scanned the lineup searching for the man who had assaulted her.

5. Looking forward to a great evening she hurried to meet her friends.

6. He found himself in a strange position liked by the wrong people for the wrong reasons.

7. Fixing up the old car Jake learned a lot about mechanics and earned himself some money.

8. Dreaming of an athletic career J.T. practiced daily.

9. She got the job done sweating in the August heat all the while.

10. Pestered by the boy in the next row Darla felt like complaining to the teacher.

B. Now write five sentences using verbals. Use commas to set them off only when necessary.

1._____

_____

2._____

_____

3._____

_____

4._____

_____

5._____

_____

TUCKED-IN *HOWEVERS* AND *FURTHERMORES*

The heavy connectives (conjunctive or linking adverbs) that we saw in the Connective Pattern can also be used in the Parenthetical Pattern. But instead of being punctuated with a semicolon and a comma as in connective sentences, heavy connectives used parenthetically are tucked in between two commas.

> We expected**,** *however,* to dance till we dropped.

> Janis heard**,** *furthermore,* how her friend had gossiped.

Used parenthetically, heavy connectives interrupt a single, ongoing complete idea. (Remember, heavy connectives that are used in connective sentences stand between two complete ideas: *I like music; however, heavy metal leaves me cold.*)

Tucking the heavy connective parenthetically inside an ongoing sentence changes the structure and makes it an interrupter.

> I like music. Heavy metal**,** *however,* leaves me cold.
>   *interrupter*

So when you tuck a heavy connective into the middle of a sentence parenthetically, tuck it between a matched set of commas.

> People found**,** *furthermore,* that the gang was cowardly.
>   *interrupter*

> Lydia seems**,** *moreover,* like she's ready to giggle.
>   *interrupter*

These tucked-in heavy connectives can help give your writing a well-crafted, polished sound.

⌯ EXERCISE 3

Practice these tucked-in adverbs by supplying the needed commas in the sentences below. You don't have to copy the sentences; just write in the commas where they belong.

1. The result of the election however was surprising.

2. Indra felt moreover that she had been wronged.

3. His sense of humor in fact makes his teachers chortle.

4. You will not furthermore abuse this privilege again.

5. Jay has succeeded however in juggling three balls with one hand.

INTRODUCTORY PREPOSITIONAL PATTERN

Another common sentence pattern is the sentence that begins with a prepositional phrase. This pattern operates like the Introductory Pattern that involves a clause, which you studied in Chapter 4. It often requires a comma to separate it from the main part of the sentence.

With the recent thaw, Luz has begun to perk up.

    prepositional phrase   *main clause*

On her way home from practice, Darcy stopped to talk with her friends.

    prepositional phrase   *main clause*

Here a prepositional phrase starts the sentence and leads to the main clause which is marked off with a comma. Prepositional beginnings are particularly useful for starting paragraphs and supplying transitions. The comma, as usual, can be heard as a pause.

Over the last five years, (pause) the number of homeless families has tripled.

    prepositional phrase   *main clause*

From the receipts of the dance, (pause) it's clear we made a profit.

    prepositional phrase   *main clause*

With the idea of finding better medical care, (pause) Kathleen visited a specialist.

    prepositional phrase   *main clause*

In the last forty years, punctuation for prepositional phrases has changed. Previously, prepositional phrases at the beginning of sentences were nearly always punctuated. Now many newspapers and magazines still punctuate prepositional phrases when they begin a sentence, but most essayists and novelists leave even longer prepositional phrases at the beginning of sentences unpunctuated. Generally, for your purposes here, punctuation should be a matter of individual style—what strikes your ear as most natural.

One possibility you might consider is punctuating longer prepositional phrases at the beginning of sentences while omitting commas with shorter ones. It is also a good ideal to use a comma if two or more prepositional phrases in a row start the sentence.

By four o'clock he had run out of energy.
(short phrase—no comma)

On Saturdays the Mercados visit their friends.
(Short phrase—no comma)

Behind Jerry and Martha's decaying old red barn, something horrible was growing.
(Long phrase—use comma)

From the way the teacher looked at Imelda's test, she figured she had flunked.
(Long phrase—use comma.)

On his way home from the dentist's, Bruce found his long-lost tennis shoe.
(Two phrases in a row—use comma.)

Near the last stretch of highway on the outskirts of town, the pavement gets bumpy.
(Three phrases in a row—use comma)

You can determine whether that first word in a sentence is a preposition by applying the "mountain" test: *of* the mountain, *above* the mountain, *below* the mountain, *beside* the mountain, *under* the mountain, *in* the mountain, *on* the mountain, *over* the mountain, *near* the mountain, *behind* the mountain, *around* the mountain, *among* the mountains, *outside* the mountains, etc.

Unless a word can be placed in physical relation or proximity to the mountain, it probably isn't a preposition. For instance, you wouldn't say: *If* the mountain he stopped for water. Nor would you say: *Go* the mountain he camped…. Only prepositions fit right in.

(Only a few prepositions won't work with this test: *during*, *except*, and a few others.)

☜ CHAPTER REVIEW

A. Write out the following sentences and supply punctuation where necessary.

1. Above the old shack the mountain loomed like a humpback whale.

2. By the final week of summer everyone was restless.

3. In thinking over the assignment Lee decided that it wasn't so difficult after all.

4. To the best of his knowledge all life forms appear to have their unique brand of intelligence.

_____

_____

5. Over the last five years the amount of drug abuse has declined in our neighborhood.

_____

_____

6. From the curl of his lip it's clear he's out to prove how tough he is.

_____

_____

B. Next, on a separate sheet of paper, write 5 sparkling sentences that begin with prepositional phrases.

BEYOND SENTENCE PATTERNS

The various sentence patterns covered throughout the book are meant to give you a starting place. They are meant to lay ground work, a foundation to build from and come back to. Unimaginative use of any pattern will make for stiff, artificial-sounding sentences. If you're lackadaisical while you write, the reader will be just as bored, and there's nothing quite as boring as boring writing.

Once you grasp sentence structure, you should move toward developing style. The easiest way to do that is to write naturally—let the words come spontaneously as they do in speech. Many times good sentences will be part of the flow of an idea or come from a rush of feeling. Sometimes part of a sentence is great while the rest of it droops. Other times good sentences are a matter of hard work and revision: the writer rearranges words and phrases, trims excess, or finds stronger, more accurate nouns and verbs. Developing your ear, listening to the rhythm of your internal voice, makes your individual style stand out as the product of the unique you.

Good SENTENCES

by Steve Wiesinger

TEACHER'S GUIDE AND ANSWER KEY

Overview

Good Sentences is a writer's approach to the teaching of sentence mechanics. Its aim is to help students produce mechanically correct sentences in their own writing. Students who complete this book should be able to write compositions that do not contain fragments, run-on sentences, and other basic errors of sentence structure. In addition, their writing should be free of major errors in the use of punctuation.

Purpose and Contents

More than twenty years ago, when I started to teach writing, I found my first students confused and annoyed about sentence structure and punctuation. My initial attempts to explain the mysteries of sentence mechanics proved troubling. Many students yawned, some rolled their eyes, and one vocal student slammed down his pencil and said, "I didn't learn this in the seventh grade, and I didn't learn it in the eighth grade, and I'm not going to learn it now."

Gradually, I developed new approaches to the problem. I showed my students how to handle sentence structure the way most writers do: by training their ear to listen to the rhythm of sentences, hearing the pauses and stops. In addition, I modeled sentences based on the patterns of the major types of sentences in the language. This combination of approaches has proved overwhelmingly successful and is the basis of this book.

The teaching material in the book is arranged in the following chapters:

1. The Basic Sentence
2. The List Pattern
3. The Connective Pattern
4. The Introductory Pattern
5. The Parenthetical Pattern
6. Semicolons
7. Colons
8. Dashes
9. Capitals
10. Apostrophes
11. Quotes
12. Paragraphs
13. Other Patterns and Beyond

Suggestions for Use

After several years of following the method employed in *Good Sentences*, several points stand out. First. it is best to teach the initial eight chapters in order. The method provides a sequence of skills for learning sentence mechanics. When I have tried shortcuts—teaching semicolons, for instance, before fully covering complete ideas—I have found that my students get confused.

An element that I have found to be crucial is reviewing the concept of complete ideas. This concept forms a clear, simple basis for sentence mechanics. In my experience students need to have this concept reviewed with each pattern until it becomes as automatic to their thinking as one and one equals two.

© EDUCATIONAL DESIG INC. 47 WEST 13 STREET NEW YORK NY 10011

Many of the students who will use *Good Sentences* have trouble learning from books. Often they feel that books offer them little except unrewarding work. Sometimes these students will do the exercises required, then sit back or visit with friends while the concepts fly out the window. I have found that this learning leakage can be avoided with some good, standard teaching practices.

Introductory work on the board giving explanations of key concepts is invaluable, as is review work when exercises are corrected. Mini-reviews of key concepts prior to regular writing assignments also does wonders. When students sense that the material is important to teachers, they often increase their attention on that basis alone.

Good Sentences is laid out to function equally well with whole classes or small groups. In addition, it can be used as a self-teaching workbook with individual students.

For whole classes, the way I use the material—I have taught writing to mid- to lower-range students for more than 16 years—is to intersperse a single chapter once or twice a week between writing projects and assignments. Usually I spend about fifty percent of the class period explaining, writing orally solicited model sentences (correct and incorrect) on the board, and checking for comprehension. Then I move through the class, checking as the students write their practice sentences. I tell students that the real test of their comprehension will come on their regular papers, essays, stories.

Over the years, I've found that this grammar-for-people-who-hate-grammar should be held to twice a week maximum. Once or twice a week gives the material a chance to be absorbed, practiced, and applied to writing. Even small doses of the most simplified grammar and mechanics day after day becomes numbing and confusing.

For small groups, I find that students get through one chapter in a period with relative ease. I give two-minute explanations of key concepts and sometimes come back with groups to explain various points, but generally the students give each other a hand and work quickly. Using the material in a school-wide writing center, student-tutors, after minimal training, have been able to initiate their compatriots into the mysteries of the comma and the semicolon for nine years now.

As a self-teaching workbook for individual students, once I get students going (again with mini-explanations) I find that I can go over their practice sentences and see immediately when they go off the track. Generally, one period will put these students through an entire chapter.

I never test on the materials, I feel that with the approach taken in this book, the student's own writing is what counts. The whole purpose of learning these skills is to have them appear in the student's papers.

Throughout the book, I try to avoid complex rules, complicated explanations, and the welter of exceptions to rules. For example, it is permissible to connect short independent clauses with commas instead of semicolons (*I came, I saw, I conquered.*) It is also OK to connect two short independent clauses with a conjunction alone and no comma (*Joan arrived and we set off together.*). But these are exceptions, best taught when the student has mastered the more customary rules covered in the book.

In the end, *Good Sentences* is aimed to lift students over and beyond the slippery slope of basic skills. I see only positive reasons for providing a simplified footing for students and helping them make their writing more cogent and fun.

ANSWER KEY

Chapter 1

Exercise 1

A. 1G or I

2C

3I or G

4F

5A

6H

7B

8E (D is a complete sentence.)

B. (Answers will differ.)

Exercise 2

(Answers will differ.)

Exercise 3

1. Ahmed (subj.) slowly walked home (pred.).

2. Dogs (subj.) frighten me (pred.).

3. The Ozark Mountains (subj.) are great for vacations (pred.).

4. A new Porsche (subj.) would come in handy (pred.).

5. The police car (subj.) pulled onto campus (pred.)

6. My apartment (subj.) is on the sixth floor (pred.).

7. Six people (subj.) qualified for the scholarship (pred.).

8. I (subj.) am learning computer programming (pred.).

9. Sheena (subj.) acts incredibly polite (pred.).

10. The grizzled old man turned out to be quite pleasant.

Exercise 4

Answers 2, 4, 6 should be checked. Remaining answers will differ.

Exercise 5

A. I my friend Claudia the other day. She was really in a bad mood. Her mother grounded her for three weeks. The spring dance is coming up. Claudia wants me to talk to her mom and tell her that everyone is going. I get along with her mother really well. Maybe she'll listen to me.

B. (Answers will differ.)

C. (Answers will differ.)

Chapter Review

(Answers will differ.)

Chapter 2

Exercise 1

Check before answers 1, 3, 4, 5, 8, 9. Blank remainder

Exercise 2

1. Parsley, sage, and rosemary are spices.

2. Jacqueline likes movies, school, and Freddy.

3. She's taking P.E., Typing III, and English.

4. The orphan felt beaten, depressed, and alone.

5. Indra came, saw, and conquered John.

Exercise 3

1. He was saving for either a jeep, a pickup, or a mini-van.

2. The hike was long, lonely, and boring.

3. Ricardo, William, and Sam made the lacrosse team.

4. My three sisters are Bea, Reece, and Callie.

5. She hates potatoes, bread, and macaroni.

6. Cheryl climbed Mt. Whitney, Mt. McKinley, and Mt. Rainier.

7. She wants to go to a city college, a state college, or a flight attendant school.

8. Irv wore tights, dance shoes, and a muscle shirt.

9. The morning broke cold, icy, and cloudy.

10. Snow, black ice, and frost covered the roads.

11. He campaigned against crime, drugs, and waste.

Exercise 4

1. After delivering the package, Mac ran down the stairs, got into his truck, and hurried away.

2. For swimming in the ocean you need a wet suit and a pair of booties and a leak-proof squid lid. (no commas)

3. Matilda got ready for the party by purchasing a new blouse, perming her hair, and doing her nails.

4. Love gives the world a lot of its joy, no small part of its sorrow, and a great deal of its excitement.

5. James strolled through the hall, sauntered by the library, and drifted into class.

6. The Chens took two tents, a Coleman stove, and an ice chest packed with food.

7. The engaged couple bought a bedroom set, a small kitchen table, and some silverware.

8. They went to the movies, stopped for pizza, then cruised the fast food places.

9. I got home and went to bed. (no commas)

10. My brother is really ambitious and has two jobs. (no commas)

Exercise 5

1. A lively, interesting, and dramatic presidential debate influenced the vote.

2. Davis brought records and drinks and potato chips to the party. (no commas)

3. Rachel, Dawn, Jeanie, and Alyssa got good grades on their group project.

4. The Rivers brought towels, a picnic lunch, and sunblock to the beach.

5. Cab driver, truck driver, heavy equipment operator—these are all jobs I'd like to get.

6. Ramon and I went to the show and met a couple girls and got their phone numbers. (no commas)

7. Mrs. Petersen says she's feeling tired, irritable, and stressed out.

8. Doing chores, getting to bed early, and not talking back are three of my non-habits.

9. The candidate seemed inexperienced, immature, and easily rattled.

10. Melissa and I hung around at the mall, had lunch at the Big T, then met our boyfriends.

Chapter Review:

A. 1. Dell and Sue like going to baseball games.

2. Apples, bananas, and tangerines are wonderful fruits..

3. My uncle is a doctor, a skilled magician, a skilled amateur astronomer, and a whirlwind of energy.

4. Frederic's grandfather worked as a cowboy, a soldier, a pilot, and an investment banker.

5. Natalie found herself thinking more deeply and looking outward with fewer prejudices. (no commas)

6. Indra was definitely excited and pleased when John asked her out.

B. (Answers will differ.)

Chapter 3

Exercise 1

1. I'm terrible in math but good in English.

2. Kids like playing and making messes.

3. Deshonne won the match and got a medal.

4. I found happiness, but it was a struggle.

5. Anger is unpleasant, and so is self-pity.

6. It's hard to know Mike, yet he's a generous guy.

Exercise 2

1. Wanda walked away, and Jim hurried after her.

2. I don't know the answer, but you don't either.

3. We drove home and parked in back of the house.

4. Selene yelled, and the window finally opened a crack.

5. No one disagreed or made a fuss.

6. I rather disliked the captain, and I'm afraid I showed it.

Exercise 3

A. I didn't know where he was going, and he wouldn't tell me. It was really bad. I had to get off the phone. After that he disappeared. It just made me extremely upset. I had to talk with someone.

B. (In the following, starred answers should be checked and copied with correct punctuation. The remainder are sentences that are neither checked nor copied.)

* 1. The lights went out, and the Franklins found candles.

* 2. Spelling is easy for me, but math drives me nuts.

3. Jeremy likes Christmas because of all the good spirit.

* 4. The dog bowl needs cleaning, but Laurie is too busy.

5. Going to the movies and going to dinner are two of my favorite treats.

* 6. Danny will bring charcoal, and Gregg will bring food.

7. Dana gets home late from practice and collapses.

* 8. Our class studied *The Great Gatsby*, and I felt sorry for Jay Gatsby.

* 9. The cost of a house is rising each year, and I'm afraid I'll never be able to afford one.

* 10. Our apartment house is getting painted, so our apartment is going to look good.

Exercise 4

1. Linda seldom gives herself credit for good work; furthermore, she simply won't take a compliment.

2. Tragedy can lead to wisdom; however, it seems a heavy price to pay.

3. People badly want peace; moreover, they are forcing their governments to listen.

4. Charles hates working at Burger Empire; in fact, he's looking for another job.

5. I like fooling around with my friends; nevertheless, I'm serious about learning Spanish.

Chapter Review

A. 1. The class nearly missed their deadline for putting out the newspaper, but they made it by a single hour.

2. The road was long and dusty, yet we enjoyed driving along it.

3. On weekends Stacy lives with her dad, and during the week she stays with her mom.

4. Karen thought Donny would ask her to the prom; moreover, she expected Donny to hire a limousine to transport them.

5. Drugs are a concern for young people; however, each year fewer and fewer teenagers become users.

6. David has cut too many classes, so he won't graduate.

7. Jim is an easy-going, sensitive man with a lot of self-doubts that he handles well; furthermore, he has learned to take his self-doubts as fuel for his courage and integrity.

8. That car is too expensive; besides, the brakes are shot.

9. Marianne thinks she's hot and the best thing ever to walk the earth. (no punctuation)

10. Jewelle wants to take a train or a bus to Las Vegas. (no punctuation)

B. (Answers will differ)

Chapter 4

Exercise 1

(Answers will differ)

A. 1. We walked to the mall as slowly as we could.

2. I nearly had heart failure when he jumped out.

3. Jake got plenty scared during his father's rages.

4-6. (Answers will differ)

7. Indra holds John's hand when he walks her to class.

8. Judy's parents allowed her to go to the rock concert, since she had already bought tickets.

9. I haven't seen Mary since last summer.

B. 1. If the assignment is too hard, people won't learn much.

2. After the camping trip Andrew needed a new tent.

3. The day was unbearable when the heat reached 107 degrees.

4. Before people could react, the man escaped.

5. Whys and wherefores are always debated in their family.

6. We will find if there is a way to make a mistake.

7. When I finally make it through this school, I'll be eighteen.

Exercise 3

1. Going toward school, James heard the last bell.

2. Since you're noisy, there will be no movie.

3. Getting curious about it, he checked for the smell.

4. When that bell rings, I'm getting some food.

5. Seeing the right answer, she marked her paper.

6. Leaping for the pass, I got blindsided.

7. Running like crazy, they avoided the rent-a-cop.

8. While Amy ate, a bug crawled from her sandwich.

Chapter Review

A. 1. Climbing the cliff, Ike nearly slipped.

2. When I'm angry, I control myself pretty well.

3. As Mara rode home, she saw the oddest scene.

4. Unless Bill asks her out, she's going to scream.

5. If you ask politely, you just might get a yes.

6. Despite Michael's smile he's often moody. (optional comma after "smile")

7. Retyping the paper, Danielle found numerous errors.

8. Reading the fine print of the contract, Marilee found she was being charged nearly 20% interest.

9. When Perry finds himself getting really depressed, it's hard for him to figure out what to do.

10. As they rounded the corner, they were shocked to discover Les standing there, directing traffic. (Omitting the comma before "directing traffic" would be OK, too.)

11. Because Silvia is so nice with her friends, they decided to throw her a surprise party.

12. Even though it's hard for Tee to actually sit down and study, he's decided there's no way he wants to be out on the streets, running around aimless, letting his friends think for him.

13. Getting the paper done, taking a long shower, and feeling utterly relieved, Racine finally plopped into bed and fell asleep.

B. (Answers will differ)

Chapter 5

Exercise 1

1. My brother, the dirty rat, tattled on me.

2. Jacob Marley, a well-known ghost, haunted Ebenezer.

3. Nipper, my dog, chases rabbits till he drops.

4. *Graceland*, an album by Paul Simon, has become a classic.

5. Mr. Adler, a friend of my dad's, has had the most amazing adventures.

Exercise 2

1. Mae, the woman next door, parades around like a queen.

2. Mae, I believe, thinks that she's related to Elizabeth II.

3. Our street, 7th Avenue, is roped off for a block party.

4. Five students, all of them sharp, questioned the speaker.

5. Mr. Markle, our beloved teacher, had a hair transplant.

6. The principal, I presume, does not want a student-run school.

Exercise 3:

A. 1. Laughter, I feel, is good for the soul.

2. Mr. Lassiter, the substitute, cannot be fooled easily.

3. Al, who is a good sport, didn't mind getting wet.

4. General Spardon, who called for an investigation, was rumored to be under suspicion himself.

5. Indra's best friend, who is usually sharp about people, warned Indra to look out for John.

6. The report, which was cited by authorities as unique and thoughtful, used only a few statistics.

7. The report cited by authorities as unique and thoughtful used only limited statistics. (no change)

B. (Answers will differ.)

Exercise 4

1. Sal, who is the number one nerd in Missouri, follows me around.

2. The one time that I really tried to be cool I spilled soup all over myself.

3. The apartment which we rent is definitely dinky.

4. Li found that popularity was overrated.

5. Ella, who invented the exercises, improved her posture.

6. Anybody else who tried them couldn't bend over for a week.

7. The sunset, which was a remarkable blaze of deep orange, hot pink, and lines of scarlet, made it look like the sky had caught fire.

Chapter Review:

A. 1. Summer vacation, which should be the most fun time of the year, can still get boring.

2. Naomi, who is my oldest sister, graduated from college.

3. The baby's toys, which are scattered through the house, need to be picked up. (It is also possible to interpret the clause beginning with "which" as restrictive and not to put in commas.)

4. The only jacket which I like seems really expensive.

5. The brain, which is a highly complicated organ, seems totally unused by some people.

6. Dana, my best friend, helped me break the habit of thinking negatively.

7. The cow that jumped over the moon landed awkwardly.

8. Anyone who likes teenagers can't be all bad.

9. Once there lived two sisters who were champion dancers and expert jump-rope teachers.

10. Jory Baba, who comes from Lebanon, has an great sense of humor despite everything he's lived through.

11. Bali, which is an island off the southeast of Java with terraced rice fields, a complex system of irrigation, and a fascinating culture, is so rich in agriculture that it exports more than thirty varieties of foodstuffs.

B. and C. (Answers will differ.)

Chapter 6

Exercise 1

(Answers will differ.)

Chapter Review

A. 1. Myra plays tennis; her sister plays basketball.

2. The man went to the creek and found a comfortable spot. (no semicolon)

3. The pigeons made nests in the eaves; the janitor had to climb on a ladder to knock the nests loose.

4. The classes' sculptures are fired in a kiln; the heat in there gets so intense, no one is allowed nearby.

5. Craig finished his painting; he set it out to dry.

6. The TV conked out; I don't miss it at all.

7. Marta started the year with great intentions; however, she quickly fell into her old habits.

8. Most week days Tito does two hours of homework; moreover, he still has time to visit his friends._____

9. Bucky has to leave school and move; he's really stressed.

10. I'm going to pass Chemistry; I also plan to get through English literature; however, typing is a horse of a totally different stripe. _____

B. (Answers will differ.)

Chapter 7

Exercise 1

1. Every Christmas Theresa has to do the following: shop for presents, cook dinner, and care for her cousins.

2. Please buy the following: bread, butter, and rutabagas.

3. Our plan is strong: it is intelligent and flexible.

4. The driveway is old: it has begun to crack.

5. The test was easy: only two questions needed thought.

6. I think you'd be silly to elope: for example, you would miss graduation and alienate your family.

Chapter Review

A. 1. Answer me this: do you like to eat dry spaghetti?

2. Her parents grounded her for three reasons: she was late, her grades dropped, and she dented the car.

3. Two things are totally clear: I need new pants and I need to run faster from strange bulldogs.

4. The chase left me in a strange position: up a tree and hollering for help.

5. Most of my friends want the following from life: meaningful work, a good marriage, and several children.

6. The philosophy known as Existentialism is also a value system: it is concerned with the meaning and purpose of existence.

7. The poet Shakespeare's words are widely quoted: "To be or not to be, that is the question."

B. (Answers will differ.)

Chapter 8

Exercise 1

A. 1. The dam gave way—look out!

2. John is a total clown—really funny.

3. Her idea of a good time comes down to one word—surfing.

4. The trip was exciting—almost too exciting.

5. We returned via the unimproved road—a mistake if there ever was one.

6. Sometimes school is fun—don't you think so?

7. Indra promises to break all her bad habits—fat chance.

8. He has a lot of ego—too much, I think.

B. (Answers will differ.)

Chapter Review

A. 1. This broken ankle really aches—I mean pain.

2. The computer is a handy tool—terrific, in fact.

3. Alice finally finished and let out a cheer—yes!

4. J.C. finds newspapers great for information—depth of thought is another matter, though.

5. They found it hard—nearly impossible—to agree with the candidate.

6. The piece sounds like funeral music—downright spooky.

7. My brother watches too much TV—his mistake.

8. The snow is thick this year—too thick, people say.

9. Jena is letting her feelings out more—just saying what she feels.

10. Nothing is worse than that inner censor—the way it tells you that you're wrong or stupid.

B. (Answers will differ.)

Chapter 9

Exercise 1

1. She loves to walk the dog on the beach.

2. Indra and John made up at the movies.

3. The Matsons found themselves near the wharf.

4. Dolores went out to walk her poodle, Rover.

5. Lilly Chen met us on State Street near Fifth Avenue.

6. We hiked near Mount Rainier.

Exercise 2

1. He likes bull terriers better than German shepherds.

2. Darrell did a report on sparrows for Biology I.

3. I saw a greyhound running in the park.

4. Eloise decided to take French instead of math.

5. Leaving home early, Marcus went to Home Ec.

6. The York rose is at least six hundred years old.

Chapter Review

A. 1. Three friends read the novel *The Great Gatsby*.

2. The delicatessen on the corner is open Sundays.

3. Cheryl and her sister went hiking in the Adirondacks.

4. The old television program *I Love Lucy* is still funny after all these years.

5. I shouted in my loudest voice, "Hey, Grandpa!"

6. My brother and I argued about which video to rent.

7. The Chicago Cubs play at Wrigley Field.

8. Tremaine wants to sing in Carnegie Hall.

9. To Simone, math is easier than Spanish.

10. Darrin never misses an issue of *Rolling Stone*.

11. Indra and John talked intently while the President (capital is optional) passed in a motorcade.

B. (Answers will differ.)

Chapter 10

Exercise 1

1. Indra's weird belief is that she can make John dance like a star in a dance movie.

2. Marcia's messy, hacked-up folder looks horrible.

3. This suspension has hurt the team's record.

4. Being left out was a blow to Jason's self-esteem.

5. Superman's latest adventure made me laugh.

6. Can you help me look for Leroy's new baseball glove?

Exercise 2

1. This year's prom was so crowded that everyone was sweating.

2. Emily envied everyone else's camera.

3. The works of William Faulkner are intriguing.

4. Sue's favorite color is electric blue.

5. The first trimesters are always the hardest.

6. The days are long during July.

7. The stapler's base is broken.

8. We crossed five streets to get to the professor's house.

9. The ragweed is in bloom now, giving me horrible sneezes.

10. Matilda's hat got blown off in the wind.

Exercise 3

1. The truckers' strike ended Tuesday.

2. The golfers' matches will get underway at 8:00 A.M.

3. The dog's tail wagged furiously.

4. The boys' treehouse stands between their houses.

5. I'll meet you outside the boys' gym.

6. The meeting will be held in the teachers' lounge.

Exercise 4

1. It's my problem; I'm perfectly able to deal with its complications.

2. His arm isn't healed yet.

3. The tiger didn't move its head for at least five minutes.

4. You called us, and we're all here.

5. That's a nasty-looking gash; shouldn't you go to the doctor's?

Chapter Review

A. 1. The lamps are damaged.

2. Della's friend is visiting class.

3. The baby's bib is stained with strange green stuff.

4. Regardless of Frank's grade on the project, he's satisfied with his efforts.

5. As we've seen with nuclear power, today's solutions can become tomorrow's problems.

6. Before they realized it, the trucks picked up speed.

7. The dance will be held in Delta High School boys' gym.

8. Buddy's coat isn't ready for the cleaner's, it's still wet.

9. Indra's new dress got a footprint on the hem, but she loved the way John's dancing improved.

B. (Answers will differ.)

Chapter 11

Exercise 1

1. "Great work, you really excelled," Mr. Roberts stated.

2. "I had a so-so time." Reed pensively walked to the door.

3. "Oh, bug off!" Indra shouted.

4. "I got all A's." Rodney waved his report card.

5. "I hate asking for help," Ty confessed. "It's a pain."

6. "Do you know Bo?" Jill asked. "Willy, this is Bo."

Exercise 2

1. "Listen to me," Jack said. "There's no other way to do this."

2. "I really have to get home," Sukie declared. "If someone doesn't help I'm going to scream."

3. "The Braves lead 55 to 51!" the announcer cried. "They are three seconds away from the championship!"

4. Mel said, "I don't think we should get into this." He shook his head. "It looks like trouble to me."

5. "I wish school was out," Benny complained. "I'm bored." "If you're bored, it's your fault," answered his sister.

6. "Man, do I like turkey." Adam said. "I could eat a ton."

7. "Give me a break," Tom said. "I'll have the money soon."

8. The book *Megathought* claims: "We need new forms of thinking. People must see interconnectedness." (Comma after claims is also correct.)

Exercise 3

1. "Serena found a really good book. It made a big impression on her. It had a quote: 'If you look for darkness, you will find darkness. If you look for light, you will find light. But if you look with open eyes, you will find both and know truth.'"

2. "Gregory didn't know what to do. The stranger came up to him and said, 'I'm going to bust you in the face. I don't like your looks.'"

Exercise 4

1. Lola said that she could easily climb the mountain.

2. "No one calls me any more," said Bill.

3. "What time is it?" asked the teacher.

4. "It's easy to get to my house," said Teresa. "First go down Green Street. Then turn left at Orchard Place. That's all there is to it."

5. "We could try." Dr. Inagaki stroked his chin thoughtfully.

Chapter Review

1. Old Jake said, "The trout are going crazy. Time to get out the poles."

2. "Check out the people down on 38th Street," David said. They do some wild things."

3. "Let's not make mountains out of molehills," the teacher warned. "There's no real problem."

4. The manager agreed that he would try to find a way to improve morale.

5. "I've got four hours of homework tonight," Matt said. "I can't believe it."

6. "English is my best subject," Dawn said. Then she admitted that she hated math.

7. "I didn't know what to do," Marnie said. "Then he asked me to meet him that night. 'Come on,' he kept saying. 'You don't need to worry. I'll talk to your mom.'" Marnie shook her head. "He didn't realize he's exactly the kind of guy my mother would die about."

B. (Answers will differ.)

Chapter 12

Chapter Review

A. Martin lifted the phone carefully from the cradle where he was downstairs below his sister's room. His sister Katie and Jana talked every night for hours.

"I swear," Katie whined, "Martin's listening on the other phone; I can hear him breathing."

"You think so?" Jana asked. "I thought he was more mature than that."

Now that grabbed Martin's interest. Jana was sleek and petite, an auburn-haired knockout who made even juniors and seniors take notice.

"Really, Martin." Jana zeroed in on him there on the extension with her radar. "I used to think you were cute. But Katie is your sister. You bug her all the time."

Martin listened, totally unrepentant. He loved his sister, but guilt wasn't part of the bargain.

"Martin," Jana said, "come on. We know you're listening."

"He could care less how anyone feels!" his sister burst in.

"You can talk to us," Jana persisted. Then softer, crooning, she said, "Please say something." Her voice made Martin think of full moons and starry nights and the scent of roses in summer. (Last sentence could also be a separate pagagraph.)

B. (Answers will differ.)

Chapter 13

Exercise 1

A. 1. Doris, Curt, and I went to the mall, and on a lark Curt and I pretended we were newlyweds.

2. When I write a paper, first I concentrate on getting my ideas and feelings down, and then I look over my paper to see if I made sense.

3. The tree outside class, an old oak, has two hundred pairs of eyes a day staring at it because the owners are daydreaming away in math or English class.

4. When I picked up my brother, which was a good idea, since he didn't want to sit at pre-school all day, I had to check for his boots, coat, sweaters, and anything else he might have forgotten.

B. (Answers will differ.)

Exercise 2

A. 1. Going home to check the mail, Grant found the letter from his father.

2. Tired from the long hike, Cheryl yawned and slept.

3. Writing carefully, he completed his exam book.

4. Michelle scanned the lineup, searching for the man who had assaulted her.

5. Looking forward to a great evening, she hurried to meet her friends.

6. He found himself in a strange position, liked by the wrong people for the wrong reasons.

7. Fixing up the old car, Jake learned a lot about mechanics and earned himself some money.

8. Dreaming of an athletic career, J.T. practiced daily.

9. She got the job done, sweating in the August heat all the while.

10. Pestered by the boy in the next row, Darla felt like complaining to the teacher.

B. (Answers will differ.)

Exercise 3

1. The result of the election, however, was surprising.

2. Indra felt, moreover, that she had been wronged.

3. His sense of humor, in fact, makes his teachers chortle.

4. You will not, furthermore, abuse this privilege again.

5. Jay has succeeded, however, in juggling three balls with one hand.

Chapter Review

A. 1. Above the old shack the mountain loomed like a humpback whale.

2. By the final week of summer, everyone was restless.

3. In thinking over the assignment, Lee decided that it wasn't so difficult after all.

4. To the best of his knowledge, all life forms appear to have their unique brand of intelligence.

5. Over the last five years the amount of drug abuse has declined in our neighborhood.

6. From the curl of his lip, it's clear he's out to prove how tough he is.

(Some writers might insert a comma after each of these introductory prepositional phrases.)

B. (Answers will differ.)